SAMANTHA'S VOICE

Lisa Hedge
Samantha's Voice

First Edition
Edited by Dave Ferkinhoff

Published by Spines
ISBN: 979-8-89569-166-3

SAMANTHA'S VOICE

First Edition

Lisa Hedge

Contents

*In memory of Jenny
2003-2021*

ACKNOWLEDGMENTS

Thanks to the ASA, the FBI, the DEA, and the USDA for all of the technical assistance.

To Jim Totton, Michael McGarrey, Laura Foster, Nancy Craig, and Eric Hedge and Ryan Hedge for creative input.

To Tom Ferkinhoff for pesky little brother memories, and to Diana Schutte for fostering so many children.

Thank you to all those who serve in the US military.

And to our furry friends: Murphy, Matilda, Jack, and Chelsey.
And a special thanks to Thor.

Jenny's Song

A war was born in the poppy fields.
The soldiers knew 'twas a long way to home.
In the morning dawn they all laid down
To fight for those lost to the poppy fields

A daughter, a sister, a mother, a friend--
Her smile like no other, another girl gone
A mother, a sister, a daughter, a friend
All of them lost to the poppy fields.

City streets dusted by the poppy fields
Those homeless so hopeless they'd nowhere to go
In the afternoon sun they all laid down
To live out their lives in the poppy fields.

A daughter, a sister, a mother, a friend--
Her smile like no other, another girl gone
A mother, a sister, a daughter, a friend
All of them lost- to the poppy fields

A weapon aimed low in the poppy fields
At a young girl so hopeful she'd a long way to go
In the setting sun he laid her life down
To rest with those lost, to the poppy fields

A daughter, a sister, a mother, a friend--
Her smile like no other, another girl gone
A mother, a sister, a daughter, a friend

All of them lost to the poppy fields.

PROLOGUE

Grand Traverse Bay
Traverse City, Michigan
August 18, 2015

Keow. Ca cow.

"Shoo."

On deck on the Sail Away, first mate Samantha Harmon took one last bite of her peanut butter and jelly sandwich before flinging the crust overboard, much to the delight of the hungry seagull waiting to pounce. After brushing the crumbs from her fingertips, she grabbed a bag of supplies, pulled a pair of scissors from her belt, and began to prepare the vessel for a trio of arriving guests. When she was done, bands of yellow streamers flew from the stern, giving color to the festivities while reggae music blared from a speaker strapped to the tan canvas roof covering the deck. Upon completion, with a slow smile meeting her lips, she laid back on a deck cushion as her feet went up to rest on a rail; she closed her eyes and waited.

In the galley, her captain laid in provisions for the day's adventure—one jar of strawberry jelly for the refrigerator, a bottle of rum for a cup.

Down on the wharf, thirteen-year-old Brian McFadden strolled along Fisherman's Pier, excited to have been invited out on his great-grandfather's boat. As he drew closer to the Sail Away, he looked up to watch a flock of gulls encircle the ship, came upon a fisherman cleaning his catch, and tripped on a line.

"Watch where you're going," the fisherman yelled.

"Come along," his mother said. A hand reached down to grab his arm. Together they hurried down the pier, followed dutifully by a young girl clad in leather sandals chosen to match the white trim of her dress. As she stopped to watch converging waves fling glistening droplets of water eight, then ten, then twelve inches into the air, Brian's mother called, "Stay with us, Jenny."

As the trio arrived at the Sail Away, a mop of curly dark hair slowly appeared over a rail, followed by an arm as it crooked to grab the side for support, and then a pair of tanned shoulders. With the vessel rocking gently on her lines, the ship's first mate rose from her resting position to point smoldering grey-blue eyes at the approaching party and, with her sunburned face wearing only the expression of an old buccaneer guarding an abandoned pirate ship, stared at the woman with two young teens standing below.

"They're here," she yelled down the galley stairs.

Captain Greg, the old mariner who'd found his sea legs in the navy, boomed in response, "Sam, change that to Buffet."

The curly-haired girl he called Sam sat tall, staring down at the people waiting to board as her fingers fiddled with a dial. Footsteps pounding up the stairs announced the arrival of her great-grandfather. Her grey-blue eyes rolled as she watched the tanned man with lean muscles and half a circle of grey hair cascading to his shoulders hop across the hatchway to land on deck with a thud. She pointed at the woman standing with two young teens on the dock and whispered, "She's beautiful."

"Aye, she is," the captain beamed. In one fluid movement, he stretched a leg up to stand on the ledge, then hopped down onto the pier, bellowing, "Permission to come aboard, get up there," before reaching across a line to assist the young teens. Lastly, he reached for the tall, fair-haired woman he called Jen.

"Grandfather!" She gave him a big hug. "This is my son, Brian. And this is my sister-in-law's foster daughter, Jenny."

"Great, great." Looking around the deck, he spied the bundle huddled on a red-striped cushion behind the cockpit. "This is her. Sam, get over here and say hello."

Slowly, the girl rose from her position and squeezed around the steering wheel to stand beside the captain. A lot taller than the other children, she stood with her head and shoulders back, poised with attitude. "Hello."

"Hello, hello," a raspy voice squawked from below.

"That would be Jack," Captain Greg said as he dropped down the galley stairs and, after a moment of squawking and yelling, returned with a lime-green feathered Macaw on his shoulder. The teens giggled at the site of the enormous bird, repeating the word, "Hello." Brian pointed a finger up at the bird's beak, a finger quickly smacked down by the captain.

A sly smile met Samantha's lips. "He'll bite that off. Hold out your arm."

Following the command, Brian crooked his forearm for Captain Greg to turn into a perch. Then, with the bird's giant talons wrapped around his wrist, he held his arm out long and tried to get the Macau to repeat, "Polly want a cracker."

"Here, gimme that bird," the captain muttered. Prying away the bird's talons, he placed them on his own arm and stared into Jack's eyes. The bird stared back and squawked, "Four o'clock."

"Stupid bird. It's five o'clock. At least it is somewhere." With a quick flourish, he replaced the parrot on Brian's arm and ordered him to take Jack below. "Prepare for departure." After hopping onto the pier and unwinding the lines securing the boat to the cleats, he tossed them aboard. "Life jackets are under that seat. Get 'em on those kids."

"What about Samantha?"

"That fish? She's old enough."

"I'm seventeen," Samantha stated.

Per the captain's orders, Jen took the wheel and reached over to push a button. The engine hummed as the boat pulled slowly out of the harbor, gliding further into the lake. Once the ship gained open water, Samantha stood ready to help with the sails.

The captain looked up at the ship's weather vane, saying, "Keep that pointed to one o'clock." Then he grabbed the main line, wrapped it around a winch and pulled, raising the canvas to point to the heavens. With the boom secured to the right, he ordered Jen to hold the boat steady so that Samantha could hoist the jib. Soon, the Sail Away flew gleefully along, gaining speed knot by knot. First at three knots, then four, and then five, plowing through waves while listing hard to starboard.

"Make a hole, make it wide," the captain ordered as he pushed past the children. "I'll take over the wheel."

Samantha watched as Jen gave up the wheel and went to sit between Brian and Jenny, encircling them in her arms. A stoic gaze of loneliness crossed her eyes as she threw on her sunglasses and turned seaward, grabbed a cable to pull herself over the ledge and then, while balancing herself with a hand pressed against the cabin, made her way to the bow. Up there, with strands of curls whipping across her face, she relaxed against the mast and hugged her knees to her chest. *Whew.* She removed her sunglasses to push the curls back and then, as the deck rocked violently, she clung to the mast. Once steady, she gazed into the waters and shrugged away the loneliness. *Grandfather made me strong.*

"Can we do that?" the young teens begged.

"When we reach smoother waters," their mother shouted.

To their delight, the boat sailed gracefully along with the bow surfing up and down through five-foot waves, rocking and running with the wind. As they raced along, the sails caught the wind at just the right angle to billow eagerly into smooth taught curves, proving the captain capable of handling the ship through the challenging waves.

"Samantha, get back here," his baritone voice boomed.

"Yes, Sir." A pair of brown legs shot feet first over the ledge to land on a deck cushion.

"Unlatch the jib. Jen, take the wheel." Captain Greg barked out the orders while handling the main line and pulled, bringing the boom about to the port side.

Now in calmer waters, Jen escorted Brian and Jenny up to the bow. As the younger teens threw down a towel and sat cross-legged facing each other, Samantha made her way back to the bow and sat facing the water. Leaning back against the mast, she threw a leg out front and studied the woman before her.

"It's nice to put a face with the voice finally," Jen said, quietly referring to the phone calls she'd had with Samantha. "You've been sailing with Grandfather for what, four years now?"

"About that."

"I'm glad you liked your adoptive parents. So tragic, that auto accident. It's hard to believe you're seventeen already."

"Just until tomorrow," Samantha replied curtly.

"Of course, that's why we're here. I'm glad Grandfather brought the Sail Away to Lake Michigan. Where's his other boat?"

As she looked sideways at the young teens, Samantha said sullenly, "It was impounded after the pirates forced him to take a load of drugs from the Bahamas to Miami."

"No. He didn't," Jen said in a voice loud enough to catch Brian's attention. He turned to stare.

"What pirates?" he asked, inching closer.

"Lunch time. Go ask Grandfather what we've got to eat."

Once the teens disappeared, Samantha re-seated the pair of large-rimmed sunglasses over her eyes. "A boy I was swimming with had a friend. They came onto our boat and the next thing I knew, Grandfather was yelling at me to stay below deck. Then, the boys brought a bag of white powder down the stairs. They snorted a little up their nose and stuck the rest in a storage compartment."

"Then what happened?" Jen asked. As she leaned forward, the sun glanced off her blonde hair to illuminate her translucent skin.

A subtle look of awe crossed Samantha's face as she sat staring at her mother, thinking the blue hue of her eyes hovered somewhere between the blue of the sky and the mirror of blue reflecting off the water. That same blue reflected from her own eyes, though hers were cloaked by a hint of grey.

"You don't look that much like me."

"I'm blonder since I went to the hairdresser."

With a quick nod, Samantha fixed her eyes on her toes and splayed them wide open. "Grandfather told me you were sick when you gave me up for adoption. I was just wondering if I look more like my father?"

"Pretty much, yes. Did those boys hurt you?"

"No," Samantha said. "The one I was swimming with got into the rum while his friend went up to make sure Grandfather didn't come down. The next thing we knew, we heard the poor guy yelling, and when we ran upstairs, his body was flying into the water. When the second guy ran up to the rail, Grandfather swung the boom over and knocked him right alongside his friend."

"The old boom trick," Jen chuckled. "Thank goodness you guys got away."

"But we didn't. Not then." Samantha bit the nail of her index finger, shortening it to the nailbed before saying, "There was a third guy who got a hold of Grandfather's flare gun. He forced us to get the other two guys back on board, and then we had to sail across to Miami. Once we could see the shore, Grandfather yelled at Jake to call the coast guard. The men thought that was funny."

"Let me guess. Jake called the coast guard."

"Sort of. He yelled out, "Coast Guard, over." Grandfather taught him that. When the guys thought it was really happening, they panicked and jumped overboard."

"I can't believe they bought it!"

"Well, probably because there really was a coast guard boat within sight."

"Did the coast guard pick them up?"

"Yes. But those guys said the cocaine was ours, and we kidnapped them. Nobody could prove anything, and Grandfather had a lot of his usual 'coffee.' He didn't argue too much."

Knowing there was always a splash of rum in her grandfather's cup, Jen let that comment go. "I'm sure he was more concerned for your safety."

"Probably. That's why we're on the lake until I leave for West Point."

"Ca caw, ca caw." The sound coming from Captain Greg's cupped hands caused the women to laugh.

"Did I just hear that?" Jen asked.

"Yes. Lunch is ready," Samantha giggled. "We better go now. He puts so much jelly on the sandwiches, they get soggy pretty quick."

"I remember that. Strawberry, right?"

"Always. With big chunks of strawberry."

"Yes!"

Samantha led the way on deck to find a tray of her grandfather's special peanut butter and strawberry jelly sandwiches resting beside four tall glasses of chocolate milk. "Grandfather, where's your milk?"

The old man held his sandwich sideways to lick away strawberry jelly oozing from the crust. "I like chocolate milk the way I like chocolate milk. Wrong brand."

"He's got something else in his mug," Samantha muttered.

"A bottle of rum," Jen replied.

As the peanut butter and jelly sandwiches disappeared, Jen licked her fingers. "I'm sorry we couldn't do this years ago."

Samantha looked at her earnestly. "At least Grandfather finally told me about you."

The women giggled together as Brian dared the young Jennifer to jump off the boat. "Mom, can we go swimming?"

Captain Greg answered that question by pointing the mast directly at the wind, quieting the sails. "Jen, grab the wheel. Samantha, get the jib."

To the delight of the teens, the sails were quickly lowered, and the anchor dropped to the depths of the sandy floor. As Samantha grabbed towels from a storage cupboard, her eyes widened when the warmth of a small hand crept into hers.

"Swim with us," Jenny's sweet voice said.

A gust of wind swept Samantha's hair forward. Pushing it back, she stared curiously at the young girl and made her excuses. "I have to watch the boat. Go ahead." Her fingers touched the girl's hand for an extra second, then released it and pointed to the ladder.

"It's freezing," Jen gasped from the water. Scrambling right back up the ladder, she wrapped herself in a towel.

"Just takes a minute of getting used to," Captain Greg responded as he floated away on his back.

The young teens swam off with long strokes. "Ahoy," they yelled to another boat moored just a hundred yards away. With laughter echoing across the bay, they swam and splashed along with the youngsters swimming with their parents.

Samantha sat back on a red and white striped cushion. "They get along well. I think he likes her," she said, pointing her eyes meaningfully at the other teens.

"Puppy love," Jen slowly admitted. "They're too young."

"Where's her parents?"

"Still in jail. Drug-related, and can't stay sober long enough to pass the drug test when they're out."

"It happens too much. I hate that stuff. The guy who killed my adoptive parents in the car crash was high."

"Come on now, don't be so sad." Jen tilted her head as she put an arm around Samantha's shoulders and squeezed. "We're here to celebrate your birthday with the canvas."

"We can't sail away from our troubles forever," Samantha said begrudgingly.

"That's why you're going to West Point. Shush now, Grandfather's coming."

They both hushed as Captain Greg climbed the ladder and stood dripping water onto the deck. Catching a beach towel thrown his way, he used it to dry his feet before wrapping the towel around his midsection. Then he sat down in the captain's chair and reached out to grab his cup. Samantha took the cup from his hand and went below to get his beverage, smiling when she heard Jen say, "You're doing a good job with her Grandfather."

"She's my baby."

"Why West Point? Why not the Coast Guard?"

Samantha returned in time to answer that question herself. "Grandfather knows he can't talk me out of the military. His father was in the military. He was military. It's in my blood. He says, if I'm going into the military then be the best, so West Point it is."

"You're just eighteen tomorrow. That's a big decision for a young woman. It will be tough, mentally and physically."

"I know," Samantha said hotly. "So is this."

Jen looked at their grandfather. "Your idea?"

"She's First Mate here. I've never seen anyone more fit to be an officer."

"You know her best."

With the young teens now aboard and the late afternoon breeze tousling his gray hair to whip behind his head, Captain Greg pulled anchor. Then, with Jen once again at the wheel, he looked at Brian and threw him a pair of gloves. "Time to start training her replacement. Raise the main," he said and walked his great-grandson through a series of maneuvers, pulling the main line through an electric winch to raise the sail. He then positioned the boom. "Never leave it so the wind comes between ten o'clock and two o'clock. Always keep it at three o'clock or nine o'clock. That's called the Beam Reach."

"Why?" a wide-eyed Brian asked.

"The breeze fills your sails, then the wind takes us away." With one hand, he tugged a line and pulled the jib port side before walking to the back of the deck. "Move away, I'm taking the wheel," he said, eyeing Samantha.

"Got it." Stomping away, she jumped over the ledge and ran up to the bow. Then, using a steel rod, she pushed the jib farther into the wind and returned to stand beside the captain.

"What's the zone called between ten o'clock and two o'clock," Brian asked.

After a moment of pause, Captain Greg finally answered with, "The place Samantha needs to stay away from when she's called overseas to fight. Jake, name the zone," he yelled down the stairs.

Jake squawked and whistled. "Dead Zone. Davey Jones, get my coffee."

"The Dead Zone? You can't protect her forever," Jen yelled at her grandfather's back as he turned to grab his cup.

"Right, right," he muttered. Pulling out a cloth bag full of small devices, he reached in and handed them out. A tambourine went to Jen, and a tin tie washboard with a thimble went to Samantha. The younger teens had shakers and wooden spoons. Captain Greg grabbed a microphone, and as the wind carried them home, the little band played along to the radio all the way back to Traverse City.

For many years after that trip, when the adventures and dangers of two wars raging overseas drew Samantha into a new realm and dark remnants of family secrets clouded her future, she would look back on that day and think, "That was the day I got to have a childhood with my family." *The sails billowing and curving with the wind gave me a feeling of freedom that I can only describe as "exhilarating." And I will give credit where credit is due.*

Thanks to the canvas, we were happy.

CHAPTER 1

Bagram Airforce Base
Kandahar, Afghanistan
June 21, 2021 11:30

First Lieutenant Samantha Harmon pulled a cap over her dark curly locks and strode out of her billets, heading for the TOC. Earlier that day, as the tactical operations officer assigned to the 2nd Battalion, it was her job to brief a platoon leader about the details of the mission his team would shortly undertake. Upon their return, she would debrief the same platoon leader to gain information about the men and equipment firing rockets onto the base.

The morning air blowing fresh off the mountains carried the sound of approaching voices to her position. Upon recognizing one of the voices as that of her battalion commander, she came to attention and fired off a crisp salute. "Good afternoon, Colonel Anderson." The senior officer stormed past.

Following the colonel was his translator, Tarik Ajabe. Curiously, today, the man Lt. Harmon normally saw walking side by side with the commander stayed several respectful steps behind. Her eyes creased as a sudden gust of wind blew Tarik's shroud aside to display the aftermath of a shrapnel fragment that had found its way across his face. First, the molten steel burned through his left cornea to deprive him of site in that eye, and then it seared through his facial skin to create a deep crevice down along his cheek.

That scar looks like a dragon poised to fight. The thought struck Lt. Harmon just as he turned to stare into her eyes. She quickly dropped her gaze. With a slight hint of displeasure, he glanced at the smile a nearby officer wore when he looked at Lt. Harmon and pulled the shroud back over his face.

"Bad day," she mumbled under her breath as he disappeared down the path.

The other officer, dressed in standard desert fatigues with captain insignia on his chest, waited until the colonel was out of earshot before commenting, "Guess he didn't like being passed over for promotion."

Her hand slowly lowered as she turned to face Captain Kramer, a tall sandy-haired fellow who, in another place, at another time, she was more than a little familiar. "How do you know he was passed over?" Standing on one foot, she raised the boot of her left foot and rubbed it down her right calf, scratching it from behind.

"Corporal Borman," he replied.

She dropped her foot and thought about the young man sitting behind the desk at Battalion, a shiny-faced boy just out of training. "Clerk, he would know. Did you see General Hays' directive to watch out for apathy?"

The green of Captain Kramer's iris narrowed. "Yes. The word is, the colonel's become a little immune to civilian casualties."

"We're aware." She stuffed a hand into a pocket of her battle fatigues and pulled out a protein bar, along with a white envelope that fluttered to the ground. The captain bent to pick up the envelope and peered at Brian McFadden's name on the return address.

"Your brother doesn't write letters. What's going on, Sam?"

"Nothing. It's just my birth mother isn't well. Now Grandfather is sick, and there's some legal stuff."

"Samantha, why didn't you tell me that your mother is sick?"

She looked away, her eyes glistening. "She's back in LaRue Carter."

"The mental hospital?"

Lt. Harmon wordlessly nodded.

"I'm sorry," he said warily. "How is Brian?"

"My brother, who got to grow up having a mom? He's doing alright."

"Ouch, that was bitter."

"Sorry. She's having trouble with her memory. She doesn't know who I am, and there's nothing I can do from over here."

"Does she know who anybody is?"

"Brian says when Uncle Benny's in town, he takes her outside to sit on the bench and talk. He says she remembers him. Now we have to take care of Grandfather's legal issues."

"Request a leave of absence. Corporal Borman has the forms."

"I will. Right now, I have a team to debrief."

"Walk with me to the TOC," Captain Kramer commanded in a wicked tone.

"West Point's gone to your head, Sir," Lt. Harmon shot back.

Puffing out his chest, he pointed to his captain's bars. "Didn't they teach you at West Point to obey a superior officer? Five minutes, Sam. In your quarters."

Giving the captain a measured gaze, she pulled her five-foot, seven-inch frame to its full height. At 122 pounds soaking wet, her frame alone did not suggest an imposing figure. That was left to the way she held her head, her squared shoulders, and the way her grey-blue eyes bored straight into his. With an about-face on the ball of her right foot, she marched away, heading for the TOC.

Captain Kramer followed with a casual gait. "Does this mean no? Because if five minutes is too much, we can make it four and a half. Or maybe three," he called teasingly from behind.

Stopping abruptly, she once again did an about-face. Her eyes pointed below his waist as she said in an impervious voice, "I'm guessing you're only good for two, Sir." Then she raised her eyes and stated firmly, "Stop kidding around Brad. The patrol's due in any second."

"I heard. That's why I'm heading to the TOC. Major Bingham flew a bird over from the brigade to deal with the situation. Any idea what they found?" he asked, referring to the potentially hazardous material a patrol encountered while on a mission to a nearby village.

Lt. Harmon nodded. "The ordinance team reported finding a truck with canisters of white powder. The EOD on site found explosive material in half the cannisters, but the other half, they don't know yet. That leaves a question about Anthrax or something else. It's all been secured by the HAZMAT team."

"Hazardous Material. Do you have any idea what it is?"

"Not yet. A few of their testing kits are on back order."

"You're kidding! Now what? Ziplocked, bagged, and flown to Langley?"

"After it's tested here. Brigade's bringing over more field tests."

"I assume they're testing for opioids?"

"In the heart of poppy territory, of course. They've also secured someone who might be a big fish. We have to go." With that, they walked swiftly to the TOC.

Inside the Tactical Operations Center, the commander and staff planned, monitored, and directed the activities of 2nd Battalion. Upon entering, Lt. Harmon removed her headgear and walked into the All-Source Intelligence Center. As the officer in charge of tactical intelligence, it was her job to create a comprehensive view of the battlespace for the situation reports she used to brief the patrols. Creating the situation reports, or SITREPS, as the military called them for short, was her favorite job.

"Good afternoon, Mam," Corporal Borman said with barely a glance up from a tactical fax he was reading.

"Have they come over on SINCGARS yet?" she asked, referring to the radio communications the patrol would have installed in the jeeps used to travel through the Afghan countryside.

"Yes, Mam. Patrol's due to roll through the gates in half an hour."

Captain Kramer stood right behind her. "MPs are ready. Ramen aware we'll need him?" he asked, referring to an Afghan interpreter. Ramen wasn't his real name; his legendary love for ramen noodles earned him that nickname. They both looked expectantly at Corporal Borman.

"They're looking for him."

The TOC, a desert sand-colored building painted the same color as every other building on Bagram, contained a small room used primarily for briefing patrols. In there, Lt. Harmon placed her briefcase on a table before walking over to stare at a grease map and traced her finger along today's patrol route. Earlier, she'd briefed a patrol assigned to travel the route that took them through a nearby rural area, a countryside lush with the fruits of agriculture and mud huts common to village life. Their mission objective was to search for the men responsible for last night's rocket attack on the base.

Outside, a Hummer rolled through the front gate carrying a group of hungry, dusty men soon to be

followed by several others. By the gate, the MPs met another Hummer to take control of a shrouded man and escorted him to a detention cell. A local's truck, dark green with the tailgate rusting away on its hinges, was also brought onto the base after being examined by EOD, the explosive ordinance device team sent out with the patrol. In the truck bed sat an arsenal of long silver canisters filled with some type of white powder, each one now individually securely wrapped to prevent leakage. Curiously, the canisters peaking from wooden boxes were labeled "High Explosive Grenades, property of the United States," though no grenades were found. Soon afterward, Staff Sergeant Aguilera walked into the briefing room, followed by his platoon leader, Second Lieutenant Adam Preston.

Lt. Harmon coughed amidst the dust kicked up from the men's boots and motioned to the chairs at her table. "Glad to see you back alright."

"Yes, thank you," responded Lt. Preston. "Glad to be here."

"I hear congratulations are in order. The baby is due in the fall?"

A wide grin quickly replaced the fatigue on Lt. Preston's face. "November 2," he replied as he relaxed into his chair.

Lt. Harmon opened her laptop and waited for pictures and footage taken by Specialist Ingram from the 1st Combat Camera to download, adding to the ones already sent from Sergeant Aguilera's phone. After refreshing her screen, she opened the file and studied the photos intently. "She's good. Poppy farmers?"

"Business as usual, brought to you by your local Afghan suppliers. Number one country poisoning the world," stated Sergeant Aguilera.

"And a lot of it here. And this," Lt. Preston said, pointing to an area in one of the fields.

"I saw our hit-and-run last night. Katyusha, no doubt left over from the Russian years. Junk weapons that actually work, and fortunately unguided. But unfortunately, very mobile."

"Anything in the barns?"

"Bunch of wine bottles in baskets."

"Full?" Lt. Harmon asked. "That town is known for wine. And pottery."

"All full in the barn. Several empties in the house. He had a fresh bottle opened with two glasses poured and a candle on the table. Looked like he was expecting someone."

"Any weapons?"

"Not that we saw. We brought in a shooter from the fields."

"Just one from that whole village?"

"Allah called."

With a nod, Lt. Harmon indicated she understood the other attackers had gone on to meet their maker and made the sign of the cross. The war in Afghanistan raged on, frequently adding casualties to both sides. She pointed to a house circled on an enlarged photo. "This where you found Assad?"

Earlier that morning, while briefing the platoon on the target, she explained that Assad Al-Jazeera was a high-value target. His communication with Jamal Haqqani, a leading anti-Soviet Islamist commander who became a prominent Taliban official and eventually a key leader in the post-2001 insurgency, was of great concern to US officials.

Lt. Preston summarized the capture of Assad. "Yes, he was there alone. We got him and his cell phone, a laptop, and a parrot. That's it."

"You brought in the bird?"

"He might talk."

"Weapons?"

"AK-47's."

"Fits the Russian connection. Good job bringing him in alive. I'll be talking with him before I brief headquarters. Grab a meal, you may be going back out."

A knock on the wooden door announced the arrival of an MP, and when a team member opened the door, his stony face told the group their meeting was over. As they all stood and filed into the hallway, Lt. Harmon wrinkled her nose against the dust cloud flowing from Lt. Preston's uniform.

"We can't all be a princess," Captain Kramer yelled, much to the delight of the other men.

"We don't all have my brain," she shot back with a note of irritation in her voice.

Rather than becoming offended, the men stared at her with admiration. Lt. Preston walked back and touched her elbow. "Nice job putting that together." He looked at Captain Kramer. "She figured out who was in a hut because he had an African Grey. The guy from Pakistan was a beach bum in Florida who used to carry it to the clubs before he returned home to his province."

"It's hard to hide an African Grey over here. Kids talk," Lt. Harmon said with a smile. "Then we got a nice picture of it sitting in the window from a photo recon specialist."

Captain Kramer looked completely lost. "What's an African Grey?"

"You know, a Psittacus."

"Which is?"

"A parrot," Lt. Preston and Sergeant Aguilera said together.

"Oh." Captain Kramer started laughing.

Lt. Preston laughed along with him. "Talking parrot kept calling Aguilera 'Mi Amore.' Guess she likes Hispanics."

"She wouldn't go for your stinky ass," Sergeant Aguilera replied. With his dark lashes hooding his twinkling brown eyes, he flashed a huge grin at everyone and walked away, saying in his thick Spanish accent, "Got to check on my new girlfriend."

"Are you going to interrogate the parrot?" Lt. Preston asked.

"Maybe later. Hang onto her. If she says anything interesting, alert the TOC."

"Roger that." Lt. Preston headed off with a smile.

Two beefy MPs stood positioned on either side of a door next to the briefing room. Soon, a man wearing civilian clothes emerged and nodded to Lt. Harmon. She understood. Mr. Owens, an interrogator working for the U.S. government, was there to solicit Assad's cooperation. From a kindly man in a white shirt he'd get the soft treatment, if only he'd cooperate.

"Ramen in there?" Lt. Harmon asked an MP.

"They couldn't find him. The C.O. sent somebody else."

The tough girl's expression normally seen on Lt. Harmon's face turned to a startled look. "That's not like Ramen. Keep looking."

"We are Lieutenant," he responded in a monotone voice.

Lt. Harmon gave him a sharp glance. "This isn't like him. Keep looking."

The MP flinched and picked up a radio. "Base alert, update on SITREP Ramen. Over."

"He's a situation?" Lt. Harmon rolled her eyes.

"He is now, Mam," the MP responded.

The radio remained silent for a moment. Eventually, a voice responded with, "No eyes on the subject yet. Over."

"Roger that. Keep looking."

"Copy that."

"We can't wait," Lt. Harmon said. While an MP held a door open, she marched into the room as the MPs walked out. Her desert fatigues, un-creased and fitting just snug enough to show off a bit of her womanly features, hid the sweat-stained collar of her T-shirt as she looked at the man handcuffed to a chair. He was gaunt, dark-haired and brown-eyed, the same descriptive adjectives she found on every member of the Taliban.

Go figure. Then she looked over at the interpreter sitting to her left and immediately rose and walked out the door.

An MP came to attention. "Mam?"

"I don't want Tarik in here."

"We can't find Ramen. The C.O. sent him."

"Get somebody else."

Captain Kramer walked back from the communications center. "Is there a problem?"

Not wanting to seem ill-equipped to deal with a situation in front of the man she'd met at West Point, Lt. Harmon glared at the MP before responding, "Nothing I can't handle." She turned and marched back in to interrogate the prisoner.

"Want us to keep looking for Ramen?" the MP asked.

"No, it's fine." Lt. Harmon gave the man a measured look as he closed the door. In the interrogation room, rather than speaking, she sat down and flipped through a file. Several moments went by before she glanced up. "When did you leave Florida?"

Tarik translated Assad's response. "Two years ago."

"You understand English?"

Assad did not respond to that until Tarik translated the question. "Not much, no."

"You lived in Florida, and you don't understand THAT question?" Lt. Harmon raised a brow. "Why does the parrot speak Spanish?"

When Tarik translated the question, Assad said with a smirk, "Not Spanish, Italian. She came that way."

"Mafia bird," Lt. Harmon said. "You lived in Chicago before you moved to Florida." *Drug runner.* She studied the man's creased face. His long, narrow cheeks presented well beneath a pair of dark circular eyes encased in lush lashes. His pink lips, once full, were already thinning with age, which Intel put at forty-two. *He looks 60.* She rose and asked an MP standing outside the door to come into the room and watch while another officer pulled back the man's sleeves.

Assad stared with impertinence as Sergeant Barrows rolled up the dirty cloth to expose the tattoo of a dagger overlaid with the number five written in Arabic. And something else.

"Track marks. Heroin?" Lt. Harmon asked.

Sweat dripped from Assad's brow as he jerked his arm away.

"Looks like he's needing a fix," one of the MPs observed.

Lt. Harmon looked at Tarik. "Tell him we'll get him over for medical care, eventually." While Tarik relayed the message, she opened Assad's phone. "Not password protected?"

Tarik spoke up. "Too old."

"What?"

"Older people don't do electronics. Have to keep it simple," he replied.

Especially when his head is snowed with drugs. With narrowed eyes, her thumb flipped through Assad's phone and found a number he'd called several times during the past few weeks. "Looks like you're buds with Jamal Haqqani. What did you guys talk about?"

Sweat poured from Assad's forehead.

"Give me something." Lt. Harmon's grey-blue eyes begged for information. Assad's eyes begged for relief as his facial muscles began to twitch. "We know you have a Katyusha prepared to launch. What is the target?" She looked at Tarik. "Make sure he understands that question."

Tarik translated the statement to Pashto. Assad spoke a few words, then Tarik responded back to him without relaying the message to Lt. Harmon.

"What did you say to him?" she asked suspiciously.

"He wanted to know what you meant by target. I told him building, people, location. You need to give him something."

Having picked up some of those words, Lt. Harmon nodded. "Where is the red truck, the one you had parked outside the barn two days ago? Our patrol searched the barn, so we know it's not there."

With his eyelids sinking shut, Assad's lips slowly moved to utter a few words. Lt. Harmon pulled open the door to the hallway, yelling, "Medic." Then she turned to face Tarik. "What did he say?"

"At the market."

"The truck is at what market?"

Tarik shrugged.

As they waited for a medic to examine Assad, Lt. Harmon stood in the hallway sipping coffee from a cardboard cup. "Could be a car bomb heading somebody's way. What's the biggest open market within a few miles of Assad's home?"

"Charikar probably has one tomorrow. There may be several in Kabul."

"We have to find that truck." She opened the door and directed the medics, "Get him awake."

"Mam."

Lt. Harmon turned to find Staff Sergeant Aguilera standing behind her. "Yes?"

"The parrot is talking."

Captain Kramer quizzed Lt. Harmon from the control room, where she appeared moments after receiving the news. "Sam, Lieutenant. What did the parrot say?"

"Not now, Brad, I mean Captain. Right now, I need to speak with Major West over at brigade.

"Already dialed the number. Here." Captain Kramer swiveled his chair around and handed over the phone.

"Thanks." Lt. Harmon's grey-blue eyes shot him an appreciative look. "Major West, this is Lieutenant Harmon at 2nd Battalion. I need a flyover."

Major West responded immediately to the urgency in her voice. "What is your objective?"

"We need to find the red truck in the picture I forwarded to your email. Based on intel we received from a patrol and an assessment by Major Bingham at brigade operations, there is significant reason to believe this truck could be used to transport biological or chemical material."

"Give me the grid coordinates."

"Three-five-zero-one-zero-eight. Those coordinates are for Charikar. Take a look at any area around flea markets, especially the market on the road from Charikar to Kabul. Last night, Bagram was hit with a few rockets launched from an old Russian artillery weapon, a Katyusha. An hour ago, one of our patrols brought in a man named Assad, who was communicating with the leader of a Taliban network. Today, our patrol secured a truck near his property. The back end was full of canisters containing some type of white powder. We have area footage of a red truck sitting outside Assad's house taken two days ago. Before he passed out, he said the truck was at a market. Why did he leave the truck at a market? Our best guess is that it was used to transport some type of weapons or materials to a transfer point. We need to locate that truck and find out what's in it."

"Did EOD determine if the white powder is an explosive?"

"Yes. Only some of it tested positive for an explosive agent. Since the powder is white, Major Bingham is concerned that it could be Anthrax."

"What makes you think the truck could be at one of those particular markets?"

"Because Assad was getting ready to open a good bottle of wine and toast a woman he was dating, Nadja Jammu. She's an al-Qaeda operative who makes baskets to look like she has a legitimate business. We found a collection in the barn. We also found a collection of wine in the barn, and the cover story is the wine was going to the market. But nobody stores wine in a barn. It's too hot."

"Good work, Lieutenant. You've got your flyover. By the way, how do you know Assad was getting ready to toast his love interest?"

"A parrot told us, Sir."

"A what?"

"A parrot. Assad kept a talking African Grey in his house."

After a few moments of silence, Major West asked, "What exactly did the parrot say?"

"She came in calling Sergeant Aguilera 'Mi Amore.' My love. Later, she added the word toast."

Major West's voice exploded over the phone. "You want me to authorize a flyover based on a parrot? How do you know it didn't mean buttered toast, or jelly, or French toast?"

"That's ridiculous- Sir. Sorry, they don't make French toast in those mud huts. And he didn't have a toaster, or butter, or jelly.

"That's all you got?"

"Yes, Sir."

"You're a little thin on this, Lieutenant, but you've got your mission."

"Thank you, Sir."

Soon, an MC-12, a liberty intelligence-gathering aircraft, lifted from a runway to fly above Charikar, collecting real-time imagery of the community and its surrounding area, then promptly transmitted the imagery back to the base.

"Toast, you got a flyover based on a parrot saying the word toast?" From the next desk, Captain Kramer's eyes sparkled with admiration.

"You can't tell anybody. It's classified." With a finger to her lips, Lt. Harmon shushed him as Colonel Anderson walked into the TOC. "Sir, we have a bird in the air gathering intel…" she started to say.

"Major West filled me in. A parrot? That's why you're calling a bird? Why didn't you report in sooner, Lieutenant?" his voice screamed.

Lt. Harmon's face remained an unreadable mask as she looked at Colonel Anderson and said, "I'm reporting now, Sir. This is my first opportunity. After questioning Assad, a prisoner brought in earlier, it became urgent that we locate his truck. Major West authorized a flyover around Charikar. It's happening right now." Breaking her standoff with the commander, her eyes looked past him at a man arriving dressed in a white shirt tucked into a pair of blue jeans. Ramen squirmed under Lt. Harmon's stare.

"Bathroom," he said.

"We have intel coming in, Sir," she finished. "The MC-12 is transmitting photos." A few moments later, she stood in the TOC reviewing the findings with Major West. "I have Colonel Anderson here with me. In one of the first photos, there's a red truck at an open-air market identical to the truck Assad had parked on his property. At the market, the truck bed is empty. A few moments later, when the Hawk circled and collected additional footage, the truck was gone."

"I see it. You think the truck might have been off-loaded at the market?"

"I believe so. Yes, Sir."

"I'll run this past Bingham."

"Yes, Sir."

Moments later, Colonel Anderson received orders from the brigade to send out a patrol to search the market. After the order passed through Captain Bruce, Team Snake Eyes company commander, Lt. Preston, once again appeared before Lt. Harmon for a briefing. Together, they stood in front of a map and studied the patrol route. She traced her finger along the line to Charikar and pointed to a spot on the map. "The market is here, along this road. The mission is to check the market for weapons, ammunition, the usual drill."

After the briefing, she followed Lt. Preston outside and grinned when he told the patrol, "Come on ladies, we're going shopping." As the men loaded into the Hummers, a figure dressed out in combat gear ran out of a nearby building.

"Ramen's going with you," Lt. Harmon said.

Lt. Preston told him to get in his Hummer and motioned for Specialist Holland, the photographer from the 1st Combat Camera, to join the second vehicle. Lt. Harmon walked up to her and said, "Good job on that last set of photos. We need pictures of the market shelves ASAP."

"Yes, Mam," Specialist Holland replied. "I'll send a video."

Soon, the convoy rolled past the gate guards heading toward Charikar. After giving the convoy a quick wave, Lt. Harmon turned to find Tarik standing behind her. Under the shadow of his stare, she winced and backed away, disconcerted by the look of displeasure on his face. Once she'd gained a little distance, her pace quickened as she hurried back into the TOC to find Captain Kramer sitting at his desk. She told him about her run-in with Tarik.

"What was that all about?"

"I don't know. Maybe he thought he should have been on that patrol, or maybe he doesn't like women in the military. Maybe his turban is wound too tight, not my problem," she replied flippantly as she took a seat. "I'll wait here for word from the patrol."

Captain Kramer's eyes looked at her approvingly.

Soon, the voice of Lt. Preston came over a speaker. "Command center, this is Snake Eyes. We've entered the market. There are containers like those at the barn in the last stall, and all appear to be empty. Over."

As Company Commander, Captain Bruce sat in the TOC with Corporal Borman, manning the Blue Force Tracker to maintain a location on the patrol. They listened over the radio to the events unfold. "Copy that. Check those containers for residue." Moments later, he sat in front of a computer, saying, "We have patrol video coming through." When he clicked on it, the command group observed a video of market scenes with booths of wares containing everything from handmade jewelry to scarves, baskets, and dishes. In the last booth where the patrol was now located, the shelves were lined with pottery. As the camera zoomed inside one of the pots, they saw that, though clean, the inside was spotted with water droplets.

"Freshly washed," Lt. Harmon surmised. "Could have been used to transport powder to the shells they found. Back that up."

Captain Bruce slowly rewound the video and stopped when the outside of the pottery came into view.

"Don't touch anything. There's powder in the corner you need to have checked," Lt. Harmon yelled.

"Roger that," Lt. Preston said.

Specialist Holland continued sending the video of the patrol as everyone sat listening to Lt. Preston give commands. After establishing a perimeter, he stood waiting for the HAZMAT team to be helicoptered in.

With fatigue etching her mind, Lt. Harmon looked up and requested someone bring black coffee. As Corporal Bowman placed a steaming cup in her hand, she leaned closer to peer at the computer screen and pointed to a small figure now standing in front of the second stall. "Who's that?"

"Just some kid," Lt. Preston replied.

Indeed, as he drew closer to the camera, they could see the figure was a small child, approximately nine years old, approaching with one hand held behind his back.

Standing silently by with his weapon aimed at the boy, Lt. Preston ordered the men to hold fire. Seconds later, back in the command center, the group stared stone-faced as the next scene played out on video.

Lt. Preston ordered the boy to drop whatever he held behind his back. The boy, though shaking and clearly afraid, held on to his possession. Through Ramen, the patrol learned the boy claimed to have a pot containing his father's ashes behind his back. Ramen instructed the boy to bring the pot slowly around to the front, which he did. Lt. Preston pulled down his mask, smiled kindly at the boy, and walked up to look into the pot. The boy brought the pot up a few inches, seemingly for a better view. Then he blew into the chamber and turned his head as a cloud of dust rose, a white cloud Lt. Preston could not avoid inhaling. He immediately fell to the ground. Seconds later, he stopped breathing.

As the boy prepared to blow into the pot again, shots rang out—*bam bam bam*. The impact of the bullets threw his little body backward, bringing his arm up to tilt the pot's contents over his head. The people in the TOC stared at the small boy lying on the ground with blood oozing in red splotches through the white powder, willing him to move.

"He's dead," a soldier said. The video ended.

CHAPTER 2

Bagram Airforce Base
  June 21, 2021

"Where's that bird?"

"Which bird, Mam?"

"The Psittacus. The parrot."

"I believe Sergeant Aguilera has that bird in his billets, Mam," the corporal replied in his thick southern drawl.

"Bring… it… here." Lt. Harmon's hands curled into fists as her eyes wildly ordered Corporal Borman to comply. He averted his eyes.

"Chelsey has to stay in her cage."

"I know," she shouted. "Get somebody to bring the damn cage. Can't anybody do anything around here? Have it brought to the interrogation room, now!" She stormed out of the office yelling, "And have the MP's report to me."

While waiting for the military police to arrive, she stopped in the briefing room and stared at the patrol map. As she thought about the scene on the ground, her finger traced along the route the patrol took to the market. *Why was the pottery empty? What was the white powder on the shelf? The same powder the boy had in his vase?* Then she thought about the boy.

Why was he there alone? This seems like a setup. Somebody tipped the locals the patrol was coming. Who? Tarik?

An MP appeared in the doorway. "You wanted to see us?"

Without taking her eyes from the map, she asked, "How's your prisoner?"

"Doing alright now. We heard about Lt. Preston. Do you want Assad back?"

"Yes, right now. Let me know when he's in the interrogation room."

"Will do," the MP replied.

Captain Kramer walked through the door and said in a softened voice, "Lt. Harmon, Sam. What are you thinking?"

"Not now." Her eyes narrowed in on the location of the barn. "Assad!" Swiftly, she turned, pushed past the captain, and ran back to the control room where all eyes were still staring at the market in Charikar. She joined them in time to see Lt. Preston, surrounded by the HAZMAT team and now decontaminated, lying naked with a tube in his throat and an IV in his arm. "Does he have a pulse?" she asked as they watched the corpsman squeeze an Ambu bag to give breaths through a tube.

"The corpsman signaled they do," Corporal Borman replied.

"Radio the Medevac. They need to know the powder is possibly morphine. Possibly heroin. That's not something they would expect in this kind of incident."

"Roger that, Mam."

As Corporal Borman re-established radio communication with the medics, Lt. Harmon pulled out her hat and walked out of the control room, heading out for a breath of air. Her eyes motioned for Captain Kramer to follow. "A word in private, Sir."

Once they were outside, his jawline became rigid as he bounced a quarter in his hand. "What makes you think the powder was morphine?"

"We're in the heart of poppy territory."

"And?"

"Assad's been shooting up heroin. The truck, that pottery. It all came from his property. Any word from the HAZMAT team?"

"Nothing's come down the pipe yet."

Lt. Harmon nodded. "Anthrax results wouldn't be back until tomorrow. They can test for morphine now. Let's take a walk."

"Don't you have prisoners on the way?"

"You're calling the bird a prisoner?"

"The bird's in a cage. Doesn't get any more prisoner than that. What else is going on?"

"What makes you think anything's going on?"

"I know you. Look, any other day you would have been talking to the medic yourself. You're not becoming jaded, are you?"

"I have a job to do!"

"I know."

"Walk with me."

Captain Kramer gave her a lopsided smile and followed her footsteps to the side of the TOC. "Now?"

"Behave, this is serious." With her back pressed against the building, she pulled off her cap and leaned forward, shaking out her hair. Then she ran her fingers through her dark locks before replacing her headgear, a desert-colored soft cap.

With a long, exaggerated sigh, Captain Kramer reached into his pocket and pulled out a pack of M&M's leftover from an MRE, then popped a green one in his mouth. "If you don't have a minute, why are you doing your hair?"

"Okay, I know what you're doing. We just watched a little boy get himself killed. It's my job to prevent that kind of thing," Lt. Harmon cried.

"Our job," he replied testily. He lifted his cap, then replaced it. "Hmmm, it does help to get a little air in your head. Want some," he asked, holding out the M&M packet as he shared a bit of survival information. "If you're going to have a Meal Ready to Eat, always get number eight. It has the M&M's."

"Of course, you would know that. How soon will the patrol head back to base?" she asked while grabbing for the M&M packet. Captain Kramer pulled it back and dumped a few pieces of candy in his palm, then handed her a red one.

"A couple of them are on a bird now. 455th's going to want answers like yesterday."

"Public Affairs, of course. So is the colonel. What about Ramen? Can you get him on a bird?"

"Why? Tarik is here."

The muscles around Lt. Harmon's eyes hardened, bringing her dark lashes up to cover the steely look in her grey-blue eyes. "I don't trust him."

The captain's jaw tightened as he said, "You have to give me more than that."

"Shush, there he is," she whispered as they watched a figure glide silently past the row of wooden admin buildings. Lt. Harmon waited a moment before walking up to the corner of the building and watched Tarik's back disappear. Then she made up her mind and returned to Captain Kramer's side.

"You've never liked him. Why?" he asked.

"I can't read him. It seems like he has some kind of hidden agenda. Somebody tipped off Assad's girlfriend the patrol was coming."

"Why do you say that?"

"Because she bailed out of the search area right before the patrol arrived."

"How do you know that?"

"She didn't touch her wine."

Captain Kramer let the comment pass. "Tarik is here, and Mr. Owens is on his way. It's too late to get Ramen on a bird. Whatever Tarik may or may not have done, he's all you've got right now. He's not going to change the prisoner's words."

"But," she tried to interject.

"You have no proof it was him. If you want to wait for Ramen, the patrol should be back in a couple of hours. My guys have to deal with the boy. Mr. Owens gets Tarik. Do you want me to talk to HAZMAT?"

"Go ahead," she replied in a strained voice. "Let me know what they say. The parrot is here. I better talk to Mr. Owens before he talks to Assad again."

"Sir, Mam." From the corner of the building, Corporal Borman stood eyeing the hidden couple and said timidly, "Sorry to interrupt."

"Yes?" Captain Kramer's voice commanded a response.

"Patrol's on their way back. They have a prisoner."

"When did that happen?"

"After the squad left, an NBC team going through the market heard a sound. It turned out there was a woman rolled up on a carpet. When they got her outside, she saw the boy and started screaming."

"She's the mother?"

"Apparently, she is."

"Did she give the patrol her name?"

"Nadja Jammu."

"Perfect." Lt. Harmon deferred the next move to the captain. "Sir?"

"Let's go."

"Mr. Owens is in the briefing room," Corporal Borman said, holding the door open for the officers.

Lt. Harmon entered first, saying, "Thanks, Corporal. Would you get Brigade on the phone for Captain Kramer? I need him for another moment. He needs to talk to the HAZMAT team, so wait five minutes."

"Yes, Mam."

Inside the briefing room, she found Mr. Owens sitting in front of a pepperoni pizza. He pulled out a slice and stuffed the hot, gooey mess in his mouth, then mumbled through the pepperoni, "Help yourself."

"Where did this come from? Pizza Hut closed."

"Church group in the states sent it." Mr. Owens washed down the remaining slice with a soda and leaned back, looking expectantly at the congregation of two.

"Mr. Owens, we sent a patrol out earlier to a market looking for a truck that was parked at Assad's place. They located the truck at a market, along with a dozen pottery vases that had been recently washed. I believe the vases were used to transport whatever white powder was in the shell casings found in Assad's barn. The vases were then cleaned and transported to the market for sale by his girlfriend, Nadja Jammu. A young boy, who we think may be her son, was also there. He blew a white powder into Lieutenant Preston's face. That powder caused him to stop breathing. I believe that white powder is a morphine crystal. Someone had to tip the market off that the patrol was coming, giving Nadja time to plan the attack on our soldiers and hide in a carpet. Tarik could be the leak."

"If that did happen, why do you think it was Tarik?"

"He works for Colonel Anderson. He knew the patrol was going out, and he knew where it was going. Who else?"

"You want me to question him?"

"Affirmative. We need to get answers before I report to Colonel Anderson. First, though, we need to finish interrogating Assad. We need to find out what the target was. Those shells were found in a box next to the Katyusha. It's possible those shells may contain a morphine crystal rather than anthrax. But why?"

"Maybe just a container for transport?" Mr. Owens said skeptically. "They do run a lot of drugs here."

"Then why the Katyusha?"

Mr. Owens had no answer for that.

"Captain Kramer, brigade's on the phone," Corporal Boorman called through the door. As he rose to leave, Lt. Harmon handed him a napkin.

"You've got sauce on your face."

"Thanks," he replied, accepting the napkin. "I haven't heard yet. How are you going to interrogate the parrot?"

"Later. Go talk to brigade while I brief Mr. Owens on the parrot."

"You're giving me orders?" he asked with a slight grin.

"Please?" Her eyes begged for cooperation as she replied with her most charming smile, "You've got the rank."

Captain Kramer straightened his shoulders and headed out to talk with the commander of the 855th Brigade. When the door closed, Mr. Owens' face lit with amusement as he opened the lid to the pizza box. "Darned, no crackers in here."

"You're so funny. You heard about the parrot."

"Word travels. You want me to interrogate the parrot, too?"

Lt. Harmon smiled. "No. If we could, I would. I just thought, if we had the parrot in the room while we're questioning Assad, she might say something. Earlier, the bird gave us Nadja, a woman the patrol captured at the market. She's Assad's girlfriend. They're bringing her in."

With a slow nod, Mr. Owens stood to leave. "Anything else?"

"The parrot's name is Chelsey."

"Officially?"

"Sergeant Aguilera calls her that. The bird has a thing for him."

Shaking his head, Mr. Owens walked out to question Assad.

As she sat waiting for Captain Kramer, Lt. Harmon mindlessly reached into the pizza box and pulled out a slice. Using her index finger, she straightened the end before biting off the tip.

"You were right," Captain Kramer said through the open door. "Brigade had the lab perform a test on the powder while I was on the phone. The reagent tested positive for opiates."

"Heroine?"

"That's the assumption since he responded to Narcan. Still, maybe not. I had them ask if inhaling heroin could have caused Lt. Preston's collapse."

"And?"

"They said no, not in powder form. It would have had to be nebulized."

Not being the answer she expected, Lt. Harmon looked momentarily confused. "Melted in a spoon and aerosolized? That obviously didn't happen. Okay, check with the hospital. See if any lab tests are back."

"I'll head over there after the team returns."

"ETA?"

"Maybe another forty minutes."

"So you have time now," Lt. Harmon said. "I'll be back."

"Where are you going?"

"To think."

Captain Kramer nodded and returned to the control room. Moments later, Lt. Harmon watched him walk out of the TOC, heading for the hospital. Once he'd left, she pulled a piece of mail from the pocket of her uniform and inside, found the Power-Of-Attorney transferring the authority to make her grandfather's medical decisions from herself to Brian.

It was just a week ago she got the call from Benny- while sailing from Ft. Lauderdale over to the Bahamas, Grandfather became dizzy and started showing signs of a stroke. The crew immediately turned the boat around and headed back to port. Fortunately, they made port within an hour of the start of the situation. Unfortunately, by then, he had slipped into a coma and now remained unresponsive. And she was told that "As your mother is in the hospital, Brian will take over his care." The legal form was no problem. She'd be able to get it notarized by the JAG.

A short note accompanied the form. Holding it up to the light, she squinted at the chicken scrawl Brian called writing.

Hey Sam,

Sorry, you had to find out about Mom and Grandfather over the phone. I just found out, too. Don't worry, just do your job. I've got things covered here.

Mom is still in the facility. Uncle Benny's been here for the last few weeks. They let him check her out of the hospital every day to go outside and sit on a bench. She seems happier, but she still doesn't remember things from one day to the next, so don't worry about not being here.

Aunt Diana is beside herself. You're not going to believe this, or maybe you will. Jenny's been staying at her house a lot. She can't find work, and now she's getting into heroin.

Burn those poppy fields down!

Brian.

No. Not Jenny! She crumpled the letter and threw it in the trash, then grabbed her cap and headed to her billet. Moments later, she walked into the workout facility and donned a set of burgundy boxing gloves.

One, two- jab- jab. One, two- uppercut. Samantha's lean, muscled arms continued to throw punch after punch, pummeling the bag until her whole body glistened with sweat. Her breathing became faster, more measured. With one last punch she dropped her hands, leaned heavily into the bag, and grabbed the sides for support. *The boy. He's gone.*

Unnoticed by Lt. Harmon, a dark figure stood against the wall watching her unload furry onto a punching bag. As she leaned wearily into the canvas, he took a step toward her and stopped. As the long shadow of a shroud engulfed the boxing arena, she turned to find Tarik hovering behind her as above the shroud, his glittering black eyes bored into hers. Silently, he turned and, without a word, left through a side door.

Mr. Owens must have talked to him.

After giving herself the luxury of a two-minute shower, she donned a fresh uniform before stuffing her gym gear into her bag, then dropped the whole thing off at her billet before walking back toward the TOC. On her way, she looked up at the watchtowers fully displayed in the sunset blazing over the white-topped mountains. The tail of an F-16, a fighter plane flown over from Wisconsin, beamed in the haze against the mountain backdrop. Soon, the *whop whop* of a Black Hawk's helicopter blades announced the patrol's arrival.

Inside the TOC, Lt. Harmon went to the control room asking if Captain Kramer had returned.

"No," Corporal Borman said, giving her a blank stare.

"Alright. Let me know when he gets here." She turned, walked straight to the briefing room, and found what was left of the patrol sitting in various stages of dress, hungrily consuming pizza. Every man in the room stood when she walked in. Sergeant Aguilera said, "Evening, Mam."

"Evening," she nodded.

"You called that one right, Lieutenant," he said with more than a little admiration in his voice. They all took a seat.

Lt. Harmon sat at her desk and flicked open a pen across a yellow legal pad. "Tell me in your words what you found. Exactly, word for word, what happened, and you're going to have to do this again. A boy was killed."

"You mean, we killed a boy," Corporal Sanders yelled, his pale face now reddened with anger.

"It's all captured on video. Let's get through this report." The soothing tone in Lt. Harmon's voice proved calming. "We'll get to that. What did you first see when you approached the market?"

Sergeant Aguilera took a chug from his canteen and then replied in a voice dripping with fatigue, "When we approached, the market looked like business had already shut down for the day, which we found odd. It's too soon for Ramadan."

"Did you see any movement?"

"Not at that time."

"The vases. Were they all in one stall?"

"Yes."

"Any odor?"

"No, Mam."

"How many vases did you find?"

"We counted fourteen."

Lt. Harmon pulled out a photo provided by the 334th Combat Camera depicting a plate of uneaten chicken and handed it to Sergeant Aguilera. He passed it around the group. "Did you see this plate?"

"I don't know. Maybe in that stall."

"Which stall?"

"The one with the vases."

"Anything else for sale in that stall?"

"Men's clothing. Didn't have time to check all the pockets. We bagged it and brought it along," Sergeant Aguilera replied.

"And Kaftans, shrouds and shoes," interjected Corporal Sanders. "And one Russian-made shotgun. And something strange. There was a huge carton of baby powder, and all the labels were in English. But that was in another stall."

"The one where you found the female prisoner?"

"No. It was in the first stall."

"What kind of baby powder?"

"The kind you put in diapers."

Lt. Harmon's eyes looked blank. "No telling how long it was there or who left it. Wait a minute." She rose and walked back to the control center.

"Mam?" Corporal Boorman asked in a quizzical voice.

"Get Major West on the horn," she said fervently. Within seconds, she was handed the phone.

"Lieutenant Harmon, what the hell happened at that market?"

"We don't know exactly, but we'll find out soon. I was interviewing the team, but I stopped for a second to call you. I need the background file on an al-Qaeda operative, Nadja Jammu. The boy may be her son. I've asked for his photo."

After a moment of silence, Major West said, "Get a positive ID on the boy," and hung up. She handed the phone back to the corporal, saying, "Print off a photo of the boy." Then she returned to the briefing room, knowing the file would be in her inbox before she completed the debriefing.

"Let's resume. How many guns did you find at the market?"

"Just one."

"Any explosives?"

"There were a few small cannisters at the site. EOD is on scene."

Lt. Harmon nodded and opened her laptop. *Come on, get me that file.* "While you were searching the stall, where was the boy?"

"We're not sure, Mam. Possibly hidden behind some artwork in another stall. We stopped searching after we found the powder. Had to wait for the NBC team. It's S.O.P., Mam."

"I know, Standard Operating Procedure. It's good you followed it." *BINGO.* The file she requested from brigade sat in her inbox. Additionally, a photo taken by the combat photographer had just come in. She clicked on the photo and turned her laptop toward the team. "It was reported that a woman was found rolled up on a carpet. Her?"

The photo Lt. Harmon displayed depicted a dark-haired woman staring up at the camera as she lay curled in a ball on the floor. The next photo followed her emotions as she rose and defiantly glared at the camera. In the next photo, she was in tears as she stared at the body of a small boy lying shrouded on the ground. That was the photo Public Affairs would shove to the bottom of the pile. These two people, the woman assumed to be a terrorist and a boy attempting to murder U.S. servicemen, that's what the public would see. She opened a file and showed the team a photo included with Nadja's family history and profile.

"This is the boy?" Not wanting to agitate Corporal Sanders further, Lt. Harmon showed the picture to Sergeant Aguilera.

"It looks like him," he replied.

"Gentlemen, enjoy your pizza. Someone from brigade will arrive soon to continue the debriefing."

"Mam, how's Lieutenant Preston?"

"I don't know yet. Captain Kramer's talking to the doctors over at Craig Hospital. He'll be back soon." Lt. Harmon picked up her laptop and strolled out of the briefing room, seemingly in no hurry to go anywhere.

But as soon as she got to the control center, she sat down at Captain Kramer's desk and reopened her computer to stare at the female prisoner. *Her eyes look vacant.* Moving on, she observed the photo of Nadja's son, petite in size for his age, staring defiantly at the photographer. The next photo gave her pause, and not just because it was in a different local than she expected. *Who is this?*

The photo, taken in the shadows of a bridge nicknamed the Rainbow Bridge, depicted a young man sitting amidst a circle of other men leaning back against a pillar. From the bundles of clothes piled into carts, they looked to be a group of homeless men listlessly watching life pass by.

"Who's that?" a familiar voice asked from behind her back, causing her to start.

Realization came as she stared at the screen and told Captain Kramer, "Apparently, Nadja has another son who used to live with that group of addicts. The area beneath this bridge in Kabul is a cesspool of heroin addicts."

"I've heard about that. A lot of drugs are dealt from under the Rainbow Bridge."

Nodding slowly as she studied the photo, Lt. Harmon looked sadly at the gaunt faces of the homeless men. "It's a place for the hopeless to survive, if just for a night. With no jobs in this country and nowhere else to go, a lot of them don't last long."

"You said he used to live there. He's gone?"

"Apparently. Nobody knows where he is at the moment. What's the word on Lt. Preston?"

"He's alive. They're keeping him ventilated. He did test positive for opioids and something else."

"What?"

Captain Kramer pulled a piece of paper from his pocket and opened it. "Have you heard of fentanyl?"

Lt. Harmon's eyes showed a moment of confusion. "Um, I don't think so." With a few quick keystrokes, she pulled up the drug information on fentanyl and gasped. "This explains why the powder was so effective!"

"Why is that?"

"It's a drug one hundred times more powerful than heroin."

"I guess that's why they're sending him to San Antonio. A Globemaster with an oxygen team is standing by for transport."

"A transport. Won't the drugs wear off?"

"Yes. But he got a huge dose, and now they're worried about heart damage. Luckily, you saved him by telling the medics it was an opioid. Those seconds counted."

"Saved him for what, to be brain damaged?"

With sinking hearts, everyone in the control room stopped to stare at the scene being played out behind Captain Kramer's desk. Eyeing the others, he stated in a low voice, "This is not the place to talk. He's young and could make a full recovery. You have a job to do. Go do it."

Lt. Harmon turned her laptop from Captain Kramer's view and asked woodenly, "When will they get here with Nadja?"

"She's already here, locked up tight at brigade. They'll have her on the next transport to Gitmo."

"They can't do that! Just because she's a U.S. citizen, that doesn't mean they can rush things."

"They can, and they are. Major West's on the phone."

"Good." With pursed lips, she took a deep breath and picked up the receiver. "Sir, it's Lieutenant Harmon. I hear you have Nadja Jammu. I need to talk to her. We've determined that Lieutenant Preston was poisoned with fentanyl. I need to find out what's going on out there."

"We know, Lieutenant. Is your prisoner, what's his name, Assad. Is he ready for interrogation?"

"Yes. Mr. Owens is with him now."

"Fine. I'll talk to Mr. Owens when he's done. You call me as soon as you've had a crack at him."

"Yes, Sir," Lt. Harmon replied. "Sir, do we know if Nadja's older son is alive?"

"As far as we know, he is. He was taken prisoner after the Helmand operation started. Word was he'd become one of the top drug lords in the area."

"Operation Enduring Freedom. I remember that brief. Helmand was in 2009, right?"

"That's when it started. Mohammad escaped from the Helmand Province and got picked up under a bridge in Kabul a couple of years later."

"He's still in jail?"

"No," Major West said impatiently. "Reread the brief. Bunch of Afghan officials were paid off to the tune of fourteen million dollars in bribes to get him out. Hasn't been seen since."

"Thank you, Sir. I didn't realize that was the same guy. I'll call you back when I have something."

"Or before that. Goodbye Lieutenant."

Captain Kramer wordlessly followed Lt. Harmon down the hall and through the outside door. "Samantha, stop. What was all that about Enduring Freedom?"

"The operation to clean out the poppy fields in the Helmand Province and replace the poppies with other crops. It didn't work, by the way. Afghanistan still produces ninety percent of the world's heroin. But they did clean up that province for a while and arrested a lot of drug lords. Nadja's son was one of them. The Taliban got him out of jail by bribing officials. Now nobody knows where he is."

"I'm glad this war is winding down. A lot of people have died in this operation, and for what?" Captain Kramer's hand clenched as he asked the rhetorical question.

Just as Lt. Harmon nodded her agreement, the rounded figure of Mr. Owens poked his head out the door and looked into the darkened sky. Fatigue lines etched his face as he took a deep breath, held out a bloody finger, and stood fuming, trying to speak.

"What?" Captain Kramer asked.

"That…damned…parrot!"

Chapter 3

Bagram Airforce Base
  June 22, 2021

In the early summer of 2021, Bagram Air Base stood surrounded by mountains where life remained traditional. Out there, the markets teaming with locals had everything from cooped-up chickens to handmade jewelry available for purchase. Occasionally, with the U.S. mission changing from one of a combat role to winning hearts and minds, U.S. service people roamed the market streets on SLEs, the street level engagements designed to engage military personnel on a personal level.

By June of 2021, with the war drawing to a close, the base where Assad sat in an interrogation room had become the last U.S. outpost in the country. And the track marks on the prisoner's arm demonstrated another facet of Afghan life, that of survival. Despite the religious edict to eradicate the flower, the poppy crops brought cash to the Taliban's pockets as well as that of the farmers and laboratories. With so many Afghans suffering from addiction problems and so much of the heroin supply headed for Asia, Europe, Russia, and increasingly, the United States, the military also participated in assisting different law enforcement agencies within Afghanistan to eradicate the poppy fields. U.S. drug interdiction teams were out now confiscating the harvests.

Inside an interrogation room at Bagram, the stench of stale body odor permeated the air as Lt. Harmon's nose wrinkled. "It's no wonder, his mud hut didn't have a shower. Air this room out."

"We're not allowed to open the windows," the MP responded. "Security issue."

"I know." The impertinence of the young woman's voice brought a smile to the MP's face. "Leave the door open while I get coffee."

With his eyes locked squarely in front of him, the MP came to parade rest and stood tight against the door as Lt. Harmon passed by. The scene, perfectly played, told Assad, who was in charge. He slumped down and stared at Chelsey in her locked cage. While fluffing her feathers, she squawked, "Bibi."

The MP's eyes turned sideways, questioning Ramen.

"Afghan name for 'Woman of the house,'" he replied.

Spit flew from the MP's mouth before he was able to straighten his face. He gave Assad a look that said, "Dude, you're in trouble."

In the control room, knowing he'd recognize her personal calling card, Lt. Harmon placed a red candy on Captain Kramer's desk, her way of thanking him for the information he'd shared. Earlier, as they stood outside waiting for Mr. Owens to finish interrogating the prisoner, a C-130 had flown overhead and landed on the far end of the base.

Captain Kramer had pointed at the plane and said, "Drug interdiction is back."

"What were they doing today?"

"They went out to assist the Afghan Special Narcotics Force destroy the poppy fields around Assad's place. How about having the guys come over for a chat?"

Lt. Harmon's eyes had blazed with fury. "Why wasn't I part of that briefing?"

"You were interrogating the parrot, and they were already out. After Lt. Preston was hit, Major Bingham called to let us know they'd been diverted over to Assad's farm," he'd replied curtly.

Unphased by his tone, she stared straight ahead and said, "You still could have told me sooner. But yes, of course, we need to dig deeper into the intel on the fentanyl issue. Bring them over." Then her tone softened as she said, "Sorry, it's been a long day. Let's get this thing done."

With a slight nod, the lines in Captain Kramer's forehead relaxed. "One of their guys took a bullet today. He's doing alright, but they're gonna be eager to help."

"Is there any more pizza?"

It was at that moment Mr. Owens had walked out holding a bloodied finger.

"Ask him."

Lieutenant Harmon did, and Mr. Owens was having a cook from the mess bring more over. "Pays to be friends with the mess."

With his interrogation of Assad complete, Mr. Owens now sat in a private office briefing Major Bingham on his results. Lt. Harmon knocked on his door and entered before he could say, "Come back later." She waited for him to realize who'd entered his domain and motion her to sit, then plopped in a chair.

"Yes sir," he was saying. "Lt. Harmon briefed me on the girlfriend after I talked with the prisoner. She wasn't part of the picture when we started. At least, not in person."

"They've got her," she whispered loudly.

Mr. Owens wagged his hand up and down, signaling he knew, and put the call on speaker. "The prisoner admitted to trafficking heroin. The Katyusha," he said, "was going to be used to launch fireworks to celebrate the U.S. withdrawal from Afghanistan."

He pulled the phone away from his ear as Major Bingham laughed, then yelled, "What else did you get? Why did they attack the platoon when they know we're leaving soon?"

"Assad didn't know anything about it, or so he said. Claims the woman is crazy and acted on her own."

"How long have they known each other?"

"A few years. She's al-Qaeda, he's a drug addict for hire. We know she's a chemist, a former U.S. citizen who traveled to India in 2007 with her nineteen-year-old son to work for a U.S. chemical lab. Met her new husband there, Dalbir Jammu, a lieutenant in the Indian al-Qaeda network. Nadja and her son were recruited, and he went directly to the camps in Afghanistan. In 2012, Dalbir and Nadja had a baby, then they moved over to Afghanistan and lived a clandestine life in a rural area bordering Pakistan. Near Torkham Gate."

"Get an address?"

"No."

"We knew about India. They lost track of her in Afghanistan. Any idea what she was doing here?" Major Bingham asked

"Being brainwashed," Mr. Owens replied.

"How?"

"She was learning the righteousness of the Taliban way and raising her children to learn about the plight of Afghanistan farmers. Especially after the NATO forces bombed the farmland while attacking the Taliban. Put huge craters in their fields and destroyed all the crops, not just the poppies."

"His tongue's that loose?"

"He's that high."

"We know what happened to the older son, or at least we did. And now the younger one. Find out anything about the husband?"

"Killed by the police. Counter-narcotics was out chopping up a poppy field. The Taliban tried to protect it, but the tractor driver had a machine gun. Husband was caught in the crossfire."

"Probably the one doing the shooting for the Taliban," Major Bingham surmised. "His death's never been recorded. Why not?"

"I don't know. Maybe he got dumped in a hole somewhere. Maybe he's not really dead."

"Maybe. Is Lieutenant Harmon around?"

She grabbed the receiver from Mr. Owen's hand. "Right here, Sir."

"You get all that?"

"Yes, Sir. We have a drug interdiction team that just arrived from outside Assad's farm. I'll be debriefing them before I talk to him."

"Very good. Call me back, it's going to be a long night."

"Yes, Sir."

A round-backed wooden chair sat in the corner of the office, the old, worn padding now sunken under the weight of many personnel who'd come in for a chat. Lt. Harmon sank into that chair with her brow furrowed as she closed her eyes to concentrate on a nagging thought.

"Are you alright?" Mr. Owens asked loudly.

"Yes." Her eyes opened and with a slight twitch, focused on a plaque on the wall, a memento given to Mr. Owens upon his retirement from the military. She lifted a desert brown boot from the floor and crossed her legs, then sat with both hands clenched in her lap. After patting wisps of dark curls back into place, her grey-blue eyes stared steadfastly at the man sitting across from her. "You were there."

"I was where?"

"In the Helmand Province. Back when we somehow decided that we could get rid of a drug problem, we can't even get rid of ourselves."

"What are you getting at, Lieutenant?"

"You've been here for a very long time, watching the underbelly of the war. Why?"

"We don't have time for this!"

"Lieutenant Preston was hit with a drug one hundred times more powerful than heroin. It could have killed everybody in the squad. We have nothing but time for this." The soft tone of LT. Harmon's voice firmed as she uncrossed her legs and rolled her chair up closer to the desk.

"How does what I did have anything to do with Lieutenant Preston? That was years ago."

With her grey-blue eyes boring fiercely into the depths of the opaqueness covering Mr. Owens' blank stare, Lt. Harmon said, "I know that you were a chemical weapons specialist. There were people involved with drug interdiction who got to know the locals in the countryside a little too well."

"Meaning what?" Mr. Owens asked suspiciously.

"Meaning some people, some soldiers, went home with more money than they should have had. You worked with a chemist, Abdul Al-Jezail. He had a little operation built into the mountainside in the province. Quite the money maker, cooking heroin from poppies, and you had government money to pay him to quit cooking. After you left the military, you were a bag man, a regular CIA guy sent over with a suitcase full of cash to pay the locals to be good."

"That's all classified, Lieutenant. And I'm not CIA."

"Whatever. A couple of people in your unit who got caught with their hand in the till are still doing time in Leavenworth. And that guy," she said, motioning to the plaque, "that's Abdul. I see that in the background his cooking skills are still in the picture."

"How do you know when that picture was taken?"

Lt. Harmon walked over and removed the frame from the wall. After taking out the picture, she flipped it over and exposed the date written on the back. The skin below Mr. Owens' eyes sagged.

"They said you were good."

"I am good. Tell me about it."

After a moment of stony silence, Mr. Owens stared at the closed door and asked, "It goes no farther than this room?"

"We're not talking in front of the parrot."

The bite mark on Mr. Owens' finger still looked angry. While keeping the finger raised, he typed with his middle fingers to bring up a file. When he was finished, he turned his laptop around to display a document.

LISA HEDGE

[TITLE] deg. AFGHANISTAN'S NARCO WAR:

BREAKING THE LINK BETWEEN

DRUG TRAFFICKERS AND INSURGENTS

A REPORT

TO THE

COMMITTEE ON FOREIGN RELATIONS

UNITED STATES SENATE

One Hundred Eleventh Congress

First Session

August 10, 2009

"That's a long document. What part are we looking at?" Lt. Harmon asked. She rose and walked around to peer over Mr. Owen's shoulder as he turned the laptop back toward himself and highlighted a section.

> As part of the military expansion, the administration has
> assigned U.S. troops a lead role in trying to stop the flow of
> illicit drug profits that are bankrolling the Taliban and
> fueling the corruption that undermines the Afghan Government.
> Tens of millions of drug dollars are helping the Taliban and
> other insurgent groups buy arms, build deadlier roadside bombs
> and pay fighters. The emerging consensus among senior military
> and civilian officials from the United States, Britain, Canada
> and other countries operating in Afghanistan is that the broad
> new counter-insurgency mission is tied inextricably with the
> new counter-narcotics strategy. Simply put, they believe the

Taliban cannot be defeated, and good government cannot be
established without cutting off the money generated by
Afghanistan's opium industry, which supplies more than 90
percent of the world's heroin and generates an estimated $3
billion a year in profits.

"Three billion dollars," Lt. Harmon exclaimed. "The growers don't make that much. So the processors get what, seventy, eighty percent of the profits?"

"Around there."

"And how much of that profit went to your pocket? Never mind. Why?"

"This," he replied.

If we're going to bleed this summer to secure these
areas, if soldiers and Marines are going to die, we need a plan
to come in behind and build long-term security through
development," said Army Brig. Gen. John W. Nicholson Jr., the
deputy commander for the six tough provinces that comprise
Regional Command South.

"We did bleed," he continued. "Families needed to be taken care of." Mr. Owens' normally jovial expression hardened under his words. "My son bled."

As Lt. Harmon's hand snuck onto Mr. Owens' shoulder and gave it a gentle squeeze, she spoke quietly into his ear. "Why the fentanyl?"

"I don't know. You need to get to Nadja."

"You know people at Brigade. Can you get me to her?"

"Done," Mr. Owens said.

"Can you hang around? I'm getting ready to debrief an interdiction team that just came back from an area around Assad's farm." The soft hand withdrew from Mr. Owens' shoulder, making the question a personal request.

He nodded. "Yes. I heard about that."

"Back in a few."

Lt. Harmon hurriedly walked over to the briefing room where the drug interdiction team sat munching away on pepperoni pizza. While staring at the rank of a man finishing a huge slice, she said, "Hello, I assume you're the squad leader." As she spoke, she pulled a map from her briefcase and walked over to place it in front of the sergeant. "Show me exactly where you were today."

The sergeant pulled a map from his pocket and opened it on top of the other, a map already marked with the area for today's mission.

"I thought it was all GPS."

"I'm old school."

The clean scent of Lt. Harmon stood in stark contrast to the grungy, dusty men who smelled of their days' work. She stood back and asked, "The first place was just a mile from Assad's?"

"About that."

"Where were you when you came under fire?"

"By the barn at the first place."

"How many Taliban were there?"

"Too many to count. It was kind of weird. Good thing the Afghans had extra forces."

"Police or soldiers?"

"Police."

After thinking for a moment, Lt. Harmon said, "That is weird. The police are often paid to look the other way. How big was the field?"

"That's the other weird part. It was one of the smallest areas we've ever hit. I think it was more about the lab in the barn."

"Lab?"

"Yeah, there were barrels of black tar cooking, and there were containers labeled with chemicals I've never seen before. The Afghan police confiscated it all."

"Did you write it down? Take any pictures?"

"Yeah," the sergeant replied with a sly smile. "I always pull out the cell as soon as I enter a building. Afghans run us off a lot."

"Keeping money and drugs for themselves," Lt. Harmon surmised. She checked through the pictures and said, "Send these to me," and gave the sergeant her email. Then she went back to a photo of a gaunt little man looking startled to see a soldier at his door. A black turban covered most of his face, but the black hair and beard poking from the fabric identified his nationality. "Who is this?"

"The chemist. Afghans called him Siegfried."

Lt. Harmon asked a few more questions that produced no new information, then thanked the squad for coming. Back in Mr. Owens' office, she pulled up her email displaying the pictures from the interdiction team. "What's your take on this? That man," she said, pointing to the

Afghan. "He's a chemist they call Siegfried, and these are chemicals the sergeant said he'd never seen before. What are they used for?"

He stared at the containers and shrugged. "Don't know. I'll do a little research while you're interrogating Assad."

"Thanks," Lt. Harmon said. "What about Nadja?"

"You'll get her tomorrow," Mr. Owens replied. He glanced at the clock. "It's 0100. One a.m. is too early to wake up the general."

"The general?"

"Old friend."

"Let me know as soon as you get anything on the chemicals. I better go interrogate the prisoner before he smells up this whole building."

"Chelsey will appreciate it. Go on." As Samantha rose to leave, he stopped her with a "Lieutenant Harmon."

She turned to face him. "Yes?"

"You've been here for what, two months now?"

"Two and a half."

"You've had some experience with this drug running before."

"What makes you say that?"

"Intuition. You put the scenario with Lieutenant Preston together pretty quickly. And a regular officer wouldn't have thought to interrogate a parrot. I think you know more."

"That was Lieutenant Preston's idea."

"You still interpreted the parrot's speech. No regular officer would have taken it seriously."

"I guess it did help that during my teen years, my grandfather and I sailed the Caribbean with a Macau."

A gleam of understanding came into Mr. Owens' eyes. "Ah, pirates in the Caribbean."

The corner of her mouth lifted. "You're pretty smart yourself." With that, the young Lieutenant cleared her mind and walked off to interrogate Assad.

Chapter 4

Bagram Airforce Base
   June 23, 2021 0100

The rules of interrogation came in all shapes and sizes, according to what Lt. Harmon learned in school. Time of day, sit, stand, all of it printed in black and white with clear directives about what could and could not be done. At one a.m., an hour that would not normally be approved by higher authorities, light beaming from overhead florescent bulbs delved into every crevice of the TOC as the MP's drank coffee. Illuminated in the light, a new, freshly scrubbed young man stood guard over an emaciated, dark-haired prisoner who was once more beginning to sweat.

"I'm glad you closed the door," Lt. Harmon commented as she entered the room.

"Had to, Mam, when the team came in."

"The men from interdiction? Yes, of course. Where's Ramen?"

"In the bathroom. He'll be right back."

"Our prisoner here speaks a little English." With an eye on Assad, she took a seat at the table and nonchalantly flipped through an open notebook. After looking at the clock, she then looked at the MPs and said, "We are in compliance. He just slept for a few hours, so this is not an EIT. You can take his chair from the room. We'll all stand."

One of the two MPs nodded and told the other that sleep deprivation is considered to be an 'Enhanced Interrogation Technique', and since the prisoner had just woke up, he was technically not sleep deprived. They walked over to Assad, grabbed him under the armpits, and hauled him to his feet. The wooden chair upon which he'd slouched was taken from the room along with all the rest of the chairs. "Geneva Convention compliance," Lt. Harmon said loudly. "He stands, we all stand. He stays awake, we all stay awake. And I'm so wide awake I can do this all night. You good?" she asked a burly MP standing beside the door.

"Fresh as a newborn baby."

Assad glanced between the two with a slight look of bemusement not lost on Lt. Harmon. "Tell Ramen to stay outside."

"Yes, Mam."

Lt. Harmon looked at the prisoner who now, with one of his own removed from the room, seemed a little unsure of himself. "State your name."

When the prisoner remained silent, she turned her laptop toward the room and looked at the MP. The screen displayed a photo of a tiki hut, and in the picture, Assad was standing behind the bar serving drinks as Chelsey cozied up against a post. The background crowd appeared to all be people of college age in various stages of swimsuit undress.

"This picture was taken in Florida. I know because I took it. How does a Muslim who doesn't speak English work behind the bar in the United States? When you were on spring break in college, you ever had a Muslim who didn't speak English serve you in a tiki bar?" Lt. Harmon asked with a glance at the MP by her side.

"No, Mam. But I never went to college."

Assad couldn't help but smirk.

Next, Lt. Harmon pulled out two brochures, one written in English, the other in Arabic. "Some words, of course, you might have trouble with. Words that aren't familiar," she told Assad. "Like when you visited Mr. Vernon. You know, the place where you met Nadja," she said as she stood right in front of him, displaying the brochures.

A sullen look crossed Assad's face.

"They found these in your house. There's security footage back in the U.S. What were you two doing in Washington?"

Assad's lips pursed as he crossed his arms and shuffled his feet.

"I understand. You don't love her, she might have a husband somewhere. She was only coming to meet you for sex."

Now, the face had a slight grin.

"We're supposed to believe that? We would, except that you're gay."

Assad's lips tightened into a harsh look.

"Okay, you're not gay. You like women. You are working for the Taliban to help line their pockets with cash, but just so you can line your own. You worked for a drug runner in the States, Harry Trot."

This time Assad's facial muscles lifted as his eyes opened wide with surprise.

"My uncle Benny is Harry's friend. He sends his greetings," Lt. Harmon said as she looked firmly into the prisoner's eyes. "The Katyusha. Your story about the fireworks was good, almost funny. Theme parks do that, too. You get that in Florida?"

Assad looked bored.

"Yes, I know. Keep going to the same parks, and it's not as fun anymore unless you're just a real theme park lover. But for someone high on heroin, that would have been too much stimulus. You must have wanted to get laid really bad to take Nadja and her son there."

With his mouth wide open, Assad gave her a, "How'd you know that?" look. "Can I have some pizza?"

"Per the Geneva Convention, we are not allowed to coerce you with pizza, or anything else, without the approval of the Secretary of Defense," Lt. Harmon responded. She looked at an MP. "You want some pizza?"

"Yes, Mam."

"Mr. Owens has one in his office. If you want to bring it in, we'll take a break and eat."

The door opened and out walked the MP, who soon returned carrying a white box with a half-open lid displaying the few remaining slices of pepperoni pizza. After reaching in to grab a slice, he carried the box across the room and leveled it when the box tilted to dump out its cargo, then he placed it in front of Assad and wiped away sauce with the back of his hand.

"Gotta go wash up," he said.

After he left the room, the younger MP said, "We're not allowed to give it to you. But if you steal a piece and eat it before we can stop you, that's not our fault."

Lt. Harmon motioned for the chairs to be put back into place. Once they were all seated, she ordered the younger MP to grab a slice of pizza and join her for a meeting around her desk. While they sat and ate pizza, Assad's freed hand grabbed a slice and soon, he too had orange sauce circling his mouth. After his second slice, an MP walked over and picked up the empty box.

"That was for our staff."

"Your name," Lt. Harmon said again.

This time, Assad's eyes remained less hostile. "You know my name. Assad."

"Not that one," Lt. Harmon interrupted. "The one you used in Florida."

A question crossed Assad's face.

"Jack. As in, you don't know Jack." The lift of one brow, along with the slight grin, softened the statement.

The MP's exploded with laughter. Assad grinned, too.

"My grandfather was at your bar quite often. Captain Greg."

The surprise on Assad's face was genuine. "Captain Greg, the pothead captain?"

A look of displeasure crossed Lt. Harmon's face. Knowing that she had to maintain a steel composure to extract vital intelligence, her grey-blue eyes squinted as she countered with, "He was a brilliant captain."

The word "was" was not lost on Assad. He slumped back into his chair.

"Tell us about Nadja."

Assad looked confused.

"Get Ramen back in here," she commanded, her tone no longer friendly. "We need to make sure he understands these next questions."

"Yes, Mam," an MP said. He opened the door to find Ramen standing right there, tucking his white billowing shirt into his blue jeans.

"Another bathroom break?" Lt. Harmon asked. "Good." She motioned for Ramen to join the prisoner.

"Ask him what Nadja was planning on doing with the fentanyl."

Assad placed his bottom lip between his teeth and let out a soft whistle, which startled Chelsey. She fluffed her feathers and let out a shrill whistle, braying in the sound of a donkey.

"Mule!" Lt. Harmon gasped.

The gleam in Assad's eye told her that he wasn't lying.

"She was carrying drugs for what? Those drugs were not being transported for sale. She was going to powder the platoon?"

A look of alarm crossed Assad's face.

"Her son wasn't supposed to drug the platoon. She was going to do it, but she thought she knew how to dust them and not die herself. Her son didn't get so lucky."

This time, Assad's face caved in.

"Yes, her son was killed. The police searched a farm close to yours. Was that Nadja's farm, or was she just operating out of there?"

Assad remained silent.

"Neighbors say she was a frequent visitor. The items we found in the house suggest she may have stayed there off and on. Where was her primary establishment?"

This brought a look of surprise to the prisoner's expression before Ramen could even translate.

"We know there was a lab in the barn. What were they cooking with these chemicals?" Lt. Harmon asked as she pulled out a list and placed it on the table.

Ramen looked at the note and read it aloud in a stilted voice. "N-phene, um, thyl-four-pi, what's this word, peridinone, four-anilino-N-phen-e-thylpi-, uum, peridine."

Assad almost smiled, then he grinned and, with a final smirk, shrugged. He and Ramen started to giggle.

"What's so funny?" Lt. Harmon asked.

"Nothing," Ramen replied.

Looking around, Lt. Harmon saw an MP's face turning beat red as he tried to withhold a laugh. Her hand covered her mouth as she said, "Read it again." Before Ramen could comply, the door opened, and Mr. Owens marched in with a copy of the same note in his hand. He laid it in front of Lt. Harmon.

"You're still here. Oh yes, what did you find out?"

"Our guest here's girlfriend had a chemist cooking fentanyl. This is the recipe to make it. They called the cook Siegfried because that's the name of the specific method they used."

"They cooked fentanyl along with the heroin?"

"Yes. From what they found in the barn, it looks like the heroin was being cut with Fentanyl."

Lt. Harmon motioned for Mr. Owens to follow her into the hallway. Once they'd closed the door to the interrogation room, she dialed his cell phone, put a finger to her lips, and pointed to his pocket. When he pulled the buzzing phone out and saw Lt. Harmon's name on the screen, he looked puzzled. She silently mouthed, "Ramen."

"What?"

"He's always in the bathroom right before something happens. He was missing for Assad's first interrogation. He has a cell phone."

A gleam of understanding crossed Mr. Owens' face. "Was he surprised by the fentanyl?"

"It was too goofy to tell. The way Ramen said it, it was funny so everybody laughed."

"You want to get ears on their conversation alone?"

"Yes."

"Take care of the phone. I'll get the MPs."

With a nod of her head, Lt. Harmon went back into the room, seemingly upset. With her back to the prisoner, she opened the pizza box and, out of view of the others, slid her phone inside.

Mr. Owens was right behind. "We have a Geneva Convention issue here," he said with a meaningful look at the MPs. "Can I talk to you in the hall?"

"But," one of them started to say as he motioned to Assad.

"He's cuffed to the chair. He's not going anywhere."

Still looking unsure, the MPs followed Lt. Harmon and Mr. Owens into the hall. He looked back at Ramen and said, "Any problems, we'll be right outside. Okay?"

Lt. Harmon also looked directly at Ramen. He nodded and gave her a look that said, "I got this."

She closed the door, then gathered the MPs to stand with them in a group a short way down the hall from the interrogation room. With a quick look around, she held a finger over her lips as Mr. Owens pulled his phone back out of his pocket and held it out so they could all listen. Tarik walked out of the shadows and nodded at Lt. Harmon. He proceeded to write down the conversation.

Assad- "What is all that fentanyl?"

Ramen- "Some kind of synthetic drug your girlfriend is making."

A- "She doesn't use any drugs."

R- "She planned to use it on somebody."

A- "How did her son die?"

R- "The patrol shot him."

Several moments of silence followed.

Ramen- "What's going on? We were just supposed to sell for money."

Assad- "With her group, I don't know. Al-Qaeda has layers of hidden agendas and they're always looking for more return on their investment. I knew nothing of this. It's not what I signed up for. How did they know about me and my part in all this?"

Ramen- "The parrot. All the kids were talking. I told you to leave it in Florida."

With that, the MPs walked back into the room and arrested Ramen. One of them pulled Ramen's phone from his pocket and, on their way out the door, slipped it to Lt. Harmon, who slipped it into her pocket.

"Please escort Mr. Assad back to his quarters," she said as she pulled her phone from the pizza box and picked a mushroom off the screen. The mushroom went in the trash before she followed Mr. Owens back to his office and closed the door. "We need to make a call."

"You can use my phone," he replied. "S2?

"Yes. Major West is waiting."

CHAPTER 5

Bagram Airforce Base
  June 23, 2021 0200

"Terrorists don't talk."

"That's what Major West said?" A bemused Mr. Owens chuckled at the look of fury on Lt. Harmon's face.

"He didn't believe me."

"Yes, he did. I think that was a compliment. You actually got Assad to talk?"

She glanced up at him. "Sort of."

"I put in a good word for you, and Bingham's already sent it through special operations. You'll be doing today's briefing."

"The general wants me at brigade?" Momentarily speechless, Lt. Harmon's eyes gleamed with admiration. "You peddle your influence well."

"I just got you in front of the General. If you want to interrogate Nadja, you still have to sell it. You're tactical, not operations." The lines in Mr. Owens' face deepened as he looked at the clock. "You've got a few hours to get some shut-eye. Better get to it." The stoop in his shoulders straightened slightly as he stood and pushed his chair up to his desk. Then he ushered

Lt. Harmon out of the room before pulling the door shut. Together, they walked down the now deserted hallway.

"Did you talk to the MP's while I was on the phone?" she asked.

"I did," he said and sneezed. "Cleaning people were here."

Lt. Harmon nodded. "What are they doing with Ramen?"

"He's in a holding cell."

"The man's for sale. We need him on the inside."

"His lawyer can work that out."

"Lawyer, already?"

"You can't surpass lady justice."

"I need to stop over at the JAG anyway. Let's go."

"Don't you ever sleep? It's two a.m." With a sigh, Mr. Owens followed along toward a building housing the base legal team. As they passed by the rec hall, the notes of country music playing loudly on a jukebox seeped into the outside air.

"They need to turn that down," Lt. Harmon said irritably as her fingers clutched the wooden door's wrought iron handle and flung it open. She stepped inside and stood stone-faced at the site of two figures dancing cheek to cheek. Abruptly, she turned and stormed out of the building.

Mr. Owens stood with his arms crossed. "Tell me you're not dating him?"

Her eyes blinked back tears as thoughts of secret trysts with Brad consumed her thoughts. A wild, distant look crossed her face as she felt his arms encircle her waist.

"No. We just went sailing once when we were at West Point." *That's when he kissed me. And he said that he'd wait for me...*

The music stopped. Mr. Owens put the force of his hand gently against her elbow and ushered her along. "We're all still human here," he muttered softly.

"I don't have time for that." Jerking her elbow away, she marched into the JAG's office to find an officer sitting at a wooden desk, doodling a picture of a dog on a piece of copy paper. The officer looked up from his drawing and laid his pencil down.

"Good evening, I'm Captain Jensen. What can I do for you?"

"My grandfather is in the hospital. I need to notarize this power-of-attorney for my brother and get it faxed over to him."

"I can handle that for you," he responded. "Do you have your ID?"

She presented her military ID and signed the form. Mr. Owens signed as a witness. With a quick stamp, Captain Jensen signed as the notary and asked for the fax number.

"Use this one," Lt. Harmon said, pointing to a number on the form. "And if somebody could call the hospital, could you get the number and fax it there too?"

Hearing the sad tone of the young woman's voice, Captain Jensen assured her it would be taken care of. "Anything else I can help you with?"

"Yes, Sir. There's an interpreter nicknamed Ramen who was arrested for working with one of the prisoners, Assad Al-Jazeera, to move drugs. Assad had a little romance going on with Nadja Jammu, an al-Qaeda operative who was captured yesterday. She's actually a U.S. citizen turned terrorist who met Assad over in D.C. There's something strange going on. Maybe some kind of terrorist attack is planned. A patrol found an old Russian rocket launcher and shells packed with white powder on a nearby farm. We need to have Ramen working with us to get more information from Assad."

"Planning an attack where? In the states?"

Lt. Harmon's eyes widened. "Why do you ask that?"

"You said they were in D.C."

"It's… we don't know. Maybe here, maybe at home," she said thoughtfully. "Of course, Sir, the sooner we get more intel on the situation, the better. We need to find out what Ramen knows, and it's been shown that he can be bought."

Captain Jensen nodded. "I don't see why they can't be neighbors. We'll get some kind of deal."

"Very good, Sir. Thank you."

After leaving the JAG, Mr. Owens walked Lt. Harmon to her billets and said good night with one final word. "Hand me the phone."

"What phone?"

"Ramen's. I know you have it. I'll take a look and hand it in over at evidence in the morning."

"But," Lt. Harmon started to protest.

"We're both good, remember?"

"Yes, we are," Lt. Harmon said reluctantly. "You're not going to bed, are you?"

"In a while."

"You'll let me know what you find before the meeting?"

"What time is the meeting?"

"Nine."

"You've got it. It's his loss," Mr. Owens said kindly before walking away.

With a small wave of her hand, Lt. Harmon called good night. After pulling the almost empty, rolled-up pack of M&M's from her pocket, she placed it on a small table, dove into bed fully clothed, and fell instantly asleep to dream of West Point and the day when wrapped in Brad's arms, she fell asleep on the boat.

Early the next morning, her eyes opened to the sound of a loud tone. *Beep, beep, beep*, a forklift blared as it backed up to the building next door. She looked at the clock and stretched. *Just a few minutes before my alarm goes off anyway.* Mindlessly, she reached over and grabbed the pack of M&M's lying next to her bunk, unrolled the top, and peered inside before dumping the last few candies into her hand. *Green, he took all the green ones.* Slowly, she stretched her arms toward the ceiling and inhaled a deep breath, then curled to a sitting position before rising to cast off her wrinkled uniform.

What should I wear today? Her closet held three sets of desert khakis, all freshly washed. She rummaged through the sets, mumbling, "I don't like the pattern on this one. Too gothic. And not this, too princess." Pulling out the last set, she held it up to the light. "This is better, casual yet formal. Enough black on the collar to make me look fierce."

Ordinarily, she let her locks flow free to curl naturally around her head. Today, she pulled her hair into a tight ponytail, then pulled it back out and twisted her hair into a French braid. Without the circle of hair, the dark lashes surrounding her eyes appeared even more lush, the pools of her grey-blue eyes that much deeper. A quick brush to her boots, a file to her nails, and off she went to the dining hall. With a tray in hand, she held out her plate for a dollop of scrambled eggs and then eyed the sausage.

"Look at you all dressed up," a voice said cheerfully from behind.

"I do my hair for important people," she retorted. Grabbing a bottle of hot sauce, she shot a few splashes of orange liquid across a pile of dried yellow eggs before slapping the now empty bottle into Captain Kramer's hand.

"Ouch! What did I do?"

Lt. Harmon's grey-blue eyes swept his figure. Looking straight ahead, she walked past the end of the serving line and gobbled down a fork full of eggs, then stuffed her tray onto a rack. As she walked toward the exit, Captain Kramer emerged from the line holding a tray full of food.

"What's going on?" With a mouth full of biscuits and gravy, he followed her outside while still chewing.

A jeep pulled up with Mr. Owens behind the wheel. Lt. Harmon climbed in and turned to flash a smile at Captain Kramer. "Off to see the general," she said, waving goodbye.

"Why, what?" Standing with a fork full of eggs halfway to his mouth, he wiped at a small trickle of gravy dribbling onto his uniform.

Once Mr. Owens turned the jeep onto Disney Drive, Lt. Harmon tensed. Named after one of the first soldiers killed in Afghanistan, the main road running through the five thousand acres of Bagram took them to brigade headquarters. "You signed this out of the motor pool. Nice."

"You're quite welcome."

"Please roll up your window. I don't want my hair messed up," she said politely.

Driving with one hand, Mr. Owens cranked up his window and swerved to avoid a chicken. "Somebody lost a pet," he chuckled.

"Parrots, chickens. This war is nuts."

"Living the Good Life. You'll be alright. Here," Mr. Owens said as he reached behind a seat and pulled out a sheet of paper. "This is a list of people Ramen called from his cell."

"Only three?"

"Probably calls his mom from a landline. Cell costs too much."

Lt. Harmon nodded. "He call anybody yesterday?"

"The first two."

"Time?"

"Once before the patrol came back. The second time, right before they left again. You were right."

"Of course, I know who Nadja and Assad are. What about this guy, Mohammed Al-Sarkis? Who's he?"

"I don't know."

"How does the CIA not know who Mohammed is?"

"I'm not CIA." Mr. Owens' lips curled to a grin. "Do you know how many Mohammed's there are in Afghanistan?"

"Not CIA? What are you, NSA, DEA, NIH?"

"What's NIH?"

"National Institute of Health."

"I'm just a civilian," he responded with a chuckle. "We have someone checking on the address this number is billed to. Probably belongs to some junkie living under the bridge in Kabul. Still worth a shot."

"SIGINT tracking the phone?" she asked, referring to signals intelligence.

"Not yet."

"Why not? Satellite turned the wrong way?"

"Patience. It's probably a burner phone they already got rid of."

"You're right, we need to stop at the prison. I'm going to ask Ramen who Mohammed is."

"You don't have time for that. If we're late, you won't get in."

"We've got forty-five minutes. This will only take one. It's just outside the gate here."

Mr. Owens slammed on the brakes and picked up his phone. After a quick call, he said, "They're bringing him right out."

"You're CIA. I know you're CIA," Lt. Harmon laughed. "Only my grandfather could pull something like that."

"He was CIA?" Mr. Owens asked with obvious surprise in his voice.

"Maybe. Or NSA, or ASA, or DIH. He wouldn't say for sure."

"I would have thought Coast Guard."

"Navy, but he evolved."

The sound of laughter followed Lt. Harmon into the prison. Inside, she removed her head gear, signed in, and was led past rows of chain link rooms containing floors littered with prayer rugs. The beds, many with a Koran lying open, were separated into rooms housing multiple prisoners with nothing more than a sheet hung for privacy. The MP stopped when they arrived at a small room where Ramen sat amicably chatting with a guard.

Upon seeing the officer, the guard stood and moved to the side of the room.

"Can you leave us for a moment?" When the guard made no move to leave, she said, "He was my interpreter. It's fine. Leave us now, and that's an order."

As the look in Lt. Harmon's eye left no room for further argument, the guard walked from the room.

Taking his place, she sat down opposite Ramen and softened her expression. "I just have a minute. You getting treated alright?"

Ramen's eyes looked at her doubtfully. "They haven't tortured me yet."

"You know the Geneva Convention doesn't protect you since you're not a combatant. So I asked them to keep you away from the general population and give us time to get you transferred."

"You're the one who got me arrested. Now you're getting me out of here?"

"I hope to. Just cooperate and do what your lawyer says. We already knew about Nadja and Assad. I suppose you were just trying to make a little side cash. Who's Mohammed?" She looked at her watch. "We have your cell phone and can see you called him."

"I want my lawyer."

"He can come, but I don't have time to stay." With that, Lt. Harmon rose to leave.

"Lieutenant."

"Yes."

"You're going to help me?" From within his sullen face, Ramen's eyes plead his case.

Her face softened. "If you agree to help us, I'll do what I can."

Ramen understood, dropped his attitude, and struggled through the next words. "Okay. I only know who he is. I never met him."

"Who is Mohammed?"

"Nadja's son."

An edge of surprise took over Lt. Harmon's voice before she gained control. "It's THAT Mohammad. Where is he?"

"Pakistan, I think."

"What name is he going by now?"

At first, Ramen made no move to respond. But when Lt. Harmon's eyes kept prodding, he finally responded and gave up the name Badhai Kahn."

"That's your name. What did you do?"

With that, Ramen stared angrily at the floor and said, "I didn't do anything. Men came into our home, took our passports, and said we were going to work for al-Qaeda."

"Your wife, too?" Lt. Harmon asked.

Ramen answered with a miserable nod.

"What is her name?"

"Sasha."

"How is Badhai involved in what happened yesterday?"

"He establishes drug routes to help move the heroin out of Afghanistan. We were just supposed to give the farmers time to harvest the poppies and move them to the border, that's all."

Lt. Harmon's eyes creased with suspicion. "You were paid well as an interpreter. Why get involved? Why not just tell us what was going on?"

The former interpreter sat back and said in a voice giving in to resignation, "Life is good while the U.S. is here. When you leave and the Taliban takes over, they will kill me. Without me and money, my wife and son will not survive."

"But the United States would not leave them behind," Lt. Harmon exclaimed. "How old is your son?"

"He's three. This is a war zone," Ramen replied. "Anything can happen. Al-Qaeda has our documents, and you're all leaving soon."

"Why the fentanyl?"

"I don't know. Not my business."

With a swift motion, Lt. Harmon stood and let out a slow breath. Before summoning the guard, she looked at Ramen and said firmly, "I'll try to help your wife and son. Just do what your lawyer tells you to do."

He nodded okay.

Out in the fresh air, she climbed back in the jeep to stare straight ahead. Without a word, Mr. Owens started the jeep and hit the gas. "You going to tell me what you got?"

"Mohammed is Nadja's son. He's currently using the name Badhai Kahn, which is Ramen's real name. And he has Ramen's passport. He functions as a transportation specialist for al-Qaeda by establishing drug routes to move heroin."

"Location?"

"Probably still in Pakistan."

A few moments later, they pulled up to a building teaming with the operation of not just the base but of the entire war in Afghanistan. Each section of the Brigade was divided into a shop, just like Battalion. Occasionally, Lt. Harmon spoke with Major Bingham from G3 in the Joint Operations Command, the area responsible for all base operations. But, as an officer assigned to tactical intelligence, her chain of command went through the G2 shop. Thus, Major West served as her immediate superior. He sat now at his desk waiting for his old friend, Mr. Owens, who was bringing the officer now jokingly referred to as the bird whisperer. As they approached his desk with their visitor badges on full display, he rose and extended a hand.

"Robert."

"Tom."

"Sir."

"Lieutenant Harmon."

Once the greetings were complete, Major West motioned for the others to sit. "Good job with the Assad interrogation. How's your prisoner?"

"He's alive, Sir. Assad is incarcerated in a cell with the interpreter we identified as working with a network of drug runners."

"Robert," Major West said to Mr. Owens as he leafed through a stack of papers. "I have your transcript. How's your finger?"

"Healing."

"And why did you let Assad talk you into sticking your finger in that cage?"

"Just making friends," Mr. Owens replied, a bit red-faced.

"You get anything more from the parrot?"

"Other than telling Lt. Harmon Nadja was carrying drugs, nothing relative to this investigation."

With a slight shake of his head, the major said, "I need that transcript."

"We have more to report, Sir," a straight-faced Lt. Harmon replied. "On the way here, we stopped at the prison."

"Oh?"

"She found out who Mohammed is," Mr. Owens said.

"Ramen is an ordinary Afghan citizen," Lt. Harmon said. "His connection to Assad is from school. They were in an English class together when they were kids."

"What's this, class reunion?" Major West asked.

"In a way, Sir," Lt. Harmon said. "Business associates now. Assad found out that Ramen was working at the base and approached him to get intel about when the patrols would be out scouting for poppy fields. Ramen, real name Badhai Kahn, saw an opportunity to make a little side money. He says al-Qaeda took his family's passports and ordered him to cooperate. Of course, he knows the U.S. is leaving Afghanistan soon and thought he'd create a piggy bank stash for his family, as without those passports, they can't leave."

"Does he know anything about Lieutenant Preston or the fentanyl?"

"He says no."

"You believe him?"

"From the conversation we overheard last night, yes. Ramen's agreed to cooperate with us, hoping for lighter treatment and help for his family. They have him locked up with Assad."

"And twenty-five other men in the same cell. He able to give you anything else?"

"He gave us Mohammed, who is using Ramen's passport. Mohammad is Nadja's missing son. Ramen told me that he's somewhere in Pakistan trafficking heroin."

"Going by the name Badhai Kahn and funding terrorism," Major West said with a gleam of understanding.

"Yes. Establishing global routes to move drugs." Lt. Harmon thought back to the letter from Brian telling her Jenny was using heroin and frowned. "And poison kids."

Major West looked at them and said, "Tell me more about the fentanyl."

With a slight shift in his chair, Mr. Owens placed an elbow on the desk, leaned forward and with a face registering battle fatigue, proceeded to say, "Fentanyl is a drug they're using to cut other drugs. It's cheaper, way more potent than heroin, and causes a lot more overdoses. And it's synthetic, which means it's manufactured from chemicals rather than plants. There are a few different ways to make it. The method being used in the lab our guys just found is the Siegfried Method."

"What's that?"

"They use N-phenethyl-4-piperidinone to arrive at 4-anilino-N-phenethylpiperidine, one of the main precursors for fentanyl."

"Maybe I'll pretend I know what that is," Major West exclaimed. "But I don't, and how does that matter?"

Mr. Owens exhaled and slumped into his chair. "Amateurs."

"We've been dealing solely with heroin here, Robert, as you know. Educate us."

"He hasn't had a chance to fill me in either," Lt. Harmon's muffled voice could be heard saying as she reached down to tighten a boot lace.

With a nod, Mr. Owens opened a file and pulled out a sheet of paper. "This is the schematic to make fentanyl, which is a synthetic drug. First, they make NPP with a chemical imported mostly from China, but sometimes from India. Then they use that to make ANPP and use that to make fentanyl." He handed the sheet to Major West. "I know it's clear as mud, but keep that. You'll get it. The main point is, fentanyl is fifty to one hundred times more potent than heroin, and it's being used to cut all sorts of drugs. In the U.S., the death rate from people unknowingly ingesting is rising off the charts."

Major West looked at the sheet of paper he'd been given and noted the title. "Interesting. The Siegfried Method?"

"There are other recipes. This one's been pretty popular for the last ten years. They called the guy cooking at Nadja's place Siegfried."

"We spend all this time destroying poppy fields, which are more plentiful than ever. Now this," Major West exclaimed. "This is what Lieutenant Preston inhaled?"

"Yes, Sir," Lt. Harmon responded.

"Why?"

She looked fervently between both men. "We don't know. Assad and Ramen both claim to know nothing about it. That's why I'd like to speak with Nadja."

"Too high up on the food chain," Major West said with a frown. "She's been assigned to a senior interrogator."

"I expect they've already tried, Sir, and got nothing."

"Lieutenant, you're at battalion level. Your job is to assist the patrols."

"I want to do this to help the patrols. We need to find out what is the risk of it happening again. Something is really off here."

"Off, in what way?" Major West asked. He once again looked at Mr. Owens' transcript and asked Lt. Harmon for hers.

"I've got it somewhere, it's in a file." As she searched through her briefcase, she started to perspire and tossed the ball to Mr. Owens, saying, "I thought it was here. I know I printed it and put it in a file. Did I give it to you?"

"As a matter of fact, you did. I gave it to Captain Jenkins. Sorry, I was supposed to pick up our copy this morning. How about I go get it while you talk to the General?"

"We don't do things here that way," Major West replied with a little frost in his tone.

"Look, Tom, her grandfather, who raised her, is in the hospital. She was seeing the JAG on a personal matter. It was my job to provide the evidence. Sorry, this old dog might be losing my touch. I'll go get it," Mr. Owens said firmly as he rose to leave.

Major West looked at him suspiciously. "You're looking tired, Robert. I'll have them send it." He made a quick call, and soon, a fax machine was humming.

"This just came for you, Sir," an airman said as he walked up and put a fax on Major West's desk.

"Thanks, Airman."

Mr. Owens picked up the fax. "I'm going for a cup of coffee. Mind if I read this while you talk with the Lieutenant?"

"Just a minute," Major West said as he grabbed the sheets of paper. "You ran this game on me before. Remember Kandahar?"

"No idea what you're talking about," Mr. Owens replied.

"Pay now, ask questions later. I assume you have the original in your briefcase. You're hiding something. Where are you going?" he called to Mr. Owens disappearing back.

"Bathroom, be right back."

As Lt. Harmon sat impatiently waiting for Major West to read through the document, she tugged at the bottom of her uniform blouse. By the time Mr. Owens returned, she was firing back a response to Major West's question.

"How did you come up with your assessment when the man didn't answer most of your questions?"

"He did, Sir. I read his facial expressions."

"First a parrot, then a bad poker face. You expect to go in front of the General with this?" Major West's tone registered frustration.

"She wasn't wrong," said a voice from behind her back. The muscles on Mr. Owens' face tightened to reflect the steel in his voice. "That's why she's here."

"Grandfather taught me to play poker," Lt. Harmon said nervously. "By the time I was sixteen, I usually beat him and everybody else at the table. Assad wasn't all that hard to read."

"And maybe you have a little more background than that?" Major West asked.

"What do you mean?"

"The transcript. You have an uncle who was involved with a major drug dealer."

Lt. Harmon shifted in her seat, looked straight at Major West, and shrugged. "My great-uncle Benny was mafia. In Chicago."

"Great-uncle?"

"Didn't affect her security clearance," Mr. Owens said. "She wasn't around that branch of the family growing up."

"You were bluffing?"

"Mostly."

"What about your grandfather and his connection to this Assad?"

Lt. Harmon's cheeks lifted as she smiled at a memory. "Assad was a bartender. Everybody called him Jack because he usually got the orders wrong. But he never got fired because Chelsey brought in the customers."

"And you just happened to have a picture of Assad on your laptop?"

"I took the picture of Chelsey while my grandfather was suffering through one of Assad's mistakes."

"Can we talk to your grandfather?"

"No, Sir, sorry," she said softly. "He suffered a stroke two days ago. My brother says he's on a vent, and they still don't know if he'll recover or what damage was done. He wouldn't know anything, wouldn't remember if he did. I'm requesting leave to go see him." She pulled out a form and handed it to her superior.

Major West looked at it and nodded. "Let's get back to the attack in the market. You said something is off. In what way?"

"First, we don't have a reason for the attack. The market was empty. Nadja couldn't have cleared it by herself, so she must have had help. They found fourteen vases that had been recently washed. There wasn't anything in the stalls. At least, not anything that could cause harm."

"Just the little bit of heroin mixed with fentanyl the boy had in the jar?"

"Yes."

The major's brow creased. "What do you think, Robert?"

"I think it's interesting they used it on the troops rather than the locals."

"Yes, it is. Why?"

"We don't have the information we need to make that call."

"What do you think?" he asked Lt. Harmon.

She bit her bottom lip before replying, "Revenge. They want us out of Afghanistan. Protecting the harvest, we don't know. Maybe even something else. Nadja is al-Qaeda."

"And al-Qaeda hasn't had a major terrorist attack since 2005," Mr. Owens said. "The cannisters found on Assad's farm had something more than explosives in them. It's too early to rule out Anthrax. And after the market incident, I'm wondering if it's something else."

"Such as?"

"Heroin, fentanyl, or any number of things. I called this morning to tell the lab about the drugs. Not something EOD would test for in a shell casing," Mr. Owens replied.

"I see where you're going," Major West said thoughtfully. "You think the market could be a small test for a large-scale attack on the base?"

"Possibly, and at a time when we're the most vulnerable while we're drawing down."

"It's a large base, well protected. Still, the 401st is here beginning to clear weapons and ammo," Major West replied thoughtfully.

"Yes, Sir. I heard the forklifts this morning." Lt. Harmon put a hand to her mouth and stifled a yawn.

"Any word from Langley?"

"Too soon. They're just now receiving the package."

"And the lab here on base?"

"We have another twenty-four hours to wait for Anthrax results," Lt. Harmon responded.

With a quick nod, Major West picked up the phone and called the base lab. "Yes, I see," he said before hanging up.

"You going to keep us hanging, Tom?"

"It's not heroin or fentanyl. You already know we're waiting on Anthrax. Any other educated guesses?"

"There are literally hundreds of things, as you know. We'll have to wait on Langley. Right now, it's not as important to know what it is as it is to know where it is," Mr. Owens replied with a grin.

"It's not as important to know, oh clever," Major West laughed. "Good thing you didn't tell me that over whiskey. You get that, Lieutenant?"

Mr. Owens winked. Lt. Harmon rolled her eyes. "You have all the intel ready for the general?" Major West asked her.

"Yes, Sir. I gave the data to Sergeant Pruitt at Special Operations. He's quick."

"Good. He'll have the PowerPoint presentation ready for the briefing. We could have quite the crowd."

"Who besides us and the general?" Mr. Owens asked.

"The usual. CIA and FBI. USDA and probably Interpol. Major Bingham, of course. A public affairs officer. General Mazdoujeh Al-Jaleesa from Afghan Special Forces, Colonel Anderson, and some guy from the DEA."

"Drug and alcohol set up shop at brigade?" a wide-eyed Lt. Harmon asked.

Major West stood and looked down at her, then at Mr. Owens. "They've been here. You really think she should be asking to talk with Nadja?"

"She's been on base for two months, still learning the ropes," Mr. Owens replied.

"I know they're here at Bagram. I just didn't know there was another office at brigade headquarters. Our battalion has a DEA unit over by the JAG," Lt. Harmon said impatiently.

As the others prepared to rise, a man dressed in a lighter shade of desert fatigues walked up to the group. The few remaining strands of his light brown mane were swept away in a comb-over gone bad by running his fingers through his hair as silence met his questions.

"This is Major Long. He's been interrogating the prisoner," Major West said by way of introduction.

"Good morning, Sir," Lt. Harmon said. She stared at Major Long's hair. "I see she didn't talk."

"How did you--" he tried to respond when he was cut off by Major West.

"Let's go," he said kindly. "Time to see the general."

CHAPTER 6

Bagram Airforce Base
   June 23, 2021 1000

"Attention," Major West barked as a door to the briefing arena opened. As military customs required, everyone rose from their seats when General Adams entered the room.

Standing at the front of the group, Lt. Harmon surveyed the general responsible for all of Bagram. A smattering of grey hair intermixed with dark strands stood thick upon his head. His bangs, evenly cut just above a forehead presiding over a long face, were smoothed straight. That, along with the even tone of his pale, unwrinkled skin, made him appear far younger than his actual years.

"ROTC grad," Mr. Owens had told her. "You have a chance."

She'd merely smiled.

General Adams surveyed the room. "Good morning everybody. Are we all here?"

"Almost," replied Captain Drake, his aide-de-camp. "I don't see DEA."

The door opened again to allow the tall figure of a man dressed in flowing robes to enter.

"Who's that?" Lt. Harmon whispered to Mr. Owens.

A brown band fixed tight around the man's head kept his shroud mostly covering his face. Upon seeing the group, he pulled it back and stood expressionless at the edge of the gathering.

"Good morning," the general greeted Tarik. "Colonel Anderson, good to see you. Everybody get coffee?"

Lt. Harmon elbowed Mr. Owens.

"Yes, Sir," replied Major Bingham. His crumpled uniform spoke of a night's work as he waited for the S2 shop to gather intel from Nadja. "Thank you, Sir, for your help," he said, referring to a phone call that took place between General Adams and the Secretary of State in the middle of the night.

"I am sorry we had to wake you," Major West said. He looked around the room. "The golden hours, those first few hours when a new captive is brought to camp, can be the most productive hours of interrogation. In order to add sleep deprivation as an enhanced interrogation technique, we had to get permission. General Adams secured that permission."

"I understand that, despite bending the rules of the Geneva Convention and keeping the subject up all night, she's still not talking," General Adams said.

"That is correct, Sir. She's al-Qaeda, well trained and knows we're not going to torture her," Lt. Harmon said ceremoniously.

The General turned to stare at the young lieutenant with a slight twinkle in his eye. "Lieutenant Harmon, I've heard many good things about you."

As the rest of the group took a seat, Major West remained standing to formerly introduce Lt. Harmon to General Adams. "Tactical intel from 2nd Battalion. She is giving this morning's briefing."

"Lieutenant." General Adams held out his hand to give the responding grip a firm shake. With a question mark still on her face, she walked up beside an easel holding the storyboards Sergeant Pruitt created from the notes she'd supplied and smiled.

The briefing room, a mostly barren area in a warehouse-type facility, was fully lit. A rumbling noise consisting of both air and ground transportation from the outside arena bounced off stark walls, down to the concrete floor, and then straight up the tall ceilings before going around again. With the speaker's voice being continuously challenged, this was not a place to divulge highly classified intel. Thus, in a voice meant to reach just to the back of the group, Lt. Harmon started. "Good morning, General Adams, Command Sergeant Major Swift, Major Bingham, Major West, and

Colonel Anderson. This is General Mazdoujeh Al-Jaleesa from the Afghan Special Forces and Tarik Ajabe. He's an interpreter."

"And represents DEA," Major West interjected.

Samantha's eyes flew to Tarik's face. *Oh.* "Two days ago, 2nd Battalion's Alpha Company and the Afghan Special Forces combined to perform drug interdiction. They were working in an area just a few miles from Bagram when they discovered a poppy field growing on a farm owned by Assad Rashid Al-Jazeera, a man known to be in frequent contact with a Taliban strongman. A search of the farm produced a Katyusha. The old Russian rocket launcher was loaded with shells containing white powder."

Lt. Harmon pointed to the screen on the computer, which showed an enlarged map of the area surrounding the farm, including another farm a mile away. "Sergeant Pruitt marked this map to identify our areas of interest."

"Good job with that map," the general said.

Sergeant Pruitt's face beamed as he sat at the computer, ready to assist with the briefing.

"You can see here the location of the barn, the weapons, and the house. The land owner is a former Afghan citizen who fled the country as a teen when he hopped on a plane during the 1996 U.S. airlift as the Taliban took over the country. He landed in Indianapolis, where he grew up in foster care."

"Really? That's where you're from, isn't it?" Tarik asked.

"No. Some of my family is there, but I'm from Chicago."

Those words brought an odd smile to the edges of Tarik's lips.

After a moment of silence, Lt. Harmon lifted her chin. "We've been able to put Assad in Chicago from 2012 to 2017, where he drove a cab, and then in Florida around the Saint Petersburg area where he worked as a bartender. He traveled to Washington D.C on six June 2018, real reasons unknown, but he claims he was on vacation. He admits that is where he met Nadja Jammu, a U.S. citizen who is now a known al-Qaeda operative. They visited Mount Vernon together and started dating. Assad has a drug problem. Nadja recruited him to help traffic heroin from Afghanistan to other countries. His interest is primarily in the money, but also a free drug supply."

"Nadja has been with him here for the last three years?" Major West asked.

"Yes, Sir. Her husband, Dalbir Jammu, was a poppy farmer. He was supposedly killed by interdiction while they were clearing his fields, but his body was never found."

"Jammu, they're not from here. That's an Indian name," Command Sergeant Major Swift commented while taking notes for his press release.

"That is correct. As you know, when a person joins al-Qaeda, he or she assumes a new first name and uses the city of their origin as their new last name. Nadja's husband was Indian. She's a U.S. citizen whose real name is Natasha Cohen."

"That sounds partially Russian," General Adams said.

"Yes, Sir. Her mother was Russian," Lt. Harmon replied. "Her father is American."

The general nodded.

"Two days ago at the farm, Assad was waiting for Nadja to arrive when the teams encountered the Katyusha. EOD was brought to the scene and determined that some of the shells were explosives, but some of them contained a white powder, composition to be determined." Picking up a stack of photos, she handed them out. "These are from aerial recon showing the same farm."

"What is the other powder?" the general asked.

"We don't know," Lt. Harmon replied in a steadfast voice. "I know Major West told you the powder is being tested for Anthrax. The test won't be back until tomorrow. Heroin and fentanyl have been ruled out."

"Was it tested for drugs?" Command Sergeant Major Swift asked.

"Yes. After Lt. Preston was dusted and quit breathing, tests at the hospital showed he was hit with heroin cut with fentanyl. So naturally, drugs became high on the suspect list, but it's been ruled out. There are a number of other substances this powder could be. We're waiting on Langley's tests. This farm," Lt. Harmon said while pointing to the farm behind Assad's, "is a place Nadja used as a lab to turn poppies into heroin. She's a chemist. They found quite the operation in the barn here. And something else. This man," Lt. Harmon distributed pictures of Siegfried, "was cooking fentanyl. They found containers of the precursors in the barn. All of that was confiscated by the Afghan Forces."

"What is this fentanyl," General Al-Jaleesa from Afghan Special Forces asked.

"It is poison," said a voice from the back of the group.

"Yes," Lt. Harmon responded, giving Tarik a puzzled look. "It's an opioid. Mr. Owens will talk more about that, he's the expert. A SITREP indicated that a truck parked at the farm was missing which aerial recon located several hours later at a market in Charikar. A patrol found freshly washed pottery in the market, which we believe came from Assad's farm. They also found white powder in a corner of a shelf. There may have been more powder in those containers, but right now, we don't know where it is."

"How do you know there is more of this powder?" General Al-Jaleesa asked. His black eyes pierced through Lt. Harmon's calm stare, daring her to validate her own words.

She met his stare and responded in a voice that only the general could challenge. "There were fourteen containers. All of them had been cleaned. Whatever was in those pots is a tangible object that has to be somewhere."

"You are guessing it was a tangible object," responded General Al-Jaleesa.

"Due to the presence of white powder on the shelf, yes."

"It could have been spices or wine," the general remarked.

Rather than argue, Lt. Harmon said evenly, "Yes, Sir, it could have been that. But an informant indicated Nadja Jammu was transporting drugs."

"Informant, what informant?" asked Command Sergeant Major Swift. "Public Affairs did not have that piece of information."

"A local."

Understanding the informant was the parrot, Mr. Owens quickly interjected with, "She wishes to remain anonymous."

"Yes, an anonymous local. The market at Charikar had been cleared of people prior to the arrival of the patrol. Unfortunately, we had an interpreter embedded with Alpha company who tipped off Nadja the patrol was coming, which we believe is the reason the local al-Qaeda network had time to clear the market." Lt. Harmon stopped to take a drink of water.

"That is a big market," General Al-Jaleesa stated.

"Yes," Lt. Harmon agreed. "The patrol was alerted to the potential for hostile activity. They were preparing to leave the area when the boy came out of hiding with an object he claimed was his grandfather's ashes hidden behind his back. When Lt. Preston took a few steps toward the boy, the kid blew powder in his face."

"Why would your soldier get so careless?" General Mazdoujeh Al-Jaleesa asked in a voice thick with disdain.

"A momentary lapse in judgment which almost cost him his life," Lt. Harmon said without emotion. She did not add the information that Lt. Preston's wife was due to give birth.

"We are getting hounded by the press to justify the killing of the boy," the Public Affairs Officer said. "Can you elaborate on the powder and why the boy had it?"

"The powder itself will be explained shortly by Mr. Owens. We can only speculate that Nadja intended to use the powder herself, and the intended target was the whole patrol. She's not talking to the interrogator."

A laptop stood on a table next to Lt. Harmon. She opened it and clicked on a file containing a PowerPoint presentation. Then, as the others gathered around to view the slides, they turned it over to Sergeant Pruitt and continued her briefing.

"Lab tests show the powder poisoning Lt. Preston to be heroin cut with fentanyl. These areas," she said, pointing to the first slide, "is acreage in Afghanistan known for growing vast amounts of poppies.

The acreage in the Helmand province demonstrates a thirty-two percent increase in poppy production in the last year despite drug interdiction efforts. Next slide. Mr. Owens is an experienced chemist, and he's been studying the fentanyl problem. He will finish the briefing," she said before taking a seat.

Mr. Owens rose and walked slowly to the front of the room.

"Your glasses," called a voice from the gathering.

"What?"

"Your glasses are on the table."

"Oh, yes," he replied while patting his pocket. "Those are mine." After going back to retrieve a pair of black-rimmed glasses, he cleaned them while walking back to the podium. "Good morning everyone. Standard army issue. My prescription hasn't changed in five years."

His words produced a chuckle from the officers, who knew that all army-issued glasses were black-rimmed-black rimmed.

"I am the civilian liaison for military intelligence between the battalions and Brigade. This slide," he said, "explains the synthesis of fentanyl which is a man-made synthetic opioid from the chemicals on the diagram. A drug interdiction team found these same chemicals at the farm Nadja traveled to several times. This next slide depicts the action of fentanyl."

Sergeant Pruitt flashed a slide with the words: Opioids mimic the brain's natural messengers. These drugs fool our receptors, activate the nerve cells, and release dopamine.

"Next slide."

A slide with the effects of fentanyl flashed on the screen: relaxation, euphoria, pain relief, sedation, drowsiness, urinary retention, respiratory depression, coma and death.

"What is that urinary retention?" General Al-Jaleesa asked.

"You can't go to the bathroom," Mr. Owens replied.

"Ah," the general responded before crossing his legs.

"Next slide. The precursors for fentanyl are being transported across the sea. Those chemicals are turned into fentanyl and then the cartels smuggle the drug across our borders."

Everyone stared at the computer which, upon flipping to the next screen, showed a map of drug routes for fentanyl to the United States. China dominated the scene, using multiple routes through Canada and Mexico. But India, a country nestled between Afghanistan and China, had a growing presence in the United States with the chemicals first sent to Mexico.

"Next slide. As the potency of fentanyl is fifty to one hundred times that of other opioids, it is being added to drugs such as cocaine, Xanax, Adderall, methamphetamine and heroin."

"And that is what the terrorists used in the market at Charikar," Lt. Harmon chimed in. "The drug slowed Lieutenant Preston's breathing down so quickly, it stopped completely before the medics could decontaminate him and get him intubated."

"After they placed an IV, Lieutenant Harmon correctly guessed the powder to be an opioid. Lt. Preston was then given Narcan. This drug binds to receptors in the brain and reverses the effects of opioids," Mr. Owens finished with one last intellectual gaze at the crowd.

"And the boy," Command Sergeant Major Swift said. "Public affairs still needs answers."

"He was shot while attempting to blow more fentanyl powder at the patrol. They needed to get to Lt. Preston," Mr. Owens replied. "Play video."

Lt. Harmon rose and walked over to the computer. After a quick search through her files, she found the video of the shooting, hovered over it with an arrow, and clicked on play.

The sound of silence echoed throughout the room as everyone watched Lt. Preston fall to the ground. When the child moved to blow into the vase again, General Adams momentarily closed his eyes. He'd previewed the video: the slight blood spatter, the white powder covering the child. Those visuals were already etched in his mind.

The rest of the video showing the medics going through the procedure to save Lt. Preston was met with equal silence.

"Why couldn't the soldiers just step back," General Al-Jaleesa exclaimed as his dark eyes pierced the room. When Lt. Harmon started to respond, he exclaimed, "Do not speak. You are a woman, not a soldier."

General Adams' voice cut through the room. "She is one of our soldiers. We are not here to discuss legalities at this time. This is an information-only briefing. Any other questions?"

As the officer-in-charge of operations, Major Bingham had several. His most crucial question came next. "How long was it after the boy was shot until the woman Nadja was located?"

"Maybe four or five minutes, Sir," Lt. Harmon responded. "During the NBC team's search for biological and chemical weapons, Sergeant Jacobs heard a cry and started looking. He found her several booths down, rolled up in a carpet."

"Anybody else?" General Adams asked.

"How many rounds?"

"How old was the boy?"

"Was Nadja his mother?"

The questions flew from multiple quarters with answers such as, "We don't know yet," "About nine," and "Yes," given as responses.

"This drug fentanyl. Why are they creating it here?" the general asked.

"In a country that is producing eighty percent of the world's heroin, that's a good question," Command Sergeant Major Swift said.

Mr. Owens deferred the question to Lt. Harmon.

"We're not certain. One reason might be to increase drug profits, another might be to weaponize it for terrorism. Fentanyl is highly addictive, but so is heroin. These are urgent questions we are trying to get answered from the prisoners. Not only did it almost kill Lieutenant Preston, but it's killing around seventy thousand people every year in the United States, and that number is expected to rise. Assad did not know the heroin was being cut, and Nadja was not talking."

Through all this, Tarik remained silent until General Adams asked him to elaborate on the fentanyl problem. "He is DEA," he reminded the room.

How clever, placing a DEA agent as an interpreter. Lt. Harmon's stare dared Tarik to come up with a better answer.

The dragon scar on Tarik's cheek glowed dark red in the fluorescent lighting. *Tap, tap, tap.* The point of a pen beat on his yellow notepad before flipping shut. "Why, indeed, in Afghanistan, a country that needs so much rebuilding."

"Ballpark answer," General Adams said.

"In this case, I do not know," Tarik replied. "Typically, drugs will be cut to increase profits. A kilogram of fentanyl will sell for around forty-five thousand dollars. And the lab doesn't have to pay growers."

"Nadja is a chemist. Could this be a test case?" Lt. Harmon asked.

"Testing for what?"

"Potency, efficiency." She took a breath. "Route of transmission."

Tarik's next words seethed with arrogance. "By blowing it into the air? Not likely."

Lt. Harmon's left brow lifted. "I'm assuming the boy took it upon himself to help his mother. Somehow, it seems uncoordinated."

Major West chewed on that for a moment. "You could be right."

"We still need to come up with the why," Mr. Owens said. "We stopped at the prison on the way over here and got a lead on Nadja's son. Lt. Harmon was able to get Assad to give up his location."

"Our S2 shop already sent the intel over to the Inter-Services Intelligence Agency in Pakistan," Major West said.

Among other agencies. Lt. Harmon looked at Tarik. "The DEA has it now. Any more questions?"

"They found twenty-two shells at the farm along with the Katyusha. Remind me, how many of them tested positive for explosives?"

"Eighteen of them, Sir."

"Eighteen, that leaves four with another substance consisting of a white powder. Do we have any idea what that powder is?"

"No, Sir. We covered that earlier with Major West. The powder did test negative for narcotics, and the anthrax test is pending. We should have results from Langley tomorrow."

"From an operational viewpoint, we don't know what level of MOPP is needed to deal with this threat," Major Bingham said.

"No, Sir. Not yet," Lt. Harmon said, knowing that the MOPP level indicated whether the soldiers needed to wear chemical suits and gas masks.

"What is the estimated time of arrival at Langley?" Major West asked.

"Accounting for the eight-and-a-half-hour time difference and the wind speed from the continent here to the U.S., they should have had it at zero three thirty this morning." Lt. Harmon looked at General Adams and added, "That's just an estimate. Changing pilots, meals, might be around four. It's been elevated."

"Which means the results could be available now," Major Bingham exclaimed.

Major West had walked from the room and soon returned looking quite perplexed holding a sheet of paper.

"What is it?" General Adams asked.

"Results for specimen A, B, C, and D: a clay mineral made of hydrogenated magnesium silicate," Major West responded.

"Which is?"

Lt. Harmon typed the results into a search engine. Everyone leaned forward as she read the results.

"It's talcum."

General Al-Jaleesa looked at Tarik, who merely shrugged. Command Sergeant Major Swift asked for the spelling.

"T-A-L-C-U-M. It's talcum, as in powder," Lt. Harmon said with a hint of humor in her voice.

"Well, I'll be a baby's ass," the Sergeant Major exclaimed.

"Exactly," Lt. Harmon replied.

"We need to know what the target is," Major Bingham said grimly. "They're plotting a blast area."

"What makes you say that?" Lt. Harmon asked.

"You ever powder a baby's ass?"

Lt. Harmon slowly shook her head no. "Babies?"

"I have four kids," Major Bingham said. "When you hold their legs up and shake the powder, it wafts out and covers everything if you don't hold it close enough."

"This could be a test market for something bigger," Mr. Owens said thoughtfully.

"Okay, everybody, we've got work to do," Major West said. The meeting ended as everyone sprang to attention.

"General Adams," Lt. Harmon called out, prompting the general to turn and stare silently at the young officer. A light breeze crossed into the room from the door left open as the others departed. She lifted her face toward the breeze. *Grandfather.*

The general gave a hint of a smile. "Yes?"

You're in command, girl. Her grandfather's words resonated in her ears.

"Sir," she said nervously. "I would like permission to interrogate the prisoner, Nadja."

"Not possible," he responded. "She's being transferred to Guantanamo."

"So fast?"

"The base is drawing down, Lieutenant. She's refusing to talk with the interrogator here, she's going away."

"He's a man, Sir," Lt. Harmon said. The light freckles on her nose took the air of impertinence in her voice to a slightly lower level, causing the general to smile.

"He is a senior ranking officer experienced in interrogation techniques." The general turned on his heel and prepared to leave. Once again, Lt. Harmon stopped him.

"That's not what she sees, General."

With his interest now piqued, General Adams turned back and studied the young officer. "Walk with me."

"Yes, Sir," Lt. Harmon said and grabbed her briefcase which had spilled open. After quickly stuffing the papers back inside, she added her laptop and snapped the case shut. Soon, she was on the heels of the general, explaining her plan to interrogate Nadja.

"And you think THAT will work."

"It's our best chance, Sir, to get information. We don't know if they were planning on using that Katyusha to attack the base or other patrols. She will see herself as my superior. Basically, she will interrogate herself."

Once they reached his office, General Adams picked up the phone and cancelled the order, transferring Nadja Jammu to Guantanamo.

"You have one week," he told Lt. Harmon. "No progress, she gets transferred."

"Actually, I only have three days, Sir."

"Then she goes to Guantanamo."

Before General Adams could pick up the phone again, Lt. Harmon said hurriedly, "Sorry, Sir. I didn't mean I only needed three days. My grandfather, the man who raised me, had a stroke. I've asked for leave, and I have a plan to continue gathering intel during the two weeks I'll be gone."

"Two weeks?" General Adams frowned. "What are you thinking, Lieutenant?"

"Our interpreter Ramen, who is now under arrest, is being housed with Assad. He was working with al-Qaeda to save some money to prepare for the U.S. withdrawal from Afghanistan," Lt. Harmon said, giving it the noblest twist she could muster.

General Adams looked at her suspiciously. "You're a sympathizer?"

Her mouth fell slightly open. "This is an intellectual exercise, General."

He couldn't help but laugh.

"Ramen's wife, Sasha, and their child are living in Kabul. We can bring her in and house her with Nadja. In exchange for Ramen and Sasha's help to collect information, the family could be transferred to the U.S. Ramen and his wife can face prosecution there, and the child will be safe."

General Adams frowned. "You do realize the whole patrol could have been killed by Ramen's traitorous act."

"Yes, Sir. But I'm in the business of collecting intel to help our patrols. The prosecutors in the U.S. can deal with Ramen when he's stateside."

"Go coordinate the interrogation with Major West."

"Yes, Sir."

"Have the woman Sasha and her son picked up," he barked into the phone, waving Lt. Harmon off. "Lieutenant, you're dismissed."

With a sigh of relief, she walked from General Adams' office, saying to herself, "Just how do I prepare to interrogate an al-Qaeda operative? I haven't had that class yet." Her eyes widened. "I'll ask Bob."

CHAPTER 7

Parwan Detention Facility
* Bagram AFB, Afghanistan*
* June 23, 2021 1200*

The guards at the detention center initially balked when Lt. Harmon requested to visit Nadja Jammu, but after a call from Major West, they led the young lieutenant to the prison block.

"I'll talk to Nadja in her cell," she said.

"Interrogation is not allowed in the cells, Mam," an MP replied.

"Oh, this is not an interrogation. Just a social call."

"Technically, the prisoners are not allowed to have visitors in their cells."

"So technically, I'm not a visitor. Just here to check on her." The blue of her eyes turned on the MP and smiled.

"You'll need a guard."

"I'd rather not. Nadja needs to see me as someone she can trust. But if I must, send a female. You have someone young and blonde?"

"Airman Whitsel, but she's new here. I don't think that will work."

"Go get her. You can stay right outside the cell but out of sight. I'll wait." As she waited for the guard to come back, Lt. Harmon reviewed the questions Major West and Robert Owens had agreed she should ask in order to find Nadja's vulnerabilities. Soon, the MP returned accompanying a nervous young airman with corkscrew blonde hair.

"Good afternoon, Mam."

"Airman," Lt. Harmon responded with a slight nod of her head. While following the guard to Nadja's cell, she told Airman Whitsel to remain silent and to stay between herself and the door. "That way, you'll project power from your little self. The power to keep her locked up or let her go." Upon entering the cell, they found the slight figure of a dark-haired woman curled on her side. Lt. Harmon studied the woman's appearance, noting the strands of hair flowing across her back were thick and tangled, and that her nailbeds were filled with dirt and bit close. And something else. *She's been crying,* she thought, noticing the trace of a dried tear staining her left cheek. "How long has she been asleep?"

"About two hours."

"Wake her up, please. Then leave us."

The senior MP reached down and gave the bed a shake. "Wake up. You have a visitor." When Nadja stirred, he stomped loudly out of the room and slammed the door. Airman Whitsel positioned herself as Lt. Harmon suggested and stood quietly observing the scene.

"Good morning, Mother."

The prisoner raised herself on one arm and turned to look at her visitor. "I am not your mother," she hissed in English.

"I know, but you are a mother. I'm sorry for your loss."

Nadja's stare hardened; she crouched as if to spring as her raspy voice echoed around the room. "Why would you be sorry? You are with the people who killed my son."

The airman moved to step forward but quickly resumed her place when Lt. Harmon waved her back.

"I lost my parents. Pretty much been an orphan my whole life so I know what it feels like to lose someone you love."

The soothing compassion in Lt. Harmon's voice, the sorrowful expression on her face. None of it could be denied as not truthful. Nadja's expression softened. "It is different. He was a child."

"I'm sorry. My name is Lieutenant Harmon. I just stopped by to introduce myself and see if you need anything."

"I'm hungry," Nadja said.

Lt. Harmon studied the prisoners' eyes, listless and encased in dark circles, sitting over hallowed cheeks. She looked at the airman and asked, "Can she have a meal?"

"Yes, Mam."

"Very well. After you eat, they'll let you sleep. I'll be back later, and we'll chat."

"You're another interrogator," Nadja spat out.

"Yes, Mother, it's my job. Right now, I just wanted to meet you. We can talk about what happened to your son when I come back." She looked around the room, driving home the point that Nadja could spend time with her chatting, or she could remain locked in her cell.

Airman Whitsel stood tight against the wall as Lt. Harmon passed through the door, then made her way down the hall with the young airman close on her heels.

"Do you want me to go down and just, like, stare at her through the bars?" she asked, her face young and eager.

"No," Lt. Harmon said sharply. She turned to the guards. "Make sure the prisoner doesn't see Airman Whitsel again. As part of Nadja's prep, only men are to interact with her."

"Yes, Mam."

As Airman Whitsel's face fell, she walked out to the waiting jeep. "I'm hungry," she said to Mr. Owens.

"Roger that. Hang on." His foot punched the gas pedal as he turned the wheel, spun the jeep in a circle, and took the Disney route to the mess hall. "Well, how'd it go?"

"She was nice."

Mr. Owens was still laughing as they entered the dining facility. "Ah, pizza."

"This is what, two days in a row?" Lt. Harmon asked as they passed through the line and headed over to a table. Using a fork, she speared a piece of pepperoni and shook it onto Mr. Owens' plate.

"No such thing as too much pizza," he replied. "She buy it?"

"I think so. At least she knows I'm an intel officer and seriously, her junior. Has Ramen gotten anything more out of Assad?"

"Just bits and pieces. He's regressed back to the days when he was part of the mujahideen."

"Men in black beards coming to liberate the world for Islam."

"Regular Muslim Armageddon," Mr. Owens agreed. "Odd thing is, back in the day, the United States supported the mujahideen when they were fighting the Russians over here."

"Maybe Assad needs to be reminded the U.S. sees him as one of the good guys," Lt. Harmon said thoughtfully as she licked pizza sauce from a fork.

"I'll get word to Ramen. Since he's locked up with the man, he can run that angle."

"I have a date tonight. Can I use the car?"

"Sure. Be home by ten."

Lt. Harmon pushed herself up from the table. "See you later."

Mr. Owens' brow creased. "It's only thirteen hundred, where are you going?"

"To study the hadiths."

"Good. When you question Nadja, be nice."

"Haven't you heard? I'm ALWAYS nice."

Mr. Owens' eyes said that she was dismissed.

"See you later," she said and headed back to her billets, where she rolled up in bed and fell fast asleep. Two hours later, after being awakened by the sounds of voices arguing outside her window, she placed a set of headphones over her ears. *Much better.*

Knowing that al-Qaeda followed the hadiths, which were the sayings of the Prophet Muhammed, she began reviewing a book written by former CIA interrogator Ali Stoufan.

I wonder if Brian got the intel I asked for.

Late into the night, she'd sent her brother an email telling him the power-of-attorney was on its way and that a copy had been faxed to the hospital. Then, as Brian had set up a security company in Chicago, she'd asked him to scour the neighborhood where an al-Qaeda operative named Nadja Jammu, formerly Natasha Brown, had lived. She checked her email. *Nothing yet.* Hours later, after reviewing information about al-Qaeda and the drug network flowing between Afghanistan and India, and the rest of the world, she closed her books and took off her earphones. Soon, the screeching of tires and the blaring of a jeep's horn drew her attention outside.

"I knew I recognized that driving," she said with a smile.

Mr. Owens studied her mop of tangled locks. "You been studying or sleeping?"

"I-- well, both."

"Fix your hair."

Using one hand to reach behind her head, she pulled the rubber band from her locks and shook her hair out with the resulting frizz leaving the resemblance of a child caught playing in the wind.

"You ready for chow?"

"All you guys do is eat around here," she grumbled.

"Military life." Mr. Owens rubbed his stomach.

The jeep's door opened and closed as Lt. Harmon climbed in and soon they were back at the chow hall enjoying a meal of barbequed chicken, mashed potatoes, and green beans. When a lump of potato stuck in her throat, she washed it down with lemonade, then she explained more of her plan to let Nadja feel superior to her junior female status. "She's been a ranking officer in al-Qaeda, in control of a big operation."

"Good call, it could work," Mr. Owens responded as he handed over the keys to the jeep.

Lt. Harmon couldn't help teasing her companion. "Are you walking home, or do you have a hot date in the motor pool?"

"Hot date in the motor pool," he mumbled as he walked off. "Like I can't get a ride."

"If you want someone to leave, leave them lonely," she called behind him. Once in the driver's seat, she gripped the wheel and sat thinking about what she'd just said. It was true. At West Point, consumed with wanting to graduate at the top of her class, she'd spent hours more than the other students studying for tests.

In his last year of studies, Brad had repeatedly offered to waylay his own study time to take her out again on his boat. She'd mostly refused, but one day, as his graduation neared, she changed her mind and ran out to the docks. There, she found him with a local woman sharing a glass of wine. He looked up as she ran off.

"Samantha, wait," he'd called after her.

They had never spoken of the incident again. Now, his sultry voice called from the curb, "How about I come over and fluff your laundry?"

"My laundry is already fluffed, thank you."

"I thought that was just your hair."

"It's my new interrogator look."

Captain Kramer studied her hair. "Floozy?"

"You would know, bye." Imitating Mr. Owens' style, she floored the gas pedal and left the captain standing in a cloud of dust. Back in her billets, she once again studied her uniforms before deciding to change into the grunge look, then she wet her hair and smoothed it flat. Now satisfied with her appearance, she sat down to check her email.

Good boy.

Hey sis. We knocked on doors this morning and found a couple of people who remembered Natasha. Her father was a minister in the protestant church. Natasha was a quiet kid, but people remembered her because she could sing. Nickname: Bubblegum because she popped gum and then stuck it under a pew.

We actually found her kindergarten teacher, Ms. Foster. She remembered Natasha because she was the preacher's daughter. She wasn't sure but suspected that Natasha might have been abused because when the kids drew pictures of their family, Natasha's picture was of her father holding a club over her head.

Natasha was an honor student in high school and graduated from college with a masters in chemistry.

Her father, as you know, passed away two years ago. I got some flowers and delivered them for her mom's "birthday." I did as you instructed and told her they were from her daughter. She was quite happy to get the flowers but a little confused. It wasn't her birthday. She didn't have much to add to what Ms. Foster said, just that Natasha was a good girl, never in trouble, and she was a good student. She hasn't heard from her in ten years and doesn't know where she is.

Sorry, but that's all I got. Hope it helps. Brian

P.S. Grandfather is still in a coma.

"Bubblegum?" Thinking back to the day she got chewing gum on a sail, she smiled. *Boy, was Grandfather mad. I wound up scrubbing the deck for hours.* In the midst of her reverie, a pounding on the door caused her to startle. Hurriedly she flung open the door to stare into Captain Kramer's determined eyes.

"One minute you're friendly, the next minute you're hostile. What the heck is going on, Sam?"

"Not now." Her eyes creased as she pushed past him with the jeep keys in hand and headed through the door. He grabbed her wrist and pulled the keys away.

"Now. We have to at least be able to work together."

"Not for long," she replied. "I'm leaving in three days." As she stood with Captain Kramer's hand holding onto her wrist, a shadow fell across their path. She looked up at the captain and smiled. "I was just leaving to interrogate a prisoner. Bye."

The shadow's creator folded his arms across his chest and looked questioningly at his watch. "At this hour?" Tarik asked.

"Once the sun goes down, prison gets a lot scarier."

A crestfallen Captain Kramer released her wrist and handed back her keys. Nodding at Tarik, she climbed behind the wheel and drove away. The sun had long ago set over the mountains, leaving Bagram bathed in moonlight. As the outline of the prison came into view, she breathed a sigh of relief. *Whew, found it!* Then she had another thought.

I'm glad Mr. Owens got Nadja an offer to go into the Witness Protection Program. He's got to be CIA!

CHAPTER 8

Bagram Airforce Base
June 23, 2001 2100

The Parwan Detention Facility, long under the control of the Afghan Ministry of Defense, stood just outside the base. Inside the prison, the interrogation room stood stark and foreboding, with one lone bulb hanging along the ceiling. Within the shadowy confines of the room, Lt. Harmon sat at the metal table across from Nadja Jammu, a captured al-Qaeda operative. The moonlight streaming through the prison window lit the shadows lining the prisoner's face as the soft overhead light glistened on strands of hair which, per LT. Harmon's instructions, had been freshly washed and deloused. Soon, the delicate dance between two women shaped by different worlds began.

While preparing her opening line, a light layer of perspiration crossed Lt. Harmon's forehead. Using her sleeve to wipe away the sweat, she calmed herself and focused her grey-blue eyes on the prisoner. "Good evening, Natasha. Or do you prefer I address you as Nadja, or Mrs. Jammu?"

Assuming a look of total disinterest, Nadja picked at the dirt packing her fingernails and set her mouth with a slight smile.

Moments of silence passed before Lt. Harmon said quietly, "Out of respect for your marriage, I will address you as Mrs. Jammu."

That comment produced a quick look of insolence. "Nadja."

"Excuse me?"

The prisoner quit picking at her nails and clasped her hands across her abdomen. "In America, the wife is dominated by the husband. She takes his last name to show that dominance and wears his ring. We are not in America."

"You are not dominated by your husband, but you have taken his last name. How is that different rom Americans?"

"In the Islamic culture, marriage means a husband is dedicated to his wife."

Lt. Harmon crossed her legs and cupped her chin in her hand. "That's how it should be in marriage,

right?"

Nadja's cheek twitched beside an involuntary smile.

"I know you both had to assume a different name when you joined al-Qaeda. Were you guys already

married when that happened?"

That remark once again produced silence.

"Just curious how it works."

The older woman looked at Samantha with a keen stare. "You are so young. What do you know about life?"

"I know what I read in books. When I lived on a boat, I read a lot of books."

"There are few worth reading. Out there is where you learn about life."

"And love?" Lt. Harmon leaned back as the corner of her lip lifted into a partial smile. Her eyes took on a bit of a dreamy stance.

"Have you ever been in love? You're beautiful, young. Of course you have. And you were

disappointed," Nadja declared with an air of superiority.

"I, well." *She's digging at me, trying to get control of my emotions. Nice try.*

"And why would they send someone so young to interrogate a hardened terrorist?"

I get it; she assumes they couldn't get anybody else. "The drawdown. Everybody's been reassigned."

"And you're the best they can do?" Nadja's eyes became cold as she crossed her arms.

"Busted." Lt. Harmon looked away. "We didn't come here to talk about my love life." With a slight shake of her hand, she opened her notes and focused on the information in a document. "I see you're from the windy city. Can we talk about Chicago? That's my hometown, too."

At this, Nadja's eyes showed a spark of interest. "Really?"

"My parents liked to take me to museums. I liked some of them."

"Me too. Museum of Contemporary Art."

"Chicago History Museum."

"And the boring ones. The Field Museum." Nadja folded her hands on the table.

"American Writers Museum." Lt. Harmon stifled a yawn.

"I liked the Museum of Science and Industry." With that, the wariness in Nadja's face completely vanished.

"Is that where you got your interest in science?"

"Maybe," she said haltingly.

"There's lots of jobs in Chicago. Why did you leave?"

"Why would you ask that?"

"Because that's where your parents lived," Lt. Harmon said casually. "Some people like to stay close to their family."

Nadja waved the comment off.

"Speaking of Chicago, my brother is there now. He said he knows your kindergarten teacher, Ms. Foster."

"Oh? She's a good teacher. How does your brother know her?"

"He doesn't really. He was at the Museum of Modern Art when I called him about our grandfather. He had me on speakerphone when I mentioned that I was going to be spending time with you. A woman standing next to him heard the conversation and said she knew a Natasha Brown, and it turned out it was you."

"How serendipitous."

Lt. Harmon thought it was strange to hear an al-Qaeda operative use that word, but this then reminded her of Nadja's advanced education in America, and she smiled to herself. "I guess weird things happen. Red or black?"

"Red or black, what?" Nadja asked tentatively.

"Licorice."

Looking at the other woman as if she were a conspirator, Nadja said, "Black."

"Me too." Pulling a bag of licorice sticks from her briefcase, Lt. Harmon handed a few to Nadja.

"Why did you ask about my parents?" she asked amicably. While holding a stick of licorice like a cigar, she bit off the end and chewed.

"It's just background information. I'm sorry about your father. Your mother says hello, and she likes the flowers you sent."

"I didn't send any..." Nadja stared hard at her interrogator. "I'm thirsty."

"Guard, water please. For both of us," Lt. Harmon called to the MP.

As the moonlight slipped behind the mountains, the creases of years gone by deepened on Nadja's face. Suddenly she remarked, "I liked finger painting."

With a slight nod, Lt. Harmon agreed. "My grandfather still has one of my art projects on a bulkhead in his boat."

"He kept it all these years?"

"Sort of." Samantha smiled, remembering the day her grandfather stood over her after her finger, covered in yellow paint, drew the rays of a sunset on the wall. "He liked the 'art deco.'" Then her eyes focused on Nadja's face. "There are like, hundreds of chemical companies in Chicago. Why go all the way to India?"

"Chemical companies that hire men and underpay women," she spat out.

"With your credentials, you still could have gotten a good job."

"Maybe staying in a place where you have to fight to get respect is not a good thing to do."

"And maybe staying around a father who abused you isn't either?"

As Nadja shifted uncomfortably, Lt. Harmon stood and walked over to the window, turning her back on the scene. Nevertheless, she could hear the captive, now seething with vulnerability, breathing in slow, steady gasps. When the breathing returned to normal, she went back to her seat.

As the MP placed two cups of water on the table, the two women sat silent, warily eying each other. Lt. Harmon gave in first. She picked up a cup and sipped.

"My brother said that Ms. Foster really liked you. She said you're a good singer."

Nadja's face remained frozen.

"She followed you through your academic years and said you were also a good student."

Again, the words were met with silence.

"I can understand why you would leave Chicago, the winters aren't fun. But why go all the way across to the other side of the world when your mother needed you?"

"Why are you bringing up my mother!"

"Your father had cancer. He died and left your mother alone. Why didn't you wait?"

The trembling in Nadja's mouth lasted for just a moment before she closed her eyes.

"I'm sorry if this part is rough. I didn't grow up with my real mother, so I'm really just not getting this," Lt. Harmon said as her tone hardened. "If you're done talking, you can return to your cell."

That opened Nadja's eyes. "And you can return to your lover."

Lt. Harmon's eyes looked distant. "I'd rather stay here."

With a slight smile creasing the edge of her mouth, Nadja sat up straight and stared at the younger woman. "Why should I have stayed near a father who abused his daughter? And a mother who knew about it and did nothing."

"Um," Lt. Harmon's voice faltered.

"Can I have some more water?"

"Guard!"

An MP walked in with a whole pitcher of ice water, placed it on the table, and quickly exited from the room.

"Ever go to that Greek restaurant just off Magnificent Mile?" Lt. Harmon asked.

"The one where they serve all the ouzo and yell 'Ump a'?"

"Probably. That was a fun place."

"Just once. My father didn't like all the alcohol, so we took our food and left."

"We went there once when my adoptive parents were alive. I just remember my dad laughing so hard at the waiters. That was in another world."

"Yes. Quite different."

"The world where you were an American."

Nadja eyed her with suspicion. "What is your point?"

"Well, I can understand why you would want to join an organization since you grew up in one. But you moved so far from the Protestant church. Why al-Qaeda?"

In a monotone voice, Nadja started to repeat a favorite hadith, the sayings of the Prophet Muhammad she'd learned in the camp. "Muhammed is the Prophet. The hadith says if you see the black banners coming from Khurasan, join that army, even if you have to crawl over ice, no power will be able to stop them."

"And they will finally reach Baitul Muqaddas, which is Jerusalem, where they will erect their flags."

"You know the hadith?"

"I told you, I read a lot on the boat. Other than fishing and swimming, there was little else to do."

"You are a true warrior."

Lt. Harmon tugged at the hem of her uniform. *We're back in terrorist mode. At least she didn't say, adversary.* "I know you were recruited to join al-Qaeda by your husband, Dalbir Jammu. I am a bit surprised that you allowed yourself to succumb to the teachings of the hadith." With that, she brushed a strand of hair away from her forehead and sat with the expression of a trusting child.

"Muhammed is the true Prophet. We follow his words."

"But many of the things people quote cannot be verified."

"Not everything is written down. My husband knew Muhammed's true sayings. 'The black banners will come from the East, led by mighty men with long hair and long beards. Their surnames are taken from the names of their hometown, and their first names are from a Kunya.'"

"Kunya, as in an alias?"

"Yes. My husband was a great leader."

"I understand he was a peace-loving Indian until he got into the wrong crowd. It's too bad, he was a good musician. His fingers were quick on those guitar strings."

"How do you know that?"

Lt. Harmon held up her phone and displayed a video of a band playing in a small venue. "Isn't that you?" she asked as the blue of her eyes locked onto Nadja's. "You really can sing."

"Enough questions," Nadja exclaimed. One lone tear slipped down her cheek.

"I know it's late. I'm just curious how you met."

Nadja buried her face in her arms.

"Well, rumor has it that you met in the break room at Bhopal Chemical Enterprises in India. I know that you were both arrested and accused of stealing drugs from BCE.

"That was a lie."

"Your husband was a foreman in the warehouse. He diverted shipments to an al-Qaeda faction in Pakistan."

"Where did you hear that?"

"Right here on this court document," Lt. Harmon said innocently. Holding up a sheet of paper, she passed it across the table.

"No, he didn't do that."

"The company records say that he did, and you told him what was in the boxes."

Nadja shook her head no.

"I'm just repeating what the court documents said. Didn't your lawyer tell you?"

"I didn't have a lawyer."

"Because Dalbir rushed you out of the country to come to Afghanistan?"

The look of confusion crossing Nadja's face could not be denied.

"It's okay, I don't mean to disparage your husband. I know he was killed in an interdiction raid. Where did you bury him?" Lt. Harmon asked in a more conciliatory tone.

With a slight tilt of her head, Nadja gave Lt. Harmon a strange look. "They took it."

"Took what?"

"His body."

"Who took it?"

"The Taliban."

Lt. Harmon held up both hands. "Who told you they were Taliban?"

"People we knew. My husband is dead."

"And your younger son? I have a video of him, too."

Startled, Nadja quickly raised her head and sat straight up. "I want to see it."

"In a minute. There are a lot of things we don't understand."

A raised right eyebrow over a smoldering light blue eye asked the question, "What?"

"What does it cost to buy a Katyusha these days?"

Nadja's laugh turned into a fit of coughing.

"What's so funny?"

"If you have to ask the price, you can't afford it."

"You shopped at Bell Ami's, nice. Me too."

"Magnificent Mile. I liked that place."

"Your clothes," Lt. Harmon said, eyeing Nadja's flowing garments, plus the headdress. "You buy that on a Webzine for '"How to be a terrorist?" Pulling a magazine from her briefcase, she opened to a page where women stood fashionably decked out in 'I want to be a terrorist' garb. "You left this at Assad's place. I saw the article you marked in al-Khansaa."

Nadja stared at the page.

Instead of the usual feminine fare of food, fashion, and furnishings, it provided tips on how to physically prepare for jihad, parenting advice on grooming future 'lions on the battlefield,' and discussions on the role of mujahid at the female holy fighters in Islamic Law. "We will stand covered in our veils and abayas (all-encompassing robes favored by Saudi women), with our weapons in our hands and our children in our arms," proclaims the editorial in the inaugural issue of al-Khansaa.

The magazine went back into Lt. Harmon's briefcase. "You're quite a long way from the Magnificent Mile."

"That is the world of the Infidels."

"Like Ms. Foster?"

Nadja looked angry.

"You're not that brainwashed. This article doesn't say that you should get your children involved. It's not your fight, it's not their world. I'll show you the video. Just tell me, how can a person around here buy a Katyusha?"

Nadja's mouth twisted into a self-satisfied smile. "An ordinary person cannot."

"But you can because your grandfather was a Russian officer." Lt. Harmon held out her phone but left the screen blank. "He was Russian, not al-Qaeda. How did you get it?"

Nadja's eyes stared at Lt. Harmon's phone. "My grandfather told me the story when I was little about a cave where the Russians left a lot of equipment. It was there." As she reached for the phone, Lt. Harmon pulled it back.

"Where's the cave?"

"In a mountain."

"I think you know you need to be a little more specific."

With a shrug, Nadja elaborated, "The mountain has a rock that looks like an eagle."

"We already found that cave. There's nothing there."

"Really?"

"The other Katyusha's were already moved. Where did they go?"

Nadja eyed the phone and provided a bland answer. "I don't know. They were both there when we left. I don't know more."

"Was there anything else in the cave?"

"Yes."

"What?"

"Death."

"From what, guns, bullets, explosives? Fentanyl?"

When Nadja's face hardened into something only one thing could change, Lt. Harmon pulled up a video on her phone and placed the phone close enough for her to see.

In the video, a little boy stood with a vase in his hand in front of the market, eagerly talking to the troops. In one swift motion, he blew into the vase, and one of the troops went down. When he tried to blow a second round of powder, his little body arched backward as bullets flew into his heart. Then he silently fell to the ground, covered in his white powder.

Nadja's chest heaved.

"Why?" Lt. Harmon asked. "Why would you attack the soldiers when you know the United States is leaving very soon?"

With words spewing in a tone of hatred she'd learned in training camp, Nadja spat out, "Because they must go home defeated in such a way they will never return."

Lt. Harmon gave her a 'You're nuts' look. "So you think the U.S. is winning?"

"They think they are winning. But we know different, and we will teach them."

"And that was the exact purpose of Osama Bin Laden when he published his second fatwa declaring war on our citizens." Lt. Harmon pulled another document from her briefcase and placed it on the table. Nadja leaned forward and stared at the words she'd been shown in another setting, on another day, in another world.

The second Fatwa on February 23, 1998

The Arabian Peninsula has never—since God made it flat, created its' desert, and encircled it with seas—been stormed by any forces like the crusader armies spreading in it like locusts, eating its riches and wiping out its plantations...For over seven years, the United States has been occupying the lands of Islam in the holiest of places, the Arabian Peninsula, plundering its riches, dictating to its rulers, humiliating its people, terrorizing its neighbors, and turning its bases in the Peninsula into a spearhead through which to fight the neighboring Muslim peoples.... The ruling to kill the Americans and their allies—civilians and military—is an individual duty for every Muslim who can do it in any country in which it is possible to do it, in order to liberate the al-Aqsa Mosque and the holy mosque from their grip and in order for their armies to move out of all the lands of Islam, defeated and unable to threaten any Muslim.

"What good did the war do for him?" Lt. Harmon asked stoically. "He's dead. Your son is dead. You have another son, and they know where he is. Give him a chance to live."

Nadja's eyes gleamed black.

With her face reflecting a mix of skepticism and contemplation, Lt. Harmon rose and, with her fingers interlaced, reached toward the ceiling. After a quick stretch that displayed her thin, muscled frame, she quickly dropped back into her seat. "You're not from here," she said thoughtfully. "You're an American woman. There we are free. Here, you're just a pawn to the men."

"What do you mean?" Nadja asked suspiciously.

"Siegfried is gone. The whole drug network you had here in Afghanistan has been disbanded. Siegfried's been arrested. Your compound on the Pakistan border has been located and confiscated by the Afghan government, along with your alias passport. If the Taliban take over this country when the U.S. goes home, women will have no freedom here. You won't be allowed to work. I know you've been offered transport to the U.S. with the potential of being in the Witness Protection Program, but they'll withdraw that offer if you don't give me something substantial. Let's talk about the attack on the patrol."

The older woman cupped her face in her hands. Lt. Harmon opened her laptop and turned it toward Nadja. "You're a Protestant. In your church, they believe you can talk directly to God and that salvation is forever obtainable. Even after this." She played the video of Lt. Preston leaning over the child, inhaling a breath of narcotics and falling to the ground. Nadja stared as the medics rushed to save his life. "That's Lieutenant Preston. He's going to be a daddy soon. Want to know how he's doing?"

The frantic movement of Nadja's eyes darting from Lt. Harmon's face to the screen resembled that of a cornered rat with tremoring paws.

"I understand. When my parents died and I had to go live on a boat with my grandfather, I had to reinvent myself too. And I'm stronger for it. This isn't who you are," Lt. Harmon said with compassion in her voice. "The fentanyl, it was a test?"

As her lower jaw flinched, Nadja's eyes continued to stare at the blank screen.

"Want to see it again?"

"No."

"We need to talk about the fentanyl."

"Okay."

"Who ordered the attack?"

"Zawahiri," Nadja said softly.

"Al-Qaeda's leader, why?"

"Because it worked when the Russians rescued the hostages at the Moscow theater."

"A lot of those hostages were killed in that indoor theater by morphine and fentanyl blown through vents," Lt. Harmon said. "And now Zawahiri wants to see how it will work outdoors, why?"

"I don't know." Nadja's raspy voice came out as a hiss.

"When is the next attack planned?"

"I don't know. I'm tired."

"Where is your phone?"

"At the farm."

"The Afghan police raided the farm. They have it?"

"Possibly." With that, Nadja's face dissolved into tears.

"And you know they could locate your son. They may already have him."

"No." Nadja shook her head. "Not likely.

"They don't have him because he's in Pakistan. Where is the second Katyusha?"

"It blew up," she said in a tone of utter defiance.

"No it didn't. There is satellite imagery of a Katyusha being transported east of the base. What was the intended destination?"

Nadja stared for a moment, then shrugged. "A barn somewhere. I don't know."

"You're not a dumb terrorist. You're a chemist. I don't suppose there is anyone else intelligent enough in this country to produce the fentanyl."

The offhand compliment worked. Nadja went into a speech about fentanyl, how she and Siegfried were the only chemists in Afghanistan who could properly manufacture it, how it was made, even the fact that the precursors to manufacture the drug came in the mail.

"From India or China?"

"China, of course." The look on Nadja's face said she was lying.

"No big deal. We'll watch your mail for a package from China."

"I thought I said India."

Busted!

"And the talcum powder," Lt. Harmon said. "We know you're using it to plot a blast area. Why not corn starch?"

After a sigh of exasperation, Nadja replied haughtily, "The molecular weight of corn starch is nowhere near the weight of fentanyl."

"And the Katyusha?"

"I don't know."

The game of cat and mouse continued for another hour, with each woman giving no quarter. Finally convinced that Nadja might not know exactly where the second Katyusha was being stored, Lt. Harmon decided to end the interrogation and looked at her watch.

"I have to go back to my other job."

"Are you coming back tomorrow?" Nadja asked timidly.

"I'm responsible for the safety of the patrols. Unless you have something else to tell me, I won't need to speak with you," Lt. Harmon replied.

"Like what?"

"Like, why fentanyl was used on the patrol. And when is the next attack planned?"

At that, Nadja remained silent.

"Guard!"

A male MP walked into the room to escort the prisoner back to her cell. "They have the woman you asked about, Mam."

"Sasha?"

"Yes, Mam."

"Looks like you've got a roommate," Lt. Harmon told Nadja. She looked back at the MP. "I'll come say hello." As she followed him down the hall, the heart-wrenching sobs of a mother crying for her child echoed from the direction of the cell. Though her eyes showed empathy, Nadja's lips remained unmoved as her steps faltered. The guard's grip tightened on her arm as he pulled her along.

Upon arriving at the cell, Lt. Harmon studied the scene between the prisoners. At first, there were no signs of recognition, but upon hearing Nadja's name, Sasha's accusations cut through the air, blaming the other woman for the loss of her child. The unearthly cries continued as Lt. Harmon walked away, telling a story of the prison holding more than just physical bars. It held the weight of shattered families.

Outside, she fired up the jeep and headed to the TOC. Along the route, she removed her headgear, opened a window, and, as usual, the wind blowing through her hair relaxed her mind enough to slowly remove all human emotion. *I have a job to do.*

"What did you find out?" Mr. Owens asked as she walked into his office. Grasping the arm of a chair, she sank into its depth.

"There's a second Katyusha out there somewhere," she said wearily. "They used talcum in the shells because it has close to the same molecular weight as fentanyl. I think she'll have more to say about it in the near future. Ramen get anything from Assad?"

"Just that he's a junkie who's crazy about Nadja."

"Who is still crazy about her husband. I suppose you have the FBI, or the CIA, or the Boy Scouts, whatever organization it is you belong to, looking for tape from their trip to Washington."

"Good work. Good night, Lieutenant," Mr. Owens said with a wide grin.

After handing over the keys to the jeep, she replied, "Thanks, Dad, see you tomorrow."

With a slight chuckle, Mr. Owens accepted the keys. As he prepared to lock up for the night, Corporal Boorman poked his head through the open office door.

"Phone call for you, Lieutenant. Red Cross on the line."

"Send the call in here," Mr. Owens said kindly and turned the phone toward Samantha. "I'll be outside in the jeep."

Her neck vein began to pulse visibly. "I know what this is," she whispered. "Someone in my family has died." *Grandfather.*

CHAPTER 9

Bagram AFB
June 24, 2021 0800

An early phone call summoned Lt. Harmon to brigade. Freshly washed and ready for her day, she headed to the TOC for a ride and frowned at the sight of Captain Kramer racing across the street. *Oh great, not now.* With her heart pounding, she quickened her pace.

"Watch where you're going," he yelled as he dodged around an oncoming Hummer. She flinched as he brushed the dust from his uniform and grabbed her elbow. "Samantha, wait."

"It's Lieutenant Harmon to you, Sir." With her eyes boring straight into his, she jerked her arm away.

"What did I do?" From below his sandy locks of hair, the eyes begging for forgiveness softened her heart.

"Seriously?" Peering up into the rugged face of the man she'd loved ever since West Point, her grey-blue eyes begged to be let go.

"She asked you to leave her alone," Tarik's steely voice said. The camel-toned color of his robes stood in stark contrast to the white shroud falling around his face, singling out the sultry black eyes commanding him to obey. With a muscle flinching down along his jowl, the scar on his cheek flashed an angry red as the two men stood appraising each other.

The green flecks of Captain Kramer's eyes dared Tarik to look away first.

"We don't have time for this," Lt. Harmon exclaimed. "Mr. Owens is waiting."

"I heard about your loss. I just wanted to convey my condolences," Captain Kramer said quietly.

"Thank you," she responded tightly. "Uncle Benny passed away in his sleep."

At that, Tarik looked down upon Samantha with an air of protection. "May life remain on you."

"Thanks, I guess."

"It's what they say in Afghanistan when someone dies," Captain Kramer said. "In our country, we say, 'May he rest in peace.'"

With her facial tone set into a flaccid stare, Lt. Harmon replied, "That might be a little hard. He was mafia." When a flicker of understanding came to Tarik's eyes, she continued, "You knew that, didn't you? Of course, DEA. There's just no privacy around here. Everybody knows everybody's business."

Honk, honk, honk.

The buzzing horn drew Lt. Harmon ahead of the men to find Mr. Owens waiting impatiently behind the wheel of a Humvee.

"You're thirty seconds late. Get in. Brigade needs us there in ten minutes."

"You take shotgun," Captain Kramer called to Tarik. Motioning for Lt. Harmon to get in the back, he pulled open a door and hopped in the other side.

Tarik looked puzzled. "What?"

"Front passenger seat."

Once his passengers were loaded, Mr. Owens sped down Disney Drive with the Hummer's windows open. Lt. Harmon flinched as Captain Kramer snuck a hand onto her knee. She grabbed the hand, threw it off, and stared at the passing buildings until they pulled to a stop in front of brigade. Just as she was about to step out of the vehicle, Brad hissed under his breath, "You're getting colder by the day. What's up, Sam?"

"Ask your dance partner," she replied with a slight catch in her voice.

A reddish flush spread across the captain's face as he followed the group into the building. "Wait!"

"You know the rules," Lt. Harmon hissed under her breath. "No dating ANYBODY while we're here."

Mr. Owens gave her a warning look as the clerk handed out visitor badges.

Inside brigade headquarters, Major West stood to greet the battalion staff as the two men sitting beside his desk slouched down in matching brown chairs. The lack of insignia on their uniforms itself didn't designate them as mujahedeen, but the short haircuts and nicely trimmed black beards screamed- "Afghan Police."

Tarik scowled at the pair. "They shouldn't be here."

"They have to be here," replied Major West. "Grab a coffee."

Lt. Harmon watched with interest as her boss pulled a file from his briefcase and spread a few photos across his desk. In one picture, the face of a young boy with the beginnings of peach fuzz on his chin beamed at the camera. The placard beneath his face read- "Forever Nineteen." All of the photos appeared to have been taken during the innocent years of life- so much to live for, so far to go.

"Who are they?"

"A friend at the DEA sent these over. They're copies of photos on a memorial wall of all of the people who were killed by fentanyl. They are forever that age because they're all dead and can never age another day."

"So young," Lt. Harmon murmured.

"And so many of them," Tarik added. He stared at Akbari, the younger of the two policemen, who shifted uncomfortably in his seat. "This is what corruption does."

Mr. Owens pulled out a packet of photos, all of men with dark skin, black hair, and long beards. Their stares, piercing the room from matching sets of bushy eyebrows, cast an eerie glow amidst the group. "Akbari, pick him out," he said to the younger policeman.

"Who are you looking for?" Tarik asked, studying the photos.

"This officer," Mr. Owens replied, motioning to Akbari, "has been selling doctored identification to assist al-Qaeda with their drug operations. Thanks to an informant, we know that one of these men is living under a new identity somewhere close to this base. We find him, we find the missing Katyusha."

"And he wiped out the old paper trail," Major West added. "Akbari here is the son of a rich Afghan family who bought him his current position as an officer. He has access to a corrupt line of officials. Not our problem, but this is." Once again, he motioned to the photos.

The young Akbari looked fearfully at the group. After a superior officer translated what the others were saying, his finger slid toward the photo of one of the men. "This one with a scar over his right eye," he said in broken English.

"What's his name?" Lt. Harmon asked. Pulling out her phone, she snapped a photo of the picture.

Tarik translated that to Arabic and said the policeman replied that he didn't remember.

Lt. Harmon's fingers flew swiftly over her phone's keyboard as she texted her brother. *Run this photo, need ID now.*

While the men berated Akbari, threatening him with imprisonment, a disgrace to his family, and financial ruin, back in the U.S., Brian McFadden reached for his phone and saw the message from Samantha. After cross-referencing the photo with various social media outlets, he replied with the message, *John Green. Current location: Dubai. Works as a personal assistant to Mojid Al-Hakeem. He was at Mojid's birthday party last night.*

"This can't be the man you're looking for." Lt. Harmon held up her phone to show the others the information her brother had just sent.

Tarik's glittering black eyes bored into Akbari's as he translated the message in a tone the others clearly understood. "Really, John Green. You don't remember John Green?"

With his hand on the butt of his gun, the senior Afghan officer said, "It looks like you have a memory problem." He looked at Lt. Harmon and asked if she could do the same thing with all the photos.

She bit a nail and studied the photos. "My source is good, but not always. It helps to get a name." She began snapping pictures of the other photos and smiled at her next thought. *This will keep Brian busy.*

"It might jog Akbari's memory if you tell him that, if he comes up with the photo and name before Lt. Harmon gets it, the government will look at him more favorably," Major West said to the senior officer.

He nodded and soon had another picture in hand, along with the name Taj Hussein. Lt. Harmon asked Brian to run that man's info. Upon receiving his reply, she closed her phone and announced that, this time, they had the right person.

Akbari's grim face nodded his agreement. "You'll be staying with us," an MP said as he was led away.

While Major West tasked his staff to locate the property of the man known now as Taj Hussein, Captain Kramer said he was going to speak with Major Bingham immediately. "We'll get an op out to shut the next attack down before they find out we have this intel on the Katyusha. Nice work."

"Thanks," Lt. Harmon replied softly, her face glowing from the praise.

After he left, Mr. Owens looked suspiciously at Lt. Harmon. "What did the message say?"

"What message?"

"I know you've been talking to your brother. He and his security company. What did he say about Taj?"

"Oh," she replied with a smile. "He said, I've got nothing."

At that, for the first time, Tarik grinned, then he started to laugh. Lt. Harmon gazed with awe at the smile allowing a set of pearly white teeth to flash amidst the chiseled features of his face. *How was I ever intimidated by this man?*

"John Green. No Muslim is named John Green," he said.

"My brother might have made that up. But for sure, Brian found his pictures on social media."

"What about this Taj? How do you know he's the right guy?" Mr. Owens asked.

"Because no real terrorist puts his stuff on social media, and he didn't have a profile."

Mr. Owens slapped his forehead. "You'd better be right about this."

"I am right. But it's good we have Akbari locked up here in case we need him."

Major West came back to tell everyone that Taj had been located and was living in a nearby village. The property, located along the same route the patrol had taken to Charikar, was just seven klicks away from Assad's. "We are getting a bird on station to gather imagery. While we're waiting for confirmation, Lieutenant Harmon, there are a couple of things we need to discuss."

"Okay," she said, her voice a little shaky as she studied the men around her. *It's no accident that a DEA agent and Mr. Owens stayed to attend this meeting.* "These photos," she said, motioning to the DEA photos from the memorial wall. "What do they have to do with finding the Katyusha?"

"Nothing," Major West responded.

"Then why are they here?"

"Lieutenant, we are asking the questions." Major West nodded at Tarik.

"As you admitted, your uncle was part of the mafia," Tarik said in a voice thick with disapproval.

"I can't pick my relatives," Lt. Harmon replied evenly. "Why are you bringing up my uncle?"

"Your uncle and some of your other relatives were involved in drug trafficking. Did you know that?"

"Nope. I know what mafia people do, but I never knew exactly what my family did. I didn't really know them because I was adopted out at birth, and nobody ever talked about it."

"Nobody, meaning your grandfather who sold a little weed in his day," Mr. Owens said in an offhand tone.

"He might have, I don't know. Grandfather had anxiety issues. But he always protected me from that kind of thing. How do you know if any of this is true?"

"Ramen got Assad to talk. He knows your family."

"You guys already knew that Assad bartended at a tiki bar."

"How did your grandfather know Assad would be at that bar?"

With a pale face and mouth slightly open, Lt. Harmon stared back at Mr. Owens. "He didn't. He just drinks!"

The men looked at each other as Major West said, "Calm down. We're not here to accuse you of anything. Tarik, tell her what this is about."

The scar on Tarik's left cheek blazed as he sat down on Lt. Harmon's right and opened a file. Everyone else sat too, including the Afghan policeman he introduced as Captain Karzai, an officer working for the DEA. In a steady voice, he walked Lt. Samantha Harmon through her childhood.

"When your adoptive parents died, you went to live with your grandfather. The stories of a quirky old man generally high on marijuana traveling with a wild young teenage girl in a sailboat were legendary around the ports," he said. "And there's more. While you were on the boat with your grandfather, there was an incident with young boys and cocaine."

Lt. Harmon's grey-blue eyes gleamed with defiance. With her shoulders squared, she looked straight at the group, saying, "With my grandfather, there were always incidents. We got through it."

"And that's what makes you so good at figuring things out," Tarik responded. "The cocaine. The boys who went aboard your ship said that your grandfather was selling the drug."

"No, he wouldn't do that!"

"And he wouldn't have willingly transported other people who were selling cocaine, or heroin, or any other drug?" Tarik asked.

"No!"

"But he did," Tarik stated. "Those boys thought they could transport cocaine on your grandfather's boat for a reason. And the reason was it wouldn't have been the first time. What they didn't count on was that if you were on board and they tried to harm you, there would be hell to pay. After that incident, your grandfather turned himself in and started testifying for the government. He had a lot to say about your family."

"Not my family. There's just me and my brother," Lt. Harmon said defensively.

"And your mother is in the mental hospital. And your uncle and the others in Chicago."

"I never met the Chicago people, not even my real father. My uncle just died, and that whole mafia thing came from his side of the family. How do you know all that?"

"Background check. You know how it works," Mr. Owens said.

Lt. Harmon wordlessly nodded.

"How did your mother get so close to Benny Harmon?" Tarik asked.

"You've been watching my mother?"

"No, just Benny. He often visits your mother in the hospital."

As Lt. Harmon stood and paced around the room, her back stiffened. "Grandfather had me on the seas to protect me from all of this. On the boat, he knew who I was around and who communicated with me. The only thing I know about my real mother is that she suffered a big trauma, mainly because of my real father, Brett Harmon. After that, Benny was going to Indianapolis to see them both, until my father died. You could ask my mom, but she doesn't remember anything from one day to the next." Her eyes looked accusingly at Tarik. "Why are you asking me about all of this?"

"Because of them," Tarik said, motioning to the photos of the deceased. "We need to know if you had any involvement in the drug trade industry and what you can tell us about your family. Assad seems to think you know something."

Lt. Harmon's grey-blue eyes pooled with fury. Her voice shook as she exploded with, "First of all, I never knew my family in Chicago or that they had anything to do with trafficking drugs. I thought they just fixed horse races. And I would never do drugs! I suppose Ramen told you this."

"Yes," Tarik said. "It was your idea to lock up Ramen with Assad. It's working, Assad is talking."

"And in my world, you have to weed out real intelligence from the stuff people make up to get out of trouble."

Tarik let out a slow breath and said, "Or stay out of trouble. Fortunately for you, as your grandfather did come forward on his own and testified that you had no involvement in any of the drug trade and that you never used drugs, I believe you."

"You should believe me anyway."

"It doesn't work that way, and you know it."

"I'm being vetted. For what?"

"I'll take it from here," Major West said.

Upon receiving the nod, Tarik rose and, along with the Afghan police captain, left the room.

"The first order of business that, we need to discuss, Lt. Harmon, is your future."

"What?" She started to protest but was cut off by Mr. Owens.

"Lieutenant, your tour is done. Everybody is going home. And since you're leaving now, you won't be coming back. The FBI is inviting you to join their organization."

"And give up my military commission? Why would I do that?"

"That's what we need to talk about," Major West replied. "The base is drawing down. The military just won't need as many people. We feel you will be a better asset if you resign your commission and go work for the FBI, or the DEA."

Lt. Harmon yanked out a chair and sat down hard on the seat. Leaning forward, she drew closer to her boss and said pleadingly, "Why?"

Major West studied the young woman's face. "What you did with your phone and with your brother, that's what they need. International drug trafficking organizations are increasingly using sophisticated tools to sell drugs. Take Snapchat."

"We know about Snapchat," Lt. Harmon responded. Indeed, she had just read an article about a young fourteen-year-old boy who mail-ordered a pill he thought was Oxycontin on Snapchat. One day, he came home from school and decided to experiment with the drug. An hour later, his mom went to his room, thinking she was going to take him for a haircut and found him dead in the shower. That was in June of 2020. Now, several people have lost family members to drugs using Snapchat."

"We?" Mr. Owens asked.

"Me and my brother. He's tracked down a few of those traffickers. You should ask him to join the DEA."

"We did. He did a phenomenal job assisting with Trojan Shield, but he refused a job," Mr. Owens replied.

"Your brother helped with Trojan Shield?" Major West whistled. "That's impressive."

"What is Trojan Shield?" Lt. Harmon asked.

"An international drug busting operation run by the FBI," Tarik said from the doorway. "We were part of it."

The blank stare on Lt. Harmon's face was quickly replaced by a thoughtful look as she glanced around the room, finally noticing the piles of brown cardboard boxes stacked along a wall. The top box was open, displaying binders of military regulations previously stored on the shelves of a steel bookcase. *They're getting ready to leave the country.*

"Of course," she said in a halting voice. "The police captain, he was part of it too?"

Tarik nodded.

"So, you were working here as a DEA agent on Trojan Shield? I remember that operation, but I forgot it was called Trojan Shield. The FBI built ANOM. It was a secure messaging service drug operatives thought nobody could monitor because it was all already encrypted."

"Yes," said Tarik in a voice mixed with satisfaction and weariness. "It was a cell phone system criminals thought we couldn't decipher. But we could read everything they were sending over their phones, and we just arrested over eight hundred people worldwide."

"Great, then you don't need me or my brother. I'm a West Point grad." With that, Lt. Harmon crossed her arms to signal that the discussion of her leaving the military was over.

"There will always be a need for you," Mr. Owens said softly. "For sure, taking down those eight hundred people was a major blow to organized crime. But they will always reorganize, and there will be many spinoff operations. Just think about it."

"Yeah, whatever. Now can we go back to finding that Katyusha?"

"That is being taken care of," Major West replied. "Due to your uncle's death, your request for leave has been escalated. You'll be flying out at sixteen hundred hours today. General Adams wants you to interrogate Nadja before you go. From what you've already told us, she is a big part of developing an organized crime network planning to transport more heroin into the United States. And probably fentanyl. She knows how to cook it."

"She can't do it from prison," Lt. Harmon said thoughtfully and wondered more about the network Nadja and her son were building. "Assad," she finally said.

The brows on Major West's face rose, prodding her to continue. "What about Assad?"

"He spent time in Chicago. My Uncle Benny was from Chicago. Assad does drugs." She gave Mr. Owens a hard look. "Tell Assad that Nadja is talking, she doesn't really love him, and that she was sent to America to recruit him."

"How do you know that?" Mr. Owens asked.

"I don't, but it's probably true. She still loves her husband, who might still be alive." Lt. Harmon bit the nail of her right index finger, a habit she'd picked up while sitting on the boat. So often she'd sat perched on a cushion, looking into the sun as her grandfather guided them to a new destination. With her index finger in her mouth and her curls blowing astray, she'd meticulously watched the weather vane above to help guide the boat into the wind, then removed her finger to call out, "Five degrees port, now ten degrees starboard."

"Lieutenant Harmon," Mr. Owens said, waving a hand in front of her face.

"What?"

"Just making sure you're still with us."

"Um, yes. I was just thinking. The network knows by now that we have Nadja in custody. And that we found the first Katyusha."

"Meaning?"

"They've probably moved the second one and will use it soon. Since it will be loaded on the back of a truck, it's highly mobile." Lt. Harmon pulled out her phone and brought up a picture of a Katyusha. They all sat and watched the video of the old Russian weapon firing rockets at some distant target. She looked at Tarik. "I assume your policeman friend is shaking his informants here for information. I'm going to shake Nadja a little more right now."

"Let's check," Major West said as he looked at his watch and grabbed his laptop. "The bird lifted off twenty minutes ago. We should have something."

"There," Lt. Harmon said, pointing to a building in a photo the MC-12 had transmitted. "That barn, the truck could be in there. But the door doesn't look tall enough to fit a truck loaded with missiles."

"I wouldn't really call that a barn," Tarik said.

"Oh, what would you call it?"

"It's more of a hut."

Everyone stared at the photo, trying to decide who was right. Finally, as another image of the brick structure flashed on the screen, Captain Kramer walked in and asked what was so important about that hut.

Lt. Harmon's fingers curled as she held up her hands, exclaiming, "Call it what you want. The equipment still won't fit in there."

"Maybe the missiles aren't loaded yet," Captain Kramer said. "That would make it fit."

They all waited while Major West picked up his phone and called an Afghan contact. "Right, thanks," he said. Then he told the others, "There's no need for a patrol to go out now. The police already searched the property. The barn was empty, and the property was vacant. They're looking for Taj. There's no telling where he's at."

"What about the other photos and video?" Lt. Harmon asked, knowing the MC-12 would have videoed the entire route.

Major West was already scanning the footage. "I know my job," he said curtly. Looking pointedly at Lt. Harmon and then at Mr. Owens, he said, "You guys go talk to Nadja and Assad. See what more you can get."

"Right after lunch," Mr. Owens said.

"We're trying to prevent an attack on the base and you're worried about lunch?"

"Not our lunch, theirs. Per the Geneva Convention, Article 46, the prisoners have to be supplied with adequate food."

"I know that," Major West fumed. The reddish tone of his Irish skin glistened with sweat as he ordered the battalion staff to leave.

"We may as well get lunch," Mr. Owens said once he'd escorted his crew back into the Humvee.

"But he's right," Lt. Harmon said. "We should be interrogating the prisoners now."

"It's eleven o'clock. They really do have to eat. Captain Karzai has his men scouring the countryside, looking for Taj and that Katyusha. Our best chance right now is to let him find an informant," Tarik said curtly.

"I'm not surprised it wasn't in the barn," she said.

"It's not a barn, it's a hut," Captain Kramer replied.

"Major West called it a barn," she retorted.

"Well, he was hungry."

"I saw a goat. That proves it was a barn."

The light banter eased the air as the group piled out of the Humvee and entered the chow hall. They continued to joke as they made their way down the line, with Lt. Harmon choosing a salad over the chili mac. Not so the men.

"Load me up," Mr. Owens said.

With their trays piled with food and a drink in their other hand, the group made their way to a nearby table. There, Captain Kramer pulled out a chair for Lt. Harmon, then sat next to her as he did in the Humvee. Unable to avoid being near him, she steadfastly ate her salad and planned in her head the conversation she'd have with Nadja. Her thoughts were soon interrupted when he leaned over and said in a voice through gritted teeth, "She's been teaching me to dance. That's all."

"Did you pack your bags?" Mr. Owens asked her.

"I started to this morning, but then you called for the meeting."

"Why didn't you do it last night?"

"Maybe I had a date," she replied. Mr. Owens kicked her under the table. "Ouch."

"You had a date with your pillow," Captain Kramer said. Looking at the other two men, he explained that Lt. Harmon spent hours awake, lying there running intel through her mind. "She was top of her class for a reason. She never quits working."

"You've done a good job here," Tarik said begrudgingly.

"Of course she has," Captain Kramer said. His eyes dared the other man to say more.

With a mouth full of lettuce and carrots, Lt. Harmon watched as Tarik jabbed a fork full of chili-mac and shoved it in his mouth. The edge of his squared jaw moved fluidly as he chewed and swallowed, then stabbed again. As she speared a mushroom and added it to the next bite, a young soldier walked by she identified as belonging to the guard who helped her prep Nadja.

"Airman Whitsel."

The woman turned around. "Yes, Mam?"

Lt. Harmon introduced the airman to her friends and explained the role she'd had in softening Nadja.

"I didn't do anything. I just stood there."

"You were a big help. We'll be going over to the prison after lunch," Lt. Harmon said. "I'll be speaking with Nadja again, and Mr. Owens here will be interrogating Assad."

With that, Airman Whitsel's eyes grew big. "Mam, you didn't hear?"

"Hear what?" Lt. Harmon asked suspiciously.

"Assad died this morning, and there's a big investigation. They think somebody slipped him drugs."

"No, we hadn't heard that yet," Mr. Owens said somberly. "Thank you for the information." He looked over to see Lt. Harmon's eyes close. "This is not our business."

"I'm done eating. So is Nadja." Nodding dismissively to Airman Whitsel, she looked pointedly at the others and stood to carry her half-eaten tray over to the rack.

"Yup, let's go," the men mumbled through mouthfuls of mac-n-chili. Tarik followed behind and put his tray on the rack, then reached in with his fork and grabbed one last bite before heading out the door.

Once they were all seated in the Humvee, Lt. Harmon said, "Stop at the TOC. I can drive myself to the prison."

"There's no time," Captain Kramer replied. "Your flight leaves in three hours."

"Yes, there is. I'm canceling my leave request."

"No you're not," Mr. Owens replied before handing her a sheet of paper. "Major West almost forgot to give this to you. He handed it to me before I walked out."

Lt. Harmon's mouth fell open. "I got transfer orders?" She read aloud the orders transferring her to the headquarters in Virginia. "You already knew about this, didn't you? That's what the whole ambush was about."

Mr. Owens put one arm over the back of the seat as he spun the wheel, performing a tight U-Turn in the middle of Disney Drive.

"What are you doing!" Tarik exclaimed.

"We're heading back to the TOC. She's right, we need to go back to work," Mr. Owens yelled over the engine noise.

Once again, Captain Kramer snuck his hand over to Samantha's knee. This time, she let it stay there. Once they arrived at the TOC, he removed his hand and climbed from the Humvee, then ran around and helped Lt. Harmon out of the back.

"Thanks." She smiled up at him before climbing behind the wheel and frowned when she looked at her watch. "I don't have much time now since I still have to pack. I'll be back in an hour."

"Take two, we're going to pack your things," Captain Kramer replied.

"No. That's my personal stuff!"

Leaning closer, he whispered into her ear, "Like I haven't seen that before. Go see Nadja."

Red-faced and not wanting the captain to say more in front of Tarik, she quickly agreed to the bargain and asked, "Who's going to tell Chelsey about Assad?"

"Leave that bird to me," Mr. Owens exclaimed.

"Watch your fingers." Lt. Harmon's eyes glowed as she headed back to the prison.

On her way down the Disney route, she drove a little more slowly than normal, taking in the sights and sounds of the base. *Hard to believe I'm actually going to miss this place, but I will.* During the past two months, Bagram was not just the place she'd called home, it was the place where she'd made a few good friends who helped each other to live and survive. *These people have been my military family.*

As she drove past the junior enlisted quarters, a soldier carrying two loaded duffels emerged and laid both green canvassed bags along the road. In her rear-view mirror, she saw several more soldiers lay their duffels in a row. Then they sat straddling the bags to wait for a ride to the airfield.

Along the way, something nudged at Lt. Harmon's mind, a thought she couldn't put aside. *The Katyusha, it's got to be somewhere close to the base. If I'm seeing signs that we're leaving soon, so is whatever informant they have here. And they want us to go home in disgrace.*

Determined not to let al-Qaeda win, she increased speed until she arrived at the prison. *This time, she will talk.*

CHAPTER 10

Bagram Airforce Base
Parwan Detention Facility
June 24, 2001 1145

Last chance. That was Lt. Harmon's thought as she passed through the gates of Parwan to be escorted through passageways of chain link fence topped with circles of barbed wire. A woman in a silky blue hajib passed by, softly weeping. Lt. Harmon walked past the woman, neither looking at her nor speaking as she entered the prison doors.

"Hello, Nadja," she said as the woman was escorted into the interrogation booth.

The burly MP, standing stern-faced with both arms flexed at his sides, waited until the prisoner was seated at the metal table before saying, "I'll be right outside."

Today, Nadja wore a rose-colored hajib embellished with paisley sketches. To Lt. Harmon, she looked a little more upscale. *She borrowed this for our meeting.* Now that she had Nadja to herself, she stared at her with the look a small child might have toward a parent they'd found had committed a crime. Her face filled with disappointment as she sat and studied her subject. Nadja stared right back at her with a look of utter defiance until she grew weary, then nonchalantly relaxed into her chair and studied the doorframe, then looked back at Lt. Harmon and pursed her lips.

For several moments, the silent exchange continued until. Eventually, Lt. Harmon picked up her phone and looked down at the screen. Using her thumb to swipe through texts, she read a message from Mr. Owens: *The bird was informed of the prisoner's demise. Chelsey's been at the bars too much. She fluffed her feathers, strutted around on her perch and said, "Four o'clock." I'm sure she meant five o'clock. Assad liked Buffet.*

Lt. Harmon's fingers moved across the keyboard, typing a message to the end user: *Lol.*

"Sorry," she said to Nadja in a kinder voice. "A coworker just told Chelsey about Assad."

"Assad?"

"Your boyfriend. He died this morning from a drug overdose. Heroin slipped into the prison and was probably cut with fentanyl."

At that, rather than assuming the sorrowful look one would expect to see on the face of someone who'd just been notified of her lover's death, Nadja looked angry. "Why would they think that?"

"Oh, I don't know. Maybe because there are so many people everywhere dying from fentanyl. Over in the States, the DEA has a whole memorial wall of victims. Like this guy," Lt. Harmon replied as she pushed her phone to the middle of the table, displaying the young face of nineteen-year-old Zach, who'd died, the same picture that broke her heart when she saw it earlier that morning.

"He's not familiar to me," Nadja said. Her eyes darted away from the picture.

"No, he wouldn't be. This boy died from taking a drug cut with fentanyl, the same way at least seventy thousand other people in the U.S. will die this year. Your older son could even wind up on this wall."

"My son doesn't do drugs!"

Lt. Harmon stared evenly into Nadja's face and said calmly, "He only transports them to other kids. I'm sure the parents of lots of kids thought the same thing. And if they did know, they'd never dream the drugs were being cut with something like fentanyl."

"I don't know."

"Just doing your job."

"Isn't that what you're doing?"

"Yes, but now it's kind of the opposite. You're supposed to be helping save lives if you want to save your own and your soul."

"My soul is just fine," Nadja snarled.

"Really? Do you believe in God?"

"Of course."

"Which God? The one you grew up believing in, or the one your husband said you have to follow?"

Nadja's shoulders squared in defiance. "I don't have to do anything."

"Then which one?" Lt. Harmon asked, her tone lighter, more questioning.

"I study the religions of all people. I decided for myself that Allah is the true God. My husband could not make me do that."

"Then I think you have a problem," Lt. Harmon said. "Muslims believe that people will be judged by their actions and will go to heaven or hell accordingly."

The picture of the boy smiling at the camera, as if he hadn't a care in the world, continued to stare from the center of the table. "This boy could have been the same age as another man whose life was cut short way too early, but in a different way. Throughout history, the stories of Jesus Christ, the savior, have been told to Christians. Even most who aren't Christians know the story of the young boy, born in a manger to Mary and Joseph in the city of Jerusalem. The boy grew up to gain a following of twelve disciples, men who would put to print in the holy bible the words of God. And Jesus, the son of God, was the teacher, the performer of miracles, and the man who suffered and died on the cross. The savior. Muslims believe that Jesus was born, right?" Lt. Harmon asked.

"Yes, he was born in Jerusalem."

"From what I have read, Muslims do not believe that Jesus was the son of God or that he died to save us from sin."

"No, he was a messenger."

"And therefore, if he was just a messenger and nobody died to save you from your sins, then murdering other people will be a reason for Allah to send you to hell. And your sons."

"No!" Nadja yelled.

"It's in your blood to believe Jesus is God's son. You sang in church. You believe in salvation, so you can't believe in all of this," Lt. Harmon said as she pointed her fingers up toward the ceiling. "Did you love Assad?"

"Why would you ask that?"

"Because from what we understand, you were assigned to recruit him for al-Qaeda since he already had a little bit of a drug network in the United States."

At that, Nadja's mouth fell open.

"The FBI has film of you at the airport in Washington, D.C. It shows you getting off a plane ahead of him, then purposefully waited for him in the lobby and followed him to luggage claim. You were pulling a carry-on bag, so you didn't even have a checked bag, but you made him believe that you did. You got him to help you get the bag out to your car and offered him a ride. The rest is history."

Nadja sat for a moment in stunned silence, then said haltingly, "Of course I loved him."

"I understand he wasn't controlling, like your husband. If you loved him, why aren't you upset that he's dead?"

"I'm just not surprised. He courted death, always doing the heroin."

"The point here is that you have a young son that just died, and now Assad. Each in some way from drugs. I'm sorry for both of your losses."

"Thank you."

"Are you willing to help save your older son?"

Though Nadja once again remained silent, she dropped the belligerent look.

Knowing an al-Qaeda member would have been trained to create some type of story filled with half-truths and misleading lies, Lt. Harmon continued to give just enough details to let Nadja know that she could sort out for herself what the truth really was.

"As you know, Assad did talk, not to us but to another prisoner. He loved you and desperately wanted to save his skin and yours. He said you were both just business people and didn't want to hurt anybody. He said you had a phone number you were supposed to call when the operation was done. The operation is not done yet, is it?"

Lt. Harmon picked up her cell phone and flipped to the next picture, the one she'd taken of Taj. She turned her phone around and showed that picture to Nadja before pulling up the next one and the next one until she'd displayed all twelve. She'd asked Nadja after each photo if she knew the man and received the same answer every time, "No." But on one, she faltered.

"He lives at your compound on the Pakistan border. You must know him. Remember, you can only be in the Witness Protection Program if you help us."

A new look crossed Nadja's face, the look of respect. "How do you know he lives at the compound?"

"When Assad was captured, word went to your farm where they found Siegfried cooking with the fentanyl ingredients. When the patrol found Assad's place, Taj took the black tar you and Siegfried already cooked and headed for the compound. The Afghan police intercepted him. An officer told us this morning that he's in custody."

Nadja's mouth fell slightly open.

"When Ramen warned you the patrol was coming, you took your younger son and went to the market. He snuck the vase of heroin along. I'm assuming that it was his idea to attack the troops because, unfortunately, he would have had no idea it was cut with fentanyl, probably didn't even know what fentanyl is."

In the light dawning on the prisoner's face, Lt. Harmon saw there was a lot of truth to her conjecture. *Whew.*

Nadja's hands curled into balls as her voice seethed with anger. "My son was only nine."

"So young," Lt. Harmon said, letting a note of sorrow creep into her voice. Leaning slightly forward, she said in a conspiratorial tone, "There was a fourth man." Her mouth twisted a bit as she dug back through the pile of pictures, looking closely at each one until Nadja's eyes slightly creased. "This guy. We know the name Taj gave is not real. What name did you call him?"

The fabric of Nadja's headdress darkened with sweat as her mouth trembled.

"Yes, your whole network has fallen apart. Help us, Nadja. Did you call him Abraham?"

"Not like that." Her voice faltered. "Ibrahim."

"We know about Taj, and we know where his farm is. The Katyusha either wasn't ever there or it's not anymore. Where is it now?"

"I don't know! I wasn't included in those discussions."

Thinking that was most likely true, Lt. Harmon picked up her phone and shoved it into her pocket. Then she picked up a pen. "What's the number?"

"I don't know what you mean," Nadja said warily.

"The phone number you were supposed to call for assistance after the third rocket attack on the base."

"How did you know that?"

"It's not rocket science, or maybe it is," Lt. Harmon said, causing both women to smile. "First, there was one attack, and then we found a Katyusha loaded with shells. That was going to be a research mission, trying to figure out the spread configuration of fentanyl. You're the scientist collecting the data. The third attack, is there talcum or fentanyl in those shells?"

"I don't know."

"Yes, you do. You know what you took to the market. You're not one of them, you're one of us and we're all going home soon. For your soul, and your son's, is there powder in the next shells?"

Nadja slowly nodded yes.

"And what is that powder?"

Air sucked deep into Nadja's lungs before she slowly expelled the words, "It's talcum."

Lt. Harmon's face remained expressionless as she asked, "Why not fentanyl if that was the point?"

"The mail is slow. We didn't get enough chemicals to make anymore."

"But you did. The chemicals were in the barn," she said emphatically. "That's what you guys were doing, making fentanyl for the shells. You just ran out of time." *We thought they were going to cut heroin with fentanyl. Maybe we were wrong. Maybe it was for both things, the shells and the heroin.*

"I don't-- I really don't know," Nadja said.

"You're a college-educated chemist, not a dumb terrorist incapable of linear thought. You do know," Lt. Harmon said, throwing theory at Nadja she couldn't compute fast enough. "When are they planning the next attack?"

A hand went over Nadja's mouth. "I really don't know. It's up to the supreme commander."

"The commander, meaning Ibrahim?"

In a voice laced with indecision, Nadja reluctantly said, "Yes. You are wrong about the shells. We always had control of the fentanyl. It was to go over to Pakistan. There is only talcum in the shells."

"Why? If one was an experiment, why wouldn't the other one be for a real attack with fentanyl?" Lt. Harmon slapped both of her hands on the table. "If you had the resources to manufacture enough fentanyl, then why the talcum? Who said they should be experiments?"

Nadja's face hardened with belligerence.

"There's another attack being planned somewhere else. Where?"

The widening of Nadja's eyes told Lt. Harmon that she, too, was just now figuring out that information.

"Give me that phone number."

"You are mistaken that I care a whole lot about saving my own life," she said in a steely voice.

"I understand. Your husband, your younger son, and your lover are dead. Your business is defunct. That leaves your older son."

"Yes, my son. That woman, Sasha, cries nonstop for her son. Why is she in prison?"

"Why are any of you in prison?"

"She's not a criminal."

"Apparently, she is," Lt. Harmon said. "Please, can I have that phone number now? Even if you don't value your own life, you can help save your soul by saving others. There's still time."

The soft demeanor of Lt. Harmon's voice worked. Nadja gave her the phone number.

"I'm going now. I also lost a family member yesterday. My plane leaves today."

"What! Who's going to be here with me?" Nadja suddenly looked smaller.

"I don't know. You need to do the work of assisting with this investigation, and then, hopefully, you'll be transferred to the States. Maybe I'll see you there." Lt. Harmon rose and picked up her briefcase. A slow breath escaped her lips as she touched Nadja on the shoulder. "I really am sorry about what happened to your little boy." With that, she left.

Outside, her eyes widened at finding Captain Kramer sitting in the Humvee, waiting for her to return.

"That was quick," he said after sipping coffee from a beverage container.

"Yeah. She doesn't know where the Katyusha is. What are you doing here?"

"Major West wants us over at brigade."

"I suppose he wants a verbal report since I'm leaving," Lt. Harmon mumbled irritably. "I still have to go file the paperwork. What time is it?"

"Fourteen thirty. That's two-thirty for you civilians."

"I'm not a civilian!"

"You will be if you take that job with the FBI, which you need to do."

"I don't know if that's a compliment or if you're telling me to stay out of your man's world. Stop teasing me."

"I'm serious. Samantha, I want to talk to you before we get to brigade."

"There's no need for that."

Captain Kramer pulled the Humvee over beside a fence, then rolled up toward the shade of a building and stopped. "Can we talk about all the stuff that's happened?"

"What stuff," she asked, deliberately ignoring his pleas.

"Well, either that damned parrot told you I was dancing with a nurse the other night, or somebody saw me. Either way, it was just a dance. I stopped by the rec hall to blow off some steam on a video game, and she grabbed my hand. It was just one dance, and it didn't mean anything."

"How would the parrot know?"

"I don't know, you get things from that bird."

"I don't have time for this conversation," she said in a strangled voice.

"Make time. You leave in two hours, and I'll be right behind you. I've got orders, too. I leave in less than two weeks."

"Orders for where?"

"Texas."

"Fort Hood?"

"Yes. While you're attending training with the FBI, I'll be in school."

"Congratulations. I'm happy for you, but I'm not joining the FBI."

"Sam, a hundred thousand kids are being killed every year by drugs. You can do the same thing for the FBI you do with the military on an even bigger scale. And you'll save way more lives, starting with mine."

"Um, what?"

"I'll die if you don't say yes to this next question." As a transport truck passed by, he turned to wave at the soldiers being taken to a distant point and missed seeing Lt. Harmon insert earbuds, determined not to hear anything more about joining the FBI.

Once the truck trundled far enough down the road to keep the troops from seeing his next move, Captain Kramer grabbed her hand and said, "I love you. Will you marry me?" Cupping her cheek in his hand, he moved to kiss her. Feeling his hot breath on her mouth, she jerked her head back.

"What did you say," she yelled. "Oh, wait a minute." As she removed her earbuds, the noise of blaring rock music caused Captain Kramer to let out a heavy sigh.

"How are you even getting that station?"

"It just comes on. We have to go."

"But I want to…"

"Not now Brad. I need to talk with Major West before I forget anything. We can talk at the airport."

As a jet roaring overhead made any other speech impossible, Captain

Kramer gave in and restarted the Humvee. Lt. Harmon reinserted her earbuds as they drove along, saying it calmed her nerves and took her mind off her family.

"Okay."

At brigade, with her visitor badge pinned to her collar, Lt. Harmon sat and wrote her final report before turning in her laptop. Upon completion, she viewed the document and thought, *I must have missed something. My meeting with Nadja really didn't take that long.* Thinking of the phone number she'd obtained, she wondered if she should make the call. *No,* she decided. *That is definitely outside of my scope of practice. It probably wouldn't be with the FBI.* She included the phone number in her report and then sent the whole thing to Major West.

"Lt. Harmon," a corporal said from the doorway. "Are you done, Mam?"

"Yes."

"Great. Major West wants to see you in the briefing room."

"He's out there?"

"Yes, Mam. I think they're just finishing."

Silently, Lt. Harmon followed the clerk to the warehouse they called the briefing arena. Upon entering, she stood perplexed by the large crowd of soldiers sporting different ranks of insignia for both officers and enlisted stitched on their uniforms.

"It's your farewell party," the corporal said.

One by one, through watery eyes, she recognized each person from her section. And on the table, there was a cake with the wording, "Farewell Lieutenant." One silver bar had been air-brushed below the lettering next to a picture of a battlefield soldier.

"Attention."

Everyone stopped and came to attention as the door opened for General Adams.

"Lieutenant Harmon, front and center," Major West called as he stood next to the commander. She immediately responded, presenting herself to stand in front of the general. With her arms pressed tightly to her side in the formal stance of attention, she soon found herself being awarded an Army Commendation Medal for her work during Operation Enduring Freedom. Then she received a second award for meritorious effort, a thank you for the work she did with Nadja.

"Goodbye, Lieutenant, and good luck in your future."

"Thank you," she responded in a voice trembling with emotion.

And just like that, the general left the room.

"Lieutenant Harmon," Major West said, holding out a hand. She scooped vanilla icing onto a utensil, then shook the hand.

"This was a surprise." After licking the fork, she placed the rest of the uneaten cake on the table.

"I listened in on your interrogation with the prisoner. We don't need to talk anymore. You need to go, and take that with you."

Lt. Harmon followed the major's finger to the corner of the room where, to her surprise, there sat a cage with an African Grey.

"Chelsey. What am I supposed to do with a parrot?"

"I don't know, Lieutenant, but with your experience, I'm sure you'll figure it out. Donate her to a rescue or a zoo. I don't care, but you can't leave her in Afghanistan."

"She's not my bird, Sir."

"She is now. Goodbye, Lieutenant, and good job. Any recommendation you need in the future, just let me know." With that, Major West left the room.

"Ready?" Captain Kramer asked.

"No, this all happened so fast," Lt. Harmon exclaimed. After taking a moment to say her goodbyes, she grabbed her knapsack and turned to stare at Tarik's chest. Holding out a hand, he shook hers with a firm grasp.

"Thank you for your help," she said with a smile. Then she turned to find Mr. Owens gobbling down a slice of cake.

"Now you like him?" he whispered as he brushed vanilla crumbs from his chest.

"Moving on." Lt. Harmon's grey-blue eyes twinkled as she gave her mentor a quick hug. "Captain Kramer, please grab the cage."

Following directions, Captain Kramer slid his fingers through the wire handle on the bird cage confiscated from Assad's home. As he moved, a few of Chelsey's red feathers flew between the bars to land on his foot. Everyone laughed as she began squawking in fear while severely chastising her courier for the bumpy ride, chanting over and over, "Hurry, human," until he placed the cage in the back seat of the Humvee.

"That's something my grandfather probably taught her," Lt. Harmon laughed.

"Why would he teach a parrot to say that?" Captain Kramer asked breathlessly.

"Grandfather had such a sense of humor, and Assad was such a slow bartender." Lt. Harmon's face glowed with the memories of her teenage years, sitting at the tiki bar while Jack, a parrot with bright green feathers, and Chelsey, a grey parrot edged with red, sat at the bar and bonded.

"He sounds like quite the character."

"Oh, he was."

Captain Kramer raised a brow as he drove swiftly down Disney Drive. "What do you mean was?"

"I meant is," Lt. Harmon stated quickly. "He's on a ventilator, so it's different now."

"Hang onto your hat. We need to speed up," Captain Kramer yelled as he gunned the Hummer and flew down the drive, passing soldiers in helmets strolling along with weapons pointed at the ground.

"Slow down," Lt. Harmon yelled as she rolled up her window to keep the air off Chelsey.

A few moments later, they passed through the VIP gate at the airfield and drove onto the tarmac, stopping in front of a C-130 Hercules, which sat waiting on a bullet-riddled airstrip built during the Soviet era.

"Here you go." Captain Kramer asked a passing soldier to carry her duffel. "I'll carry the cage."

"Look what you did to Chelsey," Lt. Harmon exclaimed. "Her feathers are ruffled straight back."

"She just needs a comb." Captain Kramer laughed as he carried the bird to the C130's loading ramp. "Wait a minute, we need to talk." Handing Chelsey to a nearby soldier, he said, "Keep your fingers out of the cage."

"Mi amore," Chelsey said with dreamy eyes.

"Chelsey quit hitting on the soldiers." Captain Kramer's green eyes twinkled.

"Five o'clock," she screeched, causing the nearby soldiers to double with laughter.

Lt. Harmon felt herself being guided with a hand on her elbow to a spot several feet away from the line of embarking soldiers. Finally, she turned to look up at her captain with a nonchalant gaze. "People are watching. What?"

"We should have had this whole talk earlier. I tried."

"The whole FBI thing. I know."

"Samantha, this isn't about the FBI. I've been trying to tell you that I LOVE YOU."

"You love me?" With rounded eyes, her face took on a soft gaze as she stood completely still.

"Yes," he said loudly. "I love you. I have for years."

"No, you don't. When you love someone, you don't hit on OTHER WOMEN."

"A man will if the woman he loves isn't giving him the time of day," Captain Kramer said defensively. The sandy locks of his short bangs blew softly in the breeze as he stood still, staring beseechingly at Samantha.

"Lieutenant," someone called from the plane. "The door is closing."

"She'll be right there," Captain Kramer called back. "She's getting engaged here."

The troops who heard the statement began cheering. As word of the proposal spread, the others joined in. "Hurrah."

"Don't you know the rules of fraternization?" Lt. Harmon asked with a frown.

"It's okay," Captain Kramer said. "You're joining the FBI. I love you, Sam. Marry me."

"Oh sure, no pressure," she exclaimed while backing away from his entreating stare.

"I love you, Samantha," he said more softly, his finger brushing a strand of hair from her eyes. "There's never been another woman for me."

Slowly, inch by inch, she moved toward the plane. Upon reaching the ramp, she placed a hand on the rail and bowed her head, feeling the rocking of the waves.

"Trust me," her grandfather said as raindrops pelted the deck.

"Trust me," Captain Kramer called as she started to slip away.

The nod of her head came first, followed by a slow turn. Finally, as those at the top of the ramp watched, Lt. Harmon turned and ran back and threw herself into Captain Kramer's arms. "Wait for me, I love you."

With pursed lips, he moved to kiss her. She moved her head to let the kiss land on her cheek.

"You are not kissing me here, in front of everybody!" Quickly, she pulled away from his arms and ran back to the plane.

"I'll see you there," he called, repeating almost the same words she'd said earlier to Nadja.

On the ramp, a red feather was crammed against the metal, having been tread on by many sets of boots. Lt. Harmon looked at the feather and smiled, knowing that goofy bird was going home with her. *That goofy bird, Nadja. Why did Chelsey say five o'clock?*

A sudden wave tipped the boat. "Grandfather."

"Samantha, watch out."

"Four o'clock. Five o'clock."

With a tight grip on the handrail, she looked at the watch on her wrist and froze. With a wild light in her eyes, she ran back to Captain Kramer's position, yelling, "I know when the attack is coming!"

"What attack?" he asked, his eyes confused.

"The second Katyusha. I don't know what day, but I know what time. You have to listen, it's already three fifty-two."

"Lieutenant, do you mind getting on the plane?" the voice of one of the pilots boomed from the doorway.

"I can't, the base. There's going to be an attack on the base using a Katyusha at sixteen hundred."

"How do you know that," Captain Kramer asked guardedly.

"Because Chelsea hung out at the tiki bar with Grandfather's parrot, Jack. Every time Grandfather asked Jack what time it was, Jack said four o'clock. Grandfather always corrected him and said, 'It's five o'clock.' You know, like 'It's five o'clock someplace.' The only reason Chelsea would be saying five o'clock now is if she heard someone say four o'clock. Then she'd change it to five. And the person she would have heard that from is Assad. He knew when the attack was planned because the first Katyusha was found on his property, and the first attack was at night, so the next one is sometime soon at four."

The pilot looked at Captain Kramer and wound his finger beside his head.

"Did you follow what I said?" Lt. Harmon yelled.

"Yes, I think so. Get on the plane, now," Captain Kramer yelled back as he turned and ran back to his vehicle.

Lt. Harmon stood for another second, then she understood and ran back to climb aboard the C-130. "There could be an attack on the base very soon," she said to the pilot. "I'm tactical intelligence. You have five minutes to get us out of here."

"Close the ramp," he yelled to the ground crew. Before they were done, he was back in the cockpit, starting the engine.

Rows of soldiers sat in the plane, waiting to be transported to another land. Knowing the C in C-130 stood for cargo, Lt. Harmon had the strange thought that they were all just cargo now. Sitting down beside a private, she strapped herself in.

Three minutes. *Captain Kramer would have called the TOC by now.* The plane started to taxi down the runway with its massive engines roaring to life.

Two minutes. The plane reached the end of the runway and started to lift off. *He's at least got to be off the airfield, driving the Humvee farther away from the walls of the base.*

One minute. As the C-130 ascended into flight, the soldiers cheered.

Four o'clock- no attack, good. Why did I believe a parrot? At least they have time to find the Katyusha. With the silhouette of Bagram Air Base fading far away, Samantha began to relax in her seat. *Whoosh*, a cylindrical object flashed by the loadmaster's window. A few seconds later, the dim illumination of the base coming under attack was lost to those being transported to another land.

Home, we're all going home.

CHAPTER 11

Lt. Samantha Harmon's long journey home from Afghanistan provided her with the opportunity to enjoy a whole two-day layover in Germany. In Landstuhl, a town where the brats were thick and the beer plentiful, a pair of flickering lanterns drew her into a back street tavern. Inside the building, she looked around at the decor of cozy charm, with vintage beer steins, hand-carved cuckoo clocks, and modern-day photos lining the walls. Wrinkling her nose as wafts of stale beer permeated her senses, she seated herself at the bar and caught a few words of the local chatter, all in German. As she asked her phone for a translation, a cheerful face, complete with apple cheeks, asked for her order.

"Was ist dein mildestes Bier?" she asked.

"Hefeweizen," the bartender replied, "is our mildest beer. Would you like a full stein?"

"Yes, danke." After receiving the lager, she sat on a walnut stool and sipped from the mug. "Ah." The brew brought back memories of her grandfather's sailboat as, inside that stein, she encountered the last dregs of her childhood.

On the Sail Away, although her grandfather never let her partake in the daily cocktail hour, or the hours of cocktails in between those hours, she occasionally nipped at the grog on her way back from refilling his cup. Until the day the usual rum was substituted for a German lager, the faces she'd made when tasting that grog were quite comical.

"That's a good beer," she'd told Jack.

Laying her phone on the bar, she texted Brad and kept checking her phone for his reply. When none came, she drank more lager from a stein large enough to match the abilities of a seasoned sailor.

"Lieutenant Harmon," a voice called from behind.

"Yes?" She turned and, upon recognizing the burly face of the MP who'd assisted with Assad's interrogation, flashed the man a smile.

"I've been looking for you. I'm your ride to the airport. Why didn't you answer your phone?"

"What?" she asked. She looked at the stone walls and stared at her phone. "I must have bad reception here. My phone never rang." *No wonder there's nothing from Brad. His texts aren't coming through.*

As people from the base joined her, the suds continued to roll right up until the moment they had to leave to catch their plane. Thus, the next day, when her brother picked her up at the Indianapolis airport and dropped her at their mother's house, the dregs of her journey still played on her spirits as she crawled into bed.

Within the safety of an upstairs bedroom, as the outside light faded to darkness, Samantha closed her eyes and started to snore. Hours later, before the first rays of sunlight readied themselves to dance across the horizon, an intruder, using the glow of a nearby street light, located a keyhole and unlocked the front door. Silently, he opened and closed the door, then crept along the hallway and froze when a floorboard creaked beneath the weight of his foot.

"Sam, wake up. I'm here."

At the sound of her brother's voice, Samantha's light snoring turned to a mighty yawn. "Brian?" Heavy footsteps pounding up the stairs announced his arrival. She blinked as his finger reached around the doorway to flip on the switch to the overhead light.

"Yeah," he said with a smirk.

"Go away," she moaned as she pulled the quilt over her head while rolling to her stomach.

"Hey, sleeping beauty, get up." With a mischievous grin, Brian snatched a corner of the quilt and pulled it all the way off the bed. Reaching down for her blanket, Samantha slid to the floor to sit with her legs splayed wide open, befuddled by her plight.

"What are you doing here?"

"You've been asleep for, like, two days."

"A day of drinking beer in Germany will do that. Why didn't you wake me up yesterday?"

"I did. You ate a muffin and went back to sleep."

"Oh."

"You've got your running shoes?"

"Where are we going?"

"Running. You said you wanted to go."

"When was that?"

"On the way home from the airport," Brian said as he threw the blanket back on the bed.

"Nobody is technically responsible for what they say after an overseas trip for at least twenty-eight hours," Samantha grumbled. "What time is it?"

"Almost six."

"A.M.?"

"Yeah."

"Masochist. What do you think, we're in the army or something?"

"You are in the army. You said that you have a lot to tell me. Nowhere is more private than the running track. See you in five."

"It won't even be fully light yet. I'm going to twist my ankle running on the trails," Samantha called through the closed door as she rubbed sleep from her eyes. *Coffee. I need coffee.* Hurriedly, she pulled on her brother's high school T-shirt emblazoned with a gold lion over an old pair of green running shorts. Her grimy gym shoes rested in the exact spot where she'd kicked them off right after Brian dumped her into bed. In a dresser drawer, she found a fresh pair of women's athletic socks.

"It's about time," Brian said when she emerged to find him standing cross-legged with his fingers reaching for his toes.

"Do we have water?"

"In the car. Ready?"

"Soon as I grab my purse."

"You don't need it. There's coffee money in the car."

"Good. I spent mine on beer." She checked her phone for a text and sighed. "My battery is dead. Do you have a charger?"

"I'm a droid guy. Mom's got an iPhone charger in the kitchen," a red-faced Brian said.

Anxious to see if Brad called but not yet wanting to tell her brother about her blossoming love affair, Samantha left her phone charging on the kitchen counter. She thought about waiting until she had enough of a charge to check her messages but decided against it. *I'm sure he's called. It's better to look at it when I can call back.*

The ride to the park wound past rows of brick buildings once housing soldiers stationed at Fort Benjamin Harrison. Now no longer an active duty fort, the firing range and bivouac sites had long ago been turned into a state park with running paths crossing through woods. After passing by the gate, Brian paid to enter the nature area and parked in a gravel lot.

"Over there," he said as they passed through a grassy area to the trailhead.

Following her brother's lead, Samantha took off running down a winding dirt path. "Slow down," she gasped as Brian disappeared around a grove of cattails. Quickening her pace, she ran down the path to find her brother waiting beneath the shade of an oak and, upon reaching him, doubled over, grasping her sides.

"Ready?" Brian asked.

"Not yet. My lungs are burning."

"They didn't keep you in shape overseas?"

"No time. I was working twenty-four hours a day."

Brian took an easy breath. "Speaking of Afghanistan, I thought you were bringing home a parrot."

"I am. Chelsey's still in Germany."

"How come?" he asked as they started walking down the path.

"Hungover," Samantha replied.

Brian tripped and caught himself. He stared suspiciously at Samantha. "Only Jack would do that."

Her grey-blue eyes sparkled with mirth. "Right. Animal quarantine."

"That makes sense."

"By the way, thanks for getting Jack here."

"No problem. Gary took care of him until I could get here from Chicago," Brian said, referring to his best childhood friend.

"Where's Jenny? I thought she was going to run with us."

The muscles around Brian's eyes tightened as he expelled a slow breath before explaining the situation with their aunt's former foster daughter.

"Jenny got arrested for possessing heroin. The lawyer is trying to get her out on house arrest."

"When did that happen?"

"Yesterday."

"This drug stuff is never-ending. Let's go." Samantha took off running. With the lean muscles of her legs pumping relentlessly, she ran faster as her brother maintained a steady pace. Together, they ran side-by-side while she haltingly told him about the things she'd seen in Afghanistan and how they tried to coerce her into joining the FBI. At the end of the trail, she stopped and leaned against a tree, panting heavily in its shade.

Barely out of breath, Brian strolled up beside her. "You done already?"

"We need to get going. Uncle Benny's funeral is today. After that, I want to see Mom." Leaning over, she allowed a breeze to blow through the front of her shirt. "Come on. We can talk more at the coffee shop."

"Wipe the mud off your shoes," Brian said. At the truck, he kicked off his running shoes and changed into a pair of tan suede sandals. After surveying the truck bed covered in dirt, Samantha kicked a shoe against the running board and laughed when several chunks of mud fell from the underbelly of the truck. Once she'd climbed into her seat, she unlaced her shoes and sat back in her seat. Her eyes closed as Brian kicked the truck into reverse and skidded backward, crunching gravel before pushing the gear forward and off they went to Arthur's Coffee Shop, a quaint little place sitting in the corner of a red brick building. After parking in one of the many empty spots, he ran around the truck and threw open the passenger door. At six feet even with long muscled limbs, he easily hauled Samantha out of the truck and carried her sideways up the stairs. Her eyes popped open.

"Maniac, let me down," she yelled.

"There," he said as he placed her on the top step.

"Typical brother and sister, always trying to prove who's boss." Arthur's eyes twinkled as they walked into the coffee shop.

"She's my older sister," Brian replied. "Much older."

"Ouch, he pinched me," Samantha complained. While massaging a red spot on her abdomen, she glanced up at the TV and caught a live broadcast showing a platoon from Afghanistan arriving at the Indianapolis airport. With the camera zooming in on family members waving American flags, the soldiers ran up to get lost in their arms. She turned to follow Brian to a table and missed the start of the next clip about a recent attack on Bagram.

Thirteen people were killed. And there was something about a white powder.

When their waitress brought coffee to the table, Samantha grasped the thin ceramic handle and gingerly took a sip. In Brian's hand sat a yellow cardboard cup steaming with his normal black coffee. Adding cream and sugar, he sat stirring the concoction with a little green straw while asking, "Why the FBI?"

"Beats me," Samantha shrugged. "I did one little briefing for a general, now they think I'm some kind of spokesperson for the drug crisis." Her air of defiance brought a smile to Brian's lips.

"You in front of a camera, hah. You're so bossy you'd wind up being the director."

"That's just it. I want to work undercover. Any job I do won't be in front of a camera."

"Either way, you'd be helping catch bad guys." Brian frowned as he picked up a paper and shook it open. "Want the sports section?"

"Nope," Samantha said, grabbing the front section from his hand. "Thanks."

"You left me the garden section!"

"The yard needs work." After reading about a series of festivals planned for the upcoming weekends, she peeked over the top of the paper and saw a man in a dark blue suit grin. He shook his own paper and held it higher, hiding his face from view. She scanned the front page headlines before crumpling the page into a ball and throwing it toward the trash.

"No news is good news," Brian said softly. "Anyway, I'm glad you're safe. When are you going to see Grandfather?"

"I have to be in D.C. on Tuesday. I'll catch a flight and go see him before I report in."

"You're going to Florida first?" Brian asked.

With the newsprint a blur, Samantha put the rest of the front section down and nodded. "That would be easiest. Maybe we can get him transferred here. How's your, I mean our, mother?"

Brian shrugged. "The same. She still doesn't remember anything."

"I'll tell her about Benny. That's my side of the family," Samantha said as she pinched cinnamon crumbs from a muffin top and popped them in her mouth.

"We're being followed," Brian said as he reached under the table.

Samantha straightened and looked at the man in the dark blue suit. Then, she peered down into the sad, dark eyes of a mutt.

"Murphy, you chow hound, what are you doing here?" Brian reached down to pet the dog. Ignoring him, the dog's tail wagged as Samantha petted his head while he licked muffin crumbs from her fingers. Soon Brian's friend Gary, a tall, lanky young man, strode into the bakery calling for his dog.

"Murphy, you can't eat that." He grabbed for the dog's collar and missed.

"Dude, he like ate my passport and my money and a case of Coke before you adopted him from me," Brian said with a laugh.

Murphy looked up with innocent dark eyes and barked. *Argh.*

Gary sat down and reached over to grab a muffin. "Where's the top?"

"She ate it," Brian said. "Remember my sister, Samantha?"

"Hey, cool, not with short hair. How was Afghanistan?"

A corner of Samantha's mouth lifted as she shrugged. "I don't know how I can even tell you how it was."

"My sis here was dealing with a lot of heavy shit. Terrorists, bombs, bad food."

"The food was not bad," Samantha mumbled through a mouth half full of muffin top. "At least not most of it. Shush." Her eyes swept the few patrons in the shop and frowned. After asking the waitress for a pen, she wrote a quick note on a napkin and handed it to Brian. *We ARE being followed.*

He looked at the note and wadded it into a ball before dunking it into his cup. As it sank into the coffee, he walked over and got a lid. Then he yelled, "Let's go. I need a shower."

"Take that with you," Samantha whispered as she stood up. Out of the corner of her eye, she saw the man in the dark suit close a paper and throw it on the table.

"Him?" Brian asked out of the corner of his mouth.

With a quick nod, Samantha walked slowly toward the door, laughing as if Brian had just said something funny. As they stepped outside, he silently handed Gary the truck keys. "We need to do a little more running, meet you at our place," he said quietly. Then, through really tight lips, he whispered, "Somebody's following us."

"What?" Gary asked.

"Shave your eyebrows stupid," Brian exclaimed loudly before mouthing the words, "That guy's following us." Without moving his head, he rotated his eyeballs back toward the man in the suit.

"Yeah, sure. I'll catch up," Gary said loudly as he stood in the doorway. Then he stared at Brian's feet and laughed. "Dude, sandals?"

"He's training his toe muscles," Samantha called as she started to run. With both fists pumping, she jumped over a curb and ran around a corner, then tripped on a crack in the sidewalk.

"Easy there," Brian yelled. Samantha gagged as he grabbed the back of her shirt and pulled her off the pavement. "What's going on?"

With her dark curls blowing around her face, she tied her laces and gasped, "I don't know. The man in the blue suit was definitely watching us."

"Let's go." Brian led the way and took off running, cut through the breezeway of a club, and ran along a wall until they reached an iron gate, pushed open the gate, and darted onto a dirt path.

"I think we lost him. Who was that?" Samantha asked as she perched on the edge of a fountain.

"Nobody I know. Why would someone be following you?"

"Me? I thought they were following you. There's something weird going on."

"If they're following either one of us, they already know where we're staying," Brian said. He pulled out his phone. "I'm calling Gary for a ride."

"Watch what you say on the phone."

With a roll of his eyeballs, Brian tried to give directions. "I don't know, dude, we're in a garden by the old officers' club. Ouch!"

Samantha raised an eyebrow.

"I got a splinter in my thumb," Brian exclaimed as he sucked at a red spot. As he dug at the splinter, the creaking of a gate opening on rusty hinges shattered the quiet. "Get down."

Samantha crouched and disappeared behind a bush. "Stay put. You're the decoy."

"You've got to be kidding." His hand found a rock.

Soon, the sound of footsteps running down the path accompanied a child's voice, daring another to come find her. Brian dropped the rock and said with disgust, "They're just kids. You're making me paranoid."

Following her brother down the path, Samantha paused when she came upon a child. The little girl, dressed in a yellow sundress with white sandals adorning her feet, had stopped in the path to dump dirt from her shoe. After helping the girl redo the buckle, she continued toward the gate and peered around the corner. From between the branches of a bush, she could see the man from the coffee shop talking to her brother.

"Where's the woman?" He flashed a badge.

"You're FBI?" Brian's voice carried into the shadows. Samantha stepped out.

"Really, Mr. Owens is having me followed? He should know better."

"Who's Mr. Owens?" Brian asked, looking suspiciously at Samantha.

"Just somebody I work with." She looked at the man in a gray cap. "What's your name?"

"I'm Agent Daniele Browne. This here is Agent John Tooley, FBI." He nodded in the man's direction.

"Yes, we're clear you're the FBI. Why are you following us?"

"We're not following you. We've been assigned to protect you."

"Protect who from what?" Samantha asked suspiciously. "There aren't any bullets or rockets in this garden. Just thorns and roses."

"This is not the place to have a conversation. Small ears around." Brian motioned to the children playing in the bushes. "How about we skedaddle over to the house. You know where it is, right?"

The agents agreed. "Gary's out there with your car," Agent Tooley said, pointing to the street with his index finger. "We'll follow you."

As they walked to the truck, Samantha's eyes gained a look of pure innocence as her hand reached out to grab Brian's phone. "I'll call Aunt Diana and let her know we'll be late," she said loudly before turning to look back at Agent Tooley. Agent Browne's face softened as he walked to a black sedan.

At the curb, Brian pulled open the back door of the truck for Samantha before running around to ride shotgun. "Let's go!" Gary eyed the black sedan in his rearview mirror as he revved the engine.

"Where are we going?"

"Drive around the corner and stop. We're getting out before they see us," Samantha said. "Hurry!" Before the agent could start his car, Garry peeled around the corner as she tucked their cell phones into the console. "Stop here. Brian, get out. Gary, go to our house. When the agents show up, tell them we're running home."

"Got it," he yelled as he slammed on the brakes, allowing his passengers to pile out of the truck before taking off again.

After diving from her seat, Samantha ran behind a bush. Brian dove after her just as the second car pulled around the corner and raced to catch up to the truck. "Why did you take my phone?" he asked.

"They'll follow your GPS. I'm assuming Gary will take the long way."

"He might play a little bit," Brian grinned. "Now what?"

"We run home."

"Of course!"

Samantha dodged ahead as they began running down the concrete walk. At the next corner, they turned and started walking slowly past an oil change business, chatting as if they were discussing the weather. "I assume this has something to do with Grandfather or Uncle Benny."

"Did you know Benny agreed to turn states witness?" Brian asked.

"No!"

"I don't think he had a choice," Brian said grimly. "Not after Grandfather ratted him out."

"That's not fair," Samantha fumed. The tone of her rising voice drew the attention of a nearby garage mechanic as he stood tinkering under the hood of an old blue truck. She waved and softened her voice.

"Weird," Brian said.

"What?"

"That looks like the same truck and the same guy," he said, staring at a dark-haired man, "who was here yesterday getting an oil change. I was right behind him."

Samantha pushed Brian's shoulder and continued walking. When they were out of earshot, he pulled her behind an office building and sat down on the curb. "I'm guessing we only have a few minutes before the FBI comes looking for you. Gary is probably going through a car wash right about now."

"You mean the FBI will be here looking for you? If this is about Benny, you're the one who's been talking to him."

"No, I haven't. I've never met Benny. He only talked to Mom."

"Why would he do that?"

"She probably knows family stuff."

"Does the FBI know?"

"Probably."

"Doesn't matter. They can't question her in a psych facility."

"No, but you can. Be careful when you see her."

Samantha nodded. "I'll go today."

"You can't go there with the FBI following you."

"Now I have to slip past the FBI," Samantha muttered.

"You'll think of something. I'm glad you're not going back to Afghanistan," Brian said as he studied Samantha's thin face.

"One other thing," she said.

"What?"

"Brad and I are getting married." With that, she bent to retied her shoe before asking, "Ready?"

"Yup," Brian said as he rose and dodged ahead of her, then tripped on the edge of his sandal. Laughing, he looked back to see her standing in place. "What?"

Samantha's chin tilted toward the sky as she looked at the clouds and started talking about the incident with Lt. Preston and the heroin laced with fentanyl, about Nadja and her now dead little boy, and about her older son in Pakistan who was setting up drug routes. In the end, she stated her belief that there was a major attack being planned somewhere in another country, possibly in the U.S.

"They want us to be totally defeated," she said. "Once we're out of Afghanistan, the Taliban will be satisfied to have that land back. But al-Qaeda, they're a bunch of would-be international power-hungry thugs. I think Nadja's husband may be alive somewhere, directing all of this."

"And she's caught in the middle," Brian said, giving his sister a keen stare. "You put the idea in her head she can somehow save her son?"

"I don't know, maybe she can. She's an American, she knows the difference between living as a free woman and living under Sharia law. And she loves her son," Samantha replied. "Did you find out anything about her husband?"

"Nope. He hasn't even bought a pack of chewing gum, as far as we can tell."

"I'd be very surprised if anything did surface. I'm assuming he has a new identity and a new look."

"Probably. Let's go talk to the FBI," Brian replied.

"One other thing," Samantha said as they started running.

"What?"

"They really do want me to resign my commission and take a job with the FBI."

"Well, you'd be good at it," Brian called as he raced by.

Samantha kicked her feet faster and faster until she caught up to Brian and jumped on his back. Laughing, he fell over into the front yard, panting for breath.

"Cute," Agent Tooley's voice said from above.

Brian and Samantha looked up at him innocently. "Just needed some air, man." Brian jumped up and brushed himself off before reaching down to pull Samantha from the ground. Wordlessly, she led the way around the side of the house and kicked off her shoes before entering the back door.

As she walked through the kitchen, her grey-blue eyes stared longingly at the cell plugged into the charger. "Would you like something to drink? I have water or lemonade."

Reaching into a cupboard, Brian pulled out a set of blue plastic cups.

"Four o'clock," Jack whistled, getting the agents to laugh.

"Shut up, Jack," Samantha yelled. Picking up the cage containing the Macau feathered in emerald green, she carried the bird to the next room, saying, "Be right back." Upstairs, after grabbing fresh clothes from one of the piles spread around her bedroom floor, she ran to the bathroom and took a quick shower before heading downstairs to rejoin the others.

"Jack, shut up," the bird whistled.

"Good bird."

In the kitchen, the agents sat at a table covered by vinyl cloth embossed with large red roses. "Nice house," Agent Browne said.

"Thank you. It was our grandparents," Samantha replied, eyeing the agent. She set her blue plastic glass of lemonade on the roses. "What can we do for you?"

Agent Tooley shifted in his chair and held up his empty glass. "Got any more of this?"

"Sure." Brian grabbed the pitcher and refilled the glasses.

Agent Tooley accepted his glass. Then he told Brian that he was sorry; they needed him to leave.

"Told you it's not about me," Brian said, gloating as he grabbed a fishnet bag full of Samantha's uniforms and headed for the door.

Her long face shot him a sisterly look. The white fabric of her top flowed over blue shorts, shielding her small waistline from view. Sure that her thin stature didn't give her enough credence, she waited until Brian left with the uniforms destined for a nearby dry cleaner before saying, "I'm Lieutenant Harmon."

"Lieutenant, we've heard a lot of good things about you," Agent Tooley said. With a polite smile, he held out a hand.

"From Mr. Owens, I expect. I thought he was CIA. He's FBI?"

"Who's Mr. Owens?" Agent Tooley asked.

Samantha gave him a sharp look. "Why are you here?"

Agent Tooley sat back and thumbed the lip of his glass. "It concerns your grandfather."

"You know Grandfather?"

"He was a key witness in an investigation," Agent Tooley said.

The bed of Samantha's nails grew pink as her index finger went into her mouth. Then she removed the finger and observed it before saying, "He's in a coma. Probably won't survive. You can go now."

"We're not here to see your grandfather," Agent Brown said evenly. "We're asking for your assistance to help continue his work." Picking up his lemonade, he took a big gulp, set the empty blue plastic cup down, and burped. "Excuse me."

That produced a slight smile. "You're not here to get me to join the FBI?"

"Maybe in the future," Agent Browne said.

"We're wasting time," Samantha said impatiently. "My uncle's funeral is today. What do you need?"

"Yes, of course. Sorry for your loss. Your grandfather was helping with a project."

"Talon?"

"How did you know that?"

"A little bird." Laughing, Samantha pointed her grey-blue eyes at Jack. "That's all I know."

"Funny," Agent Tooley replied. Then he went on to say he knew that during her teenage years when she sailed with her grandfather, there were frequent stops in Antigua and explained that, according to her grandfather, the stops along the islands' white sandy beaches included meetings with a local who claimed to be an attorney. That man, Jose Renaldo, was an import from Mexico who helped set up shell corporations, no questions asked. Eventually, there was a document leak detailing bank transactions of money laundering. Known as the FinCen Files, the documents included more than twenty-one thousand suspicious activity reports.

"FinCen, that's a global system to fight money laundering," Samantha said, her face now an unreadable mask.

"Did you meet that man, Jose?"

"No. When we were in Antigua, Grandfather made me stay on the boat. He got mad that I was doing backflips off the bow, claimed I was disturbing the fish, and punished me by making me stay back to do homework."

Agent Browne nodded and went on to explain that Carey Inc. International, the company owned by her grandfather, was a shell corporation used to assist the Chicago mob's drug money laundering operation. "He had property rented around Indianapolis and sublet for a profit. All of that information is allegedly on a laptop we recovered from the boat. Unfortunately, your grandfather went into a coma before he could give us the password."

As the room grew silent, Samantha knew the next question was going to be, "What's the password?" Before it was asked, she shook her head. "I don't know."

"Think, what would he have used?" Agent Tooley asked. He pushed a sheet of paper in Samantha's direction, then pulled a black standard government-issue pen from his pocket. "Write out a list."

She pushed the paper back. "I'm going to guess you've already tried everything to do with sailing. And his birthday-- my birthday-- my name. Right?"

"Yes, with different combinations."

With that, Samantha started to recite a litany of ways people create passwords. "A combination of words using only the first letters, that would never work for Grandfather. He didn't know a thing about computers until we bought the laptop on one of our trips. I had to set it all up for him."

At that, Agent Browne's eyes gleamed. "You set up his password?"

"No. He bought a bootleg computer in Antigua. He was the only one who knew the password. He never let me see that part."

"He bought the computer from who?" Agent Browne asked.

"As I said, I wasn't allowed off the boat," Samantha's soft voice replied firmly. "But I do know that at some point, Grandfather had to change the password. He could never remember it, had it written on a piece of paper. I told him how to change it to something he could remember, so he did."

"That brings us back to you write out a list." Once again, Agent Tooley pushed the paper to Samantha.

Her grey-blue eyes pooled with fatigue as she placed her fingertips over her eyelids. "I know this is a national security issue, and I want to help. I've just returned from Afghanistan didn't really have any sleep in Germany. I'm changing time zones, and we have a funeral to attend. Where's the laptop?"

Agent Tooley stared back and made a decision. "Here." After reaching for his leather briefcase resting against the leg of a chair, he placed the case on the table, snapped open the lock, and pulled out the small laptop Samantha recognized as one of her grandfather's. The stickers covering the case with memories of different ports were still there, all frayed at the edges.

"Leave it here. I'll figure it out," she said.

"We can't do that," Agent Tooley replied.

"I'm an officer in the United States Army with the highest security clearance, but you already know that. Trust me, you can leave it. I'll promise you two things. We will figure out the password, and we won't look at the contents of this computer."

"We?" Agent Browne asked.

"Me and my brother. He runs his own security company out of Chicago. Since he deals with installing firewalls and upgrading IT security, he's a wiz at this. We've both been asked to join the FBI. Swear us in or something if you have to."

The seriousness of Samantha's tone left no room for argument. Knowing that her help was their best chance to quickly get into the laptop, Agent Tooley made the decision to leave it with her. "This doesn't leave the house, and Agent Browne will stay here."

"Suit yourself. This drug problem is terrible. Over in Afghanistan, our drug interdiction teams were destroying poppy fields like crazy, but that didn't even make a dent in the number of drugs being transported around the country. And now al-Qaeda is trying to set up a network. And they want to kill a bunch of people by using ordinance loaded with fentanyl." Samantha put a hand across her mouth, thinking she'd probably said too much.

The agents peppered her with questions about the terrorist network and about her experience with fentanyl. She explained about Lt. Preston, how Nadja was captured, and how there was going to be another test with the second Katyusha to prepare for a terrorist event somewhere else in the world, possibly in the U.S.

"That might have been a second test three days ago," Agent Browne said. "Are you aware that Bagram was hit by an attack, and there was a white powder involved?"

"I've been traveling for three days. My phone was dead. I was just going to check it when you showed up." With that, she stood and ran to the counter, grabbed her phone, and looked at the screen. *Brad he hasn't returned my texts.* She flipped the screen around and held the phone at eyesight, pointing to a series of missed calls. "Is this you?"

Agent Tooley confirmed it was.

A series of numbers she recognized as coming from Bagram also stared back at her from the screen. *Odd, maybe Brad was calling me from a landline at the base. Saving money on cell charges.* In the background, she could hear the agents talking. Agent Tooley was saying, "Three days ago, a nontoxic white powder was spread in a three-hundred-yard radius. It was all in the news."

Samantha slowly clicked on a text from Mr. Owens. *Captain Kramer was injured in the explosion at the base. Call me when you get to a secure line. Go to the Fox Den; you're on the list.*

Of course, he knows people at INCOM; he got me on the list. It was good to know the people who would be receiving her at the intelligence communication center in Virginia were already appraised of the situation with white powder in Afghanistan.

Samantha's return text said, "Sorry for the long delay. I'm home; I just got the use of my phone. Where is he?" Blinking back tears, she grabbed a kitchen towel and wiped her eyes. When she turned around, the sound of the front door slamming gave her a momentary reprieve.

"Okay, to come in?" Brian called from the living room.

Agent Browne stood and walked over to the kitchen door. "Come on in," he said. Standing back, he allowed the young man to pass and motioned for Brian to have a seat at the table.

Brian carried the now empty dry-cleaning bag past the agent and hung it on a door handle. Then, grabbing the back of a chair, he roughly pulled it out and, with a quick jerk, turned the chair around and sat astride the seat, staring angrily at the floor. His bottom lip quivered.

"What's wrong?" Samantha asked.

"You know that guy who ran the motorcycle shop I worked for in high school?"

"I remember what he looks like. Athletic guy with big muscles, and always had a smile. What's his name?"

"They called him Bear," Brian said sorrowfully. "While I was at the cleaners, I ran into his daughter. She was picking up a suit for his funeral."

"What!"

"Yeah. She said he was working as a bouncer down at the Sports Book. At closing time, he was wiping down tables and passed out. The bartender saw him and tried to call for help, but he went down before he could make the call. In the morning, when the owner arrived, he found Bear and the bartender dead on the floor. Then, he found four more bodies out on the patio. Three more people who'd been at the bar walked down to the park and died the same night. I think you know one of them from my high school graduation. Ricky Jackson was the valedictorian."

With luminescent eyes, Samantha looked at the FBI agents and said, "We're in a war with drugs, and it's here in this country. I know we have work to do, but I just found out that a friend was hurt in the explosion at Bagram, and we need to get to my uncle's funeral. Can we talk about this later?"

Agent Tooley picked up the laptop and nodded at Samantha, his face bathed in sympathy. "We'll be back. Eight o'clock tomorrow, okay?

"Yes." Samantha cupped her chin and closed her eyes. "Eight o'clock."

CHAPTER 12

Indianapolis, Indiana
USA
June 27, 2001 That afternoon:

"I need funeral clothes." As Brian riffled through a rack of clothes in an upstairs closet, a shirt and hanger flew to the floor, followed by a pair of pants. Picking up the clothes, Samantha laid them on the bed. She surveyed the outfit.

"Floral, really?"

"Why do you want me at Benny's funeral? He wasn't my uncle."

"Go watch more TV. You know the bad guys always show up at funerals."

Grumbling beneath his breath, Brian continued searching through his poppa's closet for more appropriate clothes. "You're going to be leading the FBI straight to our mom."

"No more than you will in that floral shirt. Move aside." Ducking under his arm, Samantha's fingers dug through the rack of clothes until they happened upon the soft fabric of a woman's black dress.

"That's Mom's funeral dress."

"Mom can't go to Benny's funeral," Samantha said softly. "And on the way, I have to stop at the finance center, so we don't have time to go shopping. I'll try it on." Grabbing the outfit, she shooed Brian from the room, slipped the dress over her head, and pulled at the skirt as she walked over to a long mirror standing in the corner. While checking her reflection, she thought her overgrown mop of curly locks looked a bit civilian. Using her fingers to comb through her bangs, she turned side to side and decided that though slightly baggy in the chest, the dress fit well enough.

"I'm good," she yelled through the door and tripped on a combat boot. *Oh, shoes.* Running back to the closet, she bent down and found a pair of leather heels with pointed toes to match the suit. *They're a little tight, but they'll have to do.* Throwing the heels in a bag, she donned her tennis shoes and headed down to the kitchen, where she found Brian staring into an empty refrigerator.

"Where are all your clothes," she asked.

"All my stuff is in Chicago. I'll run over to the thrift store while you're at Building One."

"The thrift store, really? They're not going to have anything your size, not with those biceps." Grabbing a leather handbag, Samantha slung it in a high arc over her shoulder and pulled open the front door. "Yup, they're there."

Brian slammed the refrigerator door and grabbed his keys. With the FBI agents watching, they walked nonchalantly to the truck with Samantha in funeral clothes and Brian in a shirt more appropriate for a luau.

"I need to borrow your cell," she said as she buckled her seatbelt. After accepting Brian's phone, she threw both their devices in the glove box and then, with the radio volume turned high, told Brian the purpose of the agent's visit. Once they arrived at the finance center located in Building One at old Fort Harrison, she turned the volume back down and pulled their phones out of the glove compartment.

Brian jumped from the driver's seat and ran around to get Samantha's door. She pushed her feet into the high heels and, after saying loudly that she needed to check on a pay issue, accepted a hand down from the truck. As her foot turned sideways in the shoe, he laughed.

"Ouch, this isn't funny. They're tight!" While holding Brian's arm, she wobbled to the door before releasing her grip.

Leaning closer, Brian grabbed her elbow and said softly, "You know the password, it's all over your face. What's going on Sam?"

Staring with knit brows at a dark sedan parked far out in the lot, she said, "I don't know yet," and pulled her arm away. "The computer they have is the one I used for home school. Grandfather had another one he used for business. I need to find it, and then I may need to talk to a lawyer before they look at it. I don't know the password to that computer."

"What were you involved in?" Brian asked, looking suspiciously at this sister he didn't really know.

"Nothing. I just used Grandfather's computer to study geography on his sailing maps. I think our mother knows what there is to tell," she said, and told Brian the plan to sneak out of the funeral home and requested that he call Gary to come help. "Gotta go."

As Brian headed back to the truck, Samantha opened the door to the finance center, passed through building security, and stopped at the top of a stairway to check in with the armed guards. "I'm on the list."

A uniformed guard checked her I.D. against a list of approved visitors. "You may proceed, Mam."

At the bottom of the stairs, two armed guards stood flanking the door to the SCIF, guarding the ultra-secure room where officials and government contractors sat reviewing classified information. Lt. Harmon passed into the room where she quickly settled at a desk and dialed into the TOC at Bagram Airforce Base. When a familiar voice answered, she said, "Mr. Owens, this is Lieutenant Harmon."

"Lieutenant, good to hear you're safe."

"Thank you. I called as soon as I could. What happened to Captain Kramer?"

"The parrot was right. At exactly sixteen hundred hours, the second Katyusha launched another rocket attack."

"I know," she whispered into the phone. "The Katyusha hit the base."

"It did," Mr. Owens replied. "But thanks to your intel, Captain Kramer had time to warn the brigade so they could locate and destroy the Katyusha after the launch. Your captain made the call from his position on the airfield, which gave the team time to warn a Patriot battery. Most of the rockets were destroyed, but not before the first one hit the base. Unfortunately, Captain Kramer was standing outside his vehicle and got hit by shell fragments," Mr. Owens said to a quiet gasp on the phone. "His leg was badly injured when a frag sliced through a blood vessel. Your captain was darned lucky there were medics at the airfield waiting for a flight. They got to him right away and saved his life. But I have to warn you, he lost a lot of blood and may still lose his leg."

"But he's going to live?" she whispered hopefully.

"He has a good chance. The main thing I have to tell you," Mr. Owens replied in a more subdued tone, "is that a fragment hit him near the eyes. He could be blind."

"No! He can't! When will they find out?"

"When the bandages come off."

"And the powder from the launch, was he contaminated by any of that?"

"No. Fortunately, the warhead didn't go off overhead like it was supposed to. The load didn't spread far at all and was mainly just pushed into the ground. The other rockets were intercepted over an area that wasn't populated."

"Nadja said the powder was talcum. Was she right?"

"It's not an opioid. Langley's got the samples."

"I shouldn't have left," Samantha cried, causing the rest of the personnel in the SCIF to look her way.

"It was your duty to leave. Anyway, there's nothing else you could have done," Mr. Owens said firmly. "Other than get hurt yourself."

She gripped the counter. "You didn't have me call a secure line just to tell me about Brad."

"You're right," Mr. Owens replied evenly. "You can't tell anybody this, but everybody is leaving on July second. Watch the news."

"What about Captain Kramer?"

"Already evac'd to Germany."

"And the prisoners?"

"Ramen and his family have been transferred to another facility."

"Iraq or Gitmo?"

"Look, there's too many prisoners here to keep track of right now. Those of us who are left are all busy."

"That market in Charikar and the base could have been test cases. Hang on," she said hoarsely as she took a sip of water. "We're talking about the possibility of a mass terrorist attack somewhere in the U.S. Al-Qaeda wants us to leave Afghanistan feeling totally defeated. If we're pulling out next week, it will be soon."

"Get some rest," Mr. Owens said soothingly.

"I am rested. What about Nadja?"

"Um, that's the other thing I have to tell you. She was being transferred to another facility when she escaped."

Lt. Harmon stared into the receiver.

"Lieutenant…"

"What happened?"

"Her flight stopped to refuel in Kyrgyzstan. There was a fire in one of the engines, everyone was evacuated. Nadja wasn't breathing well and was unconscious. Somehow, during transit to the hospital, she slipped away."

"She just slipped away. What prisoner just slips away?"

"An al-Qaeda trained operative who knows how to put a choke hold on a person and knock them out. The young medic never had a chance."

"Where do you think she is?" Lt. Harmon asked quietly.

"Hard to say. Most likely, she's made face-to-face contact with a local in her network."

"You spooks listen to all the phone conversations," Lt. Harmon said under her breath. Her index finger came up as she bit a nail and thought back to her conversation with Nadja. "They weren't bringing her to the U.S., were they? That's why she escaped. What are you not telling me?"

Mr. Owens hesitated a moment. Then he said reluctantly, "The command here, somebody thinks you got lucky when you developed your intel. They're crediting the parrot with figuring things out."

"Good, maybe they'll quit bugging me about the FBI. Nadja isn't my problem anymore, and I already told you guys everything I know." In front of her, a computer screen flashed bright as Lt. Harmon hit a key. *What do you know that you're not telling me, Robert?* She entered the name of Nadja's mother and found her still living near Chicago. Next, she got into the mother's bank records. Several thousand dollars had been transferred to an account in India. More went to a bank account in New York. *It's no accident Mr. Owens got me into the SCIF room.*

"It wasn't the parrot," Mr. Owens said thoughtfully. "It was smart of you to have Sasha placed in Nadja's cell," he was saying as Samantha memorized the data.

"Why, what did she say?"

"Not much. It was more of an impression. She thought Nadja might be softening, especially toward you."

"Great."

"One last thing. In a market near Kabul, several people died of fentanyl ingestion. The drug was dusted on the food."

"How awful! How many people died?"

"Fifteen," Mr. Owens replied solemnly.

Lt. Harmon related the incident in a nearby bar where it was suspected that nine people died from ingesting fentanyl. "When will you be here?"

she asked as she typed Nadja's name into the system, both her real name and her alias. *Nothing new.*

"I'll be stopping in Germany to check on your sweetheart. What day do you report to INSCOM?"

Before replying, Lt. Harmon typed Nadja's husband's name into the search bar. At first, there didn't seem to be any new information, but when she clicked on a picture of Nadja and her husband playing in their band, she found a peculiar interaction happening between Dalbir and another woman. *Funny, it's not Nadja he's singing to, but she's standing right there.* After zeroing in on the woman's face, she searched the internet for the band member's names. *BINGO.*

"Lieutenant, are you there?"

"Yes, still here. There are a few weeks left on my leave, but I'm going to stop in Washington for a debriefing at INSCOM after I go see Grandfather. Today is my Uncle Benny's funeral."

"See you at Nolan Hall," Mr. Owens said, referring to the building at Fort Belvoir headquartering the intelligence community. "Where will you be on Tuesday?"

"Depends on the FBI."

"What?"

"Nothing," Samantha said hurriedly. "Just something I have to figure out. Will you call me from Germany?"

"Of course."

"See you in Washington." With that, she hung up.

Curious to see what the FBI might be looking for, she typed the words 'Task Force Talon' into the search bar and stared at a document stamped top and bottom with the Top Secret designator, a document discussing the court's decision to give the government legal permission to monitor communication systems of certain entities, and listed those entities by name: the Sinaloa Cartels, certain financial institutions, corporations involved in money laundering. *And certain individuals, including me!*

A cascade of thoughts passed through her mind. *Of course,* she reasoned, *with their penchant for doing business with the mafia, everyone in her family would be on somebody's list. But most of the bad guys are either dead or in a coma.* Switching windows, she requested Nadja's mother's bank information and learned that someone had withdrawn a large sum of money from an account in India. On several occasions, money had also been taken from an account in New York in a series of automatic withdrawals occurring every two weeks.

Wondering about her grandfather's finances, she logged into his bank account and almost laughed. *Five dollars, that's all he has?* The reports on her grandfather were a little more demonstrative of his activities and contained notations about drug running and money laundering through a rental property chain. She stared fearfully at the information. The landlord listed was his granddaughter, Samantha Harmon. *What!*

Next, she pulled up Benny Harmon's accounts and found little evidence that he was collecting money from anything but his social security checks. Then, as she looked at the intel reports on Benny, her eyes turned to fury as not only did the reports detail evidence collected to prove her uncle's connection with the cartels, but there was a photo of him meeting with a woman suspected to have connections with an al-Qaeda network. *Benny knew Dalbir's girlfriend! No wonder they're looking at me!*

The office chair flew back as Samantha stood and flung her purse over her shoulder. With the fringe of her dark lashes covering the worry in her eyes, she stormed out of the SCIF and made her way upstairs past the guard, then hurried down the busy hallway, walking steadily in heels until she pushed through the outside door and came face-to-face with Agent Tooley's puffy face. "What now?"

"A Florida congressman's daughter was murdered. TA, a twenty-year-old, got a hold of some Kratom cut with fentanyl. Her mother found her in their basement shower." His voice shook.

Lt. Harmon's eyes widened. "That's terrible. Do they know how she got the drugs?"

"Possibly. There was an emoji on a text the girl received from a friend. The picture of a plug means she'd hooked up with a drug dealer."

"I know they have a whole system of talking to each other through emojis," Samantha said. "Smiley face for ecstasy, a red and yellow pill for heroin. A little snowman for cocaine."

"A needle and syringe for fentanyl."

"I didn't see that one." Samantha's brow furrowed as she thought about the drug landscape. "I just found out about fentanyl a couple of weeks ago. Apparently, it's everywhere."

"The password to the laptop," Agent Tooley said.

As Samantha watched Brian's truck inch its way across the lot, she gave the agent her sweetest smile. "Sweets. Try desserts." Teetering in her heels, she inched her way around the agent toward the curb.

"Any particular sweet?"

"Um, popsicles. Try popsicles."

"You need to give us more than that," Agent Tooley said firmly. Using the back of his hand, he wiped away a bead of sweat dripping from his brow.

In the afternoon sun, Samantha's black dress accumulated moisture beneath the fabric as she longed for the air conditioning in her brother's truck. "I can give you something better than that. Got a pen?"

When Agent Tooley produced a government-issued black pen, along with a small notepad he kept in a suit pocket, she told him about the account in New York belonging to Nadja's mother. "And whoever is cashing checks on that account will be there cashing another one on Monday. I assume you'll be going to court now, looking at video footage from the airports, banks, streetlights?"

"Lieutenant," Agent Tooley called. She pulled open the truck door and tossed her purse on the floor.

"What?"

"Good work. You will let me know when Nadja contacts you?"

A light flashed on. With a nod, she pulled herself up on the running board and swung into her seat. "Time to go see who shows up at Benny's funeral."

"Want to grab a burger first?" Brian asked. "I'm starving."

"Sure."

The mood on his face deepened as he made a swift U-turn and headed out of the lot. "Your base just got blown up by a rocket. Grandfather's in a coma, your only uncle just died, and mom's still in the psych ward. You're acting like none of this is bothering you. How did you get to be so calloused?"

With angry eyes, Samantha replied woodenly, "Can't you just let me do my job?"

"I've seen that look before," Brian replied. "When Mom brought Jenny and me on the boat."

"Sailing was my job. I had work to do then, and I have work to do now. You want a single or a double?" Her hand dug through an oversized purse for change; her face tightened.

"Great!" Brian slapped the wheel. "Why did you say yes to a guy who cheated on you?" With his face still fuming, he studied the drive-thru menu and asked the black box for two double cheeseburgers, Number Eight.

"Pull up to the second window, sir," a robotic voice said over the speaker.

As Brian pulled up to the next window and paid, Samantha reached across to grab a sack of food from the attendant's outstretched hand, leaving Brian with the cardboard tray containing two large drinks with extra cups of ice.

"Technically, he didn't cheat. We weren't allowed to date classmates at West Point."

"Owe." Brian swallowed a sizzling fry whole and took a large chug of soda. "Where's the ketchup?"

"Here." Grabbing a red and white packet, Samantha bit off the end and squirted sauce over the fries. "Gary's in?" she asked, referring to a plan they'd cooked up to get her some time with her mother outside of the FBI's surveillance.

"Talked to him while you were in the bathroom. He's in," Brian mumbled through a bite of bacon, lettuce, cheeseburger.

"Thanks for the idea."

Brian nodded. 'you're welcome' as he pulled into the funeral home's parking lot. There, they passed by a woman standing at the front door as Brian led the way into the reception area where the requisite guest registry sat open. Samantha handed the woman a pen and said by way of introduction, "I'm Samantha, Uncle Benny's great-niece. Are you a friend?"

"Um, neighbor." After that quick reply, the woman signed the name Melisa Bard before fleeing into the reception room.

Samantha clung to her brother's arm as they followed Melissa and approached the waxy figure of Uncle Benny lying peacefully in his coffin. After several moments of paying her respects, she led the way to another room typically reserved for serving refreshments. In there, she warned Brian not to say anything a phone could overhear. "It's official, they're listening to my phone. You go take care of the bereaved while I go see Mom," she said in a low voice.

The collar of Brian's dark suit strained against his neck as he loosened his tie. "How am I supposed to explain your absence?"

"Just say I'm talking to Brad's mother. He's badly injured, and I need to find out how my fiancé's doing."

"You still don't seem all that torn up about him. Why, again, did you accept his proposal?"

"I was under pressure," Samantha replied through quivering lips.

"You love him. Hah, you love that boy," Brian said, sounding as if he'd discovered a deep, dark secret.

Ignoring him, Samantha replied, "I have an idea. You got a phone in those retro rags?" Eyeing the bulge in her brother's suit pocket, she reached in and pulled out the small device, then hit the record button. "Uh huh, uh huh," she said several times before handing it back. "Just play that every couple of minutes."

"To who?"

"Brad's mother." Using her phone, Samantha dialed the number. "Mrs. Kramer, this is Samantha Harmon. I was in Afghanistan with your son right before the attack, and I know he's in a hospital in Germany. Have you talked to anybody?"

After saying that yes, a doctor did call and said that Brad was alive and there was some improvement, Mrs. Kramer began a litany of conversation, all one-sided and all about her son as a child, her husband, and the neighbors.

"This will go on for a couple of hours," Samantha whispered. "Just play that, "Uh huh," every couple of minutes."

As her brother practiced the deception by holding one phone up to the other, Gary walked through the back door and tossed over his keys. Samantha donned his trench coat and stuffed her legs through a pair of pants; then, she pulled his hat over her curls. From her oversized purse, she grabbed a wig of curly dark locks and threw it at Gary, then she sat him down in a chair facing away from the door and hung her suit coat over his shoulders.

"You've gotta be back in forty-five minutes," Brian whispered. "Get going."

Rather than answering, Samantha disappeared out the back door. Outside, her heels stumbled over the rocks in a dirt path leading to the lot where Gary's dark maroon sedan sat waiting to take her to Central State. A short drive later, she was standing at the hospital's reception desk breathlessly asking to see Jen McFadden.

"Your relationship to the patient?"

"She's my mother."

"Fourth floor. Press the buzzer."

On four, Samantha walked up to the steel door of the locked unit and pushed the red button to announce her arrival. Once the door opened, a nurse led her to a rooftop garden surrounded by tall slats of wrought iron bars. There, beneath the shade of a tree, they found Jen McFadden sitting on a wooden bench.

"Push the button by the door if you need help," the nurse said before leaving the visitor alone with her patient.

As Samantha stood watching, sunlight filtering through a cluster of green leaves lit her mother's hair as she touched the end of one finger and said a Hail Mary before repeating the prayer on her middle finger. Samantha waited until she was quiet before slowly sitting down to fold her mother's hand between hers.

"It's me, Sam. Remember me?"

A gust of wind caught the edge of Jen's hair, blowing it backward, just as it had on her grandfather's boat so many years ago. Slowly, she nodded.

"I have something to tell you," Samantha said gently. "Uncle Benny passed away in his sleep a few days ago. They let me come home from Afghanistan for the funeral."

"Benny's gone?" Jen turned to face Samantha, her eyes belying the forgetfulness they normally assumed.

Samantha looked at her suspiciously. "I don't really have much time. His funeral is today, and there are a couple of FBI guys following me around. Have they been here?"

Jen's eyes darted around the garden. "The men in suits?"

"Yes. What did they want?"

"They… asked about Benny," Jen said haltingly, "but I don't remember things, so I couldn't tell them anything."

"But you remember that they asked about Benny, so I know you remember this. I need to know, what did Benny talk about when he was here?"

"I can't tell you," Jen whispered. Her voice became agitated as she wrung her hands and stared down at the ground. "That will only bring you trouble."

"It's too late," Samantha's voice whispered urgently. "Benny was into something bad, along with Grandfather. They were trafficking illegal drugs and laundering money through a network that's been operating rental properties, apparently in my name. Grandfather tried to get out and was talking to the authorities, but Benny's hand was still in the till as deep as anybody's."

"The Harmon family had a lot of money," Jen whispered.

"And there are people after that money, right? Our government, mafia here in the U.S., cartels in Mexico. Now they're even working to funnel money and drugs through an overseas terrorist network." *Tarik was suspicious of me for a reason.* Without wanting to elaborate more on the information she'd gained in Afghanistan about al-Qaeda's plans to traffic drugs, Samantha finished by asking, "Where is the money?"

"I don't know. Grandfather took care of it."

Finally. "Benny was after the money. Is that why he was visiting you?"

"I don't really remember a lot. I can't remember from one day to the next what people say," Jen said resolutely, her face now set in stone.

"Except that you do," Samantha said quietly. "Please, mother, I need your help. A lot of lives are at stake. Maybe even Brian's. And I know you're in here to protect him."

"You can't involve Brian in this!"

"He already is. We all are."

Jerking her hand back, Jen stared straight ahead. "All I remember is that Benny talked a lot about his childhood and how his father brought him into the mafia. Sometimes, he would ramble on about the government and executive orders and freezing assets. There was a guy in Mexico whose assets were frozen, so he couldn't pay Benny. And then there was stuff about property, but I don't remember any of the details."

"Property where?"

"It was all your father's business. I think here somewhere, I don't really know. They give me treatments that make me forget."

"How did Grandfather get involved in this?"

"Which grandfather?"

"The captain on the boat who liked chocolate milk and had a green parrot."

"Oh, him. It's four o'clock somewhere."

"Yes, him," Samantha said excitedly. "He had a laptop he used for business. Do you know where it is?"

"Maybe. It could be at his friend's place."

"What friend?"

"Jake, I think."

"The parrot?"

A look of confusion crossed Jen's face. "Jake liked Christina."

"Christina's a girlfriend?"

Jen nodded and sank onto the bench.

"It's okay," Samantha said quietly as her dark curls began to moisten in the afternoon sun. She pushed a stray curl behind her ear. "I'll take care of everything. I just have one more thing to ask. Do you know the password to that computer?"

"Password?"

"The password to the laptop," Samantha said.

"Password," Jen repeated with a tremoring voice. Her eyes reddened.

Samantha jumped up and walked quickly to the door. She pushed the red button, and within seconds, two attendants ran to her mother's side.

"What happened?" Miss Jamba asked as she strode purposefully from the door.

"Nothing." Samantha's tone grew quite defensive. "I just told her that Uncle Benny passed away."

"She's too upset. You'll have to go."

"We're not finished. No more treatments." Samantha gave the staff a fierce look.

"You're not in charge of her," Miss Jamba said.

"I am now."

"Have a seat while I call the Doctor."

With a nod, Samantha took her mother's place under the tree.

"Who is that girl on the bench?" Miss Jamba asked as they led Jen away.

Hesitantly, she looked back at the dark, curly-haired girl on the bench and smiled. "She's my daughter."

As she sat surrounded by nature and the silent whisperings of her family, Samantha's eyes watered as she listened to her mother's words and came to realize that uncovering the truth about her past could be a journey filled with both promise and heartache. *But it's a journey I have to take.* She jumped when a voice brought her out of her reverie.

"I'm sorry, but you're not on the list," Miss Jamba was saying.

"What list?"

"The list of people we're approved to talk to about your mother's case. Legally, I can't talk to you about her."

"Who is on the list?"

"I can't tell you that either."

"Fine." With that, Samantha proceeded to the lobby. *Weird, somebody drew on the wall with crayons. Do they allow that?* Observing the binders behind the unit secretary's desk, she saw her mother's name in room 408 and walked down the hall with Miss Jamba following close on her tail, yelling at her to stop.

"You can't go in there!"

"Legally, you can't touch me. That I do know," Samantha retorted as she continued to the room. Once inside, she walked over to her mother and hugged her. "Don't let them give you any more treatments. And call us if you want to come home."

Jen's face told Samantha that she was already medicated. "And stop taking those meds. They haven't even had time to take effect and remember what you told me. We have to face life."

With a steady look, Miss Jamba tried to reassure Samantha that her mother was getting good care, but she was having none of it.

"No more treatments and no more meds. Just give her cognitive therapy. That's always worked."

"That is the treatment she's getting," Miss Jamba couldn't help replying.

"What?" *She is totally faking memory loss.* With that, Samantha left the hospital and raced back to the funeral home. Gary's hat went back on her head; then, once she'd parked, his trench coat went over her shoulders. With curses rolling off her tongue, she stumbled down the dirt path in her heels to the back room where Gary sat playing "Uh huh" on her phone. In one deft movement, she threw off the coat and hat, grabbed her phone from his hand and said, "Mrs. Kramer, it's been so nice talking with you. My uncle's funeral is getting ready to start. May I call you tomorrow?" After being reassured that her call would be welcome, she looked upward and whispered to Gary, "Where's Brian?"

With his characteristic short little laugh, Gary pointed to the door. "He went out when the FBI woman peeked in."

Samantha pulled the door open and caught her heel on the door jamb. Gary's hand grabbed her elbow, and together, they found Brian sitting in the lobby across from Melissa Bard. He mouthed the words, "She's FBI," and said, "She's on the phone with Agent Tooley. They're still working on the password. Give them something."

"I think I remember. Try fudgesicle," Samantha said decidedly. "With different numbers."

The funeral director walked up to say it was time to start the service. "Is anybody else coming?"

Samantha cringed under his stare. Other than themselves, one lone man sat in the back, his thinned, graying hair telling of ageless years. "I guess he's too old because the rest of the family are gone. How are we going to do this?" she asked as canned music filled the room.

With Gary, the FBI lady who later said her real name was Agent Vargas, and the funeral director sitting in the second row, Samantha got up and gave a eulogy, talking about what a dear uncle he had been. "Such a valued member of the community. You will be missed," she told him and turned to face the funeral director. "What now?"

"I'm sorry for your loss," he said. "I understand he's being cremated?"

"Yes," Samantha said as she backed away. "We'll get his ashes later so no graveyard service today."

Brian walked her to the lobby and checked the registry. "Harry Trot?"

"The gray-haired man," Samantha replied with a start.

"Who is Harry Trot?"

"Grandfather's fixer."

"Let's go. What are we going to do now?" Brian opened the truck door and, grabbing the bag from the burger place, located one lone French fry from the bottom and stuffed it in his mouth. With the bag now officially empty, he wadded it up and tossed it behind the seat. Then, after popping open the glove box, he took out an apple. Samantha collected both their phones and placed them in the glove box, then she told him about the woman in Florida named Christine, who was Grandfather's girl.

"She might have the other laptop. And hopefully, she knows the password. Do you think Gary would take care of Jack if we go to Florida?"

"That's kind of not really a good idea." Brian's long cheeks creased. "He has a cat."

"Jack's in a cage. We can leave in the morning right after I get my uniforms."

"I can't even believe I'm agreeing to this," Brian said as he tossed the apple core out the window. "There better be something good on that laptop."

"There is."

"And you know that it's enough to link the family to a terror plot?"

"Not that in particular, but the drug running and money laundering is. It's all a network being run by the cartels. And now I think al-Qaeda wants in on the money."

"I think," Brian said, "that we're going to get Jack and just keep driving."

Home, to the sea.

"Can't yet," Samantha replied, looking sad but resolute. "First, we've got to kick some terrorist ass."

CHAPTER 13

Indianapolis, Indiana
June 27, 2021 4 PM

"How is anyone supposed to have a normal life anymore?" Brian grumbled as he shifted gears to follow the procession of cars bearing the customary flags heading into the local cemetery.

"What's normal?" Samantha asked.

"The kind where you just eat pizza and play video games. There's Bear's dad," he said, pointing to an elderly man in a brown suit hanging in folds from his emaciated frame. With his hands clasping a baby blue rosary, he knelt on the ground and wept. A funeral hearse was already parked, the dark gray casket already sitting on its perch, waiting to be lowered to its final resting place. Father Mark, the officiating priest, stood in front of the group and nodded at Brian.

"This is where Grams and Poppa are buried," Brian said. He introduced Samantha to the priest who'd officiated their funerals.

"Father Mark, it's nice to think they'll be watching over Bear." They all walked over to Jason's parents and gave their condolences to the young man the Harley riders lovingly called 'Bear.'

"He was our little bear," his mother sobbed.

Samantha's eyes narrowed with recognition as she studied a bald man with the muscled legs of someone whose hamstrings spent hours gripping the seat of a Harley. Turning, he gave a nod before walking over to chat with a gang of bikers.

"I'm sorry we don't have time to stay longer," she said to Jason's mother. "I'm flying out in the morning."

Brian's eyebrows turned to a question mark as he followed his sister to the truck. Once behind the wheel, he sat and waited for instructions. She said loudly, "Can we get another burger?"

"You're still hungry?" he asked, studying his sister's small waist.

"Yes."

"Sure."

"Bacon cheese and curly fries," she requested at the window. After receiving their order, she twirled a curly fry in circles and let the end sink into her mouth.

"I know what you're doing," Brian said angrily. "You can't avoid talking about him forever."

"Who?" Samantha asked innocently.

"What are you going to do if he's blind?"

"I guess I'll have to steer the boat."

"You can't marry a blind man and stay in the military. He'll need you at home."

"Those bridges don't exist yet," Samantha muttered. After devouring her sandwich, her lips clamped shut as she silently stared out the window.

At the house, Brian parked at the curb and waited for a UPS van to leave before pulling into the driveway. Jumping from the truck, he raced to get the package. "What's this." Reaching down, he picked up a cardboard box addressed to Lt. Harmon and held it up to his ear, giving it a shake.

"I don't know." Grabbing the package, she balanced it in one hand. "It's so light, there can't be much in here." She carried the small box into the kitchen and placed it on the counter, then noted the return address to be a P.O. box on the West Coast.

"Smoking gun," Jack squawked.

"He must have overheard the FBI guys." Using Brian's pocket knife, she slit open the tape. "What in the world?"

"What's in the package?"

Samantha held up three black licorice whips and stuck one in her mouth, then fumbled to open a slip of paper, which proved to be a receipt. On the back, a message read, "Need to talk. Urgent," along with a phone number. Pointing to the front door, she led the way outside.

"What's this about?" Taking the slip, Brian studied the words.

"It's got to be Nadja," Samantha told him more about the interview with the terrorist. "She's a fan of black licorice."

"No wonder you're worried about a terrorist attack. You have to tell the FBI about this."

"I can't yet. She's so smart, she'll run and nobody will ever see her again. I'm sure you have a burner phone or two around here. May I have one please? And the phone number for another one."

"This is just not a good idea," Brian protested as he walked back into the house, mumbling, "Not a good idea at all." His red tennis shoes took the stairs two at a time and quickly brought him back with the phone.

"The phone number."

"I, um, left it in the kitchen."

With a look of eager determination, Samantha grabbed the phone from his hand and called the number on the receipt as Brian disappeared inside the house.

"Hello, Lieutenant."

"How did you know it would be me?"

"You're the only one who has this number."

"Oh, okay. What is it that you have to tell me?"

"I want you to help my son," Nadja said in a tired, almost hollow voice.

"I don't have the power to do that," Lt. Samantha Harmon said, her voice holding a hint of remorse.

"But you know people who do. Get him a deal. He knows al-Qaeda's drug routes and about the attack they're planning."

"And so do you."

"No. I know things he doesn't know about production. He knows the business end."

"Hang on just a second." While shifting slightly in her funeral dress, Samantha held the phone away from her mouth, her face questioning as Brian returned, red-eyed with tears streaming down his cheeks, and shoved a piece of paper in her palm.

"That's for the other burner phone," he sniffed. His chest heaved beneath the fabric of a white linen shirt. Finally, he stuttered out the words, "Somebody …snuck heroin …cut with fentanyl into the jail. Jenny… got a hold of it. She's dead."

"Oh no!" With the burner phone clattering to the ground, Samantha gave her brother a tight hug, then quickly released her grip and retrieved the phone. "Sorry."

"Yeah, Jenny's dead. You're so sympathetic," Brian said harshly. When his sister's expression hardened, he turned and walked back into the house.

"What do you need?" Samantha's pleading voice fell off just a bit at the end of the sentence.

Nadja's raspy voice cut through the airwaves. "Passage into the U.S. to make sure they don't send us straight to Guantanamo before we can cut a deal."

"And then you'll turn yourselves in?"

"Of course. We'll have to."

"Do you have your flight information?"

"Not yet, I'm getting that on Wednesday. I'll be flying into the Indianapolis airport next Saturday. Security there is no problem. I'll just need to be picked up and have a place to stay for a few days."

"I cannot harbor a terrorist in my house," Samantha gasped.

"If you don't help us, a lot of people will die," Nadja said firmly.

Resisting the urge to hang up, Samantha closed her eyes and remembered the warmth of Jenny's hand slipping into hers. She continued in an even tone, "You have to give me something more. Help me help you. Where is the next attack going to take place, Mother?"

"That is a puzzle," Nadja replied.

"One that you've already solved if you're coming here. Is this where it is, here?"

"My, you are the intelligent one," Nadja murmured.

"We'll find a place for you. Got a pen?" Lt. Harmon gave Nadja the number to the burner phone. "I'll be in Washington, so my brother will answer your next call. Give him your flight details."

"No, nobody else can be involved!"

"It's fine. Brian just lost someone to drugs he cared about very much. The girl, Jenny, was like a sister to us. He wants to help. I do, too. You have my word."

A deep sigh resounded over the phone. "Very well, Lieutenant. I guess I'll have to trust you," Nadja said with just the right amount of timidity in her voice.

"I look forward to seeing you. Goodbye Nadja." *There's something really off here.* When Brian came back outside and held out his hand for the phone, she asked for another. "I have one more call to make."

"To who?" he asked as his hammer hit the burner phone. He struck it hard. *Bam.*

"I don't know, but I have a number. By the way, Nadja will be calling with flight details on Wednesday. Just write down what she says, and don't ask any questions."

Using the back of his hand, Brian wiped snot from his nose while walking back into the house. A few moments later, he returned with another phone and eyed Gary's old jalopy pulling up to the curb. The lanky young man jumped out and slammed his door yelling, "Dude, that's terrible about Jenny. What can I do to help?"

Samantha told him what he could do. After accepting the second phone, she dialed the number Nadja gave her during the interrogation way back over in Afghanistan. When a voice answered, she handed the phone to Gary.

"Sorry, wrong number," he squeaked and hung up, then handed the phone over for quick disposal. Brian's hammer angrily destroyed the small device. *Bam- bam- bam.*

"We need to be on the first flight to Florida, like tomorrow," Samantha said.

"Can't, the dry cleaners doesn't open until eight. And I'm not going," Brian replied.

"What? I need you!"

"Mom needs me."

Samantha looked at her brother suspiciously. "You're going after the drug dealer who gave Jenny that poison."

"That too," Brian said sullenly.

"Well, I don't really have all that much to do. See Grandfather, find a missing laptop, figure out this terrorist thing," Samantha muttered as she walked away. Secretly, though, she was relieved. *This will make it easier to do what I need to do. I know who that was on the phone.* Immediately upon hearing the voice, visions of a dragon scar seared across a cheek came to mind. *Tarik!* As Gary walked past with her brother, she asked Brian for his car keys.

"We're going to Aunt Diana's. Why aren't you coming with us?" Brian yelled.

"In Afghanistan, it took us too long to figure things out, and Brad got hurt. I'm not going to let that happen again," Samantha replied curtly, her cheeks flushed with heat. "I'm sorry about Jenny, but if I don't get this whole thing figured out soon, a lot of people could die. You get Agent Vargas' number?"

"Yes, it's in the truck." With a long face, Brian handed over his ring of heavy keys and another object, Uncle Benny's cell phone. "I got the phone unlocked. What else can we do?"

"Besides finding Jenny's killer?" Samantha picked a peony and twirled it in her fingers. "Maybe figure out a way to get somebody out of the airport without going through the terminal."

"Why would you need to do that?"

"Because Nadja has something planned. She's going to try to escape, and I don't think a shootout at the front door is a good idea."

The whites of Gary's eyes grew bigger as he realized what was about to happen.

"Your mom's cleaning company does the airport offices, right?" Brian asked.

"Yes. And?"

"You just got yourself a job."

"No, dude, no way! I'm not cleaning toilets!"

"They hire mentally challenged people. You'll fit right in."

"Go talk to Homeland Security, they're better at toilets."

The amusing banter gave Samantha an idea. She called Agent Vargas to set up a meeting, stating it was urgent that they speak with other agencies right away.

"See you at the JAC," Agent Vargas said.

Samantha's fingers swiped through Benny's phone. Then she jumped behind the wheel in Brian's truck and headed to an old white-bricked building sitting on the edge of town. On the way, she mentally reviewed Nadja's case. *Where's her husband? They could be planning a family reunion.*

Even though she arrived late on a Sunday evening, The Joint Analytic Cell was busy. Up at the podium, a plain-clothed man was giving a briefing on counter-terrorism, his monotone voice emitting from an olive-toned face, his dark brown eyes ringed by lush lashes. Upon finishing, he stared at Samantha.

"Yes?"

"It's okay. She's with me," Agent Vargas said. She walked over to shake hands, then introduced the men on the podium as Agent Patel from the Department of Homeland Security and Agent Baker from the National Counter-Terrorism Center.

"Gentlemen, Mam, I'm Lieutenant Harmon, U.S. Army," she said hurriedly. "Until a few days ago, I was the tactical intelligence officer at Bagram's 2nd Battalion. As part of my job, I interrogated an al-Qaeda operative who goes by the name Nadja Jammu. She will be arriving in

Indianapolis next week. You need to let her come in, or she'll disappear. Nadja is willing to hand over valuable intelligence concerning a planned terrorist attack and the manufacture and transit of heroin and fentanyl in exchange for immunity for herself and her older son. The FBI has already spoken with her about entering into the Witness Protection Program, but she won't give up any intel until she and her son are in the United States."

"You said something about a terrorist attack," Agent Vargas said. "Why here?"

"Money."

"What money?" Agent Baker asked.

"Unfortunately," Lt. Harmon shuffled her heels as her face flushed, "I know this part of the information because it's related to my family. My deceased father's side worked for the mafia, and my great-uncle Benny just died. On his cell phone, there's a message from a cartel operative about extorting the release of money owed by a Mexican national. That person's assets are frozen. Mr. Rivera, the Secretary of Finance in Mexico, has the power to unfreeze those assets, and he's arriving in Indianapolis next Saturday. With my Uncle Benny gone, it's possible they'll go directly after the money."

"Wow," all three agents exclaimed together.

"How do they plan on accomplishing that?" Agent Vargas asked.

"By kidnapping Mr. Rivera during a terror attack. Al-Qaeda was practicing dispersing fentanyl on our troops at Bagram using talcum powder. Nadja admitted it was for practice. Her husband, Dalbir Jammu, could already be here. This is his picture," she continued. "Somehow, you need to come up with a plan to capture him, and his network like yesterday."

. The group stared solemnly at Lt. Harmon. "Okay everybody, we've got work to do," Agent Vargas said. Nodding at Lt. Harmon, she thanked her for the information. Understanding that she was dismissed, Samantha thought longingly of her quarters in Afghanistan and stopped to use the restroom before heading home for a few hours' sleep.

"I'm just not into this civilian stuff," she thought as she exited the bathroom.

Back at the house, while lying in the comfort of a regular bed, she flashed back to a fishing line drawn tight on the stern of her grandfather's boat and sorted out a nagging thought. *They are fishing. And I'm the bait!* With a smile slipping across her face, her eyes closed.

The next morning, the tangled mess of blankets intertwined with human body parts flopping over the mattress's edge did little to prevent Brian from waking his sister, eager to brief her on an idea he'd dreamed up. Gently, he shook her shoulder. Slowly, she opened one eye. "You bring coffee?"

"Nope, something better," he replied excitedly. "Listen to this. Architects are the historians of our buildings, and the designs for each building are stored in city hall. But those blueprints don't account for the tunnels."

"What tunnels?" Samantha asked with a yawn.

Brian sat down on the edge of her bed, his hazel eyes burning with exuberance. "Tunnels used during prohibition that were built in secret. I know my dad has plans for one property near the airport that documents a tunnel city hall doesn't know about, and those plans are on his computer. We need to find it."

"Why didn't you say that first?" Samantha asked as she jumped up and straightened her crumpled T-shirt.

"You were asleep. Let's go!"

From the dusty bins in the McFadden's attic, bolts of fabric flew into a stack as Samantha helped her brother search for an old computer once belonging to his father and moaned, "Just one more hour. Why couldn't you let me sleep one more hour." A tickling sensation hit her nose. "Ah-choo."

Struggling for breath in the hot attic air, Brian tossed aside a bolt of red flannel, then grabbed yellow linen and threw it on the stack before finding the computer parts he was looking for. Bonus: A bundle of floppy discs wrapped in old newspaper sat on top of the computer.

"The tower, great. You left me the heavy piece," Samantha grumbled as her long arms wrapped around the computer part. Squeezing it tight, she duck-walked it over to the middle of the room.

"Just hand it down the steps," Brian said. Holding onto a rail with the monitor in hand, he rapidly descended the stairs. Upon reaching the bottom, he set the floppy discs on the floor and then walked up half of the steps to grab the tower.

"Why again are we doing this?"

"There's a video game I want to play."

"Really!"

"Just kidding. My dad used this for work. We might get lucky and find an old architectural drawing of the airport."

"Why didn't you say that in the first place?"

"Just thought of it. This thing might take forever to load," Brian mumbled as he hooked up the old computer system in the kitchen and plugged it in. Then he grabbed the floppy discs off the floor, unwrapped the newspaper, and dropped it on the table.

Samantha looked with interest at the computer system and, with her eyes on the clock, slowly backed away from the room. "I've got to get ready," she said and headed for the stairs. "Be right back." After showering off the attic dust, she stopped in her bedroom to change clothes and grabbed her travel things, then rejoined her brother in the kitchen. Using her slim culinary skills, she whisked an egg in a pan as she picked up the newspaper article used to wrap the floppy disc. "What's this?"

"I dunno."

"This is funny. It's from the prohibition years. Back in the 1920s, they caught a guy who was transporting alcohol through a tunnel when a cow's leg caved in the roof. It's boarded up, so I doubt it's being used."

"True." Brian clicked on a file labeled, 'West Side Project.' "No way. It has a tunnel by the airport!" He sent the file to his email and copied the information to Samantha while she took birdseed over to Jack's cage. His emerald wings lifted.

"Hello."

"Password."

"Shut up, Jack," he squawked.

Nothing.

Brian inserted the floppy disc simply labeled, 'Airport.' "Darned, that's the old airport. Strike two. What's that slimy stuff you're eating?"

"Scrambled eggs. Want a plate?"

"Ugh, no thanks. What time is it?"

"Almost eight. You ready?" she asked as she lifted a bag from the floor.

"Yup. Gimme that." After grabbing the bag from his sister's shoulder, Brian headed for the truck. "Why is your bag so light?"

"My uniforms are at the cleaners," she replied while climbing into the passenger seat. "Don't forget to stop."

"Jack was supposed to remind me. It's on the next block." Brian held up a pink slip, which Samantha quickly grabbed from his fingers.

"Thanks, be right back." Inside the cleaners, she wrinkled her nose against the strong odor of cleaning chemicals and handed the pink slip to a clerk who studied the slip before rotating a rack of clothes to stop at Samantha's order.

"Here you go, all paid for. Please thank your husband for his service."

Samantha's grey-blue eyes blazed with furry. Hooking a finger through the hangers, she growled, "I'm not married. These are my uniforms."

"Oh, sorry."

"I'm just back from Afghanistan. Thanks." Leaving the woman wide-eyed, she carried the uniforms to the truck, took each piece, and rolled it tight before stuffing them all into her bag. "I said no starch. These uniforms are like cardboard."

"The complaint department is closed." Throwing the truck into gear, Brian headed west toward the airport while his head bobbed to the speakers, thumping base notes from the back seat. As they entered the departure lane, Samantha turned the volume down and stared at the floor.

"Did you explain to Aunt Diana why I didn't come over?"

"Yup. You should call her."

"I will. I suppose they'll be making Jenny's funeral arrangements today."

"Nope, not until Wednesday. The jail has to do an investigation before they release her body."

"Investigate what?"

"Detective Renfro over at the Lawrence police department says they're ruling out murder. He thinks someone figured out that Jenny had the dirt on a dealer."

As the airport lanes converged into gridlock, Brian sat impatiently waiting for an SUV to drop off a passenger. Moments later, he pulled up to the curb looking not too happy, threw off his seat belt, and then ran around to open Samantha's door. "When are you coming back?"

Looking away as she climbed from the truck, she said, "I don't know yet."

"I'm glad you're home, sis." He swept her into a bear hug so tight she grimaced. After standing at the curb with the long strap of her bag hanging from her shoulder and waving at the disappearing taillights, she walked inside the terminal and made her way through security, then found a computer desk in front of her gate. As she sat with her phone charging, she searched the internet for the number to Landstuhl Hospital at the U.S. Army base in Germany.

"May I speak with Captain Brad Kramer?" she asked. Her call was immediately transferred to a medical unit.

"Hello, this is Sergeant Lanning. How may I help you?" asked a pleasant female voice.

"Good morning. I'm Lieutenant Harmon, the battalion tactical officer from Bagram. How is Captain Kramer," she asked as her long fingers tightly gripped the phone.

"He's listed as stable, Mam," the sergeant reported. "That's all I can tell you."

"Thank you." Samantha took a deep breath. "He's my, um, friend. Will he be transferred to the States soon?"

"That's up to his doctors, of course. But we need the bed, so as soon as possible."

"Thank you for your time. Have a good day."

As she waited to board her flight, Samantha searched the internet and found the usual assortment of headlines. *It's hot out west. No kidding.* "Where is this?" she asked herself as A Fourth of July festival in a west side park caught her eye. Reading through the story, she learned that during the festival, a total of ten hot air balloons would launch from the park. *Beautiful.* A thin brow raised as her grey-blue eyes studied the next article. **Indianapolis Happy to Host Delegation**. The reporter said the Mexican Secretary of Finance would be attending the festival. *Wow.*

Upon reading that a man was caught in Evansville, Indiana, transporting seventy thousand fentanyl pills, she sat astounded by the numbers and stared at the following headline. *Oh my God!* A heart-wrenching article about kids exposed to fentanyl at a daycare where a one-year-old died caused her to grip the paper so hard it crumpled in her fingers. Next, there was a school in Connecticut where an eleven and twelve-year-old had died. Several bags of white powder were found in the school. *There has to be a way to stop this!*

"We are now *boarding* Flight 243 to Miami," a voice announced overhead. "All those with active military I.D.s may now board."

Picking up the strap to her carry-on, she headed for the line and swiped her boarding pass, then walked down the gangplank and made a beeline for her seat. With her bag stored overhead, she waited for the aisle passenger to stand before pushing past her to take the window seat and pulled out her cell.

"Mrs. Kramer, this is Samantha Harmon. Sorry to call so early, but I'm traveling today."

"It's fine dear."

"How is Brad today?"

"Actually, I just spoke with his nurse. She said that Brad is breathing on his own and he's awake. You know, when he was a little boy, he loved cereal. Brad just always loved…" Mrs. Kramer's voice rambled on. Samantha stopped listening for a bit. Finally, she interrupted.

"My plane's taking off. Did they say if he has any permanent eye damage?"

"They didn't mention it, dear."

"And his leg?"

"The nurse said his foot is pink. He'll be transferred to Walter Reed on Wednesday. We went to Washington once when Brad was in the eighth grade…"

"Thank you so much," Samantha said breathlessly. "I'll call back when I can. My plane is leaving. By now." For the first time in several months, thoughts of getting her nails done, maybe doing a little shopping off South Beach, and relaxing with a mojito began seeping into her mind as she dozed off. Soon, her face lit with dreams of sailing along the East Coast with Grandfather at the helm. She smiled as Brad walked up and put sunscreen on her back. "You're here!"

"Excuse me?" the lady next to her said.

Startled, Samantha realized she'd fallen asleep. As the overhead speaker announced their arrival at the Miami airport, she looked sideways at her seatmate and picked up her phone. "I mean, we're here." While the plane taxied to the gate, a nagging thought gave her an idea. She sent Brian a text. *You need an oil change.*

I already have the appointment.

Good boy.

Outside, she stood in the long taxi line, hungry and anxious for some good Cuban food. Dressed for the Miami heat, her cotton shirt clung to her with moistened sweat. Her jean shorts, rolled high enough to display the lean muscles of her legs, glistened. She hailed a cab.

"Where to?" the cabbie asked in a thick Spanish accent. Ashes from a lit cigar spewed out the window as he waited for a reply. Samantha coughed and waved away the smoke.

"Hurricane Cove, please. I'm going to the marina. Mind if we keep the windows down?"

"No problemo."

While speeding through the streets of Miami, Samantha stared out at the pink and yellow tropical-colored dwellings lining the avenues. *What a difference from the desert mountains of Afghanistan. Was it really just a week ago?* Leaning forward, she grabbed the back of the front seat and stared at an object on the sidewalk. "That person doesn't look right. Should we check on him?"

"No!" The cabbie's foot hit the gas. "He might be sleeping or muerte. Whatever he is, there are probably drugs. Best not to get involved."

"And the people around here just walk by. I know a lot of people are dying because drugs are cut with fentanyl. Why isn't anybody doing anything?"

"Guess they don't want to get shot."

"I understand that. But why would the dealers even risk selling drugs cut with fentanyl when they know it's killing their customers?"

"Um," the cabbie shrugged. "Maybe because having a dead body around is good advertising."

"What?" Pulling back the dark locks of hair crossing her face, Samantha leaned forward.

The cabbie, who finally introduced himself as Manuel, explained that if a dealer got a client so high they died, that proved he was selling the ultimate product. "Addicts will step over the bodies for that kind of high."

"And the dealers don't care that their customers might die?"

"No. It's about the money. They know that, typically, a kid will survive for about five years. When they die, there are always new clients. Is this the right one?" he asked as he pulled up to a wooden walk.

"Can you wait a moment, please? I need to see if the boat is still here."

"Si, but pay before you leave the cab."

"Please, just one second. I'm Lieutenant Harmon, U.S. Army. I'll be right back."

Grumbling under his breath, Manuel motioned for her to proceed.

The harbor at Hurricane Cove sat filled with yachts, most used just once or twice a year. Amongst them, Samantha spotted her grandfather's sailboat occupying the usual slip. "The boat is here, be right back," she yelled as she ran down the wooden platform. As if on que, a flock of seagulls soared overhead, saluting the return of the first mate. She threw her bag over the rail and turned to find the cab driver standing beside her.

"The Sail Away is your boat?"

"Yes. You know it?"

"Of course. I'm Manuel Rodriguez. I bartended parties on this boat."

"Manuel, it is you! I thought you looked familiar. It's me, Samantha."

"Little Sammy, all grown up!"

"It's been a long time since we fished you out of the ocean." Indeed,

Samantha would never forget the day they found Manuel floating from Cuba to Florida in an ice chest, his eyes so desperate and pleading for help.

Manuel threw his arms around Samantha and lifted her in a bear hug. "How about I take you to lunch," he said when he finally set her down.

"Thanks, but I can't. Grandfather's pretty sick. I need to get to Miami General."

"I'll drive you." Manuel ushered Samantha to the cab, flipped off the meter, and headed away from the marina. On the way to the hospital, she proudly told him about her time at West Point and then in Afghanistan. Upon reaching the blue signs of Miami General, he slowed in front of the visitor entrance. With her stomach churning, Samantha rubbed her arms as she watched a family pass through the door.

"You can drop me off here."

"Want me to wait for you?"

"No." She shook her head. "Since Grandfather's in a coma, I'll probably sit for a while."

For Manuel, that did it. As he told Samantha, family was everything, and she shouldn't be going through this alone.

"I've always been alone, except for Grandfather."

With the cigar butt hanging from the corner of his mouth, Manuel hopped from the cab and opened Samantha's door. Pinching it between two fingers, he removed the stogie to say, "I'll walk you up."

"Great, great," her voice sang.

Up on the second floor, they located the door to the ICU. Manuel headed to the waiting room while Samantha pushed a silver plate and walked onto the circular unit. In her grandfather's room, she found a male nurse pushing meds through his IV and stood wide-eyed, watching her grandfather's chest slowly rise and retract to release a rattling breath.

"He's not on a ventilator?"

"No. He was extubated yesterday," the nurse replied.

With a sigh of relief, Samantha walked up and gripped the bed rail. Then she leaned over to peer into her grandfather's opaque blue eyes, open but staring into space. Tears clung to her lashes as she looked up beseechingly at the nurse and asked, "Is he going to wake up?"

"He's been awake, off and on."

When he left to answer a call light, Samantha trailed a finger across the bald spot encircled by long gray hair and said softly, "Wake up, Jack."

"Come on," he whispered hoarsely, the same thing Jack said when he wanted food.

"You're awake!" Blinking back tears, Samantha laid her head on his chest as his cool hand clenched her fingers.

"Barely," his raspy voice whispered.

Startled by the sound of an alarm beeping, Samantha lifted her head and cried, "Don't try to talk." Her grandfather's blood pressure flashed on a display, showing his pressure had dropped. When the nurse ran in and adjusted the IV pump, the flashing stopped.

"He's okay. He does this," he said. When he left again, Samantha poked her grandfather's shoulder.

"Are you still awake?" When the old captain moved his head, she smiled. "Sorry, Grandfather, I hate to ask, but it's urgent. I know why you waited for me. I assume Christina has your laptop. What's her last name?"

The old man slightly lifted his head and readjusted a hip before saying hoarsely, "Morenga."

Samantha's hand tightened on his. "One more thing, Grandfather. What's the password to your computer?"

"The password? It's…" he said with a deep rattle in his voice. As his hand relaxed, his eyes closed. She poked his shoulder with no response.

He's done talking.

Holding his phone up to his face for cell recognition, she opened the device and quickly found Christina's name. When a female voice answered, she introduced herself as Captain Greg's granddaughter. "He's sick. May I stop by your house? I think you have something of his that he needs."

"Yes, of course," Christina said.

"I can be there in half an hour."

"He said you would come."

Once she hung up, Samantha went into the phone settings and removed the password. Then she sat beside the bed and stroked the palm of her grandfather's hand, noting how puffy and cold it was, as were his feet. The urine in his catheter bag was dark orange, a color she knew indicated his kidneys were failing, according to the training the military gave her in heat injury. *But this isn't heat.* With an extra hard squeeze of his hand, she told him she loved him. "I'm glad you waited for me." Feeling a light squeeze back, their sign that he loved her, she brought his hand up to her lips and gave it a light kiss. There, the nurse found her nuzzling the hand to her cheek. "You can go now if you have too," she said, moving aside for the nurse to give meds.

The halls seemed much longer as she blindly made her way back to the waiting room. Manuel kindly took her hand and led her away. "Are you okay, senora?"

"It's hard seeing him so helpless."

"Of course it is. Ready for lunch?"

"I, um, I can't. There's this woman, Christina, who was Grandfather's girlfriend. I have to go see her. She's giving me the recipe book we used on the boat, and I have to tell her about his condition." When Manuel looked absolutely crestfallen, Samantha relented and said, "We can go to lunch right after, and I'll buy you a mojito."

Reassured that he'd eat someday, Manuel's brown eyes twinkled as he escorted Samantha into the back seat. The cab wound around Miami's streets, making its way to the address located in a suburb on the south side of the city. As they pulled into the brick drive, he stared at the pink edifice and commented, "Nice digs."

Christina's three-story home stood on a channel. From a large bay window in front of the house, a curtain fluttered as Samantha stood outside, ringing the bell. Soon, the mahogany door mounted in iron brackets swung wide open to reveal a woman with dark silver-streaked hair. Standing in six-inch red stilettos chosen to match her skin-tight dress, the smile above the neckline plunging low enough to unravel the mystery of cleavage welcomed Samantha inside.

"You're here for the captain's cookbook?"

"Yes. I'm Samantha."

"It's on the kitchen table," Christina replied.

"May I use your internet? I won't have it on the boat."

"Of course." She led the way to the kitchen, where the laptop sat waiting on a wooden table beside the remnants of a Cuban sandwich. When offered a cold beverage, Samantha accepted a glass of lemonade, sat down in front of the computer, and picked at the salted, dried plantains in a bowl.

"Do you know the password?"

"Password? No."

"That's okay."

As Christina left to show Manuel the pool, Samantha played with the laptop, trying to log on. *Why didn't he tell me the password years ago?* With different keystrokes, she tried the password to her laptop along with several nautical terms, numbers, and other combinations. Nothing worked. Frustrated, she gave it one last try and used her name, Samantha. Again, nothing.

Wait! What did Jack say? With a few keystrokes, she entered 'Shut Up Jack'. A different screen flashed before her eyes. *I'm in.* Pulling up the history, she clicked on a line and sat looking at property group charts filled with the addresses of buildings, along with the names of property owners. The leases to three properties in Indianapolis had been scanned into the files. She stared closer at the paperwork. *He signed my name! Who else knows this,* she thought as the meeting with Tarik and Mr. Owens, along with her commander, flashed before her eyes.

There was another item of interest in the history, a link to an offshore bank account. When she clicked on that line, the bank name filled the screen. Luckily, the sign-on and password to the account were stored on the computer; thus, she was able to look through all the records. "Oh my God!" The account, with a three-hundred-and-fifty million dollar balance, was registered in her mother's name. *Does the government know about this?*

"Is there a problem," Christina asked, entering through the back door.

"Um, not really. Where's Manuel?"

"In his cab."

"I printed some files. Where's your office?"

"Down the hall," Christina responded. When she returned holding a stack of papers, Samantha grabbed the printouts and stuffed them in her purse. Then, feigning a wave of fatigue, she rubbed her eyes and said, "Grandfather had a stroke. He's not going to last much longer."

"Why didn't somebody tell me!" Christina gasped.

"I just found out about you."

"I'll go see him right now. Are you going back to the hospital?" Christina's massive gold purse flew over her shoulder.

"Not tonight. I'll stop by tomorrow on my way to the airport." A touch of urgency filled Samantha's voice as she said, "I need to leave the laptop here. If anybody from the government shows up asking questions, I came to tell you about Grandfather. I'd also like to have your help with his funeral."

With a tear in her eye that Samantha judged might be real, Christina smashed her to her bosom, saying how nice it was to meet her. "Whatever you need, you call me."

Blooms of subtropical foliage lining the drive struck Samantha's olfactory senses. "Achoo." She turned from staring at the white trumpeting Hibiscus and looked beseechingly at Christina. "You have somewhere else you can store a used laptop besides this property?"

"Of course, darling," Christina said. Then she pulled the young girl behind a Gardenia and whispered, "The money is being watched by foreign eyes. Never touch the money."

Samantha's eyes blinked rapidly as she released Christina's grip and returned to the car. "Grandfather is at Miami General," she called. Waving goodbye, she climbed back into Manuel's cab wondering what Christina did for a living and how she came to pay for such a massive house.

Manuel headed toward South Beach and stopped in the district along Restaurant Row. "Fernando's is here. It's good Cuban."

"Yum."

As they dined on flatbread, salad, and croquettes washed down with red sangria, Samantha told him all about her childhood on the boat. "It was really fun, and I learned to sail."

"Can you take her out by yourself?"

"Yes. But it won't be the same without Grandfather."

"And Jack. What a funny bird."

"Thanks for lunch." Samantha's eyes danced above a quick smile. When they were done eating, Manuel led her along the cobbled streets to a spa.

"Mani/pedi time," he said.

"You too."

"Oh no!"

"Oh yes."

As the jagged nails on Samantha's hands and feet told of a desperate need for care, Manuel went along to sit by her side in the pedicurist's chair, enjoying the vibrating back massage element. His nails received a clear coat. Hers were painted pink. As they walked out of the salon, Manuel pointed to a shop. "How about a dress?"

Samantha tugged at the waist in her sagging jean shorts and smiled. "I could use a dress."

They walked through the district where many clothing shops lined the cobbled streets. There, Manuel pointed to a mannequin in a display window standing forever poised in a turquoise dress. "Senorita, it's got your name written all over it." A half-hour later, with the bodice hugging her tight around the chest, she marched out of the store, enjoying the feel of cotton fabric swirling around her legs.

"I like this."

"Hair, too?"

Samantha looked at Manuel wistfully and shrugged. "May as well." Soon, her locks were shortened and tapered into a new hairdo fitting her military style. She shook her head, felt her curls blow free, and smiled. "This feels good."

"You're a knockout."

"I have a fiancé. He was hurt overseas."

The silver streaking Manuel's temples, along with his partially lined face, spoke of his years as being close to fifty. With a manicured hand, he guided Samantha back to the cab. "You're all ready for him now."

Her grey-blue eyes filled with gratitude. "Thank you for today."

"What is your plan for the rest of the day?"

"I need to check the boat over." Samantha purposefully yawned. "Then I'm going to sleep off some sangria."

"And tomorrow?"

"I'll go by the hospital before I fly out to Washington."

"Pick you up at eight."

"Why are you doing all this?"

"Your grandfather saved me. But you were the kind one."

Still uncertain about his agenda, Samantha watched him go. After checking over the boat, she found a slip of paper and wrote a quick note, then stuck it on the side of the ship with chewing gum. The note simply said, "Sorry, I had to leave." After calling a cab, she rode past the hospital to a hotel by the airport. Once in her room, she kicked off her shoes and flipped on the TV, a luxury she hadn't done in months. Then she laid down on her stomach and looked through the documents she'd printed. *These properties. We'll need to check each one. Who's collecting the rent?*

Tomorrow, she'd meet with Robert Owens and would demand answers to questions she'd formed in her mind. *What did he know? Which side is Tarik working for? And most curiously, who are you?* Then, with her arm resting on a stack of papers, her mind turned to dreams of tunnels.

"Over here," Nadja called.

"Grandfather, which way?" she asked as he stood silently with arms crossed.

"I love you, Samantha. Take the helm girl." And just like that, he was gone.

CHAPTER 14

Nolan Hall- Washington, D.C.
  USA
  June 30, 2021

On a clear day thick with atmospheric humidity, Lieutenant Samantha Harmon stepped out of a taxi in front of Nolan Hall. She gazed at the stately building housing INSCOM, the U.S. Army's Intelligence and Security Command headquartered at Ft. Belvoir, Virginia. Standing nestled in a city plentiful with historic landmarks, its significance held a special meaning as the nation prepared to celebrate her freedom. Proud to be part of this landscape, Lt. Harmon straightened her uniform, fired a crisp salute to an approaching officer, and made her way into the red and white brick structure.

As she passed through security, a glimpse of a familiar figure changed her smile to a frown. *No, that couldn't be him. But who else has a scar like that?* Her eyes searched the hallways all the way to the Office of Counter-Intelligence, where she reported in for debriefing. Looking around the room, she stared at the emblem hanging on the wall with the words in the outer circle: United States Army Security and Intelligence Command. A lightning bolt, crossed with a torch and covered with an upside-down key, sat in the middle of the circle.

The officer sitting behind a mahogany desk looked at the new arrival and motioned to the men who'd followed her into the room. "Lieutenant, you know Mr. Owens and Tarik."

"Yes, Sir."

"Gentlemen, a few moments," Colonel Pinkston said.

The men left the room, leaving Lt. Harmon standing alone in front of the colonel. She studied the bird on his collar and noted the slight curl in his military-style crew-cut hair, which gave a bit of height to his elongated English face. *All he's missing is a monocle.*

Expecting to be offered a position in Washington, she started to sit but then immediately rose when Colonel Pinkston ordered her to remain standing. Wondering if he knew about the rental business and the bank account, her heart raced.

"I have information to provide for a course of action against the terrorist threat," she said steadfastly.

"You are way off course here, Lieutenant," the voice of Colonel Pinkston screamed as the pale of his skin took on a ruddy blush. As the rant continued, Lt. Harmon stood lost in thought as the northern lights flashed in her eyes, streaking like comets across the room. In her head, a steady voice said, "Samantha, lower the jib. Hop to it, girl, keep us on course." When the colonel got to the end of his rant, she began to refocus on his words.

"You got into a SCIF room. You made contact with a terrorist. You blew the identity of our lead agent in Talon. And worse, Lieutenant, you're taking the word of a parrot!"

"The parrot is accurate, Sir."

Her voice was so sincere, her eyes so wistful, the colonel couldn't help but lower his voice. "I, that's not how we do things here. Have a seat while I decide what to do with you."

"If I may, Sir. I'd like to be assigned to SOCOM."

"And I'd like your resignation letter on my desk right now!"

"That won't stop the terrorist event al-Qaeda is planning, Sir."

Colonel Pinkston pushed back his chair and sat looking up at his lieutenant. "You bringing up terrorists is not a reason to send you to Southern Command. SOCOM has its own problems."

"I understand that, Sir. I also know there's a focus on stopping international drug trafficking. Counter narcotics is in my area of expertise. And I think my experience in Afghanistan should count as fighting transnational crime."

"Your family IS an organized crime."

"I know, but they are mostly gone. My grandfather died last night, and Uncle Benny's funeral just happened. There's nobody left."

"You are," the colonel said.

"And I was never involved with anything illegal. My grandfather made sure of that."

The colonel tapped a pen on his desk. His fingers clenched the pen as he continued, *tap tap tap*. Finally, he told Samantha to bring the others back in. "I'm sorry for your loss," he was saying as Mr. Owens led Tarik up to the polished desk.

A row of black leather chairs bound with gold grommets stood in front of the desk. After the colonel motioned for everyone to have a seat, he eyed the men, saying, "The lieutenant here was telling me al-Qaeda is planning an attack on U.S. soil. Is this true?"

"That sounds accurate, Pinky," Mr. Owens said.

"We don't know that it's in the U.S.," Tarik said quickly.

The colonel lifted a brow bursting with white hairs and looked at Lt. Harmon. "And what did the little bird tell you?"

"There's good reason to believe al-Qaeda will hit the U.S. soon. When I interrogated Nadja Jammu, I was given a compelling reason to believe that al-Qaeda is seeking to reconstitute their organization. They have a faction in India sending the precursors for the manufacture of fentanyl across the seas to countries along our northern and southern borders, and fentanyl is making them a good bit of money. But they need more money, and in some ways, they already have it. But those assets are frozen, and they want them released."

"Assets which were frozen by Mexico," Tarik chimed in.

"At the insistence of the U.S. And without our approval, the freeze will never be lifted," Lt. Harmon said. "Mexico's Secretary of Finance would also have to get involved. His name is Jose Rivera, and it just so happens he's here now touring the U.S." She went on to outline the events in Afghanistan where talcum powder was used to test al-Qaeda's ability to spread powder during a rocket attack.

"We know about that," Colonel Pinkston said.

"Sir, I think Nadja has been playing both sides."

Mr. Owens prodded her to explain.

"The numbers just don't add up. Nadja had talcum powder put into the rockets. It is similar in molecular weight to fentanyl, but the structure is much different. The rate of particulate descent would not even be close to the same. Moisture affects fentanyl in a way that liquifies it. Talcum turns to mud. Nadja is a scientist. There's no way she didn't know about the difference."

"Maybe she didn't care. It was just a test," Tarik said.

"And maybe she didn't want al-Qaeda to have the right data."

"She brain-washed you," Tarik snarled.

"Who are you to talk to," Lt. Harmon snapped back.

"It was you on the phone." As he spoke, the look on Tarik's face was dismissive, as if having his cover blown by this woman didn't matter.

Lt. Harmon bit her nail. "What phone?"

Mr. Owens looked hurriedly between the two. "We need to focus on the problem at hand."

"I know," Lt. Harmon replied. "I already talked to a JAC in Indianapolis. As Nadja will arrive there sometime this week, they'll use her to draw out the other members of the cell."

"We don't know what they're planning. Or where," Tarik said.

"No, but Nadja does."

"There is nothing in the FBI's threat assessment to indicate any of this is true," Colonel Pinkston said.

"You need to check for updates, Sir. I just told an agent about Nadja's mother and the bank accounts she has in two different locations that I believe are being used to help Nadja and her family."

"Help them do what?" Tarik asked, now with a little more interest in his voice.

"Come to the United States to manufacture and distribute drugs along routes starting south of Mexico and transiting through the U.S. That's what Nadja's son has been doing overseas. Now they want to be here."

A discussion ensued amongst the group, talking about possible plans and events that would be of interest to a terrorist cell located within the United States. Colonel Pinkston wondered how al-Qaeda might use fentanyl in an attack if that was really part of their plan.

"It would be a large gathering in a smaller area," Mr. Owens said. "Somewhere they could get enough of a concentration in the outdoor air to cause a lot of people a big problem."

"Like a five K race," the colonel said.

"That's been done, Pinky, with a bomb."

"Or maybe a sporting event," the colonel shot back.

"Maybe a political speech," Tarik said.

The ideas kept flowing. Concerts, picnic areas, school playgrounds, nothing was off the list. Then Lt. Harmon said definitively, "A balloon festival."

"No, no way. Not going to happen." The men's conjecture as to why the hypothesis was wrong proved to be of no value. Finally, one of them asked, "Why a balloon festival?"

"The Mexican Minister of Finance will be attending a balloon festival in Indianapolis. It's at a west side park, an intercity area where they crowd a lot of people into a fairly small space."

"It still doesn't make sense," Colonel Pinkston said. "Why not just do the attack in Mexico?"

"To incapacitate everyone around him, kidnap him, and hold him for ransom," Mr. Owens replied. "The best way to get the freeze off their bank accounts so they can buy more land. They probably already have a shell company based out of Antigua. We'll need to find it."

"Al-Qaeda wants to set up an operation just south of the Mexican border," Tarik admitted. "In Guatemala."

"You have a reason why they'd want land in that particular location?" Colonel Pinkston asked.

"There's already a lot of opium production there. Some opium and fentanyl are legally sold for pain coverage in many countries. Nadja doesn't like the corporate climate in the U.S., and the chemical companies here are too male-dominated. She wants to set up her own," Mr. Owens said.

"And we know this how?" Colonel Pinkston asked.

The look on Mr. Owens' face told Samantha she was correct in placing Sasha in Nadja's cell. His words, "From a jailhouse snitch," confirmed it.

"Still, why use fentanyl? Why not just use an explosive?"

"Because Pinky, fentanyl is already killing a lot of people in the U.S. A terrorist group would like nothing more than to bring this nation to its knees. And what better way to do it than to let us know they can get to us anywhere, anytime, with a drug that's already killing us," Mr. Owens replied.

Tarik added, "And they would like nothing more than to have the U.S. go after China for the precursors they sell and to stop the Chinese influence in Mexico. They're all working together, the Chinese, the cartels and the drug dealers here in the U.S. There's a lot of money in fentanyl."

A light sweat appeared on Mr. Owens' brow. Fanning himself with a sheet of paper, he said, "China is currently being blamed for supplying all of the precursors used to manufacture fentanyl. But we know India is also in the game, and al-Qaeda has a branch there. Shutting down the Chinese would be an economic boom to the terrorist organization."

"I think Nadja originally thought she'd be part of a legitimate business if she just kept doing what al-Qaeda asked," Lt. Harmon said. Her hair swung evenly, high above her collar as she turned to look at Mr. Owens. "We actually watched as her youngest son was killed by our military."

"There's another issue," Mr. Owens said. "We'll be out of Afghanistan soon, and the Taliban will be back. They traditionally eradicate poppy fields. That leaves production wide open to other countries, so the illegal growing of poppies in Guatemala and the transport of heroin through Mexico across our southern border could become a serious cash cow for al-Qaeda." When Mr. Owens finished, his hands were clasped together across the top of his stomach. Releasing the grasp, he wiped his hands down the sides of his pants.

"What do you need?" Colonel Pinkston asked.

"Since she's already privy to our business, put Lt. Harmon on loan to the DEA."

"And help us find Dalbir Jammu," Tarik said. "Most likely, he's alive and leading this whole thing. If he's on the network, signals may be able to help locate him."

"The intel on him is slim," Colonel Pinkston said.

"That's correct, Pinky. We know he might or might not be alive," Mr. Owens said with a smile. "Whichever way it is, we need to move fast."

"Of course. She's all yours," Colonel Pinkston said.

Lt. Harmon looked at the men suspiciously. "Who's going to be my boss?"

With a smug grin, Tarik replied, "Sitting right here." After pulling a card from his pocket, he handed it to Samantha. "Give me a call tomorrow. And use this number."

"Are we done?" Colonel Pinkston asked.

"We are," Mr. Owens replied. "Call me later, Pinky. We'll have drinks while I'm in Washington."

"And dinner, on you."

"Wouldn't have it any other way, Pinky," Mr. Owens chuckled. Rising with a grunt, he led Tarik from the room, saying they were going to get the car.

Lt. Harmon started to follow, then turned and addressed her commander. "Colonel Pinkston, I was with Mr. Owens over at Bagram. I know he's a retired member of the military, but what else is he?"

"What do you mean?"

"What agency is he working for?"

A slow smile spread across the colonel's face as he shrugged and said, "As far as I know, he's just a civilian."

"So that's how we're going to keep playing it," Lt. Harmon mumbled as she turned to walk from the room. Outside, a honking horn drew her to a car parked in front of Nolan Hall.

"Lieutenant, want a ride to your hotel?"

Peering at Mr. Owens from beneath the brim of her soft cap, Lt. Harmon nodded and climbed into the passenger seat. "Sure." After map questing the address, they headed across the Potomac River while discussing the target-rich environment afforded in Washington DC and how bad it was that their own Pentagon was hit during the nine-eleven attack.

"Speaking of attacks, any word on Captain Kramer?"

Lt. Harmon looked at Mr. Owens suspiciously. "I'm sure you already know. According to his mother, he's doing well and tomorrow, they're moving him to Walter Reed. Whatever strings you pulled, thanks."

"Does that mean you'll be staying in Washington for a while?"

"I can't. We don't know exactly what day, but Nadja is coming to Indianapolis this week."

Mr. Owens nodded.

"You're not surprised to hear about this because what, you're talking to the FBI?"

"We're all on the same team."

"No, we're not. You must be one of them."

"I couldn't be, they carry Glocks. So inaccurate," Mr. Owens replied with a yawn.

"Remind me to ask Tarik for a weapon. There's a good chance I'll need one," Lt. Harmon said thoughtfully.

"You haven't been on a shooting range in what, a year?"

"Probably eight months."

"Shooting and hitting a target is much different in the field than it is on a range where everything stands still. You're not just currently unarmed, you're unpracticed."

"I used to shoot a lot. Grandfather had me do target practice all the time."

"Oh?" Mr. Owens raised a brow. "What did you shoot?"

"A harpoon."

"Funny. Speaking of your grandfather, how's he doing?"

"Rotting in hell, for all I know. He passed away last night." Lt. Harmon's face flinched under Mr. Owens' curious stare.

"My condolences. Can I take you to lunch?" he asked as he parked in front of her hotel.

"That would be nice. Be right back."

Knowing what a woman's definition of "right back" meant, Mr. Owens handed his keys to the valet and headed to the bar.

The hotel bed provided a little bounce as Samantha sat on the edge, pulled off her boots, and then laid back to stare at the ceiling. The tears she'd held back at the sight of her strong grandfather lying in a hospital bed rolled down her cheeks. Last night, Christina had called to say he would be gone before morning and, after hearing how important it was for Samantha to get to Washington, had volunteered to stay with him.

"I'm staying anyway," she'd said.

"I'll come right back after my meeting," Samantha had gratefully responded.

The second call came early that morning, telling her Captain Greg had passed at dawn. "He doesn't want a funeral," Christine sobbed. "We'll have a Celebration of Life and take his ashes out to sea."

Samantha had tearfully agreed. *Keep it together*, she told herself as she rose from the bed.

A splash of cold water revived her face. Throwing off her uniform, she donned her new dress and stood in front of the bathroom mirror, studying the blue of the fabric reflected in her eyes. For the first time in months, she felt feminine. Thirty-five minutes later, she waltzed out from the lobby.

Mr. Owens eyed her dress as she climbed in the car. "You hose down well,"

Lt. Harmon eyed him with her left brow raised. "That sounds like a compliment. By the way, I'm on leave, so you can call me Samantha."

"And you can call me Mr. Owens."

The air felt light as they sped past Mount Vernon, the plantation George Washington had called home. During the next few minutes, knowing they'd had a huge win getting the backing of INSCOM and signals intelligence, Mr. Owens said, "Maybe they'll be able to locate Nadja's husband before she gets here."

That gave Samantha an idea. "In India, he was a singer in a band. Have them sort through local bands, see who's playing."

"Interesting."

As they pulled into a parking lot attached to a long building, Samantha studied the firing range signs and asked, "Why are we here?"

"Have you ever fired a Glock?"

"I've never had a reason to fire a Glock."

"How about a forty-millimeter?"

"Never had a reason to fire one of those either. Grandfather kept a small pistol on the boat locked in a safe. He taught me to shoot, but that was a one-time thing. And you know what the military gives us."

"Well, you're going to fire one now," Mr. Owens said. As he took the weapons out of his glove compartment, his wide grin spoke of his love for firearms. The way he handled them showed his respect.

Inside the shooting gallery, they donned ear muffs and then inserted magazines into the guns. "I scored expert on the twenty-two," Samantha said.

"The range is hot, commence firing," the range master's voice rang over a speaker.

The feel of cold steel in her hand put an overlay of power into Samantha's subconsciousness. Remembering what she'd been taught, she steadied the gun in both hands and controlled her breathing, pointed the Glock at the center of the target, and gently squeezed the trigger. *Bang-bang- bang.* She fired over and over until the magazine emptied all six shots allowed by the range.

When the range was declared to be cold, Mr. Owens said, "Let's go see how you did." After walking downrange, he retrieved the paper target and brought it back to the booth, chuckling as he went.

"What?"

"You missed." When the range was declared hot again, he picked up the weapon and adjusted the sites. Pushing a button, he dropped the empty magazine and inserted another loaded with six bullets, then placed the Glock in her hand.

"Straighten out your arms," he said.

With her weight balanced evenly in high heels, Samantha pointed her arms, gazed down the sites on the gun, and fired. *Bang.* She counted three seconds. *Bang.* Three more. *Bang.* After the sixth bullet, the bolt clicked back, and she laid the gun down. This time, she walked down-range herself, grabbed the target, and carried it back to Mr. Owens.

"How'd you do?" He looked at the target and laughed. "At least you hit it once."

"Check again."

Mr. Owens brought the target up closer to his face and peered at the punctured center of the circle where he thought the sole bullet had entered the paper. "Great shot, but you only hit it once. Wait a minute," he said and noted how big the hole was. "Twice."

"I wonder where the other bullets went," Samantha said.

"Maybe in the center? Do that again."

"Okay."

Once again, with the range hot, Samantha went through the motions of shooting downrange. *Breathe, relax, aim and squeeze.* Her heel bobbled as she shot. *Bang- bang- bang.*

"You want to get it, or should I?" Mr. Owens asked.

"Go ahead," Samantha said, her face an unreadable mask.

This time, Mr. Owens carried the paper target by his side as he walked back downrange. When he reached the booth, he held it out and shook his head.

"I'm getting worse," she sighed. Indeed, the sole bullet hole perforating the paper stood just outside the circles. A hint of anger glanced across her eyes as she asked, "Why did you bring me here today? I shoot better in boots."

"You're not going to be wearing boots in the FBI. Now I don't know whether I should give you a grenade or a Glock."

"Which is why I'm not joining the FBI."

"Don't be so hard on yourself. You need to shoot the forty," Mr. Owens said.

After agreeing to try the other gun, she put a respectable shot group at the edge of the target with at least four holes sitting close together. The fifth and sixth bullets hit close to the center of the target.

"I'll frame this," Mr. Owens said. He folded the target in half and then in half again as Samantha walked outside to call Brian.

"Hey brother, it's me. I'm on Grandfather's phone."

"Oh?"

Keeping the conversation short, she described the last twenty-four hours of their grandfather's life, ending with, "He wasn't in any pain."

"I'll tell Mom," Brian said, his voice grim.

"I'm sorry she didn't get to say goodbye. I'll be back tomorrow evening, so you can get back to playing your video games at Gary's place. How's Jack?"

"That bird is weird. He keeps saying, "Free the bird.""

For the first time in days, Samantha's grey-blue eyes lit with laughter. "I told you not to let Gary around him. He's probably been playing Freebird on his guitar. I suppose he's staying at Mom's house?"

"Yup, in your room."

"He'll have cat dander on my bed!" Samantha gasped. "And I'm sure Murphy's hanging with you, so wash all the sheets in the morning before you leave."

"You intel people. Are you doing okay?"

"Yes, just keeping busy. There's news on Brad," she said quietly. "Tomorrow, he's being transported to Walter Reed Hospital here in DC."

"Really. How's he doing?"

"He's stable. Have you talked to our friend?"

"Not yet."

"Could be the time difference," Samantha said. "When we hear from Nadja, we'll contact the FBI again. Anything new at the hospital?"

"Nope, but I haven't been there yet. Been too busy watching the lube shop."

Knowing her brother was trying to solve Jenny's murder himself, Samantha admonished him to keep Detective Renfro in the loop.

"I'll take him a donut."

"Good one, brother. See you tomorrow."

Mr. Owens observed the worry in Samantha's eyes as she climbed into his car. "What kind of food do you want?"

"Mexican. Bean burritos and margaritas sound good."

"With salt. Perfect. We didn't get that at Bagram."

"They had burritos."

"I was talking about the margaritas."

"Oh."

At the restaurant, a woman at the hostess stand grabbed two menus. "Where would you like to sit?"

"In the bar," Mr. Owens replied.

"You can seat yourself."

"Great."

After choosing a high top away from the ears of other diners, Mr. Owens sat against the wall, giving himself a wide view of anyone entering the bar. Samantha perched on the stool across from him and opened a menu to observe rows of multicolored margaritas, frozen and not.

"Thanks for the firing range practice. That was fun, but I'm not allowed to carry a weapon in the civilian world," she said.

"Another reason to join the FBI. But you might want to get a gun for personal protection."

"Brian has guns over at Gary's place. I'll ask him."

"See if he has a shotgun."

"Knowing Brian, it will be some kind of Uzi."

Mr. Owens chuckled at that. "Just ask him to give you a shotgun."

"I can handle whatever Brian has!"

"You proved that today," Mr. Owens said offhandedly as he studied his menu. "But that's not the point. Weapons are not just about safety. They're about fear and power. Maybe you don't want to kill somebody, sometimes you just want to capture them, or scare them away."

"And just how exactly do I do that?"

"It's about the psychology of the gun. With a machine gun, people think they have a chance, they've seen it in the movies. But point a shotgun at someone, they know they're getting hit."

"For sure," Samantha said. "They do that in the movies."

When their waiter arrived carrying two jumbo margaritas, they ordered burritos and refried beans. While waiting for their food, she dipped a chip beneath a heap of red chunky salsa and began filling Mr. Owens in on Nadja's call. "And we're still waiting for her to call back."

"And the FBI knows about this?"

"Check your messages."

"I'm not with the FBI."

Her eyes rolled as she asked, "Did you see Captain Kramer before he was evacuated?"

Mr. Owens' eyes laughed. "I did, but I couldn't see much of him with all the bandages around his head."

"Did he say anything?"

"He was heavily medicated, so no. He took a small piece of shrapnel near his forehead. Luckily, he had his helmet on, or he might not have survived the attack."

"Thank goodness for Kevlar!"

When the burritos arrived, they dug in, hungrily devouring the stuffing made with cheese and beans. Samantha licked salt from the rim of her margarita and took a sip, then pulled her vibrating phone from her pocket.

"Hey Brian," she mumbled through the lump of food remaining in her mouth. "I'm here. What do you have?"

"Your bird flies in Saturday afternoon at one-fifteen."

"Funny. Why are you calling Nadja a bird?"

"I'm not. That parrot you were bringing back is on her way."

"What about the quarantine?"

"Chelsea was driving everybody nuts, so she's making a jailbreak."

"This is not a good time. Know anybody who wants a parrot?"

"You're not keeping Jack?"

"Not possible. I'm gone all the time."

"Hold on," Brian said. After a minute, he came back with more information. "Nadja's on her way. She'll also get here at one-fifteen on Saturday."

"You've got to be kidding!"

"Nope. See you tomorrow."

"What?" Mr. Owens asked when she returned to the table.

Taking a deep breath, Samantha said through clenched teeth, "There's a complication with Nadja's arrival. Chelsey's on the same flight."

"Want another margarita?"

"Yup." After motioning for the waiter, she excused herself to the bathroom and snuck in a quick call to Brad's mother.

"He'll arrive at Walter Reed by ten," Mrs. Kramer said.

"Thanks, see you there," she said before returning to the table where she found Mr. Owens sitting in front of three margaritas. She raised a brow.

"Tarik is on his way," he said.

"He drinks margaritas?

"Among other things."

"So you're DEA?"

"Ugh, no."

The well-defined black eyebrows on Samantha's face rose together as she stared at Mr. Owens. "There're no cows involved, but somehow I know you just have to be USDA. You're too badass for anything else." He was crying real tears when Tarik walked up to the table and stared at the two.

"We've been drinking margaritas," Samantha said.

"She said-- she's trying to guess-- oh, never mind," Mr. Owens spit out.

Tarik looked disapprovingly at the scene. "You're drinking on duty."

"Actually, I'm not on duty. I'm on leave until tomorrow." Samantha slurred out the words and hiccupped.

Tarik looked at Mr. Owens and took a sip of his own drink. "I've got the afternoon off. I have a lot of personal things to do, so tell me, what's up?"

"We all have personal things. Lt. Harmon here has to be at Walter Reed tomorrow morning by ten."

"You knew about that," Samantha exclaimed. "Why didn't you tell me?"

"Just got the text. Anyway, Captain Kramer is arriving at the hospital in the morning. There's a plane flying into Indianapolis Saturday afternoon with a person of interest," Mr. Owens said.

"Nadja?" Tarik asked.

"Yes. And one other thing, the parrot. Chelsey is also on that flight." As he relayed the news, Mr. Owen's face turned pink with laughter. Picking up his margarita glass by the stem, he licked salt from the rim before taking a sip.

Blood flowing to the skin surrounding Tarik's scar made the white tissue stand out as he laughed.

First time I'd ever seen a happy dragon. "That's not going to interfere with our plan," Samantha said. "It might even help. You know, if Chelsey sees anything, she can let us know."

A gleam of understanding crossed Tarik's face.

Mr. Owens took a sip of his margarita and placed the glass on a cardboard coaster. "The plan is to have Lt. Harmon peacefully escort Nadja and her son out of the airport, where the FBI will be waiting to take them into custody."

"What do you need from me?"

"Just make sure everyone on your team knows that if bullets start flying, don't shoot the bird. She's a cooperating witness."

Tarik sucked air through his teeth. "I'll talk to you about this in the morning." Giving Samantha a stern look, he rose to leave.

"I can't in the morning. I need to be at Walter Reed. And my grandfather passed away this morning, so I need to think about what we're going to do for him."

As Tarik walked away, Mr. Owens said quietly, "I thought you were close to your grandfather?"

"I am. I mean, I was. Why?" she asked defensively.

"You just don't seem all that broke up about it. What's happened?"

Samantha's dark curls swung forward, hiding her face. Brushing them back, she tilted her chin and stared straight ahead before tucking her phone into her purse. Mr. Owens took the purse and placed it on the other side of his chair.

"They're not that good," he said, referring to the FBI's listening capabilities.

"Maybe not." With two margaritas now under her belt, her next words slurred a little as she said, "All I can say is, it's true what they say. You just never know about somebody."

"What did your grandfather do?"

"He earned a living."

Mr. Owens nodded his understanding. "Truth overcomes all bonds."

"So they say."

"Anything I can do to help?"

"Take me back to my hotel."

"How about another margarita?"

"You too, Robert?" Samantha stood, grabbed her purse from beside the other chair, and slung it in a high arc over her shoulder.

"I just like margaritas," he said as he hurried behind the sway of Samantha's blue dress.

"I know what you're doing," she said sharply. "I don't need help with Grandfather!" Putting her fingertips to her brow, she visualized the calming waves and inhaled a deep breath. Her voice softened. "Can you give me a ride over to the hospital tomorrow?"

"Sure. Mind if we stop by Mount Vernon?"

"I've seen the house," Samantha said, remembering the day she and her adoptive parents made a trip to Washington and toured all the usual monuments.

"I hear there's a good display at the museum, and I'm buying. I'd appreciate the company." Mr. Owens looked at her so beseechingly Samantha couldn't help but agree to go.

"I guess we deserve a little downtime." Removing the top from her pink lip gloss, she applied the shimmer. "I'm ready."

To Samantha, the museum displaying the life of George Washington was more than interesting. As she observed the maps displaying the battlefields along colonial North America, she envisioned the struggles of the soldiers marching without boots, food, or the proper medications. *If they can win a war like that, so can we.*

"Come on," she said as she pulled Mr. Owens away from a life-size statue of the first President of the United States.

"Where are we going?"

"I know why I'm being investigated. We're going back to INSCOM." Standing with her shoulders squared, she made a decision and told Mr. Owens about the money.

"Your problems are not INSCOM's. Say nothing." He stared with hard eyes.

"But Colonel Pinkston thinks I'm mafia. I need to stay ahead of this!"

Mr. Owens led the way over to a corner and pointed a finger at the museum. "Guarding this country is your war. Guarding you is mine. I'll take care of the colonel."

"Who are you?" Samantha asked again.

A secretive smile crossed Mr. Owen's face as he ignored the question and walked toward the next exhibit.

Samantha wavered and made the decision that, for now, she would keep the money and the rental business separate from her work. *The FBI knows something. And why does Mr. Owens want to keep it a secret from INSCOM? When Chelsey gets here, I'm so going to interrogate that bird.*

Chapter 15

Washington, DC
  July 1, 2021

With its prominent structure located right across from a neighborhood mall, the DEA headquarters in Washington, D.C., stood out along the highway. There, the tall brick building served as the nerve center for the organization's vital mission of combating drug trafficking and enforcing controlled substance laws in the United States.

Inside the walls of the DEA, Lt. Harmon and Mr. Owens strolled through the museum located on the bottom floor. That area, open to the public, contained a wealth of knowledge concerning illegal substances, including their manufacture, distribution channels, and pamphlets one could pick up to take home for the children. While stopping at security, Lt. Harmon presented her ID. After flashing a card in the palm of his hand, Mr. Owens quickly stuffed his ID in his pocket.

"You know what keeps the director here up all night?" an employee was asking.

"Tell us," a visitor said.

"With heroin, it has a growing season. We know when it's going to most likely hit the streets. Fentanyl is different. It can be made round the clock all year long."

"The man read my brief," Lt. Harmon said as they headed to an elevator.

"You didn't invent the wheel," Mr. Owens laughed. "Are you ready for Tarik?"

"Let's get this meeting over with."

"Still feeling a little sore after yesterday?"

"My shoulders ache a little after being on the firing range. Other than that, I'm good. You were right about INSCOM," Lt. Harmon said, referring to his advice to keep her personal life private.

"The fact that you'll have two parrots is nobody else's business."

"Right. It's strange that Colonel Pinkston doesn't already know about the money. And how does the FBI not know?"

"Maybe they do. Just keep it quiet. You never know what somebody might do to chase down that kind of dough," Mr. Owens replied.

"I can't believe they're letting Mom keep the money. I'm guessing Grandfather really only turned state witness to protect it. He couldn't have gotten that kind of money legally."

"Don't touch it," Mr. Owens said. "Odds are, she owes taxes."

"What a mess. I don't even know who to trust anymore except you and my brother. It wasn't long ago I didn't trust Tarik. Still don't know if I do," Lt. Harmon replied as the elevator doors opened. "Why are you allowed up here?"

"You're working for him now."

"I know why I'm here. But who are you working for?" she asked as the elevator doors opened.

"Tarik, thanks for meeting us here," Mr. Owens said to the dark figure waiting in the hall.

"This way," Tarik said, motioning them into an office. He introduced Lt. Harmon and Mr. Owens to the agents sitting in tan leather chairs, then began the meeting. "The buzz in intel is that there could be a terrorist attack in the U.S. with the goal of kidnapping a Mexican official who froze assets owned by bad actors." He nodded toward Samantha and flashed his pearly white teeth. "Lieutenant Harmon here has proven herself to be adept at talking to-- an informant. She was a battalion tactical intel person on the ground at Bagram. Fill us in on what you have."

With all eyes pointing in her direction, Lt. Harmon began her briefing on the events at Bagram concerning al-Qaeda's goal of using fentanyl as a weapon of mass destruction.

"They performed a couple of proof of concept tests using talcum in place of the drug to validate their hypothesis that it could be put in a rocket. And though the data they've collected will not be a perfect match for what could happen if fentanyl powder was used, that doesn't matter. It won't stop them from trying to use it."

"Wow!" the man introduced as Agent Bartholomew exclaimed. "By the way, they call me Bart for short."

Samantha nodded. "We think al-Qaeda could be targeting a park in Indianapolis during a Fourth of July event. Exactly how they plan to deploy the fentanyl, we don't know yet. But there's a woman arriving soon who can possibly find out if she doesn't already know. The objective of the DEA, along with the FBI and local police, is to bring her into custody peacefully."

"And find out where they might be planning to manufacture fentanyl," Tarik said.

"Why aren't they using the fentanyl manufactured across the border?" Agent Bart asked.

"Purity. You never know what you're getting. This woman is a chemist, their chemist, who may be seeking to reunite with her husband. We think that she's planning to slip away once she's in the U.S. All the Afghans needed to manufacture drugs overseas was a cave on the side of a hill. Here, it could be a house, a warehouse, or another cave. We don't know."

"How are they getting the precursors?" Agent Bart asked.

"In the mail. They mislabel packages to get them through customs in the shipyards, then it's mailed to a local distribution point and passed through the network. The postmaster general is aware. We have SIGINT collecting intel, trying to track the distribution from the beginning to the end users over the air waves. And we have eyes on the ground," Tarik said, referring to a network of confidential informants every agency employed.

"Why not just cancel the festival?" Agent Bart asked.

"There's a lot of festivals and we don't know for sure that's the plan. The FBI is in contact with Secretary Rivera's office. A terrorist attack on U.S. soil is their baby. Our focus," Tarik said, "is to run down the drug network al-Qaeda is building and stop the manufacture and supply of fentanyl and heroin, starting with Nadja."

"I'll sniff around border security on the precursor issue," Agent Bart said.

The other agent, who finally introduced himself as Agent Franklin, said that as he was from the branch office in Indianapolis and had already been working with the police department to identify the network trafficking fentanyl into the area. "There's a Blue Wave in progress," he said, referring to the police program dedicated to capturing drug traffickers.

"We just had a family member die from heroin cut with fentanyl," Samantha said. She told everyone about the drugs that were smuggled into the jail in Indianapolis, where Jenny was incarcerated and killed.

"That's three people in your family who've died in the last few days." Mr. Owens' bushy brows scrunched as he looked at her pointedly. "You should take some time off."

Lt. Harmon shook her head. "I can't. I need to stay busy. Anyway, Nadja trusts me, and she thinks she has some control over me, so I'm the person she needs to meet at the airport."

"That is best," Tarik said quickly.

"Can we go now? I need to get to Walter Reed before my flight leaves," Lt. Harmon said impatiently.

"Of course." Tarik stood and escorted everyone to the door. Before she left, Lt. Harmon stared hard at his face. Her eyes widened.

"You're that boy!"

"What, boy?"

"The boy from the newspaper. I saw you in an article about an Afghan boy who hung out around Bagram airbase and worked his way in as an interpreter."

"Worked my way in? Before the invasion, my parents were killed by the Taliban. Like other stray dogs, I was adopted by the soldiers. And I survived just like you did."

"I'm sorry for all of our losses."

Tarik cupped her chin in his hand and pointed to the elevator where Mr. Owens stood waiting. "Go, young one."

With a flash of insight, Lt. Harmon burst out, "This explains how Nadja got my address. She called you first!" As the men stared at each other nervously, she stormed angrily from the room.

"What's on your mind?" Mr. Owens asked as they made their way to the sprawling complex known as Walter Reed National Military Medical Center.

"I'm walking in shadows, figuring out who to trust."

"You still don't trust Tarik?"

"He could have filled me in before he gave my address to Nadja. What do we know about him?"

"A former Afghan citizen who works for the DEA and has language skills. His face was scarred in the rocket attack that killed his parents," Mr. Owens said.

"Except it wasn't. The scar happened sometime after his parents were killed."

"And you know this how?"

"From a picture in the paper. His face wasn't hurt in the attack."

"Hmph. There were attacks on the base every two to three days. Could have happened anytime."

"Can I turn up the air?" Without waiting for a reply, Samantha blasted the air-conditioning, willing herself to remain calm as they pulled into the hospital lot. While picking their way across the blacktop steaming with Virginia air, Mr. Owens pulled his wallet out and checked it for currency.

"I'll wait in the cafeteria," he said as they entered the hospital. As she stepped onto the elevator, Samantha chided him to stay away from the donuts. On the fifth floor, she found Brad's parents in the waiting room.

"Hello," she said shyly. "I'm Samantha, I talked to you on the phone. Sorry, I can't stay long. I have to catch a flight."

"Of course. Hello dear," Mrs. Kramer exclaimed. "He told us about your engagement."

Mr. Kramer, a fair-haired man with striking green eyes, laid his folded newspaper on the next chair. "That was a bad business you were in, over there in Afghanistan," he said. After wiping his hand on his workman's jeans, he gripped Samantha's hand. "Brad told us about the work you did fighting the drug lords. It's just too bad we have such a problem over here." His eyes motioned to the paper. "I just saw they lost a few cadets at West Point."

"What do you mean?" Picking up the paper, Samantha read the article about three West Point cadets who went to Miami and perished after being exposed to cocaine cut with fentanyl. "I'm heading back to Indianapolis this afternoon. We just lost a family member to fentanyl." Her voice tremored as she told them about Jenny. "So young and full of light."

"Mr. and Mrs. Kramer," a red-headed nurse called from the door.

"Why don't you go back first, dear," Mrs. Kramer said kindly. "We've got all day."

"If you don't mind." The eager look on Samantha's face was more than enough reward for Brad's parents.

On their way down the hall, Samantha combed her fingers through her hair and reapplied pink gloss to her lips. She followed the nurse into Brad's room and watched as well-endowed nurse took his blood pressure; then, when the cuff was removed, his hand flopped sideways to drop onto her hip. As her smile faded, she coughed.

"Mom, Dad?" Brad asked, staring blindly toward the door.

"It's me." Samantha couldn't help it; her heart raced.

"Sam!"

"Brad," she whispered. She fell into his arms. A soft murmur escaped her lips as he pulled her close and, using his right index finger, traced the contour of her face.

"Hi, beautiful." He stared straight ahead.

She clutched his hand. "I'm a bit weathered. What are they saying about your eyes?"

The rugged lines on his face deepened. "They won't know until after surgery."

"I brought you a gift." Samantha's voice was soothing as she placed a candy in the palm of his hand.

As his thumb brushed across the smooth surface, he smiled.

"A red one, thanks. I'm glad you're here, Sam. You can help me eat and get dressed and stuff."

With a pitter-patter in her chest, she kissed the palm of his hand, then inched her way to his face and tentatively kissed his lips.

"Mm, don't stop that medicine," he said huskily.

"I had to make up for not kissing you on the tarmac," she replied teasingly. Her face flushed as she brushed a few curls back behind her ear. "Now I have a flight to catch, so I have to leave. But I'll be back as soon as I can."

When he started to protest, she explained the situation in Indianapolis with the threat of a terror attack, and with Jenny's death, and her grandfather. Rather than making her exit more tolerable, he became distraught and pulled at the bandages covering his leg. "I should be helping you!"

"Shush." Samantha grabbed his hands. "Your job is to get better. Let me go do mine. Your legs, they're both moving!"

The grim line of Brad's mouth softened into a smile. His fingers reached out to interlace with hers. "The docs revascularized my leg in Germany. We'll be dancing at our wedding," he said in a voice beginning to slur with fatigue.

"Of course we will. I love you," Samantha whispered softly.

"I love you too doll. By the way, who are you working with on this?"

"Mr. Owens is here. And you know that guy, Tarik."

"Yeah. Be careful who you trust, Samantha. I heard rumors…" His voice, now heavy with waves of exhaustion, trailed off. With a heavy sigh, his head sank back into his pillow. As Samantha rose and walked slowly to the door, the vision of the back of his hand brushing down the nurse's hip played in her mind.

"How did you know?"

"How did I know what?" he asked drowsily.

Samantha's lower jaw trembled as she gripped the edge of the door and stood with her blue-grey eyes boring into his. "That the candy was red. You can see!" With that, she stormed out of the room. Out in the waiting area, she told his parents that he'd fallen asleep. "Brad had a long flight, and he's changing time zones. I'm still a little jet-lagged myself."

"We may as well get breakfast," Mr. Kramer said.

"I'll walk down with you." As the elevator doors opened, there stood a dark-haired, olive-skinned man Samantha immediately recognized. "Tarik, hi. What are you doing here?"

"Business," he said. "We need to go."

"I, uh, these are Captain Kramer's parents. Tarik was our interpreter over in Afghanistan," she said by way of introduction.

Mrs. Kramer's face lit. "You know our son?"

As Tarik nodded, Samantha put her arm around the woman's waist and escorted her onto the elevator. On the ground floor, in the cafeteria, they found Mr. Owens with a cup of coffee in one hand and the remnants of a donut in the other. He rose when the group walked in.

Introductions were made again, followed by apologies as Samantha made her move to leave. As the men followed her through the lobby, she demanded to know, "What's this about?"

Tarik unbuttoned his suit coat and loosened the dark tie surrounding his muscled neck. "Talon. A mail carrier down along the border dropped a package today. It broke open, and he thought it looked suspicious. Sure enough, it was a precursor for fentanyl."

"Did they give you the delivery address?"

"The FBI's already watching it. The address is a PO box in southern Indiana."

"Probably wasn't the first shipment."

Mr. Owens stood back listening to the conversation and excused himself to make a phone call. When he returned, he apologized and said he'd needed to re-order his blood pressure meds. "I'll pick up my prescriptions in Indiana. We're all packed."

"You better get to Reagan. The airport will be busy this time of day," Tarik said.

"Where are you going?" Mr. Owens asked.

"To pack. I'll drive over, take about nine hours."

"Roger that," Mr. Owens said.

Before leaving, Tarik stared at the young officer who'd just visited her injured fiancé. Her grey-blue eyes looked right back into his narrowed depth of dark-brown eyes perched above high cheekbones and flinched.

"A dog will always be a dog."

As Samantha's eyes acknowledged his words, he turned and walked away. With her hand clenching the door handle, she jerked it open to sit beside Mr. Owens. "This is surreal," she commented as they passed by the Washington Monument. "Why doesn't Tarik just fly?"

"There's equipment to bring. Much easier to drive."

"Oh." Samantha understood that equipment most likely meant weapons. "What about you?"

"Checked luggage."

Her lashes swept up as she looked at him sideways.

"How's your fiancé?"

"He has both his legs. They still don't know about his eyes." *But I do!*

"Hang in there," Mr. Owens said encouragingly.

Samantha stared at the floor, then looked over to see a bulging vein in Mr. Owens' neck. Her eyes narrowed. *It looks like some kind of heart issue, but he's not taking any meds.*

"After I drop you off," he was saying as they reached the terminal, "I'll turn in the rental car while you get checked in."

"Okay. Meet you at the gate."

Inside the airport, she hurried to the ticket counter and handed over her ID. Once she'd placed her bag on the scales, she accepted her claim stub and made her way through security and followed her nose to the food court. *Food. At last!* She ordered a breaded chicken sandwich thick with pickles and ketchup, then picked up her grandfather's phone and called Brian.

"Hi, Sis. What's up?"

"I need a background report on a biker dude," she said and gave him a name. "We need our own eyes on the ground."

"Got it."

As she sat eating her sandwich, she perked her ears to the conversation at the next table. A man was talking about three people along St. Pete Beach who overdosed on drugs. "Cocaine was cut with fentanyl. People going by the apartment in the evening saw the three men sitting on the couch, looking as if they'd fallen asleep. The next morning, when the trio hadn't moved, suspicion in the neighborhood arose, and the police were called to perform a health and welfare check. When the medics came, all three men were pronounced dead. They were all just twenty years old."

They will always be twenty. This has to stop!

"I'm here," Mr. Owens said.

Samantha grabbed her purse and flung it over her shoulder as they headed to the gate.

"We are now boarding flight 2411 to Indianapolis," the gate attendant announced.

Mr. Owens checked his boarding pass and grumbled, "23A. They gave me a window seat. I asked for the aisle."

"Trade you on the plane?"

"Sure."

They walked up to 22A and watched a woman belt an animal cage to the seat. Samantha sneezed. Finally, the woman squeezed past the cat to the middle seat.

"Are you allergic to cats?" Mr. Owens asked as he stood aside to allow Samantha into aisle 23's window seat.

"*Ah-choo.* Don't worry about it. At least there's nobody in our middle seat." Before the plane ascended, she'd curled up across the seats and, in a sleepy haze, missed the rain and turbulence of the two-hour flight. "Samantha, take the wheel. I'm lowering the main. Don't be afraid to navigate these waters, girl. We'll make it through the storm." When a hand shook her awake and instructed her to prepare for landing, she grabbed her purse and was surprised to find a furry ball inside.

"Sorry." The woman in 22A reached over the seat to grab her cat, and while a seatmate held the cage open, she replaced the animal in his home. "He got away when I opened the cage to give him water."

"That's okay," Samantha said irritably. "*Achoo.*" Then she thought, "*Why is my purse open?*" Remembering that her grandfather's phone was not password protected, she pulled it out and flipped it open. *Good thing I deleted all the texts. But if Mr. Owens looked at this, he's going to know I'm making calls that might not be monitored.*

"Come on," he said as he joined the line of people exiting the plane.

Pretending to look for an item under her seat, Samantha stayed behind and texted her brother, *at the airport. Pick me up; I may need help.* Once they were off the plane, she yawned and announced that she'd be stopping at the bathroom. "I'll meet you in luggage claim."

"I'll wait here," Mr. Owens said.

She saw him stare pointedly at a young man with dark hair and olive skin, the same man who'd been seated in the row ahead of theirs. Her forehead glistened as she held her stomach. "I had a greasy breakfast. I may be a minute, so go ahead."

"Meet you at the cinnamon rolls."

Samantha shrugged and headed into the restroom. While leaning against the tiled wall, she flipped through her phone. Fifteen minutes later, she joined Mr. Owens over at the sweet shop.

"Ready?" he asked.

"Did you get me a cinnamon roll?"

"I did. But it took you so long I ate them both."

"Thanks a lot." Looking at the cashier, she held up a finger. "One, please." After being handed a pastry in a bag dripping with icing, she pulled out the gooey white mess and took a big bite. "This is so good, but now my hands are sticky. I'm going to wash up. Back in a minute."

"Bathroom again?"

"Yup." Back in the bathroom, she washed her hands and slowly dried her fingers on a paper towel before checking her phone. *Perfect. Brian's ETA- ten minutes.*

"You took so long, my bags could be in London," Mr. Owens grumbled when she returned.

"Probably. Mine too."

"Funny."

They rode down the escalator and arrived at luggage claim to find passengers from their flight huddled around a conveyor. From the collection of suitcases on the belt, Mr. Owens grabbed a black bag with an orange tag.

"Mine is blue. Can you watch for it? I'll be right back," Samantha said as she walked off.

"Where are you going now?"

"USO. I'm thirsty. Want a bottle of water?"

"Sure."

After heading into the USO located in the rear area of luggage claim, she signed in at the desk, grabbed two waters from the fridge, then walked over to a couch and watched a newscast. "An explosion in an old limestone quarry in southern Indiana is now under investigation. The blast is suspicious because the quarry had long ago been shut down," Alicia Parson from WTTV4 said. Samantha pulled out her phone and called Brian. "Where are you?"

"Out front. Hurry, security won't let me sit at the curb."

"Be right there." She slid her phone under a couch cushion and walked out of the USO, smiling. "Thanks for getting my bag," she told Mr. Owens sweetly. He tried to guide her up an escalator to the rental car area, but she insisted on going outside. "Brian's here."

"You called your brother?"

"Of course! Want a ride?"

Mr. Owens looked confused. "No. I need a rental car."

"Brian wants to talk about Grandfather's funeral."

"Okay. Call me later." Unable to say anything more, Mr. Owens trotted off to the rental car area. As she watched him go, Samantha noticed the bulge in the curve of his back. *He already got his gun out of his luggage.*

Out on the curb, she waved at a vehicle slowly creeping along passenger pickup. Then, once inside Brian's truck, she searched the curb and tensed.

"What's that on your face?" he asked.

"Icing."

"Did you bring me a cinnamon roll?"

"No. I ate it," she said while keeping her eyes on the rearview mirror.

"I should make you get out right here," Brian grumbled.

"Actually, you might want to speed up."

His foot hit the gas as he steered the truck into the next lane and shot down the exit ramp off I-70, pulled a U-turn, and took the next ramp back onto the highway in the direction from which they'd just come. Then he slowed to the speed limit and asked, "Want to tell me what this is all about?"

"You aren't even going to believe this. Mom's a multi-millionaire."

"Sure," Brian grinned. "And Gary's the king of England. So what's really up?"

With that, Samantha began filling him in on her visit to Miami and what she'd learned on Grandfather's computer. And then her visit to the DEA. "And now I'm not even sure whose side Mr. Owens is on."

Initially speechless at the news of the money, Brian finally exclaimed, "We're rich!"

"No, we're not. This money is a curse."

"A lot of people would go after that kind of money."

"Yes, and it's more than that. This whole thing with the Mexican official. He may not be the only target."

Brian's hands tightened on the wheel. "Who else?"

"Mom. The money's in her name and Uncle Benny knew about it. And if anything happens to her, you inherit it. The Mafia's in bed with the cartel network al-Qaeda is using. And Mr. Owens doesn't work for anybody, but he pops up everywhere. Something's up."

Brian frowned at the news. "What do you want to do?"

"The only thing we can do. Get Mom out of the hospital, hide her, and help Nadja get into the country and not get caught harboring a known terrorist. And then there's Chelsey."

"The bird?"

"Yes. It may help that she flies in on Nadja's flight. She could give us something, and tonight, there's a man coming in who I trust."

"Who's that?" Brian asked.

"My new boss, Tarik Ajabe. He works for drug enforcement, and I know that's real. I was with him at DEA headquarters in Washington just this morning."

"What about that guy you had me look up?"

"Cliff? What did you find out?"

"Forty-two-year-old ex-con made it through seventh grade—member of a Harley gang. Worked a series of low-level jobs, hotel desk, garbage collector, now he drives a bus. Why did you need his info?"

"He used to bring dumpsters to Grandfather's properties. Gave me his number once, in case I wanted to meet up with him."

"Why did you ask about him?"

"He was at Bear's funeral. Give me your phone, I'll send him a text."

"I don't have his number in my phone," Brian laughed.

Samantha gave him an insolent look.

"Oh yeah, you never forget a number. You know, there's only one thing we can do right now," Brian said as he handed Samantha his cell.

"What's that?"

"Shoot pool in a dive bar."

"Great." Her fingers flew over the keyboard. "Cliff wants to meet at

Bubba's. It's right over there," she said, pointing to a red and blue neon sign displaying the name "Bubba's Place."

Taking a sharp left, Brian pulled into the parking lot of the old roadhouse, a graying shack known for its pool hall.

"Standard bet," Brian said as he led the way through the door.

"Oh, you would," Samantha mumbled as she followed him into the bar. "I know what the loser gets."

"Yup," Brian grinned. "You'll be taking care of Jack."

CHAPTER 16

Indianapolis, Indiana
July 1, 2021, 5 PM

"Born to be free."

Inside Bubbas Place, Samantha's lips moved to jukebox music as she chalked up her stick and fixed her eyes on the worn green felt of a pool table. "Three balls to side pocket. This is basic geometry." Her stick flew forward, sending the cue ball into the three ball at a perfect right angle to bounce off the one ball before dropping elegantly into the side pocket. Brian's loud clapping drew the eyes of patrons sitting at the bar.

"Let me guess, that's how grandfather taught you math. And I'm guessing he taught you ounces and liters in beer language."

The merriment in Samantha's eyes matched Brian's as she called her next shot. "Eleven balls to corner pocket."

"Wrong shot," the silver-haired fox standing at the next table said. As he bent over and threw his cue forward, sending the nine ball into the side pocket, he looked at Samantha with the clear blue eyes of his Nordic ancestors and pointed at her five ball and then over at the right corner pocket. After making his next shot, he leaned his stick against the table and held out his hand. "Hello, I'm Pharmer Jim."

"Samantha." She gave the hand a firm shake. "And this is my brother, Brian. Is your farm close to here?"

"Not that kind of farm. I'm a pharmacist."

"A pharmacist! Can I ask you a few questions?" Samantha asked eagerly.

Pharmer Jim looked back over his shoulder as he picked up his stick and slid his cue forward, then he cocked an ear and listened for the ball to drop into the hole. "Did I miss?"

Plunk. The sound of a ball rolling down the ramp told everyone that, no, he didn't miss. His antics made his opponent laugh.

"Hey genius, you hit my ball in."

"That's what I was aiming for. Just helping you out since you can't hit the side of a barn."

Samantha leaned against her brother, gasping for breath. When the laughter subsided, she pulled herself up to her full height. "I'm Lieutenant Samantha Harmon," she said seriously. "And I would really like to ask you a couple of questions in private." Taking a step forward, she tripped over an animal sleeping on the floor and steadied herself by grabbing Pharmer Jim's arm.

"Woe, little lady. Watch out for my dog. Matilda, say hello."

"She's adorable!" The curly-haired mutt's tail thumped furiously as Samantha stroked her head.

After leaning his stick against a chair, Pharmer Jim walked to the next table and looked at Samantha with interest. "What can I do for you, little lady?"

"I've recently returned from Afghanistan. Did you see the last attack on Bagram where they used a white powder?"

"Yeah, my Mom's a big news junkie. They showed it a couple of times."

"Between you and me, if they had used fentanyl in those weapons, could people have gotten a strong enough dose to kill someone?"

"That's quite the question," Pharmer Jim said. His eyes narrowed as he got on his phone and started reviewing data.

"Just a ballpark guess. I know fentanyl is killing a lot of people and was just wondering, how often does that happen with aerosolized drugs?"

"Well, humans breathe four hundred and forty cubic feet of air per day. The air density of fentanyl would have to be at least twenty moles per cubic foot to be toxic. Realistically, in aerosolized form, it would disperse too much by the time it reached the ground to do any real damage, especially if there's any wind or high humidity."

"What about in a building?"

"Public buildings nowadays use HEPA filters to prevent that."

"Which is why most fentanyl overdose cases are from oral ingestion. Thanks, you've been a big help."

"Any time, little lady." Pharmer Jim tilted his hat and returned to his table.

Seeing the configuration of balls Brian left after his last shot, Samantha asked, "Can we get out of here now?"

"Afraid of getting beat?"

She studied the table. Pharmer Jim came over and hit the base of the cue ball, skipping it over the top of the black eight to hit the yellow ball, which went straight into the pocket. Then he turned and went back to his table.

"It's still my turn," Samantha laughed.

"No it's not. It's my turn," Brian said and grabbed the stick from Samantha's hand. "You had help." Nonchalantly, he walked up to the table, tried to sink the eight ball into the side pocket and missed, but the cue ball continued on its path to sink into the far pocket.

"I win. You scratched," Samantha yelled as she threw her arm in the air and high-fived Pharmer Jim.

Brian stared at a pack of Harley riders filing into the bar and noted that one of them seemed especially interested in his sister. Following them was a thick man dressed in a tan suit paired with a purple tie who walked over to sit at the opposite end of the bar and sat observing the room.

Harry Trot.

Samantha leaned forward, allowing her black curls to swing across her forehead. "Hit the bathroom, then go out the back door," she hissed through clenched teeth. "I'll make my own way out of here." Before her brother could argue, she walked up to one of the nearby leather-clad figures and gave him a big hug. "Cliff, nice to see you."

"Good to see you too, doll."

"How's your dog doing?"

"Chewed some guy's leg off yesterday. He's still picking the bones out of his teeth. Other than that, he's good."

"Your bike's riding well?"

"Perfect condition."

"Any chance you could give me a quick ride? Just up and down the street. I haven't been on a Harley in, like, two years."

"For you, of course."

With pink gloss freshly lining her lips, Samantha wrapped her hand around Cliff's bulging bicep and walked outside. "Actually, I need a ride to the airport. That okay?"

"You need me to take care of some guy in there?"

"No, just get me out of here. I'm with the military, and I'm on a case. I'd really appreciate the help," she said. With her grey-blue eyes flirting with his muzzled stare, she smiled and grabbed a helmet from his bike.

"Sure babe. Hang on tight."

Samantha's muscled leg went over the seat. After tightening her helmet, she clung to Cliff's waist. "Stop there," she said, pointing to Brian's truck.

As Cliff gunned the engine and pulled to the end of the lot, Brian sauntered from the corner of Bubba's Place, seemingly in no hurry to leave. His eyes narrowed as he stared at his sister on a Harley.

"Meet us at the airport," her steely voice said, her eyes not so sure. "But if you're followed, go somewhere else, and I'll call you."

"Got it."

As Cliff gunned the engine and pulled a sharp U-Turn, Samantha clung to his waist. "Go to passenger pickup," she hollered once they'd reached the airport.

"Hang on," Cliff yelled. Swinging to the next lane, he abruptly stopped.

"Can you wait here? I left my phone in the USO. Be right back."

"I've got you."

After running in to grab the phone she'd left on a couch, Samantha exited the terminal to find Cliff winking at a security guard. From the palm of his hand, he flashed an I.D. and stroked his beard. She threw her lean, muscled leg over the back and climbed behind him.

"Thanks for your help, officer," he said respectfully. With a twist of the handlebars, he gunned the engine and roared out of the parking area while the open-mouthed security officer put her phone back in her pocket. "Where to next, little lady?" he asked when they stopped at a gas station.

"Can I use your phone? My battery's dead."

After putting in his password, Cliff handed over his phone before refueling the bike.

"Brian, it's me. Where are you?"

"Just lost that dude in a suit," he exclaimed, sounding out of breath.

"Mom's probably safest in the hospital. When is Jenny's funeral?"

"Tomorrow, at ten."

"I can't talk right now. Lay low. Go back to Gary's and find out if he has any information about the layout of the airport. Pick me up at eight, that will seem natural to anyone watching."

"Okay, Sis. Watch your back. Where are you going now?"

"Jack's probably missing me, so I'll sleep at the house tonight. Did you leave a shotgun?"

"Roger that. Who's that guy you're with?"

"Cliff. The guy you looked up who hauled dumpsters to Grandfather's properties."

"Careful there, you could wind up in one."

"I'm alright," Samantha said with a laugh. "Talk to you later."

"Call me when you get home," Brian said stiffly as he rang off.

Cliff threw his leg up and around his seat, as he regained his perch. Samantha resumed her position and asked to be taken to her house. "Then I'm going to need a ride down to southern Indiana. Feel like taking a road trip?"

"Perfect weather for it," Cliff responded. He fired up the Harley and turned right out of the parking lot. Soon they were on I-465, heading over to the old Victorian house Samantha currently called home.

"Right there," she said, pointing to a blue-green structure with a white wrap-around porch.

In one of the windows, Jack sat calling to passersby on the street. "Blow me shivers. It's four o'clock."

"I know that bird," Cliff laughed.

"I think your motorcycle woke him up." Samantha slapped a hand on her forehead. "My suitcase, I left it in Brian's truck."

"Can't he drop it off?"

"Not today. I'll be ready to leave again in a minute. I just have to feed Jack and make a quick call. Want something to drink?"

"Got any lemonade?" Cliff asked as they entered the house.

"Of course."

"I remember your lemonade, it's the best!" Peering into the next room, he edged past the door and stopped. "There's a hairball in here!"

"What?" Samantha found the object of Cliff's comment in Jack's room, a big fur-ball with the only visible thing on the creature's face being a green feather protruding from his teeth. "Thor! What are you doing here?"

"Marauders!" Jack screamed.

Samantha grabbed her phone and called Brian. "Gary left his cat."

"We'll drop by in an hour."

"Okay, but I'll be gone. Watch your back, and can you leave my suitcase?"

"It's in my truck."

"I thought your phone was dead," Cliff said as she hung up.

"Almost, I just have one bar. Excuse me while I call my office."

Cliff nodded as he went to play with Thor. "Nice kitty. Want a treat?"

"Man overboard," Jack whistled.

Leaving Cliff to the menagerie, Samantha walked outside and called Mr. Owens.

"What was all that at the airport?" he asked.

"Sorry, my brother and I have a lot of family business between Jenny's death and Mom being in the psych facility. I accidentally left my phone in the USO and got all the way home when I remembered it, so we had to go back," Samantha said evenly.

"You've had quite a day," Mr. Owens said.

"Yes. I'm pretty tired. I think I'll take a nap until Tarik gets here. By the way, do you know anything about the explosion in southern Indiana?"

"I saw that. Word is, there were some old detonators at a mining site. They blew when a little water hit the sugar coating."

Samantha's left cheek flinched as she bit a nail. "Hmm."

"Will your mother be going to Jenny's funeral?"

"I don't know if she's ready to go outside."

"But I thought you said she would want to go."

"It's out of my control. Brian will decide that himself."

"I understand. Get your nap and call me when you wake up."

"Will do." *Click*. She walked back inside, yelling, "Ready to go?"

"Get me out of here!"

Samantha rounded the corner and laughed at the site of a muscular man with tattooed arms backed into a corner by an angry cat. "Thor, come here." The creature's fur relaxed as his claws receded into his paws. With one last yowl, he strutted over and wrapped himself around her leg.

Cliff groaned and held out an arm to display three angry red scratches. "Got any peroxide?"

"What did you do?"

"I just tried to take the feather out of his mouth. That cat's a maniac."

"Yup."

As he edged his way around Thor, Cliff kept pressure on a spot oozing with blood, complaining all the while about the scar that might mess up his snake tattoo. "It's going to look like a tree."

Samantha surveyed the arm. While Cliff sat at the kitchen table with his arm extended over the roses, she cleaned the scratches and put a Band-Aid over a spot that seemed especially deep. Then she said softly, "I know you're an undercover cop. Let's keep that between ourselves."

"How?"

"I'm military intelligence. I'm the brain, you're the muscle. Let's go." Her grey-blue eyes sent a clear message. As they looked up, pleading for cooperation, she crossed her legs and smiled.

"Where are we going?" Cliff asked.

"We need to visit an old limestone quarry south of Bloomington."

"I love a road trip," Cliff replied. "Come on, babe, let's go. You packing?"

"You know it."

State Road 37 took them south to Bloomington. As they passed under a canopy of Indiana forest, Cliff swatted bugs from his visor and gunned the engine. At a do-it-yourself car wash, he turned the bike right, headed down a winding country road to an area rife with old limestone quarry works, and stopped when Samantha poked him on the shoulder.

"Here."

As the motorcycle pulled over alongside the road, the remnants of limestone cut into blocks were barely visible through the leaves of overgrown trees,

"This is it," Samantha said. Ignoring the NO TRESPASSING sign, she ducked under a rusted wire and slipped through red mud to climb partway up a hill. Down below, she saw a woman run out of an abandoned mine to grab the arm of a dark-haired child. *Snap.* Her heart raced as a twig snapped beneath the weight of a foot. *That's not Cliff. He crossed to the other side of the road to use a tree.* Quickly, she dropped her pants and began to urinate on a rock.

"What are you doing here?"

Samantha stood and nonchalantly pulled up her pants. Behind her, a dark-haired man with olive skin matching the foreign accent she recognized as being similar to that of Afghanistan stood waiting for a reply.

"Just had to use the bathroom. Do you mind?"

"Didn't you read the sign? This is a no-trespassing area. I should call the cops."

"And maybe I should call MSHA. I'm sure the Mining Safety and Health Administration wouldn't approve of anyone being in that old mine shaft," Cliff said as he approached with the glint of cold steel in his hand.

"It's not in use," the man protested. "Our dog got away and ran into those rocks. I just don't want anybody to get hurt."

"Thank you for your concern. I couldn't make it to a bathroom," Samantha replied while buttoning her pants. "Good luck with your dog. We're going now."

The man nodded toward the Harley. With shoes caked in red mud, Samantha turned and slid back down the hill to the road. A clod of red mud flew from her foot as she flung it over the back of the motorcycle and grabbed onto Cliff's waist. Flipping a quick wave, he grabbed her knee and squeezed before gunning the engine to roar up a hill. Once they'd rounded a bend, he stopped again by the road.

The saddle bags on the bike held a special object Cliff kept for these situations. After Samantha climbed off the bike, she watched him pull a drone from its hiding place.

"This baby has a camera. Let's see what they're really doing in that quarry," he said. Soon, the drone rose above the trees, guided by the control in Cliff's hand. With a gasp, Samantha looked at the video the drone sent to Cliff's phone.

"Bring it home," she said.

"You know those people?"

"Not the kids or some of the adults. But a couple of them I know are in a band. And that guy was a passenger on my flight today. And those other two, they're supposed to be FBI agents."

"Supposed to be?" Cliff's raised brow met the edge of his bald scalp as he climbed onto his bike and looked backward.

"Those guys came to my house with a laptop they got from my grandfather. They needed the password to break into it. Wait, who's that?" she asked as she studied a photo. The wide girth of a man hiking up the other side of the hill was more than a bit recognizable to her, even from the back. *Mr. Owens!*

Hearing Samantha gasp, Cliff asked, "What's wrong?"

"Never trust anybody. I'm going to guess those two FBI guys used to be in the military unit of a man I know. That man."

"Meaning what?"

"Just a minute." *Tarik has to be in Ohio by now.* She dialed a number and was relieved when a familiar voice answered the phone.

"Hello," Tarik said.

"Hi, it's Lieutenant Harmon. I'm in southern Indiana investigating a blast."

"And why are you doing that?"

"It was at a mine that is supposed to be closed, and I was just trying to think of a place a terrorist cell might use to practice. That's when I saw the story about the blast, and you know, in Afghanistan, blasts go with terrorists. Anyway, Nadja's husband is here, in a cave. And the woman he played with in a band. And some kids. And two guys who are pretending to be FBI agents, unless they really are. And Mr. Owens is spying on all of it."

"He's supposed to be there. You're not," Tarik exploded.

Samantha pulled the phone a few inches from her ear and grimaced before mouthing to Cliff, "My boss." He nodded and pointed at the road.

"Lieutenant?" Tarik's voice said after a moment of silence.

"I'm doing my job. We're supposed to be finding the site where they're manufacturing fentanyl. Do you have the name and address of the P.O. box owner where those fentanyl precursors were being sent?"

After a slight pause, Tarik said irritably, "Don't even think about interfering with that part of the investigation. You're just supposed to bring in Nadja."

"Tomorrow, we are burying my aunt's foster daughter. Her name was Jenny. I'm going to interfere until we get answers," Samantha replied hotly.

"Lieutenant, you're not in charge here."

"And you're not here. We'll just drive past the property, that's all."

"We?"

"Me and an undercover police officer. I've known him for years. He knows about Talon."

"No! You can't just bring in anybody you want on this."

"I'm on leave until tomorrow. Anyway, he's already part of it. He's been investigating my family for a long time. I'm just giving him a little help. Maybe I'll just go knock on every shack around here, because I'm sure that's where it is."

"Don't even think about it!"

"You know they're storing those precursors in that cave. But they can't set up a lab there because it's not well enough ventilated. So what's the address?"

After fuming for a bit, Tarik pulled over and gave Samantha the address of a nearby property. While putting it into her GPS, she asked him not to tell Mr. Owens about her visit.

"And why not?"

"Because he's got some kind of agenda we're not privy to. It's weird, all the Afghan-looking kids around here."

"Thus, the FBI. They're tracking down the location of a terrorist cell. That's their job."

"Those aren't all al-Qaeda people in the cave. Some of them are just kids, and the casino at French Lick is not that far away. You know what al-Qaeda did before they attacked the Twin Towers?"

Lt. Harmon's question was met with a whisper of anger. "They went to Vegas. Just drive past the house and get back to Indianapolis," Tarik said before abruptly hanging up.

"We may not be able to see anything," Cliff said upon hearing of what they were about to do. "Some of these properties sit way back in the woods."

"Which is likely why my boss gave me the address. He doesn't know about the drone, so don't tell anybody."

A wicked smile crossed Cliff's face as he gunned the engine. Soon, the motorcycle rolled past a mailbox carved into the shape of a cow displaying the address. The box itself sat along a rugged, gravel road that curved into the shadows of the woods. Cliff continued slightly farther down the main road and waited while the drone once again flew overhead to provide surveillance video.

"It's hard to tell," Samantha said. "The windows are all open, but it is July."

"That's a pretty ugly lime-green color in the kitchen."

"Flowery wallpaper in the bedroom. This place is old."

"Old places like this may not have air conditioning."

"Wait, what's that out back?"

"Some kind of covered patio. Sure is big, maybe a party area?"

"Or an outdoor kitchen. Can you get closer?" Samantha asked.

Before Cliff could fly the drone in for a closer look, a man holding a shotgun appeared at the back door. The white cloth wrapped around his head partly covered his identity, but when he looked up, Samantha recognized the man from his picture. "Badhai Kahn. We have to get out of here!"

Cliff retrieved his drone and, as the sound of a vehicle approaching their location drew near, hopped on the Harley. He leaned slightly backward as Samantha thrust her foot over the seat, then fired up the engine and sped down the road. Just before reaching the highway, he pulled into a gravel lot and parked amongst a row of motorcycles lining the front of a bar. "The best place to hide a motorcycle is out in the open," he chuckled. "Want a beer?" Without waiting for a response, he reached back and lifted Samantha off the bike.

With her grey-blue eyes lit, she followed him into the bar.

Inside the dimly lit saloon, the Rough Riders, a sleeve-tattooed leather-clad gang, sat along the polished bar, each in their usual spot. When Cliff pulled out the chair furthest to the left, a man everyone called Tiny pushed his stool back and yelled at the new arrivals, "That chair is reserved."

"How about I take it," Samantha said with a pretty little smile as her grey-blue eyes met the chiseled chest of the pony-tailed man. With her hands on her hips, she looked up at him with only sass as her shield, daring him to rebel. "We won't be here that long."

"Sit down, Tiny," a man later identified as Rebel said. "Grainger is not coming back."

"I'm sorry, what are we missing?" Cliff asked as everyone stared at Tiny.

"She your new girlfriend?" the bartender asked as he slid two mugs of beer down the bar. Putting out a hand, Cliff caught one, leaving the other for Samantha.

"I'm Samantha. We just got engaged on his Harley. Drinks are on him," she said sweetly. Everyone cheered as she caught the other beer.

Cliff threw his muscled bicep around Samantha's shoulders and pulled her close, landing a big kiss on her head. "I forgot my wallet. You'll have to get this, honey."

The bar erupted with laughter. Eventually, the bartender walked down to stand in front of Cliff and folded his arms across the bar. "You heard what that fentanyl shit did to Grainger?"

"No. What?"

"He got some bad meth. OD'd yesterday. Took his wife with him."

"Any idea where he got a hold of it?" Cliff asked quietly. He looked down the row of bikers and sniffed, a sign he might be looking for drugs to inhale up his already damaged nose.

"I'm not sure, but word is there's a new cook around here. Be careful."

"Gotcha." Cliff turned to look at Samantha and said, "We're not going to be partying around here, babe. Let's go start the honeymoon."

Much to the delight of the bikers, she chugged her beer, hopped off her stool and said, "Okay, babe. I left my purse out on the bike, but I found your wallet. It's chained to your back pocket." Then she strode out of the building and waited.

Cliff soon followed and threw his arm around her neck. "You owe me."

"Anytime."

The ride back to Indianapolis was uneventful. Samantha smiled as she leaned back into her seat, enjoying the wind whistling past her head on the clear July night. Upon reaching the house, she asked Cliff to wait while she checked inside. "Never know who's going to show up around here."

"I'll walk you in."

Too tired to argue, Samantha allowed him to go in first. The sounds of squawking from a nearby room drew him further into the house. Cliff pulled his gun, and they edged around the corner to find the emerald-colored parrot hopping around excitedly on the perch. Thor was gone, but a spot of red mud sat beside a suitcase.

Samantha stared into Jack's cage. "Who did you have here besides Brian?"

Squawk. Jack stared back with dreamy eyes.

"Mr. Owens. He must have told Jack about Chelsey." Knowing the parrot would be thirsty after a long day alone in his cage, she went back to the kitchen for some water.

"Come on, man," he whistled after her.

"It's going to be like this all night. He's missing Grandfather."

"How about I camp on your couch?" Cliff asked, eyeing the overstuffed suede couch in the living room.

"If you can take it. Just don't let him out of the cage."

"Come on, man."

"Shut up, Jack," Cliff yelled.

"You know where the beer is. Have fun, you two."

"Love you," Jack said softly.

"Well, that's a new one." Samantha looked approvingly at the parrot. Upstairs, as the sound of the TV echoed in the halls, she fell into bed fully clothed and had one last conscious thought. She called Tarik. "I know why they want Nadja in Indiana. Her son's already here, and he's been practicing on the local population. He's killing people. They need a better cook."

Unseen by Samantha, Tarik's eyes glittered black as he said, "Good work, Lieutenant. See you tomorrow.

CHAPTER 17

Indianapolis, Indiana
July 2, 2021

TV lights flashing in the McFadden living room brightened and dimmed against the walls as the Channel 4 news anchor proclaimed, "All American troops are pulling out of Bagram Airforce Base right now, leaving behind just one thing, a piece of the World Trade Center U.S. forces buried twenty years ago. The pullout brings an effective close to the longest-running war in U.S. history."

Samantha's foot flew onto the couch. "Wake up."

Cliff's eyes snapped open. "What's going on?"

"This is what Mr. Owens was talking about. All of our troops are leaving Bagram."

"A complete pullout?"

"Yes. Completely."

With the cameras continuing to roll, the nation watched as soldiers hunched under the weight of full packs walked silently toward an aircraft. "Tragically, many Afghan citizens who helped the U.S. during the war are being left behind," the announcer continued in a methodical rhythm.

"I guess it's good they'll be fighting for their own country now," Samantha said.

"Keep in mind, we don't know who's going to be in charge," Cliff said with a yawn.

Samantha's grey-blue eyes widened. "What do you mean?"

"The Afghans will be fighting off the Taliban all by themselves. I doubt they'll hold out, and when the Taliban take over, people will die. Why are you holding a shotgun? You going to fight the Taliban with that?"

"My guard was asleep. Didn't you see the headlights that kept going past the house?"

"I think cars usually have those on at night," Cliff responded. Though his words were joking, his voice was serious as he grabbed the shotgun from Samantha. "You're going to scare Jack."

Before she could respond, a key rattled in the front door. Cliff pulled her to the floor and, after pumping a round into the chamber, aimed at the young men entering the room and screamed, "On the ground, now. Both of you!"

"Stand down," Samantha yelled as she rose and brushed off her clothes. "You remember my brother, and this is his friend, Gary."

"That's my shotgun," Brian said as he grabbed the gun from Cliff's hands.

"Sorry," Cliff muttered, his eyes flashing anything but an apology. "She was just telling me about people casing the house last night. I got a little carried away."

Brian looked questioningly at Samantha. "Got any coffee?"

"I put a pot on," she said. Her eyes, angry and unforgiving, pointed in Cliff's direction. "This is Cliff, my guard." With a fluff of the skirt on her black funeral dress, she picked her way across the living room floor to walk barefoot into the kitchen and called, "Come on in. I'll make eggs."

"Just go for the toast," Brian said loudly as the men followed behind.

"I heard that."

Gary walked around the corner to Jack's cage and found the emerald parrot lying on his back. "What's wrong with Jack?"

"He's just playing dead. Jack, all clear," Samantha called to the bird. Magically, Jack rose from the dead and hopped back onto his perch. Roaring with laughter at the bird's antics, Cliff sat at the table and looked at Brian's long face.

"What's wrong with you?" he asked.

"I'm sure you know we have a funeral to attend."

Cliff's expression immediately became sympathetic. "Sorry, man. You guys have a lot going on."

"Yeah, and we have to leave in ten minutes."

Samantha poured coffee into three cups and placed them around the table. She placed a glass of milk in front of Gary.

"Any word on Brad this morning?" Brian asked.

With a softening of her voice, Samantha replied, "His mom says he's a little better. They're starting physical therapy today."

"Who's Brad?" Cliff asked.

"Her fiancé," Brian said.

"Oh."

Ignoring the comments, Samantha spooned cereal from the bottom of a bowl and crunched on a mouthful of cornflakes. When Brian objected having Cliff in the room, she replied, "It's okay, he's undercover. I told him about Talon, and I think that we may need an extra gun today." She looked at Gary. "You got anything for us?"

"Well, actually, yes." His pale, angled features shone in the kitchen light. "One of the engineers left a program open while he used the bathroom. I've got pictures of a schematic of the airport and pic's of a computer program showing something about how they detect underground noise."

"Wow," Cliff said.

"According to the plans, before the airport was built, there was a building on the property that had a long underground tunnel used to move alcohol during prohibition. It was closed off by a basement wall in terminal one."

"I don't see how this helps anything," Samantha said. "Even if we could get behind the wall, the tunnel has probably caved in. Remember the story about the cow's leg? I doubt that it's ever been repaired, so we'll need to get Nadja out some other way. I've set something up with a federal task force. There's a plan."

"A plan. What plan, sis?"

Samantha rinsed her bowl under the faucet and shook out the water. She dried the bowl, then placed it on the second shelf in the cupboard. With her dish put away, she took a seat across from the men before replying, "I'll get her down the stairs to the tarmac. From there, Agent Vargas will take her out of a gate in the fence. If al-Qaeda has anyone waiting inside the terminal, which we're assuming they will, they'll have a long wait." She went on to tell Brian about Nadja's family already being in Indiana and had Cliff show him the video taken by the drone.

As he leaned forward to get a better view, Brian zeroed in on a rusty blue truck parked beside the shack. "I know that truck. That's the one going in for a lot of oil changes."

"Delivering drugs from the underbelly," Cliff surmised.

Samantha tilted her head and asked Gary about the staff at the airport. What were their demographics? Any middle-eastern men handling baggage? Any weird people beside you on the cleaning crew?

"Heh heh," Gary laughed. "There's a guy on the baggage crew who's a little scary."

"And knowing you, maybe you've checked out the spot where the tunnel could possibly open into the airport?"

Brian studied the diagram on the picture. "There's a drainage grate outside by terminal one that might connect to something."

"It could. I saw a guy pull his luggage dolly over there. Then he got out and reorganized a few bags before he moved over to the conveyor belt."

"Did he mess with the grate?" Brian asked.

"I don't know dude. His cart was blocking my view."

"Bingo," Jack called.

Everyone but Samantha laughed. "I agree with Jack. Nadja trusts me, which is why I'll be delivering her into the hands of the FBI. Whatever you're planning, I can't be involved." While staring at her brother, she carried her cup over to the sink and stood with her back to the group. Then she checked her texts and grimaced. "Tarik and Mr. Olsen are coming to Jenny's funeral. Guess they're keeping an eye on me until we pick up Nadja."

"At least we'll know where they are, too," Brian said. "Just bring Nadja downstairs like you planned."

"What about Mom?"

"It's too risky for her to be outside the hospital. Better to keep her inside. Gary and I will be hanging around when Nadja gets off the plane."

"Me too," Cliff said. "I'll mosey over to the airport after the funeral."

"Speaking of the funeral, we better get to the church," Samantha said. After telling everyone to leave the TV on for Jack, she put a hand on Brian's elbow and prodded him toward the door. He put an arm around her shoulders, and together, decked in black funeral clothes, they walked to the truck.

Gary looked at the coffee rings on the roses and took an extra second to wipe them away while listening to the repeat broadcast about the U.S. withdrawal from Bagram. "What! We're out of Afghanistan?" he yelled as he ran out the door.

"As of today, yes. See you at the funeral," Brian yelled back.

On the east side of Indianapolis, the spires of the Catholic church reached toward the heavens, seemingly soliciting God to end the scourge of drugs taking the lives of so many young people, or so the locals said. Still, the funerals kept coming. This day was like all the rest. As the mourners poured into the church, nineteen candles flickered on the altar, one lit for every year of Jenny's life. Nineteen flames looked like a lot, but in human years, there weren't nearly enough.

Inside the church, organ music played Amazing Grace as Brian and Samantha tip-toed their way up to the family pew to sit beside their aunt Diana. With massive tears spilling down her cheeks, she threw her arms around Brian and wept. The site of Jenny's pink casket covered with a splay of baby-pink roses sitting across the front aisle brought more heart-wrenching sobs from the congregation as Diana's cries echoed throughout the church. Soon, Brian's sniffles became more audible. Hunching down in the pew, he gasped for breath while Samantha's back remained rigid.

"I'm sorry for your loss," she said. Timidly, she patted Diana on the shoulder and handed her a tissue.

"Thank you both for coming. We need our young people," Diana sobbed.

As the notes of one song flowed into the next, the organist played a melody, "Ave Maria, gratia plena, Dominus tecum," bringing everyone to fresh tears. Then, the chaplain began the eulogy, emphasizing the importance of love, compassion, and the profound mystery of life and death. He spoke of Jenny, a young life lost too soon. She was a daughter, a friend, a family member, and tragically had a child on the way, another life lost. She was a friend to many, always ready to help. "Jenny represents every young woman with hopes and dreams of being a mother whose life was cut short," he said and urged the congregation to have strength in their faith and to come together to fight the drug crisis.

"Amen," someone called.

"Yay though I walk through the shadow of the valley of death, I shall fear no evil," he recited from Psalm 23.4.

When the organ played the last song, Brian rose and met five other men, all meeting at Jenny's side to act as pallbearers. After carrying the casket out of the church, they loaded it onto the hearse. A police escort paved the way for the procession of cars bearing funeral flags making their way down the neighborhood streets toward the graveyard. At an intersection, the procession stopped as sirens blaring from fire trucks gave them the right of passage.

"It looks like a group of motorcycle riders has joined us," Diana said.

Looking at the lead rider cloaked in a black leather vest with a red kerchief tied around his head, Samantha replied, "No worries. They're our friends."

"It's the neighborhood Fourth of July parade," Diana said as they watched a series of floats follow the fire truck.

Breathing rapidly, Samantha checked her watch and said they weren't going to have much time to stay at the graveyard.

"Yeah, we actually do," Brian said. "Gary just texted me. All flights are on a two hour delay."

"All of them?"

"There was a bird strike after a plane took off. One of its engines caught fire, and it had to return to the airstrip, so the runways are closed down."

The back of Diana's black jacket wrinkled under the July heat as she relaxed into her seat. Their car pulled forward, and they were on their way, following the hearse to the graveyard. As they gained entrance to the area where a fresh pile of dirt stood waiting beside an open grave, Brian's body started to shake. "I can't do this part."

"There's just a prayer and the rosary," Diana said.

"I can't." With that, Brian flung open the door and threw the truck keys to Samantha. He then walked back to Gary's vehicle, yelling, "See you at the airport." The roar of Harley motorcycles followed Gary's departure from the graveyard.

Samantha shifted uncomfortably as she found herself alone with Diana. "I didn't know Jenny was pregnant. I met her once, on our boat, when she was thirteen. I liked her."

"Brian told me about your grandfather. I'm so sorry."

"At least he got to be old."

Friends, teachers, and community members all stood circling the grave. With a string of blue beads hanging from her own fingers, Diana handed a pink rosary to Samantha, then they knelt and prayed together. "Hail Mary, full of grace…"

Mary, another mother who lost her son. Samantha rose and stood steady on her heels as, one by one, her fingers felt each bead of the rosary. When the graveside service came to a conclusion, she said, "Sorry, I can't stay. I have to go to work." Her downcast eyes stared at the coffin as her fingers reached out and stroked the soft pink of a rose petal before absentmindedly snapping the flower off the arrangement. Silently, she twirled it in her fingers, intermixing the stem with the rosary.

"How will you get back?" Diana asked. The petit, teary-eyed woman looked lost as she threw her arms around Samantha. Her eyes grew big when a tall man with a facial scar resembling a dragon walked up and asked if she was ready to go.

"I'll be taking my brother's truck," Samantha replied breathlessly. After releasing herself from Diana's arms, she turned and clicked away in her heels, stumbling along behind Tarik. "Where is Mr. Owens?"

"In the car."

"Neither of you can go past security at the airport. There's an off chance Nadja will recognize you."

"We know that. Owens will be down by luggage claim. Agent Vargas and her team will be in the terminal, and my team will be outside."

"Okay, see you at the airport. I have to change and get Brian's truck from the church."

Tarik looked at Samantha's black funeral dress. "I like what you're wearing."

Suddenly, at a loss for words, her face flushed. Finally, she muttered, "Nobody catches terrorists in heels," before walking over to a motorcycle occupied by a muscular, tattooed man and once again threw her lean, muscled leg over the back seat. She nodded at Cliff. "My cousin."

Tarik's lips pressed into a flat line. "We'll meet you at your house." His words, lost to the roar of the motorcycle, went unacknowledged.

With the rosary protecting her from the thorns, Samantha clutched the pink rose firmly in one fist as she wrapped an arm around Cliff's middle to enjoy the winds of freedom blowing through her hair. With it being less than half a mile to the church, she'd decided to go without a helmet. Thus, Cliff made his way slowly down the city streets, where he found Brian's truck parked along the curb.

"Thanks," Samantha said. Lifting a leg off the back seat, she caught her heel.

"Woe there, little lady." Cliff steadied her. "Your eyes are dark. Did you get any sleep last night?"

"Not much. I woke up early to go over some leases I printed from Grandfather's computer. My name is signed for them, and I don't even know who's living in these buildings. I've got a few hours. Think I'll check out a couple on my way to the airport."

After Cliff said that he would follow her, she gave him an address.

"Let me do a drive-by first," he said. "I'll case the place."

"Great!"

The Fountain Square neighborhood in southern Indianapolis seemed a favorite place for her grandfather to do business. Samantha found the first address near a duckpin bowling alley and, as Cliff watched, knocked on the door.

"Hola," a Hispanic woman said, standing with the door half cracked. The squeals of children resonated from upstairs. "No English."

"I'm Samantha Harmon, apparently your landlord." Samantha held out a copy of the lease and pointed to the occupants' signature. "Carlita, is this you?"

As the woman stared at the document, a look of fear crossed her face. "Pablo," she yelled. A child appeared at her elbow and said, "Hello" to Samantha in English.

"Hello," she said back. "Do you speak English?"

"Si, yes."

"Where are you from?"

"Guatemala, but here now."

"I'm Samantha, it's very nice to meet you. My grandfather died. Captain Greg. Did you know him?"

The boy spoke to his mother who gasped, "El abuelo es muerte?" With a hand over her mouth, she grabbed the boy's shirt, pulled him back and started to close the door, but Cliff's foot intervened. He said something in Spanish to the woman as his eyes demanded an answer and received one in a long, rapid-fire Hispanic response.

"She says the captain brought them over on his boat. They became refugees after her brother and his son were killed by the cartels."

"Ask her about the rent. How does she pay it?"

Cliff repeated the question. At that, Carlita said they didn't have to pay rent. The captain just let them live there.

"Don't worry," Samantha said. "I'm just trying to figure out how his business works."

The shadow of a man holding a shotgun appeared in the next room. After yanking his foot from the door, Cliff interpreted Samantha's words and told the family to have a nice day. Grabbing Samantha's elbow, he led her down the porch steps, asking, "What was that about?"

"Grandfather liked to help people."

"Want to give me those other addresses?"

"No." Her young face looked aged. "We're going to keep finding the same thing. I need to drop off a rose from my mother's funeral. She's in a psych hospital that's on the way to the airport. I'll change into uniform there."

"You're wearing your uniform?"

"Yes. Nadja knows me as Lieutenant Harmon, so that's who I'll be."

"I'll follow you."

"That's not necessary."

"There's a guy sitting in a car down the street who's been behind us for a while. He says it's necessary."

Samantha checked her mirror. "That's Harry Trot, the guy who followed us to Bubba's. I'll take the street."

Cliff nodded. While Samantha pulled a U-Turn and headed toward Harry's car, Cliff hopped onto his bike and road down the sidewalk, then pulled off the curb and stopped with the car sandwiched between their vehicles. Cliff gunned his engine and motioned for the man to roll down his window. The kickstand on Cliff's bike went down; he walked over to the car and asked to see the man's I.D.

"Harry, you here all the way from Chicago?" he asked.

"Yes," Harry replied. "Just doing a little business."

"Your business is over," Samantha said from where she'd walked to stand behind Cliff. "There's not going to be any more rent. My grandfather passed away, as did Benny, and the IRS confiscated all the money. You know, all the money. The account is closed. We're just informing the tenants they'll have to move."

The front door of a nearby home slammed as people emerged to stare from the porch. With police sirens echoing in the distance, Harry glanced at the witnesses. His hands tightened on the wheel.

"I run a large organization in this town. Make sure we don't cross paths again," Cliff said. He slapped the hood of Harry's car and walked back to his bike.

Samantha shot him a look as she got back into the truck and pulled forward, heading for the hospital. The roar of Cliff's motorcycle echoed in the background as she called Tarik. "I had to run an errand and got delayed. I've got my uniform with me, so I'm heading to the airport now."

He let out a sigh of exasperation. "This is not how we do things in the DEA."

"Sorry, just all these funerals. I have to sign papers for people and take care of personal business. I'll see you in an hour."

"All right," Tarik replied. "Meet us in baggage claim at half past one."

"I'll be there." At the next red light, she hopped from the truck and ran back to Cliff's position. "Here," she said, handing him the other two leases.

"What's up?"

"I know you'll get the addresses from city hall. Now you can say that I cooperated. I'm not part of this."

With a nod, Cliff pulled up in front of the truck. Waving as he turned left, he punched the bike and roared off. Samantha proceeded to the hospital alone.

Other than a teenage boy who picked up his phone as she entered the hospital, all was quiet in the lobby as Samantha entered the elevator to ride to the fourth floor. Outside the unit, she pushed the buzzer and was informed that her mother was waiting for her in the garden. Once again, she found her mother sitting on the bench.

"She's been very quiet today," Nurse Jamba said. "I'll leave you two alone."

"Thanks. Hello Mother. I brought you a flower."

Jen's eyes drifted sideways as she murmured, "Pink roses. They were Jenny's favorite."

Still in her black dress, Samantha sunk onto the bench beside her mother. "We missed you at the funeral."

"I wanted to go, but Brian said I had to stay here."

"So I heard. I have to tell you that I went to Miami and saw Grandfather." Her mother's eyes welled with tears as Samantha said quietly, "He died too. He's up there now, sailing the deep blue skies." Her eyes pointed upward as her hand reached sideways. Jen took the hand, and together they gazed at the heavens. "I met Christina," Samantha finally said. "And I got into Grandfather's computer. Did you know he was laundering money through rental properties he leased in my name? And he put the money in a foreign bank account. That account is in your name."

"I don't remember!" Jen exclaimed as she snatched her hand back.

"It's me, Samantha. You remember me. And you remember what Grandfather always said."

"'Face into the storm, ride the waves. Navigate the waters.'" Jen recited the whole litany of instructions, followed by, "'Me father was King Neptune.'"

"'All me blooming life.' That old sailor. We can't let our family go down with this ship. Especially with Brian at risk."

"And you."

"You sitting in here pretending not to remember anything isn't doing anybody any good. Tell me, what do you know?"

Jen clasped her hands together and placed them over her right knee. "What do you know about your birth father."

"Just what Uncle Benny told me. His family was mafia, and he moved to Indianapolis to get away from that."

"Yes. Brett had issues from his childhood, but he was trying to be a good man. Before your father died, he had his will changed and put everything in a trust for you. And as you were a minor when he passed away, your grandfather volunteered to manage everything."

"Are you talking about the account overseas?" Samantha asked.

"No. There's another account worth almost two million dollars in Chicago. That was your father's private account that he kept away from the mafia."

"How much of the money in Chicago is mine?"

"All of it."

"Holy cow!" Samantha thought about the will her grandfather had kept from her. "I was too busy at West Point, and then with the military, to really look at it. Grandfather said his attorney was handling everything. Why was the rent money going to your name?"

"I was the beneficiary on Brent's account. He was being used by the family, and he didn't dare say anything because his parents would have gone to jail. He didn't care about his father, but his mother; she was a good person."

"That is sad. But hundreds of millions of dollars is a lot of money. How did he get so much?"

Jen rubbed her forehead. Then she said nervously, "Benny and his mafia people have been putting money in that account since the fifties. Rumor has it, some of it was stolen by skimming casinos."

"Grandfather," Samantha said haltingly, "was your mother's father. Why was he handling my father's will?"

"It's simple," Jen said with a shrug. "Grandfather was there when your father was dying. As I was having difficulties with my mental health, he offered to handle all aspects of your father's will. And as we didn't trust my ex-husband, who is Brian's father, my lawyer thought that was best."

Samantha let out a sigh of disgust. "All of this. The boat. Him raising me, managing our affairs. It was all about the money."

"No! Between the marijuana and alcohol, Grandfather was a mess, but he loved his family. We were more important to him than anything. He turned states witness to protect us."

"Was Uncle Benny there too?"

"When?" Jen asked, her voice strained.

"During that time when my father was dying."

"I suppose he would have been."

"And that's when those two met and cooked up the whole rental scheme," Samantha surmised.

"We're not safe from Grandfather's legacy. Or Benny's."

"What legacy?"

"You know, laundering mafia money. We're going to need a forensic investigation into everything. I assume he was transporting people here illegally, giving them housing and depositing huge rent sums in their names. That's a creative way to launder money."

"That may have been true many years ago, but not anymore. The foundation pays the rent."

Samantha's eyes widened. "What foundation?"

"The one Christina runs."

"We need a lawyer and an accountant to sort this out before the feds get ahold of it. By the time we pay all the back taxes, I doubt there will be anything left."

"Why is that?"

"Grandfather never paid taxes."

"He never made anything. But I'm sure we filed mine. Did you check the laptop for tax documents?"

"Um, no. I didn't have time to go through every file."

"Was there a file called Mayflower?"

"I think so."

"Check that one."

"Is this what you and Benny were talking about?"

"Well, he tried to bring it up, but Grandfather asked me not to talk to anybody about the business. I told Uncle Benny I couldn't remember anything."

"Men, you just can't trust them." Samantha looked at her empty ring finger.

"Brian is good," her mother said. Pointing to a hummingbird suspended above a flower, she smiled. An aura of peace surrounded them as mother and daughter stood and walked toward the door.

"We'll get you out of here soon. I have to leave."

Jen merely nodded and returned to her bench.

In the lobby, before departing the unit, Samantha stopped to watch a bird-like woman add an element to the crayon drawing on the wall. *The cigar with a red band hanging from the superhero's mouth looks like the exact same brand Mr. Owens smokes. He was here!* She went to the nurses' station and asked the clerk, "Robert Owens. When was he here?"

"What does he look like?"

"Medium height, rotund. Could double for Santa Claus, but his hair's not that long."

"Oh, him. He left right before you came out of the garden."

"What did he want?"

"The man asked to see your mother, but as he's not on the list, he departed after leaving a card and some flowers from her niece's funeral."

"She doesn't have a niece. Throw them away." With a curt nod, Samantha turned and headed out the door. During her short ride down to the lobby, she leaned against the elevator wall and enjoyed a moment of peace. Breathing deeply as the elevator doors opened, she ran out, grabbed her uniform from the truck, then headed back inside and changed into a bathroom. Her growling stomach sent her to the gas station for a sandwich.

"Here you go. One hot ham and cheese," the attendant said.

On her way to the airport, she swiped at cheese dripping onto her uniform; then, she fumbled beneath her seat and sure enough, the cold steel of a barrel met her hand. Her eyes narrowed as she pulled out a sawed-off shotgun and smiled.

Good boy.

Chapter 18

Indianapolis, Indiana
  USA
  July 2, 2021 2:15 PM

"Nadja's flight arrives in forty-five minutes. Where are you?"

"Sorry. I'm stuck in a traffic jam on I-70 behind a couple of semis that collided. We're finally starting to move," Lt. Harmon said as she slowly edged forward. "I'll see you in ten to fifteen minutes. The first two hours in the garage are free, right?"

"I think so. Do we know for sure that Nadja even got on the plane?"

"Yes. They put an agent on her flight."

"Good. See you in a few."

As traffic picked up to normal speed, she jerked the wheel to the right, exited I-70, and shot onto the airport express lane as up above, the shadow of a yellow-blue Caribbean carrier passed overhead. Taking a deep breath, she slowly exhaled. Well aware that Nadja's arrival might be accompanied by people who didn't care so much about other people's lives, she thought back to the psalm read at Jenny's funeral. 'Yay, though I walk through the shadow of the valley of death, I shall fear no evil.' *No fear. Navigate these waters.* Reaching under the seat, her hand reconnected with the cold steel of a gun. *Whew!*

Once inside the parking garage, she circled her way through two floors before finding an open spot. *Finally!* After sliding into a spot, she climbed from the truck and walked quickly over to the escalator. With her military boots clamoring down the stairs, she clung to her purse, jumped down the last two steps, and ran across the terminal to baggage claim where she found Tarik pacing the floor. As agreed, rather than approach her boss, she headed inside the USO.

A stocky man, slicked black hair wearing a brown uniform stitched with the yellow trimmings of security, picked up his radio and followed the lieutenant into the military lounge. Soon, another guard arrived and handed her a badge. After loudly thanking the desk clerk for her service, she headed out with a bottle of water in one hand while munching down a baloney sandwich with the other. The tip of her tongue swiped at a bit of white bread sticking to the roof of her mouth as she rode the elevator up to the first floor. Upstairs, in a food court packed with visitors, there sat a solitary man whose garb identified him as a priest. As he picked up his fried chicken sandwich, she stopped to say hello.

"Father Mark, what a surprise."

The collared man stopped mid-bite to ask, "I'm sorry. Have we met?"

"Yes, Father. First at Bear's funeral and then today at Jenny's." With the image of young Jenny on the forefront of her mind, her grey-blue eyes turned to mist as Father Mark's gained recognition.

"Of course, Samantha. I didn't recognize you in uniform."

"I'm with the army." A man at the next table looked up. "I just returned from Bagram."

"Dirty business over there, especially that last rocket attack. I'm heading to my nephew's funeral now." Laying his chicken sandwich on a napkin, Father Mark pulled off a half-eaten dill pickle before taking another bite.

"I'm sorry for that. We lost Jenny to fentanyl," Samantha said sorrowfully.

As the priest peered over his sandwich, his brown eyes gleamed with understanding. "I'm praying for your family. Is there anything else I can do for you?" he asked as he laid the sandwich down.

"Pray harder." Samantha's next bottled-up words spilled out. "And Father, on the third Sunday of the month, can you ring the church bells once for every fallen victim killed by fentanyl this year?"

Startled, his eyes widened. "How many are there?"

"About seventy thousand."

"I, that's a lot. That would take, I don't even know how long, even if we did it round the clock."

"Four days, Father."

"Impossible!"

"Then we need all the churches to ring the bells for a few hours."

"Still!" He threw up his hands. "Ring the bells?"

A woman sitting close by stared at the priest excitedly. "Oh, Father. My son was killed by fentanyl at a college graduation party. He was supposed to start his new job today. Can you ring a bell for him?"

"I, uh, have to call the Pope."

"I'll pray for a miracle," Samantha said. After waving goodbye as the priest hurried off, she lifted her boot to retie a lace and noticed a dark-haired man standing idly around the food court. Two other men in tailored dark suits sat drinking coffee near the security exit, heatedly exchanging conversation about a baseball game. And then there was the familiar face of a man in casual dress sitting alone.

"Lieutenant, thank you for your service," he said as he pushed back his chair and extended his hand. Lt. Harmon's fingers curled around a small device he left in her palm as she gave the hand a firm shake. "Can I buy you a latte?" he asked.

"Thank you, but no, I have to go." On the monitor, she saw that Nadja's flight was about to land and made her way to Terminal A's security. One of the dark-haired men followed her to the line and stopped.

"Boarding pass and identification," the security guard said.

Am I imagining things, or was he at the Joint Task Force meeting? After the officer verified her identity, she walked through the scanner and made her way to Gate 3, where she found Brian standing at a window with his eyes fixed intently on a luggage cart.

"I'm here," she said softly. "You get a badge?"

Nodding, he pulled out a laminated picture of himself attached to a silver clip. "Think it will work?"

"Is that real?"

"Yup."

"I won't even ask."

"What took you so long," he asked, his eyes almost angry.

"Sorry to worry you. Cliff and I stopped to check out a property Grandfather leased in my name, and that was just one of them. There are three others. Grandfather, apparently, was running some type of game. I don't know if he was just laundering money or if he was flying under the radar and helping to set up a trafficking network."

"Drugs or humans?"

"What?"

"What was he trafficking?"

"Oh," Samantha said as she got what Brian was asking. "I don't know. Whichever it is, we'll deal with it later. Where's Gary?"

"Out there." Brian pointed to a group of people standing beside a luggage cart. "There's the security officer, and the other guy's an engineer."

"What are they doing down there?"

"Watching that plane unload." Pointing to a group standing by a DC-10, he said, "That baggage handler, that's the one who likes to stop by the grate."

"On the way here, I was wondering. Why was there a Fourth of July parade today? Shouldn't it be on the fourth?"

"You've been out of touch for a long while, Sis. They don't always do holiday stuff on the holidays anymore. That doesn't give government people enough time off."

"The balloon festival is a Fourth of July event. When is it?"

With a 'wait one minute' finger held up, Brian surfed the net and said, "It's today."

"You're kidding! Why didn't anybody tell me?"

"Now you want to be in the FBI?"

"Huh?"

As they watched the surreal events unfolding on the tarmac, a guard lifted a grate to shine a light into the space. The men joined the guard and bent to look inside; the engineer shook his head. Then Gary walked over and disappeared through a door. The engineer and the security guard soon followed.

"What was that all about?" Samantha asked.

"Guess they didn't find anything in the storm drain," Brian replied.

"What are they doing in the building?"

"I have no idea."

Glancing across her shoulder, she checked to make sure no one was in hearing range before whispering, "I stopped by the hospital and found out that Mom knows about the overseas bank account. She thinks it's being used as a charitable foundation." She went on to explain about the mafia's money. "Mom inherited it from my father, and Grandfather was taking care of it."

Brian flinched. "She was suckered?"

Samantha placed a trembling hand on her brother's arm and steadied herself. "I suspect that Mr. Owens knows everything and he wants to blackmail us into helping with whatever nefarious thing he's up to." The lashes surrounding her eyes creased. "If anything happens to Mom, we're next to inherit. And she said there's a two million dollar trust fund in my name. I don't need a hundred million more problems right now. Why is that luggage cart stopped by the door?"

Brian studied the cart and darted toward the stairs, saying, "Gotta go check on Gary."

"Meet you down there."

Looking around the waiting area, Samantha spotted Agent Vargas, dressed in a violet tank top and designer jeans, sitting casually reading a magazine. Agent Bart sat in a black leather chair on the other side, appearing to nap. The feeling of a hand on her shoulder propelled her away from the window. *There's no one there. Grandfather?* She walked over to stand in front of the door leading to the gangway and waited.

The disembarking passengers arriving from LA contained an assortment of people, everyone from students sporting a laid-back sense of fashion to the sun-kissed skin of a blonde man who, Lt. Harmon imagined, might ordinarily be on a surfboard. As the only dark-haired woman in the crowd, Nadja looked a bit out of place as she entered the waiting area. Seeing the woman dressed in modern-day clothing with her short-sleeved blouse hanging lightly over Capri slacks, to Lt. Harmon, the green stripe in her running shoes did not match her outfit. A startled look crossed Nadja's face.

"Lieutenant! I was told to meet you in the food court."

"Yes, Mother. That was the plan, but I thought it would be much nicer if I met you here." Lt. Harmon reached out a hand and grabbed the handle of Nadja's carry-on. "How was your flight?"

"Turbulent."

"Your son. He is with you?"

Nadja's eyes dropped to stare at the floor. "They couldn't get him on my flight."

"Chelsey was on your flight."

As she spoke the parrot's name, a tall man dressed in flight attendant attire carried the Pittacus from the gangway, laughing heartily as the bird squawked, "Touchdown."

"Assad watched football?" Lt. Harmon asked.

"Dolphins fan," Nadja replied. She glared at the bird, who peered back with recognition in her eyes.

"Hi you lonely hefe asumbra," Chelsey shouted.

Lt. Harmon laughingly asked, "What did that bird say?"

"I think she's hungry," Nadja snapped.

"Oh. Can you take her down to the USO? There's someone waiting for her," Lt. Harmon said to the steward.

Mesmerized by Chelsey's antics, he agreed and trotted off with a smile.

"Aren't we going with him?" Nadja asked.

"No. We're taking a shortcut." Reggae music blared from a uniform pocket. "Hang on a minute, I need to take this. It's my fiancé's mother."

"So you have found love." A smile creased Nadja's weary face.

Ignoring her, Samantha said, "Hello," and listened for a moment. "That's good. I'm sorry I can't talk right now," she was saying when Nadja interrupted.

"I need to use the bathroom."

"Alright."

As the other woman disappeared into the restroom, Lt. Harmon followed and stood by the door. Quickly, she unzipped a front pouch on the suitcase and slipped in the silver object. Then, she closed the zipper and continued her conversation with Brad's mother. "Goodbye, Mrs. Kramer," she was saying as Nadja rejoined her. At the stairway, she swiped a badge to disable a door alarm, pulled Nadja's suitcase along, and bumped her way down the stairs leading to the ground floor.

"Where are we going?" Nadja asked suspiciously as she grabbed the rail and followed along.

Lt. Harmon's boots pounded down the stairs. Feeling the glare of the older woman's eyes on her back at the bottom step, she turned to look her in the eye. "If you have anything to tell me, now would be the time." Slowly, she lowered one foot to the floor; her grey-blue eyes looked into Nadja's. "My fiancé was almost blinded in your last rocket attack. That was his mother on the phone, calling to tell me that they just took his bandages off and thank God, he can see. Tell me, what's going on with your network?" The pleading in her voice brought a slight smirk to Nadja's face. Lt. Harmon looked deliberately at her watch and waited.

As she looked back from her position on the bottom third step, Nadja's mouth turned to a wry grin when she saw two people waiting at the top of the stairs. "I should have known you wouldn't come alone."

"I'm with the U.S. government. You know that. We know that your son and your husband are already here. What are they up to?"

"Get me out of here," Nadja hissed with her eyes darting fervently around. "Or people will die."

"People are already dying. Your son is cooking bad fentanyl. Why should I trust you?"

Nadja grabbed the rail and took another step down. Now within inches of Lt. Harmon, she asked, "Who else do you have?"

The agents began slowly descending the stairs, chatting as if they were a married couple having a disagreement about the kids' homework. Lt. Harmon gave the carry-on a firm tug and, while pulling it along, walked through a door leading to the tarmac. "We have a car here."

Two security guards stood waiting to escort the women over to a parking area. As they walked along the building, a door opened and the slim figure of a woman dressed in a purple top emerged. She pointed at an approaching luggage carrier.

"Look out," she yelled.

Lt. Harmon pulled Nadja closer to the building just as the carrier brushed within inches of their position. "Where's the car?" Nadja asked, staring wide-eyed at the luggage carrier.

"Right outside the gate." Releasing the suitcase handle, Lt. Harmon rubbed an elbow and coughed in the dusty air mixed with white smoke billowing from the drainage grate. Suddenly, she ran for the door where she'd seen Brian disappear, yelling for Nadja to follow.

"Samantha, man overboard." The words echoed in her mind as she searched frantically through the oncoming mist for the door. Behind her, Agent Vargas's purple top stood out through the fog and then disappeared, along with her prisoner.

"Nadja. She's gone," a voice yelled.

"How did she get away so fast?" Tarik yelled. While staring at Lt. Harmon, his angry dragon flinched on his cheek as she coughed out wisps of smoke and stared straight ahead.

"I don't know. But the transponder is in her suitcase. Is she tracking?"

Tarik clicked on a phone app. In a voice mimicking the furry emanating from his black eyes, he said, "Got her. She's back inside the building."

"I assume someone is watching the luggage carousel?" Lt. Harmon asked.

"We've got that covered," Mr. Owens' voice thundered from behind. "FBI has a team in place. How did you pull this off?"

"What?"

"They're following a bag. You got the whole FBI team and a faction of infidels off our ass. Where's Nadja?"

"Right now, I don't know," Lt. Harmon replied honestly. A shiver of fear ran up her spine. "We have to find my brother and Gary. For added security, they were supposed to meet me right here."

"Who's Gary?"

"Cleaning crew."

Mr. Owens leaned over to look in the grate, then straightened and hiked his britches up as security ran onto the tarmac. After the guards lifted the lid and found an empty smoke cannister, Tarik led the group inside the building and stopped short at the site of globs of congealed blood streaked across the white marble tile. It started off as a few drops, then turned to a giant smear leading to a body lying crumpled in a heap beneath the stairs. With their weapons drawn, the guards stealthily advanced.

"Clear," Mr. Owens yelled as he checked around the room.

The first guard knelt to feel for a pulse and barked at his partner, "Chris, radio for help." Then, with two fingers, he picked up a weapon lying next to the body and tossed it aside.

"Watcha got Hank?" Mr. Owens asked.

"Gunshot wound. This guy is one of our engineers." Taking a handkerchief from his pocket, he applied pressure to the wound. The white kerchief immediately turned red. "Get help here, now!"

"Ambulance is on the way," Chris said. Using his radio, he warned security to be on the lookout for someone using Paddy McCready's badge. Once again, for the second time in one day, the Indianapolis International Airport was shut down.

Feeling powerless without a weapon, Lt. Harmon's heart pounded as she stood back and observed the scene. As she thought back to the building with the tunnel sitting at the edge of the airport, her eyes narrowed with unease. "Shouldn't someone be here at the desk?"

"Not right now," Chris said. "Eric's only here when there are passengers disembarking on the tarmac."

Waves crashed into the boat from all sides. "What's the heading?" Samantha cried.

"Study the current girl." Captain Greg's words resonated in her head.

"Mr. Owens, can I see you outside?"

"What's this about?" he asked after following her through the door.

"I saw you at the limestone quarry yesterday with two FBI agents who came to my house. They're your guys."

A shadow fell across her back. "What's going on?" Tarik asked.

"He was about to say that he and those two FBI agents following me around were all in the same military unit together. In Helmand. And they know something about my family, which is why they want to get into Grandfather's laptop."

"Yes. They got in, by the way. You were great at math." Despite the situation, Mr. Owens grinned and told Tarik, "Homeschooled."

Lt. Harmon's face relaxed. "Where's the tunnel entrance?"

"What tunnel?" Tarik asked.

"There's a tunnel under the airport leading to a house across the road built during prohibition. I imagine it was extended to open somewhere around that desk inside. The opening will either be in the floor or the wall," Lt. Harmon replied with narrowed eyes.

"A tunnel. Really?" Mr. Owens said with a slight tremor in his voice. "Why didn't you say something before this?"

"We just figured it out. Nadja's people took my brother and his friend Gary."

"You were deceived," Tarik snarled.

"Why didn't you arrest them all when you had the chance?" Lt. Harmon snapped.

Tarik scowled at the tone of her voice, accusing him of dereliction as he replied, "We will. First, we have to find the rest of al-Qaeda's network."

"You don't even care that my brother's life is at risk, along with many others!"

Tarik's eyes glittered black as he crossed his arms and remained silent. Mr. Owens remained quiet during the heated exchange. When it was over, he stepped forward and said in a moderating tone, "I've got things from this end. Meet you at the house. I'll take my men through the tunnel." Without waiting for a response, he walked swiftly into the building. Tarik's eyes followed his back.

"Your plan goes sideways?"

"A little."

Her boss ran toward the security gate, yelling, "Let's go. My car is waiting," Lt. Harmon stayed close on his heels. Outside the gate, he stopped in the parking lot beside the sleek body of an aerodynamic car. Her eyes grew wide as she observed the ride.

"You're driving an electric car? How did you even get here?"

"It's a rental. It's airtight, so better in a chemical or biological attack." The scar on Tarik's face deepened as he unlocked the doors. Lt. Harmon pointed to a back window on the passenger side that had been smashed in with a rock.

"Watch out for glass."

"Why would someone do this?" After yanking open the back door, Tarik found the rock and swore.

"Your car's going to stand out like a sore thumb around that old house. Drop me off in the garage. I'll take the truck."

As he opened the front passenger door, Tarik's black T-shirt clung to his body, defining his muscles with sweat. After checking to make sure there was no glass on the cushion, he escorted Lt. Harmon into the car. She looked up at his frame, long ago defined by poor nutrition and noticed the tattoo of a dagger with the number five written in Arabic stenciled on the underside of his arm. *The same one we found on Assad!* Her eyes narrowed. "Are you al-Qaeda?"

"No," Tarik said through gritted teeth.

"Taliban?"

"No! Why are you asking these questions?"

"The prisoner they brought in, Assad, the man who owned Chelsey. He had your same tattoo."

Tarik's fingers gripped tightly around the wheel. "He was my brother."

"What?"

The muscles in Tarik's face stiffened as, in a tight voice, he spit out the words, "Assad was a C.I. for the DEA."

"C.I. What's that?" Lt. Harmon's grey-blue eyes genuinely looked confused.

"Confidential informant, like your grandfather," he said with a smirk.

A light dawned on Lt. Harmon's young face. "Oh, yeah. Trading information to fund his own drug habit. For sale to the highest bidder."

Tarik brushed aside that comment. "Whose side is Nadja on?"

"I can't say for sure. I just know that we need to be prepared for anything."

"Agent Vargas has her?"

"She does."

"What do you think is going on? Give me your honest assessment,"

Tarik said as his foot hit the gas. Lt. Harmon clung to the seat as he headed for the parking garage.

"I think it was no accident she used Talcum in both experiments. I think she was supposed to use fentanyl in the second attack, but it wasn't ready. I just don't know for sure if she delayed production on purpose," she said breathlessly. "Did you get city hall to call off the balloon festival?"

"That's not going to happen. We have no concrete information to call off a public event."

"But you at least warned Mr. Rivera not to go?"

"His security personnel are aware of your concerns, but nobody believes that fentanyl could be used in a mass incident like the balloon festival. Homeland Security is doing downwind tests along with all the other usual stuff. Mr. Rivera is scheduled to stop by the festival at five."

Lt. Harmon checked the time. "We have two hours," she said as Tarik dropped her off at the truck.

"We'll both take your truck."

"May as well. With that hole in your window, you're not bio-protected anymore."

A slight smile actually crossed Tarik's lips. After reaching down to grab a pair of black heels lying on the floor, he tossed them into the back seat and climbed in.

On the way to the house across from the airport, Lt. Harmon thought back to the architectural drawings as she described the property. "It's a two-story structure with a pitched roof. The living room is at the front of the house, kitchen's at the back. Upstairs, there's a widow's landing between two small bedrooms. Oh, and there's a basement. The door opens into the back of the kitchen." When they stopped behind a red SUV parked at the edge of the driveway, she continued, "I'll go in through an upstairs window. Mr. Owens should be approaching through the basement right about now. You watch out front." Her eyes widened as she stared at the SUV parked along the road. "Whose car is that?"

Using a hand to shield his eyes from the sun, Tarik said, "Looks like the rental car Owens is driving."

"He didn't use the tunnel? We can't trust him."

"First me, then him," Tarik snarled. "Who do you trust?"

"Just myself." Lt. Harmon looked at him suspiciously. "You were with him in Helmand. I remember hearing about a young Afghan boy who was translating in the province when he got hit with a mortar round. Mr.

Owens' unit saved him and got him transferred to the States. You were that boy."

"He saved my life," Tarik said quietly. "Backup's on the way."

"I'm not waiting for backup. My brother's in there." Before her boss could object, Lt. Harmon pulled a gun from behind her seat, stuffed it into a cargo pocket on her uniform, and climbed from the truck. Then she grabbed the shotgun and slung it over her shoulder.

"Get back here!"

Too late, she was gone. Ducking behind a line of peonies, she made her way to an elm tree growing at the corner of the house and stood studying the branches hanging over the roof. *Perfect. I can use that branch to get onto the widow's landing.* The only problem was the lowest branch was way above her head. After making a few jumping attempts to grab the branch, she'd just about decided to go back to the truck when Tarik appeared at her side. Silently, he motioned for her to step into his hand.

"Get into an upstairs bedroom and stay there, and that's an order," he whispered.

"Why didn't you help me sooner?"

"I was having too much fun watching you jumping up and down in those boots."

"Hmph." Samantha stepped into his hand. With the gun weighing down a pocket and the shotgun strap across her back, she made her way up the tree and slipped onto the widow's landing, then quietly opened a window and stepped across the window ledge as her phone vibrated against her leg. Pulling out the device, she whispered, "Hello."

"Lieutenant, are you here?"

Upon hearing Mr. Owens' voice, she said quietly, "We're outside." As she crept to the bedroom door with her phone pressed tight against her ear, a voice she recognized echoed up the stairway. *Agent Daniels!*

"I came in through a storm passage. All clear in the basement, but people have been here recently," Mr. Owens said.

"How can you tell?"

"Water bottles, empty airline snack packets."

"Why didn't you use the tunnel?"

"And get shot like a rat? Nope."

I have two more agents here, Tarik texted. *Circling the back.*

Mr. Owens is downstairs with the FBI guys, she texted back.

"Come on in," Mr. Owens said.

"Okay. We're approaching the front door."

Lt. Harmon texted Tarik that Mr. Owens said he would meet them at the front door. *But don't trust him.*

He's not the bad guy, Tarik texted back.

Proceeding to the lower level.

Army boots would not have been her first choice to try to creep down wooden stairs without being detected, but knowing she might have to run, she kept them on and made the descent. On the way down, she heard Agent Daniels offering to get someone a glass of lemonade.

"Lieutenant Harmon. Please join us," he said.

Gingerly, she walked into the kitchen and stared at the scene before her. Standing against the kitchen counter with their arms crossed were Agents Daniels and Tooley. A hint of steel glistened in their hands. In the center of the room, Mr. Owens sat at the table playing cards with Brian and Gary. Unstrapping the shotgun, she leaned it against the wall.

"What are you guys doing?"

"Go fish," Gary said.

"Give me all your fives," her brother said.

Mr. Owens handed Brian three cards. "I'm out."

"I win," Brian said dully.

Lt. Harmon studied the men. Gary's brow was sweating profusely, and the normally competitive look on Brian's face when he played games was missing. *Who shot the engineer?* She walked over to the table and slid into a chair. While pretending to scratch an itch, she reached down and unbuttoned her cargo pocket.

"You in, Sis?" Brian asked as he shuffled the cards.

"Yes. Deal me in."

After receiving five cards, Lt. Harmon said, "I'm first. Brian, give me all your two's."

"Darn it," he exclaimed and slapped a card down on the table so hard it sailed over the edge toward the floor.

"You're such a baby," Samantha said as she leaned under the table. "It's on our side. Pick that up." She pulled out the gun from her cargo pocket and laid it by her foot, then, using toe of her boot, slid it forward.

Grumbling under his breath, Brian bent down to retrieve the card. Seconds later, he was standing and holding a gun pointed at the agents. "Drop your weapons in the sink."

The sound of metal clattering against porcelain soon followed as the agents, surprised by Brian's actions, dropped their weapons behind their backs and moved over to stand against the wall.

"I'll get them," Mr. Owens said eagerly. He started to rise from his chair but was stopped by Lt. Harmon.

"Stay seated. It's your turn."

"What are you doing?" he asked. Above his smile, his kindly eyes had turned to rounds of steel.

"You weren't all that surprised the engineer was shot, and you're missing your Glock. He had one lying by his body. That makes you somebody I don't trust."

"I didn't shoot him!" Mr. Owens exclaimed. "The guy decided to play hero and grabbed my gun right out of my belt. He shot at the wall, and the bullet ricocheted and caught him across the chest. He's okay; just passed out at the sight of his own blood."

"We're not the bad guys," Agent Tooley said calmly.

"You're not the good guys either," Lt. Harmon snapped as she walked over to the sink and stared at the weapons. "Looks like we've all developed trust issues. Good, a Glock. I'm sure I won't miss from this distance." Pulling the weapons from the sink, she walked over to her brother and tucked one in his belt while casually holding the other pointed at the ground.

"You've got about twenty seconds to tell us what's going on," Brian said.

The men looked at each other and remained silent. Gary stood and grabbed the gun from Brian's belt. Then, with his pasty skin glistening beneath his mangy brown hair, he ordered the agents to sit down. "I know part of it," he said as they took a seat.

"Yeah, what do you know?" Agent Browne asked.

"I work on the cleaning crew at the airport. Yesterday, I saw a few people who looked like Afghans walk down the stairs from a plane onto the tarmac. The baggage cart blocked my view for a minute. When it moved away, I thought the group looked much thinner."

Lt. Harmon's eyes widened as she realized what the group had done. "You've been smuggling people into the country through that tunnel!"

The agents stared at the table, unmoving.

"Human traffickers," Gary said accusingly.

"Humanitarian," Mr. Owens said in a reasonable voice.

Lt. Harmon demanded that Mr. Owens tell her who they worked for. "And what do you mean, humanitarian?"

Ignoring the first question, he rubbed his eyes and said, "A lot of Afghan people put their lives on the line to help us during the war. People like Ismael. He was a man who worked for eleven years with our forces at Bagram as a translator and armed guard and frequently put his own life on the line. After he started being threatened by the Taliban, he applied for a special immigration visa to move his family over here. Sergeant Kevin Owens wrote a letter to support his visa application." Mr. Owens' hands clenched into balls. "Sergeant Owens died by suicide, so the letter could not be confirmed to be valid."

"I see. Sergeant Owens was your son. Now you're the immigration office. How much is Nadja's mother paying you?"

"People make donations to foundations," Mr. Owens said defensively.

"Where are the Afghan people now?"

"In a hotel in Chicago. They've all applied for asylum. They'll show up in court."

"You've been paying their legal fees and hotel rooms. Your donation money is frozen, and some of your honorable refugees are not quite as honorable. The Jammu's son was supposed to turn on the cartels and go into the Witness Protection Program, but it's payback time for what happened to his brother. Now he's gone rogue," Lt. Harmon said. "And now you're after the money in my family's overseas account. You wanted us here for insurance."

"These guys are after our family?" Brian asked, his voice holding the scorn of betrayal.

From the door, Tarik said, "They worked you as they did me."

Agent Daniels finally found his voice. "No, we're not the bad guys. We've been following Nadja and her family. They're leading us to al-Qaeda's network here in the U.S."

"In other words, you've lost control of the situation," Lt. Harmon said.

"As you know, they've killed a lot of people with fentanyl," Mr. Owens said softly. "Those victims need a voice."

"Whose?" Samantha asked. Then her eyes widened. "Mine? That's your plan?"

"Who better?" Tarik asked as the dragon tattoo glistened feverishly on his face.

"There's a lot of agenda's going on here," Lt. Harmon said. Her grey-blue eyes searched Tarik's face. "Is Nadja talking?"

"She's refusing to speak with anyone but her lawyer," he said firmly. "We cannot violate her rights."

"Everything is going to be fine," Mr. Owens said. "She's trying to keep her son out of trouble while leading us to al-Qaeda."

The weather vane moved as the winds headed south. With the deck shifting beneath her feet, Samantha steadied herself and read the currents.

"Coming from a man who needs a lot of money, I'm thinking your credibility is shot. You need the DEA to get rid of Badhai so that Nadja can take over because she's a chemist who knows how to cook. You wanted my brother to get Mom out of the hospital today to kidnap her for ransom. Then you didn't get her, so you thought you'd get us."

"It's the FBI's job to look into mafia money." The sullen look crossing Mr. Owens' face was matched only by the two FBI agents. "And fentanyl is legally used in hospitals. She wants to start a legitimate company."

Lt. Harmon looked at Tarik. "Check his ID."

"Enough! Drop your weapons. We have to get to the festival," he replied. Looking at the young people, he pointed to the front door and told them to wait in the truck. "And you guys, not another word."

"Lieutenant," Mr. Owens barked.

"Be careful," she said. "I told you, I shoot better in boots."

The steely glint shining from Tarik's black eyes, along with the metal of his gun pointing at Mr. Owens' head, quieted the man. Lt. Harmon walked over to Tarik and hissed in his ear, "What are we going to do with them?"

"We work for the DEA," Tarik said as he holstered his gun. "There are no drugs here, and Nadja is in custody. Anything else is outside of our jurisdiction. Let them go. My guys outside will be dancing with them."

"Fine. We'll drop my brother and Gary at the airport. His car is there." With that, she turned and marched out the front door. "Come on," she said to her brother. "I so would have beat you in Go Fish."

CHAPTER 19

Indianapolis, Indiana
USA
June 2, 2021 3:30 PM

Outside the house, Lt. Harmon went to grab her gym bag and ran behind the peonies. Soon, she returned, hobbling along in her heels and dress. Tarik walked out and looked at her approvingly.

"Your guys are keeping those goons here this evening, right?"

"Yes. They're playing poker while we're at the festival."

"Does Mr. Owens know the Mexican official isn't staying for the fireworks?"

"Probably."

"You trust him, don't you?"

"He's given me no reason not to."

"And Agents Tooley and Daniels?"

Tarik shrugged.

"So you're letting them all go. We better get to the park. Somehow, I just know they'll try to kidnap Mr. Rivera at the balloon festival."

"You can be so weirdly right about stuff," Tarik said begrudgingly as he dropped Gary off at the employee parking lot.

Gary looked dazed. "What should I do?"

"Go home. You'll be debriefed tomorrow."

"Wait a minute," Samantha said.

"What?"

"What was the engineer doing in that part of the terminal?"

"He was checking the circuit box and found an extra breaker that wasn't labeled," Gary said. "The guy was flipping it back and forth, trying to figure it out, when Mr. Owens walked in with his gun. The engineer got all excited and grabbed the gun from Owens' hand. He fired at the ceiling, and the ricochet caught him in the chest."

"Just like Owens said." Tarik nodded.

"What was the circuit for?" Samantha asked.

Brian's eyebrows had formed into a question mark. As he worked out the answer, they lowered to a period. "Probably how they bypassed the sensors when they transported people over to the house. There was some kind of weird noise when they took us over in a golf cart."

"They were setting up to grab Nadja when Brian and Gary walked in!" Samantha exclaimed. "At least we know his game."

"It's not Owens who's after your Mexican official," Tarik said grimly. "Let's go."

"And Brian?"

"You'd like a balloon festival, wouldn't you?" Tarik asked with a slight grin.

Brian nodded.

"No," Samantha shouted. "He stays with Gary."

Tarik stared at her. "The two of you can drop me off, then he'll be taking you to headquarters for debriefing."

"You guys planned this!" Samantha looked at her brother. "Why didn't you warn me?"

Brian merely shrugged.

On the way to the park, a small gleam shone from her grey-blue eyes as she checked her messages. "They're flying Brad to Roudebush for rehab," she said softly.

"Where's that?" Tarik asked.

With her index finger, Samantha pointed at several brick buildings highlighted against the skyline across from the park. "It's the VA hospital next to where Mom's at."

Lines of disproval deepened on Tarik's furrowed brow. He said nothing.

As they approached the west-side city park, a kaleidoscope of color dotted the skyline, drawing everyone's attention to the different hues of greens, blues, oranges, yellows and reds in multiple spheres of floating canvas as a flotilla of hot air balloons rose above the trees.

"How do they control where they're going?" Lt. Harmon asked.

Tarik shrugged.

"Hey, Siri, how do you control a hot air balloon?" Brian asked his phone.

"Eyes on the road," his sister shouted.

He handed the phone over as she read the information aloud. "Hot air balloons don't have steering wheels, but hot air balloon pilots use the wind direction and speed at different heights in order to steer the balloon. Hot air balloon pilots control their ascent and descent but can't steer the balloon in a different direction without changing altitude."

"That makes sense," Tarik said.

As someone who'd used the wind to control a vessel, Lt. Harmon said the job of a hot air balloon pilot was probably much harder than they made it look. "They have to find the wind at different altitudes."

"You only had to worry about the wind across the seas. And the currents. And waves," Brian said.

"And seagulls and dolphins," Samantha said with a roll of her eyes.

"And whales," Tarik chimed in.

Lt. Harmon smiled at him curiously. "There were three children in that picture of you outside Bagram. I assume one was Assad. The other was Ismael?"

Tarik's black eyes stared straight ahead. "Yes. My friend who was forgotten and left behind."

"Until Mr. Owens helped you get him out. Now you owe him."

"Enough!"

Samantha looked at her brother. His eyes answered in agreement. "We're not leaving until Mr. Rivera leaves safely," she stated. "At least I can identify Badhai if he's here."

"Very well," Tarik said. "You will both stay far away from the ambassador. As soon as he leaves, you leave."

"The air current at the park," Brian said as he studied a weather app. "It's blowing right toward Mom's hospital."

"That's nice. She'll be able to see the balloons from the garden," Samantha said.

A row of black limousines with small colorful flags sat parked along the road. Motioning in their direction, Tarik muttered, "There they are. Anybody in the cars?"

Brian studied the black limos and replied, "I think there's a driver in the first one." He tried pulling up alongside, but a policeman waved him away. "Don't you guys have a badge to flash around?"

"We're undercover," Tarik replied.

"Like anybody won't notice a woman in heels walking around with a guy who looks like he belongs in a turban," Brian said, laughing at his own joke as he found parking farther down the road.

"Okay, smartass, stay with the truck." Grabbing the handle, Tarik pushed open the door and stepped out to follow the gravel road back to the festival.

Following closely behind, Samantha teetered in heels as her eyes searched the crowd. "I'm sure this place is crawling with FBI, DEA. Lots of regular cops." Leaving the road, she walked past a line of food trucks and stumbled in her heels as she caught a shish-ka-bob cook looking at her with a menacing grin. Tarik grabbed her arm and steadied her feet.

"Why are you wearing heels?" he asked, his eyes ever searching.

"Combat boots didn't match my dress, duh," she replied in an impertinent voice. Then, in a more serious tone, she said, "I can't believe Mr. Rivera came here. Tell me they're not letting him eat or drink anything."

"Why is that?"

"Because most fentanyl deaths are from ingesting the drug orally."

Tarik looked at her approvingly. Spying a group of dark-haired men standing at the edge of a field, he touched her arm and said, "There he is."

"Why is he out in the open?"

"Not my call. It's going to be a minute before the next balloon takes off. Let's get something to drink."

"Seriously?"

"There's a food truck right here. We can keep an eye on everything from the line and be inconspicuous."

"Okay."

With Tarik leaning against the red food truck, Samantha looked at the back of a man climbing into the basket of a yellow balloon patterned with purples and blue. "What's he doing?"

"Who?"

"That man." As they stood by the shish-ka-bob van, she pointed toward the man in the basket. "He's messing around a lot with something on the floor."

"Maybe ballast?"

"I didn't read anything about that. Something about him seems so familiar."

"You've only seen him from the back," Tarik said dismissively.

"True. Hang on, my phone's ringing." With a finger in one ear, she listened to a message from Cliff telling her that when he checked out the first property, it was empty. Then he heard the back door slam and ran out to see a woman running down the alley. She called him back. "Who's the woman?"

"Hey. Good to talk to you too, babe. I um, couldn't catch her."

"A woman outran you?" Samantha imagined Cliff's big thighs thundering down an alley and grinned. He described the woman as thin with long black hair.

"I went back inside the house and found an AK 47, so, given the situation, I called for backup to meet me at the third house. It was lucky I did because we found two dead bodies."

"What! How were they killed?"

"Overdosed. There's a kid here, approximately two years old. He's crying and dirty, but otherwise okay. Social service is on the way."

"Thanks for the report. Come to the park when you're done," Samantha said woodenly. "We're at the shish-ka-bob truck."

"What happened," Tarik asked when she hung up. When Samantha told him, he merely nodded. "It's nothing new. Over three hundred-thousand kids in the U.S. have been orphaned because of fentanyl."

"Being an orphan is no fun, as you know," Samantha said sullenly. "We need to do something."

"You can always join the FBI. Or come work with us." Tarik flashed a smile.

"Right."

Out in the field, more pilots prepared their ships for flight. Using gas-powered fans, they cold-inflated the balloons while two people held open the 'mouth.' A third crew member walked up to the top of the envelope to install the parachute, held in place during flight by pressure and lines.

"I like that one," Tarik said, pointing to a nearby balloon. As he and Samantha watched, the red, white and blue display of patriotism sailed elegantly into the sky. When the second balloon rose from the ground, it seemed to Samantha that its blue zig-zag stripes infused over a canopy of dark green created the allure of two brightly colored parrots beating their wings in flight.

"Did you get me a lemonade?" she asked.

"Here." As they leaned against the back of a red food truck, Tarik handed over a cup of sweet tea. "They were out of lemonade."

"Why don't they make more?"

"Closed for break." Leaning against the truck, he asked nonchalantly, "How's your Captain Kramer?"

Samantha turned her head away to study the road. "He's getting better. Why?"

"I hear you're engaged. What a surprise, somebody like you, in love."

"Why do you say that?"

"Because," Tarik said with heat in his voice. "People like us, our work is our love. I've watched you. You're so jaded, you don't know the first thing about being in love."

The stubborn look crossing Samantha's grey-blue eyes intensified. "I thought that before, now it's different. But how does anybody know if they're truly in love?"

Tarik slammed his hand on the side of the truck. "When the thought of losing them forever makes you fall to your knees. You should be with him, not out here chasing terrorists!"

"What do you know? Have you ever been in love?"

"I loved my parents."

A look of understanding crossed Samantha's face. "Your parents were killed by the Taliban in a rocket attack. So you did everything you could to help save Ismael. I assume he and his family are in Chicago?"

"Yes."

"Well, if we don't catch all the bad guys, my family is next."

Tarik gave a slow nod.

Samantha's eyes narrowed. "Why is Mr. Rivera still here?"

As he sucked sweet tea through a straw, Tarik shaded his eyes to watch the balloons. "History tells us that if there is going to be a terrorist event using fentanyl, it will be tonight during the fireworks," he said.

"What makes you think that?"

"They used powder in the rocket attacks."

"Launched from Katyusha's. Did you send the real FBI to check out the fireworks?"

"DEA is working with Homeland Security. They'll take care of it."

Lt. Harmon's voice tightened. "Maybe. I wish Chelsey were here."

"Why do you want a parrot?"

"She's the only one who has intel on Nadja and Assad's time together." Samantha giggled and yelled out the sentence she'd heard Chelsey say. "Hi, you lonely hefe as umbra."

Tarik locked eyes with Samantha. "Don't call me a traitor!"

Captivated by his smoldering eyes, she stared back and blinked. "I didn't. Why would you say that?"

"Hialonelyhefeasumbra is what the word 'traitor' sounds like in Pashta."

Samantha took a sip of tea and gagged. "Yuck." A wide spray of froth hit Tarik's arm.

"Clean that off," he roared.

Grumbling under her breath, she walked around to the front of the vehicle and stared down the line of food trucks. *Where are the women? Traitor. Where did Chelsey hear that word? From Assad? He called Nadja a traitor for what? Because she wasn't supposed to substitute the fentanyl with talcum. Assad was working both sides of the fence.* Returning to Tarik's side, she asked, "Where are the workers? They're not back here smoking."

He shrugged. "Not in my job description to keep track of a bunch of cooks."

"They've completely closed up the trucks. Why? And why are all of the food trucks staffed by ethnic men? Even the hot dog vendor?"

"It's not uncommon."

"This is not New York."

Samantha looked at the scene on the field and saw a father standing near his child, watching him play in the dirt. She saw three tow-headed children laughing and crawling over a pile of rocks while the older adults stood near the balloons, stretching up on their toes for a look inside the baskets. A young couple smiling, eager to watch the balloon launch as their dog stood on back paws, also peered into the basket.

And then there were a few individuals standing by themselves, scanning the faces of the crowd. She spotted agent Bart, looking hot in a suit. "Let's go talk to him." As they moved toward the field, she told Tarik about Nadja being called a traitor by Assad.

"What does that mean?"

With her eyes anxiously scanning the skies, Lt. Harmon replied, "I think it means she didn't buy into the terrorist lifestyle."

"How do we know this is true?"

"Nadja's younger son wasn't supposed to die. Now, she's trying to save her older son, but he's not cooperating. Unfortunately, he grew up in the terrorist camps."

"And you think he's here."

A man came running up to a yellow balloon, yelling something the others on the ground apparently couldn't understand as he kept pointing to the ground while angrily stomping his foot. Ignoring the scene, the pilot in the basket motioned for his ground crew to release the lines. He looked over at the crowd, his eyes searching. A smaller man with black hair and olive skin ran up and jumped into the basket.

Looking back behind her shoulder, Samantha pointed to the yellow balloon and yelled, "Stop him!"

As if in a dream, she held steady on her feet as giant waves crashed over the side of the boat.

"Samantha, get everybody below," Captain Gregg bellowed. With his biceps straining against the fabric of his shirt, he cranked a handle to lower the main. "A storm is coming."

She felt herself running, calling for the dark-haired man they knew as Mr. Rivera to come hither. "Get inside. Get under cover."

The wind blew her hair sideways as drops began to fall. A hand pulled her back.

"No," she yelled to Tarik, who couldn't see what was going on to his left, thanks to his blind eye. "The attack, it's coming from that balloon."

As Samantha moved toward the field while shielding her eyes and holding her breath, Tarik stood frozen in place, absorbing the white cloud of death billowing around.

"Cover your eyes. Hold your breath," she yelled to the crowd. "It's fentanyl."

Screams pierced the air as people ran to get away from the white powder being thrown into the air from the basket of a balloon ascending from the festival. A stampede ensued. A few people who were struggling to breathe stopped and bent over, gasping for breath before falling to the ground.

The sound of tires screeched beside her and a door slammed. She started to run toward the field, but a hand drew her back. "Sam, get in the truck."

"Brian," she cried. Together, they sat in his truck and watched the scene. By now, officers on the ground were aiming at the men in the balloon. Bullets whizzed into the air, but the balloon was already too high.

"Stop shooting," Agent Bart yelled. "The bullets have to come down somewhere. Get in your cars."

With a hand on Mr. Rivera's shoulder, he started pushing him toward the road but was quickly surrounded by a group of dark-haired men.

"He's having trouble breathing," one of the men said in broken English. "We treat him."

"Looks like the food truck chefs are al-Qaeda," Samantha said with a fierceness in her voice her brother hadn't heard before.

"Stay in the truck," he yelled. "There are people on the ground needing help. More ambulances are on the way."

As if in a nightmare, she watched as dozens of people fell to the ground, lured into sleep by the soft lapping of the waves. "The children. Samantha, get the children," Captain Gregg called from the stern. Her wooden legs carried her to the spot where she'd just moments ago seen the children playing by the bow. "Grandfather, they've gone under." She climbed from the truck, frantically searching for the right course to help.

"The children, they're not breathing," she yelled to a nearby fireman. "They've been contaminated by fentanyl."

"We have to decontaminate this whole area now," he yelled. Thinking quickly when the attack started, he'd already begun attaching a small diameter hose to a nearby fire hydrant. With the nozzle aimed high over the field, he let the water fall over the victims to wash away the drug. Once the white powder was gone, the firemen and medics on scene set to work giving life-saving Narcan and breaths.

"Lieutenant, over here," Agent Bart yelled.

"They're trying to kidnap Mr. Rivera," she yelled back. As her black dress was spotted with flecks of white, she carefully pulled Brian's shotgun from the truck and teetered in her heels to take a position in front of the group surrounding Mr. Rivera while Brian circled from the back.

"Get out of our way," a man up front yelled. His hollow cheeks made his eyes seem extra big and bulging as he stopped to stare at the woman holding a shotgun. Slowly, he put his hands up.

"All of you hands up." Agent Bart grabbed one man from behind, twisted his arm into a pretzel, and soon had him in cuffs. Brian and Samantha held the other suspects in place until they could be taken peacefully into custody. Moments later, Mr. Rivera lost consciousness.

"Don't touch him," Samantha yelled. "He's contaminated with fentanyl."

"Medic," Brian called from a squatting position as he leaned over the victim.

"Is he breathing?"

"No, and he's pretty blue," Brian replied. As the ambulance sirens drew near, he rose, pulled a bottle of water from the truck, and poured it over Mr. Rivera's face. Then, with a rag, he wiped away the water and looked to see if his chest was rising.

"Be careful," Samantha said with her voice slightly slurred.

Brian gave mouth-to-mouth until the medics arrived. "Don't touch anything," he said breathlessly as they took over. Grabbing a bottle of water, he decontaminated himself by pouring it over his face. "I'm okay."

After giving Mr. Rivera Narcan, a medic yelled, "He was breathing, but now he's stopped again," and placed a tube down his throat. After another dose of Narcan, Mr. Rivera began having spontaneous breaths and the tube was removed.

"We'll take over from here," Agent Bart said.

"No way dude. He's going to the hospital," the medic said firmly.

"We'll follow," Agent Bart replied.

Mr. Rivera was packed into an ambulance and taken directly to a nearby hospital that had been alerted to prepare for a mass casualty. After Mr. Rivera's ambulance left for the hospital, it was then Samantha noticed that Tarik was missing.

"He was standing right here before you grabbed me," she told Brian.

"Where did you see him last?"

"By the red truck."

They started toward the area but were stopped by a police officer. "We're keeping this path clear for the ambulances."

"We're with the DEA," Samantha said. "We've lost an operative. He should be over by that truck."

The police officer let them through. Brian looked over at the field and started to run. "Come on!"

In the field, multiple ambulances flashed red and white lights as medics quickly triaged people into those who needed immediate assistance and those injured in falls by the rush of people. As the medics worked to resuscitate the victims who'd inhaled fentanyl, one by one, the people who were alive were either released or intubated and taken away for further treatment. Those who'd passed were left in peace and eventually placed into body bags for a respectful departure.

Over by the food truck, Brian found Tarik lying unconscious and yelled, "He's not breathing!"

"Get the medics!" Samantha exclaimed. Yanking open the door to the food truck, she grabbed bottled water and washed Tarik's face by pouring the liquid over his skin. "Tarik!"

Beginning mouth-to-mouth, she slowly gave breaths, coordinating with Brian as he started chest compressions. As her air intermingled with Tarik's, a calm came over her body. *Breathe.* The blood coursed through Tarik's vessels, forced along by the pumping actions of Brian's compressions.

The medics came and gave Narcan. Still on her knees, Samantha forced more air into Tarik's lungs. *Breathe.* Tears coursed down her cheeks. "Breathe."

"We've got him, mam," a medic said, forcing Samantha out of the way. Her head swayed.

"Breathe," a medic yelled to her.

A police officer standing nearby pulled out a dose of Narcan. From her position on the ground, the kaleidoscopic blur of color filled Samantha's vision. Looking at Brian, she muttered, "Mom. The balloon is heading for Mom."

The roar of Cliff's motorcycle echoed in the background as he arrived at the scene. In a daze, she saw him walk up, yelling at her to stay awake. She moved her mouth and tried to reassure everyone that she was okay. And just like that, she lost consciousness.

"Give her another dose of Narcan," the medic said.

"She has powder on her dress. Stand back," Cliff yelled.

Repeating the decontamination they'd used earlier, water was poured over Samantha's body; then the medics reported they'd used their last dose of Narcan on Tarik. She never felt the discomfort of a tube going down her throat, or the sting of a needle from the IV catheter inserted into her arm.

An Ambu Bag was placed over the tube. "Breathe," her brother begged.

"I've got Narcan," Cliff yelled and pulled vials from the stash he kept in his saddlebags. "Here." He threw a couple of vials to the medics. A dose was pushed into Samantha's IV. With bated breath, everyone watched as she started to struggle, then she coughed. They cheered when, in one fluid motion, she reached up and pulled out her breathing tube.

"She's breathing on her own!" Cliff let out a long breath.

"That could change," a medic replied. "A lot of people need three doses of Narcan."

"What are you guys doing?" Lt. Harmon asked. She struggled to push herself onto an elbow and, in a daze, stared at the IV dripping into her arm. She demanded that it be taken out and flopped weakly back down.

Grandfather.

In the clouds of a snowstorm, she watched as the sails of a mighty ship chased down a marauding pirate, the weather vane bouncing in the winds.

She watched as her mother lifted her face to smile at the sun, taking in the beauty of an approaching balloon.

Grandfather.

She watched as a harpoon flew toward the balloon, puncturing a hole in the side.

As the air current caught the balloon, bringing it too close to the ground to unload its deadly payload onto the occupants of a hospital balcony, the eyes of Badhai Kahn grew wide as he stared into his destiny right before he crashed into the ground.

Tarik.

She looked beside her and saw Tarik's body, still not moving.

"Breathe."

"Lieutenant."

"Captain," she said into the smiling eyes of the blonde man standing beside her.

Another dose of Narcan coursed through her veins.

"Breathe."

She knelt on the bench, facing the waves, laughing as the wind tangled her hair. Her young face, illuminated with the sun, looked toward the skies, watching the seagulls fly. "Oh, that bird. He's a big one. Is that a Hawk?"

The Captain shaded his eyes against the sun and gave Samantha a strange look. "You know what that is. That's Tarik. He's going away."

"No. Tarik, come back," she cried.

Two dark-haired apparitions appeared to take Tarik by the hand. "Come, Son."

"He's supposed to stay here. They gave him the medicine," Samantha said numbly. "I'm on my knees."

Looking back, Tarik gave Lt. Harmon a reassuring smile and saluted, right before he slipped into the light.

"Breathe."

Chapter 20

Indianapolis, Indiana
 USA
 July 16th, 2021

The bells at St. Michael rang, calling the procession into the church just as they had so many times all summer. *Ding dong. Ding dong,* the bells of weddings, and the bells of funerals had resounded throughout Indianapolis. And on the Fourth of July, the bells of every church in the city rang twenty-one times, once for every victim killed in the terror attack.

"Everyone please rise," Samantha's brother said, using words similar to the bailiff's in a courtroom the day Nadja was arraigned.

Dressed out in her Class A uniform, Lieutenant Samantha Harmon stood and saluted the steel gray casket positioned in the middle of the aisle. Throughout the month, she'd done the same thing for every victim killed by fentanyl. Today, the funeral was for Tarik and for him, the stoic look on her face matched the crisp line of her salute. After several extra seconds, she dropped her hand to let her fingertips curl beside the black stripe on the side of her Class A trousers, the stripe signifying her status as an officer.

"Why are we having a church funeral for a Muslim," Father Mark had asked.

"He wasn't Muslim. He was an orphan and wasn't anything religious. We are his only family," Samantha had responded. "And the only church we know is on our mother's side, which is the Catholic church. Tarik was a good man, and he was saved. I saw it myself."

Surprisingly, for a man not from the U.S., much less Indiana, the procession of people flowing into the church was long. Suits and dresses, blue jeans and shorts, scarves and hajibs, at this funeral, the style of clothing didn't matter as people from all walks of life gathered to honor the DEA agent who gave his own life to help stop the scourge of drugs killing their family and friends. The procession slowly wound down a side aisle as people shuffled into the pews, leaving a few mourners to stand in the back.

Lt. Harmon went to sit with several people occupying the upper church balcony. There, two solitary figures sat handcuffed together, surrounded by authorities from the DEA, the FBI, and Colonel Pinkston. It had taken some doing to convince a judge to release Nadja into Mr. Owens' custody, but with the argument that seeing the after-effects of her family's actions might influence Nadja to reveal the location of Dalbir Jammu, the judge had agreed.

"Thank you, everyone, for showing so much love for humanity," Father Mark said, raising his hands in praise. He continued the sermon with an explanation of the importance of the procession he'd organized, starting with a prayer out in the parking lot.

"Mystically, the procession calls to mind our status as pilgrims. All of us are journeying toward our heavenly homeland, for "here we have no lasting city, but we seek the city which is to come.""

Audible sniffling emanated from the congregation, none louder than Mr. Owens. Colonel Pinkston put a hand on his shoulder, a move Lt. Harmon observed through her tears. *Guess all is forgiven.*

Seething with annoyance, Nadja held her gaze on Samantha's empty ring finger until the final amen.

"Amen," the congregation chanted.

Organ music flowed from the pipes with the melody, Amazing Grace, signaling the start of the recessional hymn. From the balcony, Lt. Harmon watched as Agents Tooley, Browne, and Vargas joined Gary, Brian, and a sixth pallbearer, dressed in traditional Afghan garb with a turban wound around his head, to lift the casket out to a waiting hearse. She studied the man.

Ismael.

One by one, the stone-faced DEA agents filed out of the balcony, followed by a group of FBI agents, all in shiny dark suits. As Colonel Pinkston rose to make his way toward the balcony stairs, he gave Mr. Owens a nod.

"Sir, thank you for coming," Lt. Harmon said quickly.

"Of course," Colonel Pinkston replied and handed the men tissues. "Bob, take a moment."

With that, Mr. Owens burst into tears, removed the handcuff from his wrist, and slapped it around the arm of his chair. "Pinky!"

Colonel Pinkston raised a brow at Lt. Harmon. The grey-blue of her eyes relayed her understanding as Mr. Owens was led away, saying he'd be back in a moment. While keeping her eyes glued to the front of the church, she said softly, "Hello, Mother."

"Your men are weak."

"Your men are dead."

"As are some of yours."

"Just one."

"One that mattered."

Lt. Harmon kept her hands folded in her lap as she thoughtfully asked, "How many more does there need to be?"

"What do you mean, need to be?" Nadja's defiant tone turned to one of curiosity.

"For your group to obtain the objective. How many more mothers have to lose their sons?"

"It's not—."

"And daughters. I almost lost my life in that attack, Mother. So let's not forget the daughters."

"You are not my daughter!"

"I am a daughter. And Badhai was planning to kill my mother. Did you know that?"

"No!" The pallor in Nadja's face, the shadows under her eyes, it all deepened in the glare of the church lights.

"I'm sorry you've lost your sons," Lt. Harmon said. Her pert face glowed pink in the heat of the balcony. "What happened to your plan to go into the Witness Protection Program?"

As her chest rose up and down with a few soft breaths, Nadja's bottom lip began to quiver.

"You loved your children, just as the parents of the kids killed in the attack loved their children. Did you know the youngest child that died was only six years old?"

"That wasn't the plan!"

"Then why did it happen?" Lt. Harmon's hand snuck into Nadja's. "Their parents need answers."

Silence pierced the air as Nadja closed her eyes.

"I remember what we talked about over in Afghanistan. The United States needed not just to leave the country but to leave thoroughly defeated. Your sons are dead, and your mother is in custody. Your husband is missing. Nobody won here."

"Because you lost the man you love!" Nadja snapped.

"My fiancé?" Lt. Harmon's curls dampened on her head as she withdrew her hand.

"The man you are burying."

"First of all," Lt. Harmon replied in an even voice, "Tarik is not going to be buried, he's going to be cremated."

"I saw the way you looked at his casket. You loved him," Nadja said with a little laugh.

"And second, my fiancé is still in the hospital." Lt. Harmon ran her fingers through her hair, sweeping it back from her forehead.

"So you are still going to marry a man you don't love?"

"How did we get on this topic?"

"You can't even say the words."

"What words?"

"That you love him."

Samantha turned her head to stare into Nadja's eyes. "I love him."

"You couldn't convince a jury," Nadja said.

"I'm not the one who has to do that," Lt. Harmon exclaimed. "You could wind up in prison for the rest of your life if you don't start cooperating. Is that what you want?"

Nadja studied the medals pinned onto Lt. Harmon's Class A uniform. "What are those for?"

Footsteps echoed on the wooden stairs, signaling the men were coming back. Lt. Harmon pulled out her phone and found the picture of Dalbir staring into the eyes of the woman in his band.

"Sorry, we don't have time for pleasantries. Assad called you a traitor because you were switching the fentanyl with talcum, right?"

Astonishment lit Nadja's eyes. She blinked. "How did you know?"

"And you purposefully substituted talcum in the rockets that were supposed to hit the base. How did Badhai find out you did that?"

"My son is clever."

"You mean was. The men who tried to kidnap Mr. Rivera talked. Badhai wasn't supposed to be up in that balloon. He stole it at the last minute, and he used his own powder he's been making, which really was badly cooked fentanyl. It's been killing a lot of people in southern Indiana, his own personal jihad."

Nadja remained silent.

"And he wanted to kidnap Mr. Rivera himself, get all the glory. Prove to al-Qaeda that he could be the next leader."

"It wasn't my son's fault that he was indoctrinated with their ideals," Nadja cried.

"I know. Dalbir lured you to take him to Afghanistan. Then you tried to control the damage."

Nadja's chest heaved as she slowly nodded.

"Where is your husband?"

"I don't know."

"But he would come to you if you called?"

Nadja stared at the picture of Dalbir looking into the eyes of the silky vixen and said, "Of course."

Lt. Harmon handed her a phone. Suddenly, Nadja withered into her clothing. Looking small and frightened, her free hand clasped the phone as she sat with indecision on her face. Feeling the heat, Lt. Harmon removed her jacket. "We can't help him if we can't talk to him."

"And if you were me, would you be calling your fiancé?"

"To get him away from another woman, yes."

"What should I say?"

"That you escaped. You'll meet him at an abandoned house over on the river."

"My husband is not a bad person," Nadja sobbed.

"We know what he is." The feminine silk in Lt. Harmon's voice was soothing.

"It's his girlfriend," Nadja continued. Asseya is the number one arms dealer in the Middle East."

No wonder they let Nadja come to the funeral. They want the girlfriend.

"Call him," Lt. Harmon said and recited the address of the house on the river.

With her trembling hand still locked in a cuff, Nadja held the phone and dialed a number. When no one answered, she left a message proclaiming in a haughty tone, "I escaped. Meet me at this address in an hour," and gave the address of the house on the river.

With that, Mr. Owens thundered up the stairs to assume control of the prisoner. Lt. Harmon shot him a warning look. *Don't screw this up. As* she clicked away in her heels, she announced that she'd meet everyone at the river. "I'm going to change."

"You're taking me too," Nadja declared while staring at the hardened expression on Mr. Owens' face.

"We can't. The agreement with the judge is you go straight back to prison," he replied.

"Dalbir will call to me. He'll run if he doesn't hear my voice."

Lt. Harmon's heels clicked their way back to Nadja's side. After pulling out her phone, she instructed Nadja to say, "Dalbir, over here." Her finger hit the record button before she held the phone up to let Nadja speak into the mic.

"Dalbir, come here."

When Lt. Harmon replayed the recording, she noticed that Nadja's voice sounded hollow, unsure. She gazed into the older woman's eyes, spinning her magic. "Do it again. Call to your love." An arch of whistling wind shot through the church as she held out her tanned hand to the dolphin, "Come here, my love."

Rising out of the water with an air of joyful exuberance, the dolphin stood on its tail and smiled, it's trusting eyes looking into the face of the young girl holding out a fish.

"Dalbir, it's you! Over here," Nadja's soulful voice pleads.

"Perfect." Lt. Harmon snapped her phone shut and, with a nod to Mr. Owens, headed toward the stairs.

The sound of trumpets echoed outside, formally ending the recessional parade. As Lt. Harmon pulled open the heavy wooden door to the church and carefully made her way down the three concrete steps, a young man came across the pavement, walking in her direction. His scrawny physic clad in a rocker T over thread-bare denims drew the scrutiny of Cliff, who stood ready to give Samantha a ride on his bike.

"Mam, you're Lieutenant Harmon?"

With her grey-blue eyes scanning the young man, Lt. Harmon stood holding her Class A jacket over her arm. "Yes, I am. Can I help you?"

"I just wanted to thank you for your service."

"What's your name?"

"You know me. I'm Benjamin. You asked me and my friends to mow your mom's yard when she got sick."

"Oh, Benjamin, from next door. How's Bobbie?"

"He died, mam."

"I'm so sorry. What happened?"

The young man's feet shuffled as he stared at the ground. Finally, he said, "Fentanyl."

"And Kenny and Donny?"

"Them too."

"Jerry?"

Benjamin nodded.

"I heard about that party. I'm glad you're alive."

"Samantha," Father Mark called from across the pavement as he strolled over to her location. She held out her hand.

"Thank you, Father. That was a very nice service."

"No, thank you for your service. The bells are ringing on Sunday, a memorial for all fentanyl victims, just as you requested. Can you be here to ring the first bell?"

"I, uh, don't think so. I have to be in Washington. Sorry, I have to go," she stuttered hurriedly. *My picture can't be on national TV.*

Father Mark smiled. "It will all work out for the best. Good day."

"Can I ring the bells," Benjamin asked excitedly as Lt. Harmon backed away.

"That's a great idea," she murmured as she watched Nadja being escorted to the back of a police cruiser. When the woman turned, they locked eyes for a moment, a final farewell. "Ring the bells."

"Come on," Cliff hollered from his bike. "We got to go."

"Okay," Samantha said as she walked slowly toward the bike, now watching the hearse pull away from the curb with Tarik's body. "Let's go kick some more terrorist ass."

"Lieutenant," a nervous voice called from behind.

Samantha turned to find Benjamin still standing by the church steps, a hint of eagerness on his face. "Yes?"

"My dad was working in the garage where that al-Qaeda guy was changing his oil." He shuffled his feet, his eyes wide, appealing for clemency.

With her pulse quickening, Samantha's voice softened to a tone that said-just me and you, two people talking on the street. "What did your father see?"

"My dad's afraid of losing his job," Benjamin said, a bit of trepidation now creeping into his voice.

Taking a step closer, Samantha nodded reassuringly. "There's lots of mechanic jobs. If we have to, my family will buy that garage. What do you know?"

Benjamin smiled and nodded. "There was one guy, Grady, who always changed the oil in that truck. And when the al-Qaeda dude went to pay Al, he's the owner, he'd put a cardboard box in the back of the truck. Told everybody they were tomato plants, but my dad knew different."

"What was in the box?" Samantha asked.

"Al, he left a box by the register when he used the bathroom. My dad just wanted to make sure the tomato plants didn't need water, so he peeked inside the box. I heard him on the phone talking to Al about it. He was asking about the gun parts."

Startled, a wide-eyed Samantha said, "Thanks, Benjamin."

"You're going to tell the police?"

"We'll take care of everything."

Smiling, he nodded and walked off.

While standing in the shadow of the steeple, Samantha realized that the mission had just become much more dangerous. *Badhai was trading drugs for guns.* As the risk she was about to undertake loomed large, the memory of the bells ringing for Jenny and Tarik and for thousands of others fueled her resolve.

'Be strong and courageous; do not be frightened or dismayed; God is with us, girl.'

Remembering those biblical words, quoted by her grandfather during an intense storm as they battled through torrential winds and ten-foot waves, a renewed sense of determination entered Samantha's heart as she picked up her phone.

"They're trafficking guns out of that garage, exchanging them for drugs," she told Brian.

"Got it. I'll let Renfro know."

"I've got your clothes. Where do you want to change?" Cliff asked, making no mention of the call he'd just overheard.

"Gas station. I'm hungry."

The bike roared out of the parking lot with the tip of Cliff's ponytail flicking Samantha in the face. Pressing up against his back to avoid the sting, she kept her face hidden until they pulled into a gas station just before they reached the river. In the parking lot, a trucker just finishing the task of refueling his rig stared at the picture of the leather-clad biker with a curly-haired woman in Class A uniform and smiled.

"Do you want anything from inside?" she asked. Hopping off the bike, she pulled her street clothes from the saddle bag. A playful grin spread across Cliff's face as he patted his rounded abdomen.

"Nope. I'm saving all this for my woman."

That brought a smile as she ran into the gas station and asked for the bathroom key. In there, she wasted no time changing out of her Class A uniform and carefully folded it to be placed in her bag. Then she slipped into a dark T-shirt with straight-legged jeans and shoved her feet into a new pair of black running shoes. In this casual clothing, her mounting tension eased. Outside, she tossed her uniform to Cliff and dodged back inside the gas station for a breaded chicken sandwich. Then, she stood watching the parking lot from a plate glass window. Soon, a dark van rolled into the lot and parked around the side.

They're here.

As she emerged from the glass door, she found Cliff standing with Agent Vargas next to the dark van. Twisting a handle on the back door, he pulled it open, then caught a bulletproof vest thrown his way and wrapped it around his barreled chest. *Click.* The sound of a bolt sliding back came as Cliff held a weapon out straight and chambered a round.

"We need more firepower than this," he said.

"Take your pick," Agent Vargas replied as the women donned body armor. Agent Bart stood inside the van and opened a case displaying an assortment of weapons. Picking up an AK 47, he handed it to Samantha. Next, he handed over a magazine full of bullets.

"Those are for Tarik," he said. She nodded grimly.

Anticipating that Mr. Owens would be arriving soon, they donned more protective gear, put sliding helmets in place, and checked their communications as she explained the layout of the house.

"It's similar to what we found at the airport. The bootleggers moved grain during prohibition using tunnels to avoid detection. There's a tunnel going from the river to the house, but it caved in when a cow's leg sank through the ceiling. Still, it would be a good hiding place for anyone using an abandoned property for illicit purposes. The living room is seated in the front of the house, kitchen is in the back. The bedroom's on the left side."

"We better get you over there before Dalbir arrives," Agent Vargas said.

"How do you know he's not already there?" Agent Bart asked.

"Got a guy with eyes on it," Cliff replied. "He checked the place out.

It's empty. Got there before Nadja made the call, so it's verified nobody's there yet."

"Good!"

A black sedan pulled into the lot. As it stopped, Samantha caught a glimpse of Mr. Owens as he lowered a window. From her position on the back seat of the motorcycle, she wrapped an arm around Cliff's waist and waved, 'Follow us' as the bike sped off.

"What is he doing here?" Cliff yelled.

"He cares."

The drive to the river was short, less than a quarter of a mile away. When they rounded a bend, Cliff's bike slowed to a crawl as he peered at the river through tree-lined banks. A lone otter paddling rapidly toward a damn froze. After a moment, with no one coming to bother him, the otter continued with his busy task, observed only by eyes on the other side of the water.

The house stood at least fifty yards back off the road. *Perfect.* "There's plenty of trees to give you cover," Samantha said.

"Our orders are to wait out here," Cliff replied.

"Where we'll do no good?"

"And you are to stay down way back in the woods."

"Where's your guy?"

Pointing to the man standing across the river watching the house with a pair of binoculars, Cliff waved and gave the guy a thumbs up.

A motorcade passed by, crawling along the road, halting just long enough to drop off passengers. With his gun drawn, Mr. Owens started to make his way toward the house when he was stopped by Agent Vargas.

"You're taking the left," she said.

Noting the shadows of people framed in the window, he nodded and led Agents Tooley and Browne to a grove of trees, leaving Samantha in the woods. Then Cliff gunned his bike and roared out of site to take a position along the upper road.

"Everyone down," Agent Vargas said as she dropped behind a bush.

"What's happening?" Samantha asked.

"One car coming down the road. And two Kayakers paddling down the river."

As the car pulled into the dirt drive, it slowed to a stop. Through the windshield, Dalbir's face was visible through the glass.

"Shows on," Mr. Owens said quietly into Samantha's ear. Nodding her understanding, she waited until Dalbir emerged from the car before hitting the play button on the phone.

"Dalbir, come here," Nadja's voice said.

"Nadja, where are you?" he called back. While shading his eyes, he yelled, "I don't see you."

"Dalbir, over here," Nadja's voice rang again.

"In the woods?"

"Over here."

After the car door opened, the man Samantha recognized as Dalbir Jammu stood clothed in traditional American garb, his face encased by the beard of the mujahedeen. As the man stepped away from the car and approached the woods, he pulled out a gun and aimed toward the trees.

Samantha stood and held up the phone. "Dalbir, I'm over here," echoed Nadja's distant voice. As he aimed his gun toward the voice, a shot rang out, dropping him on the spot. Mr. Owens looked admiringly at Samantha.

"Nice shot."

"It wasn't me!" She hugged her weapon closer to her body.

"Who's in the house?"

"Cliff's guys," she said as a bullet whizzed by, splintering a tree branch overhead.

"Get down," Mr. Owens screamed as he fell behind a log. Following his lead, Samantha dove to the ground.

"Over there. The kayakers," she said, pointing to the river.

More bullets whizzed into their positions, forcing them to stay ducked behind the log. When the shooting stopped, Samantha listened to the rapid exchange of fire between Agent Vargas and her team shooting at the people on the river.

The kayaks, now empty, sat lodged against the shoreline. Beside it, bullets flew from a submachine gun carried by a dark-haired woman as she fired from the hip.

Samantha peered between the sites on her weapon and watched as the woman dropped behind a kayak to reload. Using the log to steady her aim, her grey-blue eyes pierced the route. *Breathe, relax, aim and squeeze.* A lead bullet sliced through the air, propelled in a parallel line by forces unseen to lodge between the eyes of Ashira Jammu. As large droplets of blood spewed five, then eight, then ten inches into the air, she laid on the ground, lured to a peaceful rest amongst the rapport of weapons continuing to fire.

"Stay down," Mr. Owens yelled as more shots rang out, coming from the direction of the car. He grabbed the weapon from Samantha and pushed her to the ground. "Stay there." Putting the weapon on automatic, he fired a rapid succession of bullets, decorating the car with a figure eight. One lone blast flew into the woods before the door opened, and two bloodied hands appeared, held high in the air.

On the ground, covered by a mass of twigs and shell casings, Samantha rose to a sitting position and stared at the bloodied man beside her. "Mr. Owens!"

Moving stealthily through the woods, Cliff walked up from behind with the telescope of his rifle pointing at the ground. The muscles in his face hardened as he said grimly, "He's gone," and grabbed her arm to pull her away from the scene.

A police van arrived on scene, followed by four ambulances. With weapons drawn, the officers moved to help and pulled two people from the car, cuffed them, and escorted them to the van.

Samantha sat on a log, hugging her knees to her chest as she watched the scene unfold. Tears streaked through her dirt-stained face as Cliff walked up, holding Mr. Owens' wallet in his hand and flicked it open. "Want to know who he worked for?"

While pulling a few leaves from her hair, Samantha replied in a dazed voice, "I know who he is. He's a man who's just rejoined his son."

"He did," Cliff said firmly.

"Why wasn't he wearing a bulletproof vest?"

"It didn't fit."

Samantha stared at Cliff suspiciously. "The trail to Ismael and the others. It ended here?"

"It did," he said and led the way back toward the house.

"Where are the FBI guys?"

"Gone. Filing their reports."

"They're working Talon?"

Agent Vargas walked over to Samantha, saying, "Nice job."

"Not really," she replied sadly. "Tarik should have been here."

"He was, through you."

"What happened in the house?"

"Bunch of drug dealers. They read about the tunnel in some news articles and rebuilt it. Used it to traffic their drugs down the river. Cliff's guys found them huddled in there along with a brick of fentanyl."

"Come on," Cliff said. "I have orders to get you out of here."

"But, I need to wait for the investigators. I shot someone."

"Mr. Owens' orders. Officially, you were never here."

Agent Vargas motioned for Samantha to leave. "Get out of here before the news vans arrive unless you want your face all over TV."

Samantha nodded. "You'll be at the church on Sunday, right? Ring a bell for Tarik and one for Mr. Owens."

"You too," Agent Vargas replied. "I'm the face. You're their voice."

Samantha removed her vest and handed it to Agent Vargas. "You be both. I'm done. No more orphans. I'm joining the FBI." Looking into the back window of the police cruiser holding the young boys captured in the tunnel, her voice became tight. "How old are they?"

"Sixteen."

Using the back of her hand, she wiped away the smudges on her face and knocked on the window. As it was lowered, she pointed to the body bags lying on the ground and said, "Keep doing those drugs, you're next."

Samantha, you are the voice girl. Her eyes softened.

Grandfather.

CHAPTER 21

Indianapolis, Indiana
USA
July 18, 2021

The cloud is dark. A burst of lightning flickers through the cloud, backlighting it from within. But we know lightening doesn't come from clouds, it comes from the ground.

"Sam, what are you doing?"

"Ruminating."

"Really!" Brian exclaimed. Closing his hand around the straps of her backpack, he pulled her upright from the couch. "The truck's loaded. We have to get out of here!"

Samantha stared at the TV shimmering in red, white, and blue. A flag waving behind a newscaster reflected the American colors as he blared the announcement: "The pope gave permission. The bells will ring once for each person killed by fentanyl this past year."

"The phone's been ringing nonstop. How did the media find out about you?"

"From Father Mark, I guess."

Using one finger, Brian pulled back a curtain and peeked outside. "Yup, there's already a van in the driveway."

"Out the back," Samantha yelled. With her face registering alarm, she ran out the back door and kept going straight through the hedge. Before she could reach the driveway, Agent Browne stepped in her path. Brian stopped short behind her.

"Where are you two headed?"

"The VA," he replied.

Agent Browne frowned as he looked at Samantha. "You should be at the airport."

"She needs to see her fiancé," Brian retorted.

"I'm not going there," she said fiercely. Her eyes narrowed suspiciously as Agent Browne held open the door to a dark sedan and yelled, "Get in."

"Brian is taking me to the airport, and all my things are in the truck. You need to stay here and make sure we're not followed," Samantha replied curtly as she climbed into the truck. Her face looked startled as she lifted her hips when she sat on a lump.

Meow.

"Thor!" Clenching the cat by the scruff of the neck, she placed him in the back seat. Then she pointed to a news truck blocking the drive and said sweetly, "Please get that van to move."

Flashing her a scowl, Agent Browne walked up to the curb and ordered the truck to move.

"What was that all about?" Brian asked as he slid into the driver's seat.

"They want me in Washington."

"But they know you're going to Grandfather's Celebration of Life. Don't they have to give you leave?"

"I already took it. Colonel Pinkston wants to know today whether I'll be staying in the military or getting out to join another service."

"That's why you won't help ring the bells. If you join Talon, you can't have your face on TV," Brian muttered. Slamming his foot on the gas, he made it through a green light. "Why aren't we stopping to see Brad?"

"Because we can't talk to each other," Samantha replied in a voice so low Brian almost didn't catch her last words. But he did. Rather than heading toward the airport, he threw on the brakes and turned toward the VA. Peering into the rearview mirror, he noted that the two cages securely tied in the truck's bed remained steadfast as a bright green feather arched in the air.

Bam. "Ouch!" Samantha yelled as her head hit the dashboard.

Brian looked at his sister suspiciously as she rubbed her head. "Since when is the word "can't" in your vocabulary? You were so hot to have him transferred to the U.S. Now you won't see him. What's going on?"

After a moment of quiet, Samantha admitted her suspicion that Brad might be faking his blindness. "He was able to see the color of a candy I gave him. And he's angry they're discharging him from the service."

"And you're resigning your commission on purpose, so he broke off the engagement," Brian muttered.

"He actually told me to join the FBI and he doesn't want to get in my way. Just take me to the airport."

"Nope. You don't deserve this."

"I'm not going in there," Samantha snapped.

Ignoring her, Brian stopped in front of the red-brick building housing the VA. "Hurry up, or you'll miss your plane. Get in there."

"No, I'll take a cab!"

"Coward."

Under the glare of her brother's stare, Samantha angrily climbed from the truck and leaned against the side. Taking a moment to collect herself, she stood staring up at an American flag waving from a tall silver pole. Eventually, she calmed and asked contritely, "Did you bring that other phone?"

Brian held out the burner. "Promise not to call a cab?"

With an exaggerated sigh, Samantha grabbed the phone and dialed a number. "Christine?"

"I'm here."

"Is everything ready on the boat?"

"It is," she answered. "He's in an urn, down in the brig."

"I'm surprised he fit. Will you be there?"

"Of course."

"How's Mom?"

"She's doing very well. It was so nice of your brother to bring her."

"Just keep her safe. What about the laptop?"

"Buried where she'll never see it. Or anybody else. And Samantha, never touch the money," Christine said in a voice mirroring the ominous warning.

"Eyes are watching," Samantha whispered.

"Always."

"I understand. See you later."

"Adios Senora."

The emergency parking lot nestled next to the front door was empty as

Samantha walked toward the entrance. Before she could push the door open, a blue and white ambulance pulled into the lot and abruptly parked.

"Hang on, I'm coming," the driver yelled into a phone as he hopped out and ran to open the back door. Upon recognizing Agent Tooley's slick haircut, Samantha hid behind a pillar as he walked through the emergency door, then she ran around and peered inside the hospital. In the lobby, the agent stopped at a desk and spoke with the clerk, and then headed for the elevator. Her feet slowly carried her through the same door, right up to the same desk.

"I'm Lieutenant Harmon. That man who was just here. I'm supposed to meet him, but I forgot my phone. What room did he go to?" she asked with wide-eyed innocence while applying pink gloss to her lips, seemingly unconcerned with the answer.

"Room 368," the clerk replied graciously. As he offered to write the room number down, Samantha disappeared onto the elevator through the closing doors, waving and giving him a big smile.

As luck would have it, she rode up the elevator with a housekeeper's cart. A woman in purple scrubs pushed the cart off the elevator. Using it to shield herself from view, Samantha followed the housekeeper down the hall.

"Can you run a mop in that room," she asked, pointing to room 368. "There's a water spill."

"Sure, baby," she replied. Grabbing the yellow mop handle protruding from her bucket, she knocked and slowly opened the door. "Housekeeping."

From behind the cart, Samantha's eyes widened at the site of the patient lying in the bed. *Mr. Owens! It figures.* Agent Bart turned as she ducked back behind the cart. From her crouched position, she ran to a nearby stairway and took the metal stairs two at a time, not stopping until she reached the fourth floor. Barely out of breath, she made her way down the quiet hall to Brad's room. Upon finding his lights off and window drapes closed, she hesitantly took in the sight of him lying in a hospital bed, looking thinner and paler than she remembered.

"Why are you sitting in the dark?"

"Sam," he said hoarsely. "You shouldn't be here."

"I know Owens is here. And he saw you in Germany. They got to you."

Brad's lips pressed into a stubborn line. "They're not wrong."

"I don't want to work for some homegrown terrorist network!"

That produced a slight chuckle, followed by a frown. "They're not terrorists. A lot of people are dying in this country, more every year. That fentanyl, it's bad stuff."

"Are you joining the FBI too?"

"In a different capacity."

"I still don't want to…"

"Yes, you do. It was all over your face."

"I know you can see," Samantha replied with a trace of anger in her voice.

"That was the point of the operation," Brad replied curtly.

With her fingers curling by her side, Samantha cried, "How could you let them do surgery when you could already see?" As she stared at Brad, his mouth slightly opened.

"Why would you say that?"

"Because!" Samantha took a deep breath, trying to control the shake in her voice. "The candy I gave you at Walter Reed. You knew it was red."

"Huh?" Brad's green eyes popped open, his mouth now a wry grin. "That's why you called off our engagement? Because of a red piece of candy?"

"It's not funny," Samantha exclaimed. Her finger pushed a black curl from her eye. "Why are you laughing at me?"

"Sam, you always give me red. Maybe the intelligence officer isn't quite so intelligent," he said haughtily.

"That's not… but…" Her mouth worked to form a further reply, but none came.

"But you're still beautiful." He reached out a hand. She took the hand between her slender fingers. Her heart melted as she timidly reached up and traced her finger along the scar, trenching an ugly line from his right eye to his jaw.

"Then we should work together."

Jerking his head back, he stared at the wall. "You shouldn't be here. You need to keep your picture out of the press."

"I know." She rolled her eyes. "Undercover, clandestine, saving me for fieldwork. Blah blah blah."

"You need to stay safe, Samantha. I don't want to be in here for nothing."

Slowly, she understood. As they gazed reluctantly into each other's eyes, the door burst open.

"Brian, why aren't you with the truck?"

"Why aren't you answering your phone?"

"You took it from me."

"Oh." His eyebrows rose together as he saw the scar along the opaque glaze in Brad's right eye.

"Brad, you remember my brother?"

Nodding, Captain Kramer turned his head away.

"What are you doing here?" Samantha asked.

"Jack's gone," Brian replied in a tight voice.

"What! You didn't secure the latch?"

"Don't blame me. You left your window open. Thor jumped out, and the next thing I knew, he was in the back of the truck, and Jack's cage was open."

"Thor did not eat Jack!"

At that, Captain Kramer grinned and turned to look at Brian. "Who's Thor?"

Spitting each word out slowly, Samantha replied, "His friend's big, hairy, vicious cat."

With a glance at the ticking clock, Brian asked, "Where would Jack go?"

"Just about anywhere," Samantha shouted as Brian's phone pinged. "Who's that?"

Brian peered at his phone. "It's Gary. He has a line on Jack. Turn on the news."

Grabbing the remote, Brad turned the TV to Channel 4, and they all watched as a helicopter news team captured video of a green parrot flying across the skyline to perch in the belfry at Saint Michael's church.

"Jack. It's Jack," Brian yelled.

"That bird!" Samantha exclaimed.

"Why's he in the belfry?" Brad asked.

"He's missing Grandfather. We had a big dinner bell on the boat."

"Gary and I will get the bird," Brian said, hurriedly checking the time. "I'll drop you at the airport."

"No." Samantha shook her head. "He won't come to you. I'll go, it's not that far."

"The bells. They'll be ringing soon," Brian said worriedly.

"Then we better hurry. Come on," Samantha cried as she ran to the door. Abruptly, she stopped and walked back to the bedside. Her eyes gazed at Brad with pure trust, and then she was gone.

"Sis, stop," Brian yelled as, once again, she entered the stairway and ran down the steps to the ground floor. "You can't leave without me."

"Where's the truck," she asked as they burst through the front door.

"Over here."

Fortunately, a quick check assured them that Chelsey was still in her cage. As they pulled out of the lot, Samantha reprimanded Thor, "Bad Kitty," while Brian ran a red light and sped toward the church. Twelve minutes later, they arrived downtown to find a crowd standing in front of the cathedral.

"Wait," Brian said, giving Samantha a hard stare. "I'll take Chelsey. Maybe Jack will come to her."

Samantha grabbed Brian's ballcap from his head and pulled it over her locks. "Good idea." Climbing from the truck, she looked up to see a mass of green feathers poking from the belfry.

As Brian stood with Psittacus talons wrapped around his wrist, he held her up and called to Jack, "Come on, man."

Jack rested his head against the bell, appearing to fall asleep.

"One of his tricks," Samantha said.

"What should we do?" Brian asked.

"I don't know." Taking off the ballcap, she called to Jack, hoping he would see her face and come. "There's too many people here." Spotting Benjamin in the crowd, she put the cap back on.

"Ring the bells," a voice squawked.

"Chelsey!"

Brian's eyes implored her, "Let's do it for Jenny."

"I can't." A tear slipped down her cheek.

"Ring the bells."

His arm encircled her, his eyes brimming with tears.

"Ring the bells."

"I can't. Our family… the government will go after us."

Thunderstruck by his sister's words, Brian yelled, "I knew it! They're forcing you into the FBI. Screw the government, do this for Jenny. Ring the bells."

Propelled forward by Brian's words, Samantha's grey-blue eyes looked wildly around. Together they reached for the rope. As she started to draw back, saying, "I can't," a strong hand closed around hers.

"Brad!"

He nodded. "Now."

"Ring the bells for Jenny," Brian said.

They pulled the ropes.

Clang.

"Ring the bells for Kole."

Ding dong.

"And for Meghan."

Ding dong.

"Ring the bells for Dawan."

The bells chimed in a mighty wave.

"And for Bear," his mother's voice said. "Ring the bells for Bear."

"All across the land, the bells are ringing," the announcer from Channel Four proclaimed as, one by one, people took turns ringing the bells for a loved one lost. "A mother, a sister, a brother, a son, a father, and a daughter. A friend."

Up above, the wings of an emerald green parrot flapped slowly in the sky as Samantha ran outside and stood with her head buried in Brad's chest, protected from the cameras. As Jack's wings carried him down to land on her shoulder, she made her decision and threw off the ballcap. Squinting her grey-blue eyes toward the sun, she saluted.

"There she is," Benjamin yelled. The cameras swung to point in her direction. A rumbling went through the crowd, echoing the words "There she is" as they walked back toward the church.

"Go ahead," Brad said and placed his hands on Samantha's shoulders. "I love you, you don't have to give up your commission. Samantha, you have a voice."

As the crowd cheered, Samantha looked into his eyes and nodded. With both hands, she grabbed the rope again and gave a mighty tug. Then, with her eyes pointing toward the stained glass window depicting the picture of a man who gave his life to others, she rang the bells again.

"Tarik. This is for you."

Donnng.

Sail Away

On the deck of the Sail Away, Captain Kramer studied the ship's GPS and gave the order. "Weigh anchor."

"Aye, ay, Captain," Samantha said. Her grey-blue eyes looked with amusement at the sandy-haired man wearing a patch over one eye. "What's our heading?"

"Your choice, Lieutenant," he responded.

The soft curve of a smile lit the young woman's face as she watched a dolphin jump over a wave. The crystal blue water flowing off the coast of Miami, now carrying her great-grandfather's ashes, had beckoned the crew to anchor near a sand bar. With an impish grin, she climbed onto the rail and did a backflip off the bow.

"Samantha, wife. Get up here," the captain bellowed.

Floating on her back, she looked at the sky and yelled, "SOCOM, here we come."

From her deck chair, Christina sipped from a margarita and laughed at the young people's antics. "Fish her out," she called. The corners of her eyes crinkled as she nodded at Jen. Together, they stood and walked over to the stern and gave the captain a mighty shove.

"Man overboard," Jake screeched from a perch high on the mast.

"Coast Guard," Chelsey chimed in.

"Ship ahoy," Jake yelled, preening his green feathers.

"Shark," Chelsey squawked, bringing the young people back on board.

"Four o'clock," Jake squawked as he flew down to the deck and pecked at the margarita glass.

"Five o'clock," Chelsey corrected him.

"Who are you?" Jake asked with a flutter of his wings.

"Shiver me timbers," Chelsey squawked back. "I'm just a civilian."

AFTERWORD

This book is the brainchild of my friend, mentor, and man I cannot name, who was a former member of the ASA. It was his worry over the potential for fentanyl to be used as a weapon of mass destruction that created the impetus for the creation of Samantha's Voice.

Jenny was a young mother who was gone way too soon. She leaves behind two boys. This book is dedicated to them.

Ring the bells for